Well Armored

Hearts

A Novel By

J.D. Harrison

Well Armored Hearts

Cover Photography copyright © 2016 Jessica Post
Author may be contacted at: j.d.harrison.author@gmail.com

ISBN-13: 978-1533350176

ISBN-10: 1533350175

Published via
CreateSpace Independent Publishing Platform
An Amazon Company

Dedicated to the men and women of the full contact jousting community, for the blood, broken bones, bruises, swear words, sweat and tears that go into bringing this wild bit of history to such tangible life in the present day. Thank you for letting me take care of your horses and for being my friends.
You know I love you.

To: Pat
Never give up on the
Strength found in a dream!

Love can finde entrance, not only into an open Heart; but also into a Heart well-fortified, if watch be not well kept.
Francis Bacon

As I slid through the air, a victim to gravity and inertia, it wasn't my whole life that flashed before my eyes, just the last several months. Among them were seven weeks of the hardest work I'd ever done, all having led to this breathless moment as more than a hundred pounds of armor dragged me toward the ground. My leg scraped roughly across the saddle as my horse continued galloping, a few seconds of raw adrenaline that somehow slowed to a crawl, and my brain flashed back to spring.

It felt like an incredibly ordinary day, one that easily could have taken the place of many other days, before then and since. Through the open window of my childhood bedroom, the whole world shone bright with promise, the elm tree outside shivering in the warm breeze as I worked on fleshing out the final project for my marketing degree. As a senior in college, I had the whole world spread out before me, and the future tasted as sweet as the Oreo I nibbled on.

Fiddling with the end of my long, dark brown braid, I tried to focus on the numbers in front of me, but after a repeated lack of correct answers, I had nothing to show for my efforts but a lack of cookies. A tension headache also threatened my equilibrium and even the acupressure trick I usually resorted to didn't touch it. Numbers and I had never been the best of friends, and we were now skirting nemesis territory with alarming regularity.

Groaning my frustration, I shoved the pile of papers inside a drawer, needing a break.

For a distraction, I pulled my tablet off my nightstand and flopped gracelessly onto the bed, landing on my stomach and propping myself up on my elbows. The mindless distraction of social media lured me in and I flicked my finger over the screen to scroll through all the status updates. Stopping here and there to like or comment, I lost myself in other peoples' lives until a chime let me know I had emails waiting. Pulling up the app, I answered one message marked urgent from my strategic management study group, then eyeballed the remaining five. Tucked between a reminder for my internet marketing project and a note from Mom, I found an email from an unknown address. Short, to the point, it still pounced on my unsuspecting psyche with all the subtlety of a sledgehammer, as I had given up any hope of hearing back from the sender.

'Dear Miss Bowen,

We apologize for the short notice, but our apprenticeship program has an unexpected vacancy, and you are the next qualified candidate in line. Please let us know by the end of the week if we should expect your arrival in Kentucky for the start of our summer program, and we will send you more information.
Sincerely,
Sir Bartholomew Clark
Quartermaster
Gallant Company of Knights'

As I stared at the email, a thousand thoughts ran through my mind, no one voice drowning out the other. So I did the one thing that always worked when faced with a seemingly unravelable knot—I ran downstairs hollering for my Mom. Torn between the responsible answer and the selfish desire, thankful for the opportunity and terrified all at once, I felt at a loss. I had been attending renaissance faires since birth, thanks to my mother, no matter where my father's military career had led us. In all that time, I'd never wanted to be a wench or a princess or even a pirate. I wanted to be a jouster, a knight of noble virtue and strong heart, unswayed by fear.

When the troupe at my favorite faire near Louisville had put up applications for interns on their website, I had spent winter break filling in the required information, pestering my father and my old horseback riding instructor for references, and selling myself like a prized filly. After three months, I had written it off as a pipe dream and intensified my focus on achieving my degree. A bachelor's in marketing seemed a far more practical bet in the long run anyway, something to pay the bills and at the same time, I could help the family ranch expand its organic meat sales. *Cynefin* Farms had already enjoyed a jump in business when I overhauled our ancient website.

"Hey Squeaker." The warm boom of my father's voice always gave me strength, and I turned toward the living room when I didn't find Mom in the kitchen. In this instance, disappointment filled me, needing my mother's penchant for balance over my Dad's practicality, but I'd take what I could get. I found him sitting in his favorite chair, a deep leather wingback that had traveled with us all the way from Italy. "What do you need?"

Dad looked up from the book in his hands with a calm mien, his thick black hair heavily regimented from years in the military. Hazel eyes only a shade darker than mine, studied me carefully as if he could pick the answer from my brain. Between his fit musculature and a firm jawline, he'd always cut a handsome figure in his officer's uniform. Now he wore the ubiquitous jeans and cotton button up of a cowboy with the same air of competent command.

"I'm looking for Mom, actually." Guilt colored my confession, well aware I'd been hoping to dodge the responsibility bullet until after Mom bolstered the urge to follow my dreams. It's not like I planned to make a lifetime career out of working at renaissance festivals, but it didn't take a genius to understand that something so physically demanding would be best done while young. After all, I'd have the rest of my life to talk marketing with bigwigs who would mostly ignore me, and I could do that just as easily from a desk chair as anywhere else.

"You know, Jo, you can talk to me too. Even if it's about boys, I'm generally a good listener." The combination of hope and admonition in his tone felt comical to my skewed funny bone, and I gave him a reluctant grin as I sat on the ottoman at his feet. "No, Daddy, it's not about boys or even school. But it is about something foolish, and I know that isn't really your bailiwick."

"Hey, I've been known to act on a whim." The mock indignation laced through the statement did the job he wanted it to do, and I laughed easily. "Dad, the only whim you've ever pursued was Mom, over 25 years ago."

"I've had a lot of whims though. And look how well pursuing that one moment of lighthearted frivolity worked out for me," he replied seriously, thick brows lifting toward his faintly receding hairline, which in no way detracted from his looks. "How about you give me a try, at least?"

For a moment, the bold truth of his declaration rang in my ears, realigning my viewpoint of the universe with little effort. It took a second to find my voice around the compelling honesty vibrating through my bones. "True enough, Dad." I sighed heavily and looked up at the ceiling, trying to order my thoughts coherently. "Here's my quandary. I'm all set to do the responsible thing and start job hunting right after graduation, but I just had an exceptionally rare offer dropped in my lap that I'm torn about pursuing."

"Ah, did that Clark fellow get ahold of you then?" he asked matter of factly, stunning me into speechlessness yet again.

Swallowing a few times, I stammered. "How did you know?"

"He called me last week, checking your references, and I told him all about your riding proficiency and work ethic. Caroline Grant rang me the next day to let me know he called her too, but we didn't want to get your hopes up."

"He did? You did? She did?" I squeaked. Now you know why he called me Squeaker, because that's what happened whenever I got excited. Like a Jack Russel waiting for someone to throw a ball. Ugh.

"Sure did. And I imagine you think I'll tell you to focus on doing the responsible thing, to not pursue something so foolish." Taking my silence confirmation, he chuckled before continuing. "Well, my Jo, you are also responsible for fulfilling your heart, and you'll probably question your decision for the rest of your life, if not outright regretting it if you don't at least try. Bart said they take four interns, and they'll weed you down in the first month, so you won't be losing much time if it doesn't work out."

When Mom got back in from the garden she also threw her blessing in, sharing in a bit of childish squealing. It wasn't until that night, when we walked over to Gran's house for the *cawl cymraeg* she served every time I came home to visit, that I encountered real opposition. Half way through my bowl of lamb and veggie soup, Gran shoved away from the table with a frown, professing to need to finish working on a pie. Considering Gran's hunched shoulders, and the way she'd broken her own rule about getting up from the table during a meal, I stared after her in shock.

Mom touched my elbow, her soft smile and chocolate brown eyes sweet with support. "Honey, I think she's probably just worried about you. How about you go see if you can help? Let her know why you want to do this so badly."

Sighing, I stood up from the huge family table that only ever reach capacity at holidays and pushed through the swinging door to Gran's well-ordered kitchen. The old gas stove gleamed against the far wall, the counters immaculate and well ordered, but I found Gran bent over the massive island, rolling out dough. She wore a braid that matched mine, though her walnut brown had slowly become gilded with silver threads, and her shoulders were still hunched defensively.

"Gran?" I queried softly, sneaking around her side to snatch a small piece of raw pastry, just as I had since childhood. As she smacked my fingers, at least it prompted a smile. While I had spent most of my life traveling for Dad's military career, many summers were spent on the home ranch as well. *Cynefin* would always call to me, no matter where I went, because this is where my roots lay.

"Precocious child." She chided, gently wrapping the dough around the rolling pin so she could place it on top of the apple plum pie laid out beside her. I held my breath, another childhood holdover, as if one wrong move would ruin the result, but there could be no doubts. A magician of the highest order when it came to the kitchen, Gran never failed.

Then she pushed the dish toward me, having long ago given over crimping the edges to me; she'd claimed it to be a young woman's work, that her hands were becoming bent and feeble with age, but it was a fib. I'd sooner hand her a jar I couldn't open as I would my Dad. Bending to my task with due diligence, I ventured to talk as I worked.

"I gather you don't approve of this jousting thing?"

She harrumphed faintly, but I knew it too well to not hear it. "I can't say as I'm excited about anything that involves you getting hurt, *fy annwyl*."

I couldn't help a soft chuckle, her years of quoting Welsh proverbs at me finally paying dividends. "*Adfyd a ddwg wybodaeth, a gwybodaeth ddoethineb*." Adversity brings knowledge, and knowledge, wisdom.

"The cheek, throwing my words back at me!" Despite the verbal chastisement, a glint of pride shone in her amber eyes. "You cannot want this, my darling. You've your way to make in this world, and now that school is almost over, a life to create. So much you've put on hold to reach this goal, mainly your heart. How can you hope to find love, to add to the story of our family, when you are being pummeled at every turn?"

Wincing under the weight of her hopes, I responded quickly, pushing the finished pie toward her. "Gran, this *is* a matter of the heart. You've always taught me to push my own limits, and I know you understand the need for me to love myself. To write my own tale before joining my story line with another."

Indeed, this lingered as a sore subject between us. I'd never truly risked loving anyone but family, the two boyfriends I'd had warranting mere paragraphs in the epic adventure of my life. To Gran, love meant the world, and after losing Grandpa Llewellyn five years ago, it had gained in esteem.

Quietly, she turned to put the pie in the oven and I marveled over the woman I resembled so much in both work ethic and looks. She gestured me to join her at the sink, where we both washed our hands, and only when she'd handed me a flour sack towel to dry my hands did she finally speak. "If you are determined in your course, *fy annwyl*, I know I shall not dissuade you. We raised you with tales of heroes and it is no wonder you wish to have your own adventures." She cupped my cheek, and looked up at the height I'd gained from my father, smiling wistfully. "My grand adventure was your Grandpa, and I just hope when love comes calling, you'll be brave and answer the door as readily as you have for this."

I bent to hug her, burying my nose against her neck just as I had all my life, and she tugged my braid playfully before I stepped away again. "I can do no less, with the brave example my family has set for me." I didn't bother to tell her that jousting remained the least of my worries when it came to finding a boyfriend—I could run them off with my smart mouth and unwillingness to be a doormat all on my own.

Ah, there she showed me the smile I loved, years falling from her face in an instant. "Yes indeed. A Bowen woman's heart is her own, and I'm glad you know yours." Then we headed back to our dinners, and I let her ply me with a fresh ladleful of *cawl*, grateful down to my bones for a family that would love me no matter where my heart led me.

Later that night, I wrote a short, pointed email that barely scratched the surface of my excitement over the adventure to come.

'*Sir Clark,*

Glad to hear from you, starting the legwork to clear my schedule. Looking forward to joining the troupe for the summer, please send further instruction so I can arrive prepared to learn.
Respectfully,
Josephine Bowen'

❤❤❤

After that, finishing classes and walking for my degree in the humid Indiana heat seemed anti-climactic, but it sure made my parents happy. Being an only child sometimes led to a lot of pressure to achieve, since Dad and Mom had just one shot to get it right. Then I spent two intensive weeks at home, working not only my own horse but several others. Add in a hefty dose of my Mom, eager to spend time together before I left again, and the workout regime Sir Clark had recommended, and I fell into bed early every night.

The day of my departure, I got up before dawn, sneaking out to the barn to saddle up in the quiet hush of darkness. Abby, my dear partner of twelve years, nuzzled my neck with her long whiskers before I slid on her bridle, tears coming unbidden at the rare show of affection. Horses in general weren't affectionate the way people were, and Abby herself qualified as a veritable ice queen.

I thought back to the first time I rode her, how standoffish and cranky she had been, kicking out every time I applied my leg to ask for more. It had taken many long hacks around the countryside, and two moves to different Air Force bases, to convince her that I refused to give up on her. She'd been incredibly angry when I disappeared for college, reverting to old habits the first couple visits home, until I promised her I would always come back. Her moon-white face looked more familiar to me than my own, her long grey legs having carried me through countless adventures, and even now, it stung to realize I'd be leaving her alone yet again.

"I'm sorry, Abs. I'd take you with me, but these guys use draft horses, and I don't want you getting beat up." I murmured, laughing when she pinned her ears in response, as if insulted by the insinuation that she couldn't hold her own with a bunch of clunky plow horses. I knew she didn't understand a word I said, but sometimes, I thought her intuition read the meaning of my words. No doubt her thoroughbred speed would be an advantage in some situations, but I still couldn't envision her carrying me around in armor. "You really don't want another horse running at you anyway. Add in some crazy person with a huge stick trying to hit me, and I think you'd hate it."

Her answering yawn rolled her eyes back in her head and squinched her nostrils closed, demonstrating her boredom with the subject. I tightened her girth one more notch, earning a further look of disgust, but when I swung into the saddle she sighed gustily. We turned as one body and headed out into the pale silver of the lightening sky, losing ourselves in each other and the morning. I claimed that selfish hour of calm before the frantic storm of activity likely to ensue when I returned, and closed my eyes to listen to the birds greeting the day as we slipped deeper into the cattle pastures my father managed.

Before joining the military my Dad had been raised in a close knit rural community, and just before I entered college he had retired to take over the family ranch. That summer before college started had been one of the best of my life, no longer gauged by well-planned vacations, just early morning feedings and late night barn checks, mutual effort knitting our family closer together. Grandma Pearl still ran everything from behind the scenes, growing prize winning gardens and canning enough vegetables to feed the whole town. I waved at her as I passed the house my father grew up in, and she waved back from her regular station on the screen porch, her rocking chair in perpetual motion.

Abby took us back to the barn in her own good time, relying on me to manage gate latches, and only spooking once as a cow and calf popped out of the bushes. Still wet from being born, the calf's coat showed a deeper red than his mother's in the rising sunlight. I snapped a picture with my phone so I could remember the cow's tag number for my father—he would no doubt go out and check the little creature over after I left.

After a good curry and a few carrots, I turned Abby loose in the pasture with one last pat. Not one for undue affection, she turned on her hindquarters in a display of athleticism that put a lump in my throat, throwing dust in the air as she galloped toward the herd in the distance. As I turned to walk away I noticed a long coil of her silvery tail hair, left on the ground like some sort of parting gift. The strands glittered like precious metal under the now full light of the sun and I picked it up, twirling it thoughtfully in my fingers as I headed up to the house for breakfast.

Mom plied me with waffles and bacon, my two favorite things, though I asked for some eggs as well. She fussed about how much weight I had already lost getting ready to go as she prepared them. I didn't have the heart to tell her I'd actually gained muscle weight, despite the smaller size jeans I now wore, but the freshman fifteen had finally melted from my negligible waist.

After slowly savoring every bite, I swiped leftover syrup from my plate with an extra slice of bacon, knowing how much I would miss the food from home. Everything on the plate except for the wheat for the waffles and the maple syrup had come from our farm, even the meat. Don't judge—I'd been in 4-H or something like it since I'd been big enough to raise a rabbit, showing everything from chickens to cows, and enjoying the byproducts thereof for just as long.

Looking up from sopping the yolk on his own plate with a slice of toast, Dad grinned. "If you make it to the second round of internship, Squeaker, Mom and I can drive down to visit. We'll bring you a care package with all the good stuff, so you get enough protein. You'll need it. And I imagine Grandma Pearl will send along some jams and cookies."

I rolled my eyes and laughed, though admittedly, my mouth watered at the idea. "I don't know, Dad, I'll be living with a bunch of guys. Unless you bring it in a safe that I can lock, none of it will probably last long."

"Well, as long as those boys are good to my little girl, I imagine I can pack some extra for them too." Mom responded, squeezing my hand where it rested on the table. "I'm still not so sure about you living with a bunch of strange men, Josie."

Mom had refused to call me Jo my whole life, telling my father it sounded too masculine, but I didn't mind. After all, he'd gotten a daughter that could be just as much a son, and I liked that they each had their own way to cherish me. Even when it

10

made me crazy to have the weight of all their hopes hanging off my shoulders. With Mom, I could be girly, and go shopping, get pedicures, watch chick flicks. She'd been my one constant friend throughout our transient lifestyle, and the older I got, the stronger our friendship had become.

On the other hand, Dad got his hunting buddy and extra cowhand, who preferred driving trucks and getting her boots dirty. His only complaint remained my refusal to fish. I'd never once enjoyed standing on a river bank casting a line for hours. I'd go with him, but from ten years of age onward, I had used the quiet hours listening to the running water as an excellent chance to read. Stories were the one vice our family shared, the love of words written into our Welsh DNA.

I flipped my hand over and squeezed hers in return. "Don't worry, Mom. Sir Clark has repeatedly told me the men in the company are expected to behave chivalrously toward all women, that honor is their strongest code. Likely, this is going to be like having a nosey, over protective passel of brothers. And if you come down to visit, you'll get to see that for yourself." She mustered a trembling smile, but I'd done what I could. Now, it would be a matter of time, for the proof to win her over.

They helped me pack my car, which didn't take long, since I had only packed clothes and a few books. If I only lasted the first four weeks, it would be foolish to take more, and if I stayed longer, home was really only two hours away. Dad smiled and simply hugged me extra hard before heading toward the barn, leaving me alone with Mom.

"You promise me you'll call if you need anything, Josephine?" she asked, sniffling to keep back the tears trying to drop off her eyelashes. "And you'll take care of yourself, and you'll come straight home if things aren't going well?"

"Mom, you've known these guys as long as I have. You know where I will be unless we are traveling for a show. It's not like I'm about to hitchhike across America with a bunch of drug addicts. I have my phone, there is Wi-Fi, and once I know my schedule we will make plans to Skype, okay?"

I stilled the hands wringing the edge of her shirt with my own, wondering when I'd grown up enough to realize sometimes my own Mom needed some mothering. Hugging her tightly, I let her cling, pushing away my impatience in the hopes it would comfort her. Smooching my cheek noisily, like she had since my first day of school, she stepped back and folded her arms around her middle, forcing a smile. Eager to go, not just because I felt excited about the adventure ahead, but because I knew only time would ease her worries, I slid in the door of my little compact car and started the engine.

I waved at Gran one last time as I drove past her house, her form slim and strong as she stood on the front stoop, and hoped I'd do our family name proud. Pausing at the end of the drive, just before the cattle guard that marked the end of our property, I looked through my rear view mirror, memorizing this last sight of home. As I fiddled with my MP3 player, hunting for an upbeat playlist for the drive, movement back by the barn caught my eye. I saw Abby's big grey butt lifting in the air, bucking a small circle and shaking her neck, the silky hairs of her mane waving in the wind of her own creation. Smiling, I put my foot on the gas, headed off toward the unknown with a far lighter heart than I woke up with that morning.

I arrived at the farm in good time, traffic minimal for a Saturday, greeted by an unexpected quietness as I pulled down the long drive. No whinnies came from the barn, no barking of dogs or even the ever present hum of chewing horses marred the silence. Sir Clark had given me his cell phone number, so as I put my car in park between a sleek Porsche and a rusty Chevy pickup I dropped him a text to let him know I'd arrived.

By the time I called Mom to let her know I'd safely reached the farm no one had appeared, and my own curious nature got the better of me. Softly closing the door of my car, I slipped around the end of the barn to find the main doors open wide. The interior, while a little dark, felt cool, and neat as a pin, exuding a sense of peace that seeped through my pores. Admittedly, I'd been worried that the standards of horse keeping might be lax— I'd known big time riders who were an absolute shambles whenever they weren't in the public eye. Reassured by the tidy row of manure forks along one wall and the freshly raked aisle, I emerged from the other end of the barn and lifted a hand to shade my eyes from the brightness of the sun.

On a far hill, a group of riders broke through the tree line. They were too far away for me to pick out details, just a mob of large horses blending together, the humid air blurring everything.

Then one broke from the group; even from so far away I could hear the pounding of the horse's feet, and my heart stuttered like a snare drum at the thundering reverberation.

The lone rider came on at a reckless clip, bent forward over his horse's neck to urge him on. For one moment, a naive part of me got caught up in the romanticism of the image, but then, my horsewoman's heart won out. My nose wrinkled at the selfish display; I remembered the time I got grounded for running my pony toward the barn when I was eight. I'd never forgotten the disappointment in my mother's eyes, and the banked anger in my father's as they'd explained why you always brought your horse in cool.

The big black, well past 17 hands tall, and no doubt breaking in over a ton, already sported lather on his chest and neck, taking my eyes away from the attractive man on his back. It took real effort to disguise my irritation as the rider sat up hard to slow his mount, the bit dragging through the horse's mouth as they circled tightly to keep from running me over. Eyes rolling, the huge Percheron danced sideways, agitated by the rough handling, and unable to contain myself any longer, I hooked two fingers in the horse's noseband. Immediately, he quieted, bringing his head down to my level with a grateful sigh as a frown sketched over the model perfect face of his rider.

"May I cool out your horse, Sir?" I asked, trying to keep my tone civil, but some hint of my displeasure must have come through. The young man's lips thinned and his pale blue eyes narrowed with suspicion, humanizing his smooth face in an instant. Before he could address me the sound of hoof beats filled the stable yard.

As I looked past the pretty blonde idiot and his long suffering mount, my eyes went round with excitement as two men led in the rest of the cadre. Side by side, one on a towering steel grey and another on a muscular sooty black, they sat tall and quiet in the tack. Hands soft on lifted reins, their bodies moved to the metronome rhythm of their horse's foot falls. I could describe it no other way than dancing, the horse's knees lifted high, their hocks flexing deeply beneath their bodies, belying their size with incredible lightness. Like they had done it a thousand times before, without so much as a whispered whoa the two horses rooted themselves to the ground, and while I stood momentarily awed by the spectacle I lifted my eyes to their riders.

Closest to me, his shrewd blue eyes taking in the scene without an ounce of emotion, I studied a face I knew well from years of attending the renaissance festival. Sir Aaron Drew of Carrington, the leader of the company, known for his absolute honor and flawless aim. Women were known to affect a swoon or drop hankies in his general direction without provocation, as much for his manners as his looks. While not quite as pretty as the dimwit I just saved the horse from, his features were striking nonetheless. Wild brown hair framed a strong, clean shaven jaw and nice lips, for a man. Those lips were currently as thin as the idiot's as he took in my hand on the horse's bridle, and I lifted an eyebrow in response, jutting one hip out in defiance.

Laughter wrecked the tension in the air, a gruff bark that pulled my gaze to the other man. This unknown fellow, a rougher specimen than the other two, sported strikingly green eyes, currently twinkling with humor, though something made me suspect it was a rare look for him. His full lips were struggling to stay firm against the amusement he found in the situation, a pale, puckered scar peeking up from the scruff texturing his jaw. A faint similarity echoed between him and Sir Drew, though aside from the color of hair, I couldn't put my finger on the specifics. Instead of long hair he wore a more conservative style, reminiscent of my lifetime as a military brat.

"Aaron, I believe you can relax." He finally rumbled, amusement fading as he looked over at the idjit still sitting on his heaving horse. "And Trace, you can get yourself off your horse. He looks like he's going to need a long walk to cool off."

The moron started to open his mouth, the sudden paling of his face making me look back at the nameless supporter. An unyielding firmness filled those eyes now, all hints of early lightness lost.

"Miss Bowen, if you'd be so kind as to let Cappy go, Trace will take care of him, I assure you."

15

The directive in that voice, and a surety in his face made me drop my hand without qualm. This man was to be obeyed, which bothered me not in the least. In fact, it reassured me a great deal, knowing none of the horses were likely to be ill-treated on his watch. As the moron now known as Trace stalked back toward the barn with his horse in tow I stepped closer to the two men and tipped my chin up a little so I could see them better.

"Miss Bowen." The more cultured voice of the Captain drew my attention, his clipped diction reminding me faintly of one of my professors. "I am Aaron Drew, and this gentleman beside me is Sir Bart. Bartholomew Clark, I believe is how he addressed himself to you. His word is as good as mine, and you will be spending a good deal of time under his tutelage for the next several weeks."

I looked to the rough edged man, barely lifting a corner of my mouth before I nodded my head in acknowledgement. No doubt, this fellow would push me to my breaking point, but I sensed an infinite fairness in him. If he pushed me that hard he'd be doing the same to everyone else.

"Now, if you'd be so kind, we need to take care of our mounts before evening feeding. Join us in chores, then we will get you settled in."

This time, I stepped back, hands lifting toward the bridles of both horses, allowing the men to dismount without worry. A tip of Sir Clark's chin indicated approval as Sir Drew barked over his shoulder to the rest of the company for them to dismount. As a unit, six legs lifted over their horse's backs, six men dropped to the ground with remarkable grace for their size. I began to detect a theme, which gave me a little thrill. I was no little woman, but it seemed finesse played into the equation as much as brawn, and that would play right into my wheelhouse.

"That is a good habit to get into, Miss Bowen." The timber of Sir Clark's voice sounded like what I imagined a bear would, if it could talk. "Armored knights aren't the most graceful creatures, and sometimes that armor makes the trip toward the ground a little more cumbersome. It helps to know someone is at your horse's head should anything go wrong."

Filing that away, I nodded, using a finger to scratch under the chin of Sir Drew's mount, the big grey canting his head toward me for more. Rather than taking it amiss Sir Drew also scratched his mount, rubbing vigorously under the thick mane until the horse bent around him like a pretzel, trying to reciprocate the attention. If I'd had any doubts about the horsemanship of this outfit that alone would have dispelled them—to care for the small comforts often meant the larger needs were well provided for.

Then the man turned to me, holding out a broad palm, several long fingers thickened at the joints. We shook hands as my father taught me, firm enough to convey resolve, but not forceful or testing. Nodding as if to himself, he grinned and pointed toward the barn. "Alright, Miss Bowen, let's put those capable hands to work."

An hour of pleasant diligence saw the horses untacked and rinsed clean of sweat, and most of them rewarded our efforts by immediately rolling in their stalls. My jaded opinion of Trace softened slightly when I caught him crouched in the shavings of his horse's stall, whispering unintelligible nonsense as he fed the horse a carrot. Once horses and equipment were sorted out evening feeding began, conversation drowned out by the horses banging impatiently against the walls. Still, at the end of it all, the rest of the men acted more comfortable around me, and Sir Clark led us out of the barn to the steady grind of horses consuming their supper.

On his heels, I noticed a very faint limp, kind of like the one I sported the last time Abby bucked me off for being stupid. It had been a long time ago, but the bruises to my ego and thigh had taken a long time to fade. I briefly wondered at the source of his discomfort but shook it away. His business, not mine.

We trooped down a gravel path toward an old, outdated brick ranch house, the paint starting to peel from the porch railing. The brass handle rasped as he shoved open the door but the interior surprised me, everything neat and in good repair. Considering how many men lived there my expectation of a locker room scent would be reasonable, yet it smelled almost pleasant. While the wretched pea green carpet wore the additional ugliness of countless pair of boots treading across it, it too appeared fairly clean.

"Make yourselves comfortable." Sir Clark dropped himself into a sturdy wooden dining chair with a barely perceptible wince, donning an expression of patience belied by his crossed arms.

The men all responded to the underlying tone of command and folded themselves on to the available furniture, while I settled on the worn leather recliner. The seat looked too deep to sit all the way back in without looking ridiculous, so I leaned forward, elbows on my knees, keeping my eyes on the two men in charge.

"I wanted to only do this once, but since our last candidate had car troubles, she won't be in until tomorrow morning at best. For you newbies, expect it's going to be a thankless couple of weeks. While we don't believe in hazing, outside of this house, *you* are going to be doing most of the grunt work around here, proving you've got the work ethic required to thrive in this company. That's going to mean getting up early for chores, lots of cleaning, and moving more manure than you've probably ever seen in your lives." His smile pulled an answering one to my lips, even if it looked a bit grim around the edges. "If anyone is rude to you, come see me, and I will straighten things out, but don't be a whiner. This is going to be tough, physically and mentally, and if you can't handle this, then you aren't going to be able to hack the jousting either."

A snort from one of the guys on the sofa made Sir Clark's eyes narrow, and I looked out the corner of my own vision at a guy probably a couple years younger than me. Everything about him screamed frat boy, from the Tommy Hilfiger jeans to the highlighted and styled hair. Like an imbecile, he stared right back at Sir Clark with all the smug superiority of an entitled brat.

"You think this is funny, Cranston?" While it wasn't directed at me the ice in his tone still sent a shiver down my spine. "Because I'll happily boot you right back out the door if you are going to waste my time with juvenile pissing contests like this."

Frat boy proved to be smarter than he looked, dropping his eyes just enough to no longer be challenging and clearing his throat. "No, Sir."

"Cranston and Lee, you'll be bunking together, last door down the hall. Bowen, you'll be on the other end of the house with Brantley, when she gets in tomorrow. We've only got a few rules here. One is to always behave honorably. Failure to do so will result in your immediate removal from the property." I noticed he looked straight at frat boy when he said it. Sir Clark's radar and mine were apparently reading the same frequency of douche bag. "Two, the horses come first. You take care of them like you would family, because we'd all look damned stupid jousting on foot."

Sir Drew covered a chuckle with a cough, and innate curiosity left me wondering what sort of inside joke they shared. But then the Captain straightened in his seat to address us, his razor sharp gaze pinning each of us down individually. "This is a team. We have a good group already, and we are looking for people who fit into the established company. That doesn't mean you have to act like everyone else, or bend who you are to fit. We are here to find out which of you we can bend ourselves around too. You know myself, and Sir Bart, already."

Every time he said it I immediately imagined the man in an eye patch with a peg leg, and I shook my head slightly to dispel the picture.

"On our roster we also have Sir John Barry of Kent." A lanky older man with a chaotic mop of reddish blonde hair unfolded himself from the loveseat, his legs perpetually bent as if astride. The bow he offered felt one part sincere and two parts comical, as if he made fun of his own chivalry. I didn't recognize him, but without his heraldry to identify him by it didn't surprise me.

"We also have Sir Alex Black of St. Sebastian's." Long, raven sleek hair swept back from sharply drawn brows and a narrow nose, he wore a faint sneer like one might wear a favorite hat, almost as though daring you to pick a fight with him. This fellow read classic dark knight from head to toe, and I recognized him as the villain from the past few years at the fair.

"Pleasure, I'm sure." He intoned, barely sketching a bow of his head, but part of me wondered at the truth of his abrasive sarcasm.

"And lastly, the newly knighted Sir Trace Davies of Montrose."

As the young man stood it took an act of will to shake off my earlier irritation at him. He couldn't be blamed for being pretty, genetics being what they were. His long blonde hair shone fair enough to glitter in faint light, and he had ocean blue eyes framed by lashes women would kill for. Nor could I hold him responsible for my own suspicions against the physically perfect, from his narrow waist and wide shoulders, all the way to his dimpled cheeks. When you are no classic beauty, like myself, gorgeous people sometimes put your back up. No doubt the girls in the audience screamed the loudest for him, and while I'd been less than impressed with his negligent gallop, his seat looked solid enough. If the Captain and Quartermaster had seen fit to knight him there must be something virtuous beneath the shiny exterior.

"Great to meet you all." Trace grinned, looking around at all of us, though his eyes stuttered and then jumped over me. I saw a bit of over eager golden retriever in his manner, and it softened my earlier snap judgement.

"Sir John and Sir Alex do not live on site, and have day jobs, so you won't be seeing too terribly much of them until the weekends. Sir Trace is in the first bedroom on the right, and you can ask him about anything you require during off hours. Sir Clark and myself both live above the barn, and our phone numbers are posted on the refrigerator if you need us. For the newbies, I suggest you get settled into your rooms, then we will all head to town. Pizza is on me; beer is up to you."

With that, Aaron rose from his seat, practiced elegance in even that simple movement. His spurs made a faint chinking noise, distracting me enough that I nearly missed the stiffness in Sir Clark as he unbent from the unforgiving chair. His first few steps were crabbed but he quickly lengthened his stride, leaving all of us alone in the room. Sir Alex stepped forward to fill the gap and cleared his throat harshly to garner our attention.

"When we are here on the weekends, John and I occupy the left hand bedroom. To say I value my privacy would be putting it mildly." The sneer appeared again, twisting the corner of his mustache. "Touching my things will certainly guarantee my recommendation for your removal from the house." With that, he started down the darkened hall, leaving John to shrug apologetically and follow him.

Trace stepped up next, greeting Lee first, giving me a chance to evaluate the other candidate. This guy appeared unassuming, not too tall or too short, his hair a nondescript brown in a vaguely in between haircuts sort of shagginess. Even his body looked squarish and plain, though the muscles in his arms definitely came from hard work. Asked to pick him out of a crowd, I don't know that I could, but intelligence shadowed his dark eyes, reminding me to judge no book by its bland exterior.

Cranston shook Trace's hand next, his grip the testing kind, proving that while smart enough not to mess with the big dog he had no qualms challenging everyone else. "Hey there, man. Toby Cranston, looking forward to working with you." While his tone declared him all hail fellow, well met, something in his eyes made my shoulders tighten.

"Yeah, same here." Trace replied, extending and flexing the fingers of his hand once Cranston released it. "Looking forward to having some people around closer to my age, you know?"

Reflexively, my eyes rolled. While these guys were in my age bracket, I felt so much older, and I worried I'd be finding myself without friends to relate to. Don't get me wrong, I didn't generally mind being considered mature for my age. That trait had helped me get along incredibly well with my parents and nearly every teacher I'd ever learned from. But it did make finding peers a little more difficult. Maybe the girl arriving in the morning would be better.

A shadow fell over me, and I looked up, schooling my face into a facsimile of friendliness. It wavered slightly under the calculating scrutiny of Cranston, almost revealing my utter distaste. He positioned himself too close, invading my personal space, testing me, I felt, but in this he would not find me lacking. I rose to my full height, almost bumping chests he stood so close, and reined in a smile when he stepped back. I owned an inch of height on him, and when it forced him look up slightly his lips curled unpleasantly.

"Hi, I'm Jo Bowen." For a moment, he became confused, since I'd taken away his verbal high ground by attacking first. "Pleasure to meet you."

Though slightly delayed, he returned fire. "Yeah, a pleasure." Never had such a pleasant word held so much disdain. "What brings you here?"

"I want to joust." Smiling vacuously, I hoped to disarm him with sweetness. Posturing exhausted me, and while I hated playing the girl card I hoped it would take some of the wind out of his sails. "Just like the rest of you."

A glimmer of pure viciousness sprang up in his calculating eyes, and I braced for whatever vitriol he could come up with. Luckily, Trace and Lee saved me the trouble, stepping forward to introduce themselves and Cranston's mouth remained shut.

"I'm Fillmore Lee, though everyone but my Momma calls me Fill." Lee said, reaching for my hand to pump it amiably. "Great to meet a girl who thinks this is cool."

"Oh, you'll find no shortage of girls who think you are the most wonderful thing since the invention of selfies if you are around for the faire." His ears pinkened, but he grinned readily, revealing an easy going manner that would disarm his opponents faster than a riposte.

Trace offered me his hand next and I grasped it without qualm, fighting a smile when his eyes widened in surprise. Pretty as he might be, he seemed like a sweet kid and I felt willing to let our earlier encounter go if he would.

"Sorry about earlier, I was eager to meet the next candidate, and I think Cappy picked up on it. Before I knew it, we were flying, and I was having too much fun to rein him in. He's usually the laziest horse in the barn."

"Bygones and all that." I grinned and squeezed his hand encouragingly, and he smiled so widely I almost expected a lolling tongue to pop out and his butt to start wagging. Yeah, golden retriever, all the way.

"Can I help you carry anything in?"

I shook my head. "No, I've just got one big bag. Only brought the basics, but I'm two hours from home, so I can go back for more if needed."

"Alright then, we'll leave you to it."

As he swung his sculpted jaw back toward the other two candidates I took my leave, stretching my arms over my head to dispel the tension in my shoulders. The air outside felt reasonably pleasant, just humid enough to make the hairs touching my forehead stick, but not enough to render my clothes damp, and I sucked in a big lungful before exhaling the last of my worries. While Cranston had already worked his way under my skin like a splinter, my heart felt too full of hope for the future to let it ruin my mood.

I slept like a rock after our pizza dinner, a combination of carbohydrates and a long day putting me right out. Luckily, I jumped right up at the first sound of my alarm, and while my brain objected to being up before the sun I stumbled from the bed with excitement. Day one of my adventure was about to begin in earnest.

The room I would be sharing had once been the master bedroom, and while I didn't usually like preferential treatment for being a girl I sure appreciated not having to share a bathroom with a bunch of guys. Mind you, Sir Alex and Sir John had left last night after supper, so there were only three other people to concern myself with. All the same, as I scrubbed my face free of sleep and dragged a brush through my hair, I counted myself lucky. As clean as the rest of the house was, the quick peek of Trace's room last night as we all parted ways had revealed a veritable pig sty, further humanizing the walking, talking piece of art.

Honestly, the kid had proved himself funny—not witty, or sarcastic in the least, he had been self-deprecating without being ingratiating. When Sir Alex had sniped at him about being the pretty boy, he had replied with "God asked me if I wanted brains or looks, and I said looks. Good thing too, because we all know jousters don't have brains anyway." I almost shot Coke out my nose at the pole axed expression on Sir Alex's face and Sir John had laughed so hard his face turned purple.

The evening became a relaxing way to get to know each of them better, even Sir Bart unbending enough to challenge us to air hockey. He'd wiped the floor with all of us, beer held negligently in one hand, despite our desperate sweaty efforts. The deceptive casualness of his posture changed only twice, once when I smacked the puck hard enough to make it bounce, clipping one of his knuckles. His wince made me worry for a moment, but then he took advantage of my awkward embarrassment to score the winning shot.

The second came as he faced Sir John, who proved a more formidable opponent than his mild mannered exterior would lead you to believe. Their contest traded goals evenly for some time, then there had been no score for several minutes, my head swiveling back and forth like a bobble head at a high speed tennis match. That all changed the instant Bart set his beer down on the edge of the table, never taking his eyes off the puck. Two moves later, he scored the final goal, setting his mallet down with casual indifference despite the back slapping congratulations from Trace. John good naturedly called him a bastard, and they all laughed it off on the way back to the table.

"Get a move on," came bellowing from the family room, shattering my musings and hurrying my fingers, finishing off the plait in my hair with a rubber band before I dragged on a baseball cap. Hurrying out the door with my boots still in hand, I relaxed slightly, noticing Cranston and Fillmore remained unaccounted for. Still couldn't bring myself to call Frat Boy by his first name. I didn't like him well enough to behave that familiarly toward him.

Sir Clark nodded at me perfunctorily from his seat at the kitchen table, one hand drumming against the hardwood and the other lifting a steaming cup of coffee to his lips. Leaning against the counter at the edge of the kitchen, I laced up my short paddock boots, wiggling my toes in the familiar embrace of leather. Just as I straightened the two boys entered the room,

Cranston perfectly coiffed and coutured, while his roommate glowered at him, still tucking his shirt into his jeans. I didn't miss the miniscule grin of mischief on Sir Clark's face, and restrained myself from joining in on it. No doubt, Fillmore now regretted having to share the bathroom with the resident fashionista.

"Alright, plebes, we have chores to do." Admittedly, the early morning growl in Sir Clark's voice came off a little intimidating, my nerves strung slightly tighter at the first word. "First, we feed grain, then turn out, then clean stalls. If you get that done before nine you get a riding lesson after lunch. If you don't you'll be helping shovel the old manure pile into the spreader for the rest of the day. Grab coffee and a power bar off the counter if you want them, then get your asses to the barn. If you aren't there by the time I get feed buckets mixed you won't like the consequences."

He quit us without a backward glance, and by dint of my position, I grabbed my power bar first, leaving Cranston and Fillmore to sort themselves out. I didn't particularly care for coffee, unless desperate, so it only took a second to snag a bottle of water out of the fridge and head out the front door.

The cool morning air tightened my skin, but not enough to raise goosebumps, the sun just peeking over the horizon as I hurried toward the barn. Deep, guttural nickers sounded out from the stalls, several horses poking their heads over the bottom of their Dutch doors to stare down the hall at the feed room. I stroked the soft nose of Eros, the sooty black Sir Clark rode the day before, chuckling when he shoved his enormous head against me as if to hurry my feet toward the source of his breakfast.

In the tiny room relegated to grain storage I found Sir Clark bent at the waist, head and shoulders deep in a plastic bin, scraping the dregs up with a scoop. "Grab me another bag of oats." he said, grumbly voice muffled inside the bin, not even looking up from his task.

I snatched the fifty-pound paper sack off the appropriate pile and laid it over my shoulder to carry it across the short distance, at home in the familiar routine of taking care of animals. Yet when Sir Clark straightened, clearing the way for me to step closer, his eyebrows shot up. Wrinkles appeared in his forehead when I yanked the string to open the bag, allowing its contents to hiss straight into the bin.

"Good morning, Bowen. You look like you've done this before."

"Yes, Sir. Rancher's daughter." My simple explanation didn't seem to satisfy him, and the quirk of apparent disbelief that rode his lips put my back up. "I thought my father would have made that clear."

Sensing my irritation, he held one hand up, palm toward me. "Well, rancher's daughter can mean different things. I'm sad to say I didn't query much beyond your riding skills, imagining you were some sort of rodeo queen or barrel racer." Sipping casually from the mug he picked up off a shelf, he offered a faint smile of apology, waiting me out for a response.

"Sure, I've run barrels. Got boring pretty quickly though, and I'm allergic to glitter." I responded dryly, smiling to myself when he almost choked on his swallow of coffee. "I've done everything from brand and doctor cattle to feeding in a spring blizzard. I hunt better than most guys I know, and can drive a forty-foot gooseneck with one arm tied behind my back. Anything my Daddy did, I did too. Which means I expect you to push me just as hard as you do these boys."

One eyebrow arched quizzically when I mentioned hunting—not a surprise, as most men got pretty bothered by the idea of a woman with a gun. But when I spit out the word boys, he obviously heard the veiled irritation I'd been attempting to disguise. His mouth opened as if to comment, but then he looked toward the door, focusing on the shuffling footsteps coming from the aisle way.

"Welcome to the party, gentlemen." The greeting came out so exceedingly mild my own eyebrows shot up, but I smoothed my expression before anyone could note it. "Cranston, grab the pile of buckets, Lee, you'll be opening doors. Bowen, you get to run the gauntlet and drop the feed."

It took some willpower not to turn toward the challenge I heard in his assignment, making me wonder which of these gentle giants behaved less than gentlemanly about his food. A one-ton animal definitively won the size advantage from me, but if I stayed quick on my feet maybe I'd get through this unscathed. Back in the hallway, all the horses now stared pointedly at us, several flinging their massive heads around wildly. I swallowed any nerves, determined to exceed his expectations. The challenge in and of itself may have been a test, to see if I would let it get to me.

The first three went smoothly, each stepping back politely to allow me in the corner to attach their buckets to the wall. Number four, a strapping red fellow with a bright white blaze, had the name Tuck painted on his door. His only issue proved to be the profuse amount of drool pouring from his mouth as if someone had neglected to turn off a spigot. I dodged all efforts to smear some on me, sneaking under his neck as he attempted to shove his head in the bucket and had it securely clipped before he was on me. While I moved quickly he still managed to mark me with a lengthy string of saliva by flinging his head in excitement as he moved toward his grain.

The airborne moisture landed with a wet *swack*, running from my chin to my waist and while certainly not the most attractive thing, I laughed on my way out the door. It still beat out a momma cow snotting all over you as she thrashed in the stocks for palpations. Cranston eyeballed the long trail of slobber with intense disgust as I pulled the next bucket from the stack in his arms, and I resisted the urge to wipe some off on his designer polo shirt.

My next customer, Hawk, proved pushy, but I easily dissuaded him from plowing me over by pinching the thick skin of his neck, mimicking a bite from another horse. Memory sprang up, providing me with the image of Cranston on the sturdy, bright bay Clydesdale—unsurprising that the pushy guy ended up with a pushy horse. In that pairing the universe displayed a marvelous grasp of comedy but since Sir Clark assigned the horses I probably should thank Sir Clark's sense of humor.

Eros behaved exceedingly sweetly, softly whuffling under his breath as he waited for me to hook his bucket, and it gave me even deeper appreciation for Sir Clark's abilities as a horseman. Clearly, he'd done a great job with his mount.

Byzantine, Sir Drew's dappled grey Percheron, proved most wicked, considering I'd thought him sweet yesterday as I scratched his chin. He came at me with wrinkled lips and laid back ears, clearly used to cowing people with a dirty look. Luckily, I'd never been a wilting violet, and I wadded into the fray with a vengeance, fending him off with a quick tap on the soft skin of his nose before darting to the corner. Experience with the other horses had given me enough practice to snap the bucket in by feel alone, allowing me to keep my eyes on the huffy gelding. Offering a snap of his teeth to the air in my general direction he stepped back in shock when I growled and drew up to my full height, giving as good a dirty look as I'd received. His hesitation gave me enough of a gap to hurry back toward the door, wide eyed Lee slamming it behind me.

"Tactfully done, Bowen. Most people drop the bucket and run the first time I send them in." Sir Clark intoned, the compliment so off hand as to seem bored. Narrowing my eyes, I grabbed the next bucket and pivoted on my heel, quitting his presence with haste. Part of me harbored anger that he would send anyone uninformed into that horse's stall, the other felt a little proud that he considered me capable enough to handle it.

As the horses munched on their grain we pulled out all of their water buckets to scrub and refill them. Turning them out became a thrilling experience, the horses well aware of where they were headed, and we simply opened their doors and got out of the way. A ton or better of charging horseflesh took my breath away, the earth beneath my feet vibrating with the concussion of their hooves against the ground.

Sir Clark led us out the end of the barn, down a broad dirt path that wound around the house, following the dust lingering in the air from the horses mad cap gallop to freedom. We emerged through a tree line to find an open gate, beyond it at least forty acres of thigh high grass, the drafts already bent to the task of stuffing their faces. Without prompting, I turned toward the trough along the fence to check its contents, and looked to Sir Clark in inquiry when it proved half empty.

"Lee, there's a hose behind the gate, if you please." Sir Clark directed. Fillmore jumped to the task with alacrity, while Cranston stood around with his thumbs hooked in his pockets, looking bored. "Cranston, right beside it, you'll find a scrub brush. I expect that trough clean enough for me to drink out of when you are done. Bowen, fall in with me."

Without a word, he headed back up the hill, leaving me scrambling to catch up, unable to enjoy the visual of Cranston actually doing manual labor. What I didn't miss was the narrow eyed look of anger the frat boy leveled at me as he stalked toward the trough. Yeah, we were definitely in a mutual antipathy society.

"You've got a problem, Bowen." The remark came off so blasé I almost didn't respond, but the tip of his chin in my direction appeared to be waiting for an answer.

"I just got here." If he wanted to play it cool, well, so could I. "Did I do something wrong?"

"Not actively, though I sense that could change fast if things escalate. Unless something happened last night that I don't know about." A question framed as a statement, to keep the pressure off. Interesting.

"I went straight to bed when we got back." Unvarnished truth, right there. I barely stayed awake long enough to shower.

"And yet, I sense trouble brewing." Still no specifics, leaving it to me to fill in the blanks. I needed to do a better job disguising my aversion to Frat Boy. Starting with not calling him frat boy in capital letters anymore, since even thinking the words made my lip curl.

"No trouble on my end, Sir." He regarded me with one eye as we approached the barn, as if surprised by my matter of fact response. "I'm not here to play games, I'm here to work, and I won't let anything get in the way of that."

"Glad to hear it, Bowen. I've got a good feeling about you."
For a moment, my inner child danced circles in my heart, but
then he yanked the rug out from under her. "Don't make me
regret giving you a shot."

While we waited for the guys to return from the field Sir
Clark tasked me to hose out the back of the manure spreader.
When Cranston strolled up he smirked nastily at the backsplash
of watered down manure on my jeans. He probably found it
entertaining, but I just smiled. Still better than a calf with the
scours any day.

Our last member arrived shortly after we finished cleaning
stalls, parking her bright yellow Kia next to my old Subaru just
as we walked out of the barn, at nine on the dot. I'm pretty sure
we would have finished sooner, but it took Cranston twice as
long to get his work done up to Sir Clark's standards. I shook out
my arms, already aching from the labor. While I felt more than
comfortable mucking stalls, I neglected to factor in the sheer
volume of manure a draft horse produced. On the upside, I'd
gotten a great upper body workout, lifting bushel buckets of
manure and wet shavings to dump them into the spreader.

The girl exiting the car appeared to be everything I thought
Sir Clark might have been expecting from me. Lithe and blonde,
with more curves than a racetrack, she waved cheerfully in our
direction. As she walked around the front of her vehicle it
revealed the blinged out belt and fancy boots indicative of a
rodeo princess. While I wanted to give her a fair shake I simply
couldn't imagine this pretty bambi enduring getting struck with a
lance.

"If either of you gentlemen start howling, I'm going to be
assigning extra manure moving." Sir Clark murmured before she
could get close enough to hear him. "Is that understood?"

Both of the boy's nodded, but while Lee turned his head
toward Sir Clark to give his acknowledgement Cranston kept his
eyes firmly on the approaching target. A mile-wide protective
streak reared its head and I stepped forward to meet her first,
determined to keep her away from the douche bag as much as
possible.

"Hey there, I'm Josephine Bowen. Glad to have another female around, the testosterone is thick on the ground here." A genuine smile sprang up, lifting her sun kissed cheeks, and I swallowed a bitter pill of jealousy. No amount of makeup could ever make me as pretty as her natural beauty and the sun preferred to mark me with a burn, slowly increasing the population of my freckles over time.

"Hi! I'm Annabelle Brantley. Sorry I'm so late, I had a tire blow out on the way through Nashville, and the repair shop had to order in a replacement." The southern accent both charming and saccharin sweet, leaving a bitter aftertaste that would take some time to recede. Beauty queen material for sure. The professionally manicured hand she offered me felt soft, though at least she'd kept the nails short, and the grip hinted at unexpected strength. "Bart said we will be roommates?"

"Yes indeed, we get our own bathroom and everything." Oh Lord, I'd need to beat her out of bed in the mornings if I wanted to have time to get anything done. Under my breath I said a prayer of gratitude for my low maintenance routine. Turning to the side, I waved to Lee first, whose eyes widened in panic. "This is Fillmore Lee, and then there is Toby Cranston." Really, someone should have given me a cookie for how friendly I sounded.

While Lee managed to shake her hand without passing out it was a close call, since he forgot to breathe the whole time. Cranston took a completely different tack, lifting her hand to his lips for a smarmy kiss, pouring on the charm. "A pleasure to meet you, dear lady. I look forward to sharing the field with you."

To her credit, at least she didn't simper. "And the same to you all." she answered, pulling her hand from Cranston's grasp and looking around at the rest of us. "Bart, is it okay if Josephine shows me where I'm bunking?"

A grunt and nod released us, and I followed her back to her car to help carry bags. Yes, bags, plural. Multiple plural. Matching baby blue luggage, five total, left Annabelle struggling to pull two bags with another shoved under her arm. Thankfully,

Lee recovered from his previous shyness, and jumped forward to relieve her of the heaviest. I shook my head when he looked back to see if I wanted help too—best not to overtax the poor boy when he looked ready to trip over his own feet at any moment.

It took a half hour for Annabelle to get unpacked, fussing over each item as she hung it in the closet, brushing at non-existent lint and faint wrinkles with a frown of displeasure. Despite a clothing collection that probably beat out Cranston's and a flawless face, I found myself warming to her sunny chatter, listening to stories about the rodeo circuit. We exchanged sympathetic platitudes when discussing the horses we left at home, and shared pictures from our phones. The broad palomino quarter horse she showed me looked gentle, but action shots of them barrel racing revealed a sharper side to the gelding and his mistress.

"I was so tickled when Bart told me I'd be riding a palomino here too." Chuckling faintly, she unzipped another suitcase to line up her boots in an exact row along the floor of the closet. As she placed the last set she blanched and looked up at me in distress. "Oh, Josephine, I haven't left any room for your things!"

"Please, call me Jo. And don't worry about it, I didn't bring much with me." I pointed toward my abbreviated selection at the foot of my bed, and her eyes widened at the sight of one set of flip flops, my favorite cowboy boots and a pair of sneakers. "Counting the boots on my feet, I've got a third of what you have to worry about."

"Oh Lord, you must think I'm awfully vain!" she exclaimed, worrying her bottom lip with her teeth. "But really, if this doesn't work out, I'm headed straight to Texas to be a hostess at my Uncle Terry's dude ranch, so I just brought everything with me."

"Well, that certainly makes more sense." I conceded, smiling to reassure her. "But what I really want to know is how you found out you'd be riding a palomino, because I still haven't received my horse assignment."

"My Uncle Vince runs an auction yard in Ohio, where Bart goes to buy horses sometimes. He emailed Bart about her when she came in a few months ago, and when we found out I made the cut, Vince recommended the pairing. I guess Bart agreed."

"Her?" I hadn't seen a single mare in the barn. Curious.

The staccato pounding of a fist on our door stopped any answer she might have made, and we both jumped slightly. Sir Clark filled in the doorframe as much with his personality as the breadth of his shoulders. "Ladies, you've got free time until 12:30, I expect you to report to the barn properly attired for a riding lesson."

Not even a breath later he disappeared, and it surprised me when the door didn't slam in the force of his wake, as if the very air sought to leave with him. The man wore an air of mystery, a ball of humor and anger and patience by turns, all clothed in terrible practicality and a rough exterior.

Glancing at my phone for the time, I sighed. "Okay, we have an hour to eat and relax, then about twenty minutes to get changed, so let's get a move on."

Annabelle nested all her suitcases together and shoved the bulk into the back of the closet before falling in with me. "That's the one thing I forgot to grab on the way here." Gesturing toward the kitchen, she elaborated. "I'll need to hit the grocery store later."

"Well, my Mom made sure I was well supplied when I left Indiana, so if you don't mind tuna salad, I'd be happy to share with you."

The offer widened her eyes in surprise, but she accepted readily enough. We sat down at the worn vinyl table top to toast our friendship with a Coke and a sandwich, laughing when the boys looked at us in confusion. Yeah, I might be harboring a growing dislike for Cranston, but now I didn't feel so alone.

By Friday, we settled into a steady routine, up early to feed and clean, with random chores until lunch. After lunch involved riding lessons, then grooming and tack cleaning before we fed again. Sleep came easily every night, and despite the rigorous demands on my body, I popped out of bed in the morning looking forward to more of the same.

I'd been assigned Ivan, a surprisingly speedy Percheron that demanded tactful handling to keep him calm, leaving me little time to pay attention to the dirty looks I still received from Cranston. Not that I knew where he got the energy from. Our lessons were generally without stirrups, and if I felt the strain I could only imagine the boys were taking a beating.

As we rode up the hill toward the arena for our lesson I glanced over at Annabelle, who ran her fingers through her horse's pale mane, daydreaming. Buttermilk didn't mind the arrangement, happy to pack her rider around without interference from bit or leg. The mild mannered mare tended to be gentle and sweet with people, but she embraced the hell hath no fury method of dealing with most of the geldings. Ivan and I had figured out exactly how close we could get without raising her ire, which I couldn't say for anyone else.

Proving my point, Cranston kicked Hawk up to a trot to come up on the other side of Annabelle, and Buttermilk immediately fired a shot off the port bow to warn him away. The big bay shied hard in self-defense and Ivan took a half step away, just in case her wrath spread, though I prevented further movement by closing my leg against his side.

"Buttermilk!" Annabelle chastised, though the way she barely lifted up the reins and gently booted her in the ribs, the effort fell flat. While she maintained an amazing seat and great focus, I began to doubt whether Annabelle possessed the heart to joust. Neither the woman nor mare struck me as the kind of creatures to enjoy being hit. To be perfectly fair, I didn't feel thrilled by the concept either, but I balanced it out pretty well with the screaming desire to hit someone else.

As we crested the hill and entered the arena my eyes immediately went to Sir Clark, no longer perched on the fence rail as on all the days before. Today, he sat on Eros, and while I completely respected him on his own, the two of them combined drew on me like a magnet. They melded in a rare fashion, as if their nervous systems were woven together like fabric. The pair remained completely still as they waited for us to form up around them, and I held my breath against their potential power, like anticipating a lightning strike.

"Good afternoon, ladies, gentlemen." He shifted slightly, and swung a leg over Eros's neck, catching the pommel of the saddle behind his knee before leaning his crossed arms on the bent limb. The posture appeared casual, as if a predator could ever be said to do something casually. "Today we add in a new element. You've proven quick studies about making passes in the lyst," While waving an arm at the rope alleyways used to keep the horses on course, he smiled as though pleased with us. It had taken all of us a little time to become comfortable releasing the reins during the passes, but when I learned it prevented yanking on our horse's mouth if we fell I'd immediately improved. "Now let's see how you handle a weapon."

Cranston and Lee high fived each other, Lee's horse General pinning his ears at the excessive display. More evidence of Sir

Clark's dry sense of humor, giving a guy named Lee a horse named General. Yesterday I'd quipped, "The South will rise again." under my breath as they practiced making passes with Brantley and Buttermilk, unaware of Sir Clark at my stirrup. Then I heard his faint chuckle, flushing scarlet when he shook his head. Surely, he must have thought me a hopeless case.

"You'll be tilting at rings, which will give you an opportunity to practice several skills at once. One is your stops and starts. I expect them to be controlled. We can add speed later, but control is your main objective. Two is your ability to keep your leg on the horse, so he stays straight. We've gone over it before, but these ropes are just suggestions to them, and it is your job to keep him focused. Three is going to be aim, but I'll cover that more after you get a few practice runs."

Straightening in the saddle, he unfolded his leg, Eros moving beneath him with no noticeable cue. As if he knew what came next, the stallion swung past a weapon rack, close enough for Sir Clark to snag up a longish pole with a sharpened tip, its length marked with a candy swirl of red and white paint. They came to a halt just inside the lyst, allowing man and beast to gather themselves, and Sir Clark adjusted his grip on the lance by a hairsbreadth to find the right balance.

Breathing effortlessly into a canter from a standstill Eros carried his rider toward their objective, a four-inch metal ring that hung from the arm of a stanchion, immobile except for the flutter of ribbon dangling from its bottom. It slid onto the lance with barely a hiss of friction, Sir Clark's eyes already on the next ring thirty feet away until it joined its brother, wreathed around his knuckles. Just as effortless as the start, they finished in infinite stillness, Eros softly mouthing the bit when Sir Clark leaned forward to pat his neck.

I'd have sat there in silent admiration forever if not for Annabelle, who set up whooping and hollering like she'd just witnessed a winning bull ride. The boys added to the ruckus, hooting like deranged owls, and when Sir Clark looked up his eyes landed right on me, one eyebrow lifted in what I could only take for inquiry. Still quiet, I dropped my reins for a moment, bowing in the saddle in acknowledgement. Hard wired to tease, I offered them an incredibly slow pantomime of a golf clap, rewarded by another smirk and shake of his head.

Before the din died down completely he cued Eros to round the end of the lyst, pivoting hard to sling themselves into the other lane, and the lance snapped up with a surety that proved hours of practice. This pass came at speed, Eros's hooves flinging clods of dirt with the force of his passage, and I could hardly see the rings as they slithered onto the lance. Despite the velocity of travel the black stallion slid to a stop at the end, the hairs of his mane rippling as they came to rest on his neck again. This time, I joined the fray, whistling and clapping—audiences paid to see that sort of mastery, the adrenaline pumping speed as horse and rider skirted the edge of disaster and glory.

As he then put each team through their paces I hung back, studying everything, comparing it to the standard set by Sir Clark. The way the lance laid firmly along the bottom of his forearm, how he aimed down the length of wood, and lifted himself slightly from the saddle to absorb his horse's motion. It reminded me of when I'd tried my hand at team roping during my junior year of high school, the way the rope went where you aimed your hand like an extension of your arm. Hopefully, I'd prove better at this than that—I'd ended up roping Abby's feet at my first and only competition.

When Sir Clark called my name I took a deep breath to dispel tension before taking up the reins. Ivan preferred to do a power takeoff, and hated to wait for direction when he got his blood up. Like we had all the time in the world, I strolled past my fellow candidates with a leisurely grin and lifted a blue and gold stripped lance from the rack before assuming our start position. It took a minute to convince Ivan to stand, but if I nipped it in the bud right away it would get better and better throughout practice.

Giving him a few breaths to relax once he stopped prancing, I tested the weight of the lance in my hand until it seemed balanced, then squeezed my legs, the right further back than the left to cue for the correct lead. The sudden acceleration left me behind the motion, and I didn't have time to sight in on the first ring, coming nowhere close. Then the second loomed large in my vision, like the selective focus on a camera, the tip of the lance aimed just above the ribbons that trembled in the breeze. I leaned forward eagerly, determined to be the first to catch one, only to watch it fall from the stanchion like a lead weighted butterfly. Disappointed or no, I managed to collect myself, sitting deep to slow Ivan down, and patting him when he halted like a good boy.

"Don't be so eager." Sir Clark's voice came from much closer than I expected, and I looked up at his approach. "You have to let your horse get you there. If you hadn't leaned so far forward you might have caught it." He reached down, using a long pole with a blunt hook on the end to scoop up the lost ring. "Try again."

Between the rocket propelled take off and my own nerves I totally blew the second pass, but he reset the rings and offered me another chance. This time, I almost sighted in on the first ring, but it came too quickly, the second glancing off the tip like a rim shot in basketball. He directed me to level my elbow just a little, and like magic, I watched the golden rings slide down the lance, settling over my wrist like gaudy bangle bracelets. While I wasn't much into jewelry, I could admit to a certain amount of vanity in seeing them there.

Over the sound of my heart and the whoosh of air heaving from Ivan's lungs it took a second to hear the cheers of my teammates. I didn't even look to see if I pissed Cranston off, grinning like an idiot when I caught Sir Clark returning my golf clap with that damned raised eyebrow for accompaniment.

Saturday we faced a completely different animal, up well before daylight to feed horses and load the trailer for the short drive to the renaissance festival grounds for the first of two dress rehearsal days. The horses remaining behind almost seemed reluctant to head to the pasture, even Ivan stopping to look back at me on the way out of the barn. The massive trunks full of armor that we hoisted into the bed of the farm truck were heavy, but Annabelle and I levered them in quickly, while Lee pushed them up toward the cab. Cranston stood around and watched, under the guise of supervising, until Sir Aaron walked around the end of the barn. Then he jumped forward and deadlifted the last trunk by himself, nearly shoving Annabelle off her feet as he swung it up. When he dusted his hands off as if pleased it took a good deal of willpower not to smack the smug smile right off his face.

Instead, I walked toward the barn, on the hunt for something else to do. Before I could even ask, Sir Clark emerged from Eros's stall with the horse in tow, handing me the lead rope. "Wait here." He bit off gruffly, leaving me to wonder what had gotten under his skin.

He returned momentarily with Byzantine, and waved me to fall in after him, leading the way out to the trailer. The horses walked in the narrow stalls like the well-practiced soldiers they were, tucking into the hay in their mangers with gusto. We also loaded J.T., a black Clydesdale, and Tuck, then he sent me after Cappy, who paced his stall nervously, afraid to be left behind.

Closing the doors to the trailer with brisk efficiency, Sir Clark winced faintly when he bent down to lift the ramp, and I jumped forward to help, hanging on despite his instantaneous glare. Yup, someone definitely peed in his Wheaties. He stalked off in a huff, headed for parts unknown, and after a moment's thought I headed back to the house. Grabbing the bag packed with costumes for Annabelle and me from the foot of my bed, I detoured back through the kitchen, struck by inspiration.

As I jogged back out the door a few minutes later Annabelle hollered at me from the top of the path. "Hurry up, Josephine! Bart is waiting on us!"

I picked up the pace, tossing the bag in the bed of the equipment truck before I climbed in the back of the crew cab, frowning at the sight of the horse trailer already headed for the gate. Cranston rode shotgun, no surprise, and Annabelle squeezed in the middle of the back seat, right up next to Lee, giving me plenty of room to fold myself in and slam the door.

"Seat belts, ladies." Sir Clark growled, his hands tight on the steering wheel, and I hurried to comply, having a hard time balancing the travel tumbler full of coffee as I secured myself. The vehicle lurched into motion the instant he heard the metallic click, and I took a moment to compose myself before leaning forward to reach around his seat back, holding the coffee up as a silent peace offering. Wordlessly, his thick fingers closed around it, and I sighed before sitting back, hoping it would help ease whatever bothered him.

We passed the blessedly short ride to the site with Annabelle filling the tense air with a hundred questions about what it will be like to work behind the scenes at the faire. Apparently, she'd gone to quite a few as a patron, but usually dressed as a princess or fairy, and once more I silently questioned her ability to take a hit. On the other hand, she'd shown a remarkable amount of endurance over the last week, never once complaining about the work load, so I hoped that would equate to the toughness required to joust.

At the gate a robust looking gentleman in a commemorative t-shirt from last year waved us in, and we drove through a half full parking lot, many of the cars serving as impromptu dressing rooms as people donned their costumes. Dropping down a hill behind a line of buildings, we emerged in a sizeable field where several paddocks were roped off with electrical fencing. Parking beside the trailer, Sir Clark exited the truck before the engine even quieted, leaving the keys in the center console, and we all scrambled after him.

Each of us took a horse and followed Sir Clark through an arched wooden gate which delivered us to the knight's encampment. We made busy getting the horses settled in their open air stalls, providing hay and water to keep them occupied. Surrounded by the familiar shop fronts of faux Olde England I sucked in a deep breath, relishing the unadulterated scents of the soap vendor and smiling at a woman putting a fresh coat of paint on her shutters, enjoying this calm before the storm.

Byzantine behaved himself as I got him settled, though I got the idea it amused him, allowing me to pretend I had any control over him. He surely knew this place far better than I did. Just as I bent to tie a loose bootlace Sir Alex and Sir John arrived, prompting a new flurry of activity. With their help we dragged the awkward armor trunks into the small building attached to the horse area, shoving them into their assigned places. As we dusted off our hands Sir Aaron cleared his throat and we all turned toward him like one body.

"Candidates, today you will be assigned to a knight. It is your job to help him armor or whatever else he needs to get ready. We have two rehearsals to do, one pair of knights for each turn. Trace, you'll be paired with Brantley, and I get Mr. Lee. The two of us will be in the first round. Alex, you get to break in Cranston, and Bowen, you get to ride herd on John."

Confusion must have been plastered all over my face, because Sir Barry stepped forward to slap me on the shoulder. "What he means, dear girl, is I am both notoriously late and absentminded. You get to be my nanny for the day." I smiled immediately. Compared to keeping work study groups on track during school, he couldn't be that bad.

Thank goodness I got to watch the first go from the sidelines—well, nominally speaking anyway. Once we got changed into our costumes, in my case a tunic and flat cap I could drag on over my t-shirt and breeches, I made myself useful. Carrying lances and weaponry to the arena and tightening the ropes that made up the lyst kept me occupied and gave me a chance to get to know the four squires that usually managed the chaos.

Hillary, a lanky seventeen-year-old girl, had wild red hair that reflected her energy level and a devotion to the horses that echoed my own. I liked her immediately. A forty something fellow named Steve appeared to be the organizer, directing everyone wherever they were needed, while Jeff and Kory, a brother and sister duo, spent most of their time getting lances assembled. They had a system down for fitting the caps and plates to the long wooden rods, so I left them well enough alone, simply volunteering to be grunt labor when enough lances were ready to move to the arena.

The thirty-minute call went up as I returned from delivering the last load, and I dodged through the people now populating the street, all of them costumed cast members. Popping in the door of the armor room, I looked around for something to do. Sir Clark was nowhere to be found, but Sir Aaron caught my eye immediately, gesturing me closer from his bent position over the armor trunk. "Bowen, you can watch what Lee has to help me with. John isn't always very helpful with directions."

Fascinated, I watched the layers of protection come together, overlapping smoothly to protect the joints and critical areas. No amount of watching armor demonstrations or studying charts could quite convey how differently I looked at things now, hoping to soon be wearing it myself. Sir Aaron's incredibly ornate kit bore etched designs along the edges and brass chasing here and there to draw the eye, clearly marking him as the leader of the crew. He wore dark blue trews beneath his leg armor, and a matching arming jacket on his torso, trimmed in an old gold color. In comparison, Trace's kit looked hard used, wearing sweatpants on his bottom half and a generically off white arming jacket, faintly stained and worn at the seams. The armor appeared beat up and scarred, possibly even hodge podged together from different sets, though it fit just as well as Aaron's.

"Well, if this isn't a case of city mouse vs country mouse, I don't know what it is." I murmured conversationally, looking between the two disparate men. Aaron's soft huff of a chuckle surprised me, and I found him shaking his head. Not for the first time, it struck me that Sir Aaron and Sir Clark reminded me of each other, speaking to a long history together.

"Bart said you were funny, Bowen." he said casually, grinning when my eyes widened. "But really, the reason Trace gets paired with me is that he's still learning his craft. We wouldn't have knighted him last year if he hadn't earned it but until he gets a little smoother and consistent he gets to joust against me. No one else should have to risk getting hurt going against him, he is my responsibility."

"So kind of like the horseman's adage, green on green equals black and blue?" I queried, truly excited to be having this sort of conversation. As much as I appreciated Sir Clark when it came to actually doing things, trying to pry extra information out of him remained tedious. Frankly, I felt a little flattered to be getting such attention from our leader.

"Exactly like." The confirmation set the wheels spinning in my head, and while I tried not to let it puff my ego too much, I realized of all the candidates, I had received the more challenging of the available mounts. "That, and I've competed against a lot more people than the rest of these guys, so I can take better care of myself in the event my opponent has issues." His sense of responsibility for everyone reassured me, adding new depth to my gratitude for the chance to learn with this team. Between him and Sir Bart, I would be given every opportunity to succeed.

"Ten minutes," boomed loudly through the open door, and I visibly flinched, turning to face the voice. Bart filled the rectangle of light with his broad shoulders, considerably changed from the grumpy goat on the ride over. Now attired in full heraldic panoply, a split tunic of blue overlaid by a golden two headed eagle, he seemed more comfortable in his own skin, and my mouth fell open. "What Bowen, no smart ass remark?"

My teeth met with an audible click, and I narrowed my eyes at him, fishing my addled brain for some kind of response. That taunting eyebrow lifted and he quit the room before I could manage it, victory making his swagger absolutely infuriating.

"Yeah, Bowen, absolutely funny." Aaron laughed, and heat crept up my cheeks, anger and embarrassment a potent cocktail to choke down. I never lost. And I never blushed. I just did both.

The knights mounted their horses at a huge wooden block specifically built to accommodate the weight of their armor and the height of their horses, a squire holding the horse's head to keep them still. I slid in on the right side of Byzantine, and placed weight on the stirrup to prevent the saddle from twisting as Aaron mounted, thinking first of the horse's comfort in all this. If a horse could develop a sore back just from the regular weight of a rider, then one in armor would only exacerbate the issue. I slid the stirrup on each rider's foot without thinking too much about it—I might as well help if I could. I didn't even notice when I did the same for Sir Clark, at least not until I felt his leather clad calf under my hand, a divot that should not be in the muscle making me freeze. Quickly, I pulled away, moving off to find something to fetch or carry, anything to avoid the eyes I felt burning a hole in the back of my head.

Luckily, as soon as we reached the arena, a cheer went up and the drummers on the royal dais pounded out a welcome. However conflicted I might feel about my inadvertent discovery, my heart had no problem beating just as hard as the drums when Eros started to dance to the deep bass cadence. Sir Clark lifted his hand to the crowd, then bowed slightly, his steed not missing a step. All three riders processed around the arena to the catcalls and whistles of the crowd, the cast members playing up admirably to the theatrics provided by the knights. They halted as one unit in front of the King and Queen, bowing deeply this time.

"Your Majesties, long have we lived in darkness, unable to bask in the light of Your glorious reign." Sir Clark greeted the occupants on the dais, and goosebumps went up on my arms. Holy spotted purple parasol, not just his demeanor had changed; his voice as well, sounded richer, reminding me of my father's parade ground command, becoming the stuff of legends before my eyes. I didn't remember him from my years at this faire, thinking back. The master of ceremonies had been a narrow shouldered, scholarly looking fellow, full of pretty turns of phrase and a wretched penchant for puns. If I had seen Sir Clark, I have no doubt I never would have forgotten him. No one would.

"Ah, Sir Clark, pleased are the Queen and I to have you returned from the Crusades, to grace us with your noble spirit. Pray thee, who competes today to lay claim to the title champion?" My brain worked in two directions at once, partly studying the jovial, yet serious man playing the King, his white hair an excellent foil for the golden crown glimmering on his head. Having always been on the bleacher seats, I'd never been this close to the dais, able to see so much nuance of facial expression. The other half of my mind sat in stunned silence, circling around the implication left by the King's welcome— returned from the Crusades. From the wars still going on in the Middle East? It felt like an intimate piece of knowledge, and I clenched my fingers with the remembered feeling of his twisted muscle, hating knowing what I felt I shouldn't.

"I bring before you our esteemed Captain, and my brother, Sir Aaron Drew of Carrington." The cheer of the crowd gave my brain a moment to do a loop-the-loop without anyone noticing. Brother in arms, or brother for real? And why did I care? Their relationship should be none of my business, but for reasons unknown, I wanted it to be. "He answers the challenge of our younger compatriot, Sir Trace Davies of Montrose." A bone shaking roar came from the crowd at his name, at least half of them screaming "Scotland!" so loud and long, even steady Cappy danced in place.

When the noise began to quiet, the King waved his arm magnanimously at the knights. "Then, by all means, Sir Bartholomew, Guardian of the Queen's Heart, let the games begin."

A wrinkle of confusion formed on my forehead, unfamiliar with this script. I had thought my four years of attendance would have given me a leg up, but it felt like someone pulling the rug out from under me. I hated being under prepared, but I covered it in a flurry of activity, letting Hillary point me wherever she needed me. Hold a ring up for the knights to spear? Sure thing. Grab Byzantine's reins while someone secured the latch on Sir Aaron's helmet. You bet. Hand up lances to the riders? Absolutely. Look anywhere but at Sir Clark? Yeah, I had that one well in hand.

Trace lost by the barest margin, the squires scrambling to clean up debris as they traded broken lances, but on the last pass he only scored a touch. To my uneducated but eager eye his arm appeared tired on the final pass, letting the lance skip off its intended target. He met Aaron in front of the crowd, and they clasped arms in a show of goodwill that felt incredibly genuine. When one of the squires helped him remove his helmet, it became obvious he couldn't be more thrilled with the result, his smile stretched so broad it approached comical.

We listened to a brief exchange between the King and Queen, encouraging the crowd to return at the ringing of one to find out which knight would be victorious. Sir Clark delivered a pretty bit of speech promising spectacle and awe, then we processed back out the way we came, following the knights to the encampment. As Sir Aaron vaulted to the ground he grabbed my shoulder and handed me Byzantine's reins, an earnest light in his eyes.

"I'm trusting you with him, Bowen."

Thankful for something constructive to do I took my charge to his stall, both of us heaving a sigh as we entered the shade. In the excitement and awkwardness, I hadn't noticed the sweat that sprung up on my skin, and I shoved a few loose tendrils of hair back under my cap to keep them off my sticky forehead. Byzantine lowered his head when I slid the bit from his mouth, and grunted with pleasure when I rubbed the sweat marks left by his bridle, though I had to growl at him when he shoved me for more.

His saddle proved slightly more complicated, having to unbuckle the decorative leather barding draping his chest and hindquarters before I could pull the tack from his back. The instant I removed it he turned toward the big rubber bucket in the corner for a lengthy pull of water, and I left him to it for a few minutes, arranging his equipment on a rack built specifically for the heavy saddle.

Hillary came by with more hay, a couple carrots surreptitiously tucked between the leafy flakes, though I noticed she didn't linger like she tended to with the other horses. Clearly, Byz owned a well-known reputation for poor table manners. As he chewed on his richly deserved snack I lost myself in the mindless and meditative rhythm of curry and brush until the sweat marks on his dark grey coat faded to memory.

"Every time I turn around I find something else to like about you Bowen." My hands stuttered at the compliment, the brush slipping from nerveless fingers as I turned toward Sir Aaron. Byz covered my clumsiness by twisting his body around to face his person, accepting a few affectionate pats before beginning a search of pockets. "You've been capable with every horse in the string, and I've a feeling with a little schooling, you could probably outride most of us." Aaron continued conversationally, smiling indulgently at the fierce war horse as Byz wiggled his lips against the pouch hanging from his belt. I snatched up the fallen brush and ducked past horse and man, still unsure what to say in response, or if I should say anything at all.

I managed the rest of Saturday without making a further idiot of myself, getting Sir John kitted and on his horse admirably well, I thought. Not to say it happened easily—no, it would have been simpler herding cats high on caffeine. His standard answer every time I asked him if something was tight enough was "Oh, that's fine, dear." Fine quickly became my least favorite word in the English language.

I didn't mind the dear part so much, as it seemed a very uncle-like thing to do. I had a feeling if Sir Black did it, I would want to deck him. John's arming jacket bore a divided field in red and white linen, stitched so finely my Gran would be impressed. The armor as well looked beautifully wrought, though scarred by usage.

By the time I had him ready to mount he realized he forgot his spurs, and I had to rummage through the detritus lining the bottom of his trunk to hunt them up. I buckled them on once we got him on Tuck's back, grateful for the big Belgian's dog like personality, though I had to dodge a string of saliva when I walked around him to get to John's other leg.

Running back into the armoring room I snatched up the linen coif meant to cover Sir John's wild mop of hair, only to find his helm missing from the shelf over his trunk. Scrambling, I checked behind the trunk, even behind the neighboring boxes, my stomach plummeting into my boots when the helm did not reveal itself.

"Everything okay in there, Bowen?"

Of course it would be Sir Clark who brought my downfall to everyone's attention. I flung myself into the doorway to answer him, the words stuck in my throat—but just beyond the man in question, Lee stood, the lost object tucked under his arm, completely oblivious to my panic.

"Nope." I squeaked, then swallowed hard before waving the coif in the air. "I found it."

"Well, since this is the closest to on time John has ever been, I guess I'll just have to be grateful." No eyebrow this time, just his normal, dry sense of humor. "Let's get this show on the road."

The joust kept me so busy I hardly looked up to enjoy the spectacle of it all. I lost myself in the minutiae of tightening a girth or scrambling for an extra cotter pin when the one for Sir John's visor slipped from Trace's fingers, immediately lost in the deep footing of the arena. The level of jousting felt markedly different, more intense, as the men were testing themselves against each other, giving no quarter.

I rose on my toes, ready to sprint for the lyst as Sir John wobbled in the saddle, but he righted himself with a twist of his torso, aided admirably by Tuck, who made a slight shift to center his rider. On the third pass, John and Alex both bobbled in the tack, our dark knight pin wheeling his arms to keep from tipping to the side. The crowd grew in intensity, both in its expectant silences and savage roars of appreciation, but I barely heard them. In fact, my focus became so pinpoint I heard Sir Clark's no doubt pithy byplay as muffled honks, like an adult in the Charlie Brown comics.

Pass number four happened with all the crescendo of a finale on the fourth of July, the explosion of Sir John's lance throwing colorful shards high in the air and two of the squires ducked to avoid flying debris. But that all became backdrop to the sharp thwack of Sir Alex's lance catching in the sweet spot of his opponent's armor, the lance bowing in slow motion before the kinetic energy sprang back, flicking Sir John from his horse's back like an insignificant insect.

I expected a screeching of metal, like a car wreck, dirt spraying up like water as he hit the ground. Yet I could hear nothing over the din of the audience, like the bloodthirsty Roman mob of two thousand years ago chose that moment to appear in the present. In motion before Tuck even reached the end of the lyst, I left the horse in Hillary's capable hands and went to my knees beside Sir John, placing a hand on his shoulder. Before I could roll him over Sir Aaron was beside me, staying my actions with a calm voice.

"Give him a second, Jo. Impact takes the wind out of you." As if the words were prophetic, a rattling, indrawn breath came from behind the slitted visor of the helmet, and Sir John moved, his gauntleted hand gripping the earth for leverage. "Alright, grab him under his armpit. We'll get him on his feet before we pull his helmet."

Amazingly, once his legs were under him, John pulled away, lifting his arms in the air to the renewed enthusiasm of the crowd who had quieted while we got him up. Sir Aaron gripped along the exposed edge of his breastplate to keep him from walking off and used the other hand to open the visor of John's helm, revealing a surprisingly fierce grin on the bumbling, good natured man. Seconds later, we pulled his helm off and he jumped to the top of one of the big mounting blocks, bellowing, "Are you not entertained?" to the throng. Yup, Roman mob, all the way.

Sir Alex greeted him in the middle of the field, right along the fence line in front of the dais for an arm clasp and back slap, showing their brotherhood intact. The King presented a bonus to the dark knight for the unhorsing, yet Sir John did not go unrewarded, receiving a ribbon and a kiss on the cheek from one of the Queen's ladies in waiting. The woman's full cheeks colored warmly when he bowed over her hand and delivered a kiss to her knuckles.

"That's his wife, if you can believe it." Sir Aaron, back at my elbow. "She's the whole reason he pursued jousting, wanting to truly be her knight in shining armor." Okay, yes, my girly heart, deeply suppressed though it may be, gave a mushy sigh. It certainly made me like Sir John even more than I did before.

Back at the encampment I helped Sir John out of his armor, remarking on a busted leather strap on his left cuisse, and he told me to toss it in the box with the rest. While I complied I kept it to one side so I could fish it back out later. Absentminded professor would probably forget all about it the instant he left the room. Truthfully, it surprised me not to find more damage to his kit; just a bit of dirt and some scratches lingered along one arm to mark his meeting with the ground. He did give me a quick side hug and perfunctory kiss on the cheek before bolting out the door like a racehorse from the gate, leaving me staring after him in shock.

"Don't take it amiss, Bowen. He's a hugger, is John, but right now, riding that adrenaline high, he just wants to see Caroline." My head swiveled hard toward Sir Alex, his classic villainesque mustache and goatee ruined by the grin quirking his mouth. The jousting left him much more relaxed than I would have ever expected.

While I smiled back at him I took in Cranston, the way he was negligently throwing things in the trunk without looking, making more work in the long run. Without asking permission I slid around the two of them and begin sorting the armor, trying to remember how Sir Aaron had nested his together. After shifting a few of the blackened pieces around it all began to come together like a puzzle, and this time, my grin of accomplishment could not be dimmed.

"What the hell are you doing, Bowen?" Everyone but Cranston could say my name with respect or humor, and he managed to make it sound like he was chewing on glass.

"Just helping." I bit off, though I plastered a sweet smile on my face. "Many hands makes short work." Before he could respond I quit the room, taking the little victory while I could get it.

During cleanup efforts I grabbed the broken piece of Sir John's armor, and went in search of Sir Aaron. He had commissioned me to look after John, and I didn't want to go into next weekend's rehearsal still needing it fixed.

"You looking for something, Bowen?" Cheeks pink with the anticipation of some sort of verbal duel, I pivoted toward Sir Clark, losing my facility for speech momentarily. He'd changed clothes again, and while I had seen him in riding breeches, one of the most revealing garments known to either sex, something about any man in a pair of wranglers and scuffed cowboy boots made him instantly more masculine. Dammit if it didn't make my rancher's daughter knees go a little jello-y. What the hell?

Mute, I held up the cuisse, the broken strap flapping in objection, grateful when understood my intent. "Alright then. I haven't brought the armor repair equipment over yet, so we'll just take it back to the farm with us. Grab Byzantine, we're about ready to load up."

I snatched up my bag, obviously out of time to change, and clipped a lead on Byz, who behaved remarkably more content with me than at the beginning of the day. For that alone, I'd call the day a win.

Sir Bart locked up the armor room and followed behind me with Eros, but it didn't take him long to pull abreast of us, walking along in companionable silence. I found myself sneaking glances out the corner of my eye and chewing on my chapped lips as I puzzled over everything I knew about Bartholomew Clark. I still couldn't think of him as Bart without the stupid eyepatch manifesting in my imagination, which I found entirely too humorous. But that sort of comical farce didn't fit him at all, and I couldn't bear making fun of him that way.

The sound of a horse shoe striking a rock made me look back, finding Annabelle with Tuck on our tail. Strung out behind her, Lee walked with Cappy and Cranston with J.T., though Cranston spent more time flirting with Kory than paying attention to the horse. The steeds loaded like the old pro's they were, and we all piled in the truck with Sir Clark again, united in exhausted silence. For me at least, I knew it stemmed from the emotional rollercoaster as much as the actual work.

Back at the farm, the horses that worked for the day got turned out in a nearby paddock to graze and roll while we plebes did the chores that didn't get done that morning. The sun just touched the horizon line when Sir Clark ambled back into the barn, waving us all in as I emerged from Ivan's stall, where I'd been apologizing for not taking him with us with a granola bar. His weakness for anything in a crinkly wrapper had been a pleasant discovery, and he'd accepted my atonement with particular relish.

"You are officially off the clock until your riding lesson on Monday afternoon. I will come out myself to feed and let them out in the morning, as they will be getting time off as well. This coming week is going to be rough, and I want you well rested. There is no curfew, but we also don't want you bringing home hook-ups, so whatever fun you plan that requires a partner will not happen here. Is that clear?" Eyes that missed nothing pinned Cranston and Lee in place, though they briefly flickered sideways to Annabelle and I, and his lips flattened out as if something bitter crossed his tongue.

"Yes, Sir Clark." I answered while everyone else just shifted from foot to foot in silence, the tightness in his jaw lessening minutely.

"You answering for everyone now, Bowen?" The eyebrow moved, just a tick, and in response, so did my smile. Just a tick.

"No, Sir Clark. But my Daddy raised me to answer when someone asks a question."

"Fair enough. Cranston, Lee, Brantley, what say you?" He turned the full weight of his gaze on them, the air in the aisle way thick with the possibility of a storm.

They finally responded to the affirmative, Brantley and Lee both pink cheeked, and it made me wonder if hooking up would go on in the house anyway. Cranston looked a millimeter away from a sneer of disdain, but he saved himself with a clear, "Yes, Sir Bart." I closed my eyes on the stupid eyepatch image, praying my self-control would prove itself better than this someday.

"Also, no drunk driving. Get your alcohol and bring it here, sleep it off in a hotel, get a cab or call the farm. But do not get behind the wheel, under any conditions. The least of your worries will be getting pulled over if we find out you did so."

"I'll be staying in at night, so you guys can call me." I offered, flinching at how fast those green eyes landed on me. He no doubt now thought me the world's biggest goody goody, but after losing a friend to drunk driving my freshman year my desire to party had vanished. "I've got books to read, so aside from a grocery run tomorrow, I'll be here." Unable to face the censure likely in his eyes, I headed for the house, looking forward to losing my over thinking brain in a pile of books and a box of Oreos.

♥♥♥

I turned off the alarm on my phone, but even after staying up until two AM finishing the epic fantasy I started reading while I ate my supper, I still woke at 6:30. Rubbing the crust of sleep from my eyes, I stared at the dim grey of the ceiling, letting my body come awake slowly. Alas, that notion vanished at the sound of hooves on the road, a small tremor of excitement prompting me to roll up on my knees to look out the window.

I expected to see the herd break slowly from the barn doors, barely trotting, but what followed them lifted the small hairs on the back of my neck. Eros's sooty black coat caught the sunlight as he came in at the tail end, with Sir Clark anchored to him by a handful of mane. Nothing lay on the horse's body but his rider, the naked freedom of the moment so incredibly moving that goosebumps ran the length of my arms. I might have even leaked a tear, though you couldn't make me swear to it. They were lost to my sight in seconds, swallowed by the trees, leaving me bereft in a way I'd never experienced before.

My chest ached, longing for that sort of partnership, that sort of trust. Don't misread my love for Abby, she and I were good partners, and my gratitude for everything I'd learned working with her defied measurement. Yet, in the deep, quiet places of my soul, I didn't think she wanted to be the sort of partner I really dreamed about. She always reserved a part of herself and so did I, much as I did in many of my human relationships. I'd felt love for my boyfriends but I never thought it the kind of love that lasted a lifetime.

Then I cried, silent and aching, shedding tears for the beauty I witnessed and releasing the bitter questions that still plagued me. No longer would I wonder over things that were a shadow of what I truly desired in my heart, either in the saddle or in my relationships. I took a few minutes to mourn what I lost, mourn what had never been, but when the last of the tears dried hope flooded in behind them. The future might be unknown, but I felt perfectly okay with it because that left it open to a world of possibility.

Since Annabelle hadn't returned yet by the time I fell asleep her empty bed did not surprise me. Let's face it, if you aren't in by two AM you aren't coming home before morning. There were no messages on my phone, allaying any worries about sleeping through anyone calling for a ride. I dragged a pair of shorts on under my oversized sleep shirt, smiling groggily at the cartoon unicorn that adorned the front. The pajamas had lasted me all through college, and though threadbare and developing holes at the seams, I could not part with my old companion. Armor of a whole other kind, I'm afraid.

Padding into the kitchen, I filled a mug with hot water and popped it in the microwave, mindlessly watching the turntable spin for the entire two minutes. Boil achieved, I fished a tea bag from the cupboard, grateful no one indulged in my tea the way they had in my Oreos. Finding the box of cookies half empty left me cranky, but Annabelle admitted right away to stealing them, and promised replacements, so all would be well. Wrapping my hands around the warm ceramic I strolled toward the front window, content with the silence as a squirrel ran across the porch. I could imagine having a place like this all to myself.

The illusion tremored along with the pane of glass in front of me as one of the trucks rumbled to life, the diesel hooked to the trailer by the sound of it. Curiosity prodded me on to the porch, then along the brick pavers leading toward the barn, my bare feet splaying on the comfortable smoothness. It put me in perfect sight of the road, though a stand of trees kept me from seeing the barn itself and the vehicles parked on the other side of it. It also put me in perfect sight of Sir Clark as he drove past, the powerstroke engine gurgling in protest as he momentarily slowed, eyes widening when he noticed me. For a second, I thought he would stop, but then his jaw tightened and he sped up, making the engine protest again. Once more, silently judging me and leaving a confused mess in his wake.

Letting my frustrations fuel a cleaning jag, I scoured the kitchen and our bathroom until they both gleamed, glad when no one came out of their rooms to object to the racket I made. Laundry too gave me an outlet for the stew of emotions cooking in my gut, attacking stains with a vengeance.

By ten o'clock I slowed down but still felt too restless to read. I finally ran a brush through my hair, trying not to overthink the fact that Sir Clark saw me with a righteous case of bedhead. I wouldn't give a rat's patootie if anyone else saw it, so it shouldn't matter.

Changing out the sleep shirt for a tank top, I realized he also saw me without a bra, and damned if I didn't blush like a tween girl. My disgust had little to do with being seen without proper underthings and everything to do with my reaction, completely refilling the well of anger. It drove me up to the barn where I vented my spleen on cleaning stalls, losing my outrage in effort and sweating away the confusion until it coiled quietly in a corner of my heart, hoping I wouldn't notice its presence. After dumping the last load of soiled bedding in the manure spreader I jumped at the sound of boots on the stairs, relaxing marginally when Sir Aaron emerged from the door that led to his and Sir Clark's apartment.

"Hey Bowen, you know you have a day off, right?" The lopsided grin he offered in no way reduced the amount of respect I felt for him, but it went a long way toward lightening my heart. He peeked in one of the stalls as I set my tools in the utility room, heading outside before I could answer him. All that sweating took the starch right out of me and I plopped on the bench beside the tack room to rest.

He returned in an instant, a bag of shavings gripped in each hand but rather than heading to the stall, he stacked both in front of me and sat down on them expectantly. "Why are you out here working, rather than dragging yourself in around noon like the other three probably will?"

"I'm not really the bar bunny type, and this morning I needed something to do." I answered vaguely, shoving a tuft of hair back behind my ear, wishing I had remembered my ball cap. "I'm not one for being useless."

"Yeah, we get that impression." Tease filled his smirk, but I hoped the glimmer in his eyes meant approval. "But you don't have to do stuff like this to get ahead. We know what a hard worker you are."

"I'm not trying to curry favor." The growl of frustration I had been biting on must have come through anyway, because he sat up and held his palms out in front of him.

"I never said you were." The words were calm and matter of fact, not placating, smoothing my ruffled feathers. "I just want to know what prompted the spate of activity."

"I had some things to think about." His eyes sharpened at the purposefully nebulous response, spine going blade straight.

"You need someone to talk to? Is someone making you feel unwelcome? Because everyone who counts wants you here."

"No, it's not like that." I shifted on the bench, pressing my back against the sun warmed wall with a sigh. "I'm just not sure what to make of certain people."

Understanding bloomed on his face, and I forced myself not to look away. "Certain people probably don't know what to make of themselves either. Particularly certain people like my brother."

Apparently, Aaron's accuracy remained as precise off the field as on. "I wondered if there was real truth in that spiel yesterday, not that it's any of my business. It's just that one second I think he might be taking me seriously, and the next it's like I'm twenty shades of disappointment."

"Don't take it personally, please. Just know that what you are seeing has more to do with what's going on with him than you. If you are around long enough, I'm sure he'll probably share his story, but in the meantime, cut him and yourself some slack."

Forcing out a big breath I looked out the barn door, needing a moment to mull it over. Aaron rose from his improvised seat and headed toward the stalls to begin bedding them down, giving me plenty of space. Everything he said left me with more questions than I started with, but it did give me at least one answer to cling to. They wanted me there, and as long as that remained the case, I would throw myself wholeheartedly after my goal.

♥♥♥

I drove into town after a shower, indulging in a milk shake for lunch before heading to the Super-mart for groceries to get me through the week. It didn't take much brain power to pick a bunch of single serve frozen meals, then grab a bag of apples and a larger bag of carrots that I could share with the horses. Add in some microwave popcorn, and two dozen assorted meal bars that I could grab on the go (and ply Ivan with), and I headed back out the door in under thirty minutes.

Two storefronts down the scents coming from a Chinese food restaurant tempted me in the door. I yielded to an order of crab rangoon and beef chow mien, taking it to go so I could eat it for supper. On the drive back I popped in my Bluetooth and dialed home, grinning when Mom picked up before the second ring even finished.

"Josie, my beautiful flower, it's so good to hear from you!" Distance couldn't disguise the relief in her voice. I'd texted her every night with an update, hoping to reassure her, but nothing could compare to hearing my voice.

"Hi Momma, how are you?" I asked, prepared to settle in for a good long listen. She didn't disappoint, giving me a full report on her book club, the women in her church group and the current state of affairs at the beauty shop. My mom, the social butterfly, had finally landed someplace long enough to develop a real community connection.

"But enough about me, tell me all about the knights." A breathless quality laced through the inquiry I couldn't really blame her for, since each of them were charming in their own way. They certainly owned a fair bit of romanticism that lingered in their wake. But I'd seen the men behind the characters now, and become aware that their manners were armor just as surely as the steel they wore.

"You'd like them, Momma, not just as knights, but as people. They're a mixed bag of nuts, mostly, with a few bruised fruit thrown in for sweetness, the kind of people we'd be fortunate to invite over for dinner."

"Oh, I'm so glad to hear that. I hope we can come meet them all in a few weeks."

"I hope so too, Momma." Crossing my fingers where they rested on the steering wheel for good measure, I sighed. "I really love this, and we haven't even gotten to the good stuff yet."

"I still don't know why you'd want to be knocked from your horse, Josie." The exasperation in her voice made me grin. Some things just couldn't be explained.

"I don't rightly know either Momma, but I'm looking forward to finding out if I've got what it takes to get back up when I fall."

"Oh, you will, my dear." Such matter of fact surety startled me a little. "In that respect, you are one hundred percent your father's child, and nothing in this world has ever stopped either of you from rising to the challenge."

"Speaking of which, Momma, is Daddy there? I've got something to ask him." I expected a twist to form in my stomach, even thinking about the topic laying on my heart, but it remained remarkably relaxed.

"Sure thing, here he is."

A bit of fumbling filled the air, but then Daddy boomed in my ear, the familiar voice reassuring if overly loud. He'd never quite figured out the improvements in cell phone technology, and kept yelling like he still had an old Nokia flip phone. "Sweet girl, how are things treating you?"

"If the guys here heard you calling me sweet girl, they'd all laugh." I answered, grinning at the truth of it. My sweetness only benefited those I loved, and none of them had become that dear in so short a time.

"Aw sugar, they'll learn better if they treat you right. Just takes us fella's a little longer to warm up and be friendly than it does you ladies."

"Speaking of friends and ladies, I've got a favor to ask you, Daddy." I sucked in a big breath, prepared to force out the next words. "I'd like to find Abby a new girl." Silence followed the declaration, and my brain filled it in with guilt and admonitions. How could I betray the mare who had given me so much? So many years of adventure and freedom?

"Oh, sweet girl, I'm so proud of you." Quietly spoken, it took those words a few seconds to filter in past the self-recriminations.

"You are?" I squeaked. Seriously, I needed to work on that.

"I am." A big sigh closed the distance between us, and I forced myself to pull over as tears stung my eyes. "You've been ready to move on from Abby for a while now, but you were clinging to her like some kind of safety net. Like you needed a reason to come home. But you never need a reason, Jo."

Oh crap. Now the tears came in earnest. What was it about this day and tears? Hormones maybe? I tried to think past the lump clogging my throat, and remembered that yes, my cycle should start soon. Honestly though, I didn't do hypersensitive, hormones or no. Maybe I was just about due for some tears? Yes, mourning the loss of the old me so I could be ready to embrace the new.

"Sorry, I didn't know." My reply came a little thick and stilted as I swallowed that realization. "It's just I'm seeing such amazing levels of horsemanship here, and I don't think that's something Abby wants or needs. I have to do what's best for her."

"See, Jo, you make me think I couldn't be any prouder of you and then you prove me wrong." Oh how I wished he were close enough to hug right now. "Your momma and I, we hoped you'd develop roots even though we kept having to dig you up and transplant you. I guess it worked, because you are growing like crazy."

I chuckled weakly. "Stop it Daddy, you're going to make me cry more."

"Just keep growing, honey, and don't be worried about the future so much. All you can do is prepare, then let it come to you in its own good time. And know that you've always got someplace to call home."

We said our goodbyes and I finished the drive back to the farm, moving quietly in the house when I noticed everyone's cars were back in the lot. Well, all of them but the truck Sir Clark drove off in that morning. Tamping down my curiosity about his destination at that early hour, I got my groceries unloaded, then snuck in the bedroom to pull another book from my pile and a blanket from the top shelf of the closet.

Annabelle didn't move a muscle, or at least the pile of bedding vaguely shaped like her didn't, though I winced in sympathy at what her condition must be. The room felt too warm to be huddled under all those layers, and she would be a miserable, sweaty mess when she woke. On the upside, maybe she'd detox a little faster that way. I dropped my burden on the threadbare sofa and headed back in the room to leave a bottle of ibuprofen and a glass of water on her bedside table, proof that maybe I was a sweet girl after all. Then I headed to the pasture to curl up under a tree for the afternoon, the humming of insects and the slow grind of chewing horses the only soundtrack I needed.

This time, I set my alarm on purpose, even though I didn't need to. Though I turned off the irritating tone from my phone in seconds, Annabelle threw a pillow at me, screwing up her face and rolling back over to sleep a little longer.

Braiding my hair and brushing my teeth took mere minutes, and I pulled on jeans, needing the comforting embrace of denim after the last week in riding breeches. Don't get me wrong, breeches were okay, and I could care less that they revealed my decided lack of badonkadonk—Welsh girl butt would do just fine for me.

Then I headed outside, needing to move—nearly fourteen hours of reading had left me rested and restless. Halfway to the barn, I hesitated, realizing there were no stalls to clean since the herd spent the night outside, but then I saw Sir Clark moving across the aisle toward a stall that had been empty the whole time I'd been around. Spurred on by curiosity, I let my feet carry me inside, worry slowing my steps. Who knew what my reception might be after yesterday's embarrassment.

My arrival coincided with his exit from the stall, and he startled slightly, but a faint smile encouraged me forward. "You have a problem with sleeping in, Bowen?"

"Not any more than you, early riser." I teased experimentally. "I heard you roll in after dark last night, so a sleep in probably would have been warranted."

"Yes, mother hen." Ah, the dry reply felt reassuring even as it nettled. "I went on a mission that took a little longer than expected, but the needs of the horse come first, so here I am. That still doesn't tell me why you are out here just past dawn when the rest of the house is still dark."

I leaned against the wall just beside the door, shoving my hands in my back pockets. "Well, I was going to do chores out here, because I'm fairly certain no one in the house wants me running the vacuum at this hour."

"But the chores are already done, or so Aaron informed me when I got home last night." He leaned his elbows on the bottom of the Dutch door, looking at me sideways, but a shift from the inside prompted him to straighten, pointedly facing away from the interior. "Taken care of by a rare breed of woman, or so I'm told."

"What's that supposed to mean?" I kept my voice low, something in his posture telling the stalls occupant wouldn't appreciate an increase in volume to match the level of my affront.

The eyebrow got me every time, and he upped the potency level by tipping his face to sight me along his nose. "Seriously, I pay you a compliment and you get huffy? You really are an odd duck, Josephine Bowen."

"And now I'm a duck?" The smirk on his full lips let me know he thought he'd hit his mark, so I straightened from the wall to deliver my blow, masking it in a pleasant smile and a mild tone. "Well, Bartholomew Clark, since you can't even identify what species I am, I'd bet you couldn't spot a rare breed if it bit you on the ass."

Both eyebrows closed the distance toward his hairline as he fished another arrow from his quiver of barbed commentary, but he never got a chance to fire it as Aaron came spilling out the door to the apartment. His laughter came out completely unrestrained, eyes almost disappearing in his face as he looked us over.

Sir Clark whipped around, caught between the uncomfortable sounding rustling that came from the stall and his reaction to our audience, holding a finger to his lips to quiet his brother. Immediately, the laughter was silenced, though you could still see it in Aaron's eyes. He approached more reservedly, lightly clapping Sir Clark on the shoulder.

"Oh Lord, you two are funny. Bowen, even if you don't work out as a jouster, I might have to keep you around to needle him."

Sir Clark stepped away from the touch, briefly checking on the horse before turning narrowed eyes on Aaron. "Just wait, big brother, one day she's going to turn that sharp wit on you, and it will be me laughing."

Again with the complement that felt razor sharp. Surreptitiously, I rubbed at the ache in the area of my heart, but when they both leveled a smile on me it eased. I peeked around the edge of the stall door finally, barely able to make out heavy dapples on a broad butt with the dim lighting, a full white tail catching the light. Then I mulled over the dropped information— big brother. I never would have guessed it, as Aaron seemed so much more lighthearted, though physically they looked very similar in age. But the welcome back from the war comment slid across the back of my consciousness, providing perspective. That would age the hell out of anyone.

"Hey, I've got to head over to the faire and hash out some details on the contract, so I'll leave you two alone as long as you promise not to kill each other." Aaron teased, and I turned back toward him, offering a sideways grin to Sir Clark.

"I'll promise if he will."

"I won't touch her, I swear." The absolutely deadpan expression made a giggle tickle at the back of my throat but I swallowed it down, along with an unexpectedly bitter pill of random disappointment that confused me to no end.

"I'll hold you to it, Bart." He strolled out the barn, his ever present swagger making him impossibly likeable. Once the farm truck rolled past, I turned back to the door, peering more intently.

"So, what's up with the new guy?" I asked casually, though it took effort to keep breathing while I waited, like the answer would hold weight.

"I don't know much." He sighed and dragged a hand through his hair, ruffling the dense, short cropped strands. "He came in to the auction via a broker, with every indication of being broke as hell, and he's pretty to boot, so Vince called me. We always need new horses, so I went to look at him. But what this horse is telling me is that he's been through hell. I couldn't leave him there a second longer, but it took us an hour to get him loaded and the paperwork was just as exhausting."

I swallowed hard around the lump of anger gathering in the center of my chest, knowing it wouldn't do anyone any good, least of all the horse. At least now he was in a better place. "What's wrong with him, then? Beaten? Starved? Neglected?"

"I don't quite know. Maybe all of the above, though I can't find a mark on him, and he doesn't flinch when you raise your hand. He's about a hundred pounds under ideal weight, and his feet are a little overgrown, but nothing we can't fix with one good trim."

"Then what?" I asked, keeping my volume low, but crossing my arms over my chest in impatience.

"See for yourself." He grumbled lowly, conveying just as much frustration as I felt, and I shook the tension from my shoulders as he flicked on the stall light.

Holy bejeebers, he hadn't been kidding about the pretty. Maybe even understating the obvious. The horse's coat appeared steel gray, with dapples across his body in a constellation of bright white stars that I wanted to trace with my fingers. His feet were almost completely concealed by thick feathering, the yellowing of the silvery strands revealing he'd spent a lot of time standing in soiled bedding. The hair itself looked brittle though, smacking of poor management and his belly was distended, though the flesh hung too thin over his hips and back. But the neglect went so much deeper than the skin, a cloud of hurt

hanging around him like a disease. He stood with his head in the
far corner, not looking at us with his eyes or ears, purposefully
shut down to the world around him. The resulting ache in my
chest would not be rubbed away.

"Jesus." The whispered word hit Bart like a visible slap, and
for the first time, I thought his name without humor.

"Yeah." A wealth of heartache lived in that syllable.

"I can't even wrap my brain around this." I rubbed my arms,
suddenly cold despite the growing heat of the day, my tank top
completely inadequate to combat the chill trying to root itself in
my chest.

"Don't, Jo. Don't try, don't go there. It won't help him, and it
will only hurt you." I trusted the experience coloring his
statement more than the words themselves, and looked over to
find a reflection of my roiling emotions in his eyes.

"So what do we do?" My whole body itched to move, to do
something in the face of this travesty.

"Who's this we, white girl?" Sharp humor again, and I finally
recognized its function. Armor, protecting himself from the
harsh reality before us, and no doubt from all the other little
hurts life could throw at you. Look at me, being all wise and
stuff. Don't get used to it.

I smiled easily enough, momentarily allowing him deflect
both our real feelings on the matter, then gestured between the
two of us. "Yeah, we. Mother hen, remember. I can't un-see
this." No response except for a direct stare that seemed to weigh
me more thoroughly than it ever had before. "You said he's
broke, but it looks like what he needs right now is care, and if he
wants one, a friend. That I can do."

"Bowen, you are here to learn to joust, not help with extra
projects." He framed it as a chastisement, but I recognized the
out he tried to offer me. I could no more take it than I could walk
away from a tease.

"Please? Let me at least try."

Ah, a rare smile then, the warmth from it finally shunting the
icy shard of despair away from my heart. "Alright. Let's see
what he thinks of you then, since it's his choice anyway."

I reached for the latch of the door, pausing there for permission, which I'm sure surprised him, but he nodded. It slid smoothly beneath my hand, and the horse barely flicked an ear as I let myself in the stall, moving toward the open corner so I could get a better look at him. The angle of his hip and shoulder spoke of tremendous athleticism, the length of leg and depth of chest whispering the temptation of speed. I admired the short back, meant for carrying weight, and the elegance of his neck, though it needed muscle to fulfill its potential for grace. I could barely focus on the finer planes of his face past the dull orb of his eye, emotional response coloring my vision as I visually traced the wide forehead, unwilling to touch him when I hadn't been invited. His ears, a trifle large against the sculpted perfection of the rest of him, depressed me as much as his eye, hanging listlessly to the sides with hopelessness. "What's his name?"

"I think he needs a new one. That's the only negative reaction I've gotten from him so far, trying to use the one they gave me." Worry tightened Bart's cheeks and I flicked my eyes back toward the horse. "R-O-S-C-O-E" he spelled out slowly, and I mentally chewed on the name while leaning against the wall in an obvious show of relaxation.

"How about Ro?" I asked conversationally, as much to the horse as the man. "Can I call you Ro?" Nothing from either camp. "Well, until you tell me otherwise, sweet boy, I'll call you Ro." My heart leapt, though I remained perfectly still at the slightest twitch of his ear my way, and I took a moment to observe his environment. Most notably, his breakfast remained completely untouched. "Is he not eating?"

"He didn't eat last night until I left, I imagine today will be much the same."

"So food won't be much of a motivator." I sighed, and rubbed my cheek, surprised at the faint sting of the touch. Apparently I'd gotten a bit too much sun the last couple days.

"No. And I can't put him out with the others just yet. We're pretty strict when it comes to quarantine, but extra careful when they come from a dealer. Too many unknowns, and we can't risk the other horses getting sick." Now Bart took his turn to sigh, scratching at a couple days' worth of stubble.

"Can I take him out for walks?" Memories of hours spent lounging with Abby prompted the idea, needing her to know I didn't just want to ride. I valued her for herself too. While she'd never really gotten buddy, buddy about it, it taught her to relax in my company, and this horse needed that even more than she ever did.

A light came on behind Bart's eyes after a second of thought. "Tell you what, I don't want him touching anything anyone else might get to, but you could take him out to the paddock on the other side of the trailer. Let him hand graze there, if he'll relax enough for it, just make sure to close the gate when you are done. He can use that for the next week, and we'll reevaluate." I let myself out of the stall to hunt up his halter, but Sir Clark stayed my hand, his fingers light on my knuckles. I froze at the touch, lifting an eyebrow in question. "Let him eat his breakfast Bowen, and you go eat yours. You'll have plenty of time before lunch."

We went our separate ways, but in a way, we were closer than we'd ever been. He might put my back up in the worst way possible, which conflicted entirely for the respect I had for his natural authority, but in this, we were one hundred percent united.

After breakfast, I helped Annabelle get her laundry going and took the time to shoot an email to Mom. At ten, I ambled up to the barn, finding a new halter and lead hanging by the stall as if waiting for me, a tiny key tag attached to the cheek with Ro written in blocky letters. Practically speaking, I knew it would prevent Ro from contaminating anything the other horses came into contact with, but it still felt like a silent blessing.

I caught Ro working on his hay, my heart breaking again when he froze—it took a lot to make a horse stop chewing, their survival dependent on remaining constantly moving and eating. Ivan, for example, would have shoved his head further into the pile and stuffed his face until I pulled it out, working over the giant mouthful he had horked down while I got him ready to ride. I waited Ro out, leaning against the door without looking at him directly and held a one sided conversation with the air in his general direction.

"Hey Ro, I heard there's some mighty fine grazing outside. The boss said we could go check it out if you want, but only if you want to." The litany continued for much longer than I usually talked, until my mouth went dry, but then miracle of miracles, the grind of teeth began again. I slid the latch, the chewing stopped, and so did I, beginning my monologue all over again. One painful step at a time, I approached him, stopping whenever he did, not wanting him to turn for the corner because I put too much pressure on him. The first contact felt too important for me to rush, even if I missed lunch for it. If I did this right it would set the cornerstone for everything that came after, and give us a place to fall back to when needed.

I didn't touch him more than necessary as I slid the crownpiece across the freshly shorn bridle path in his thick mane. Holding the bulk of the halter by that one strap as the other hand guided the noseband over his muzzle, I stopped every time he did. My arms burned with their own weight, fatigue making them tremble, and I tried not to think about the spear I would have to manage later. If I could make this happen, I would happily miss every single ring today, while Cranston laughed, no less.

Finally, the halter was buckled on, and I turned for the door, breathing a sigh of relief when he fell in at my side. The lead rope I left draped over the door looked longer than most of the ropes we used, and I blessed whatever impulse prompted the gift, as this would allow him to graze a little more freely. We traveled out to the paddock, his manners absolutely perfect, but it felt like leading an automaton, no life in the creature beside me. The energy traveled through the lead rope like a conduit and the deadness, the utter lack of spirit made my skin crawl.

In the paddock, he stood, waiting for me to give him a direction with all the feeling of a chalk board waiting to be written on. No warmth, no will existed, his wide nostrils pinched with defeat, and his eyes glazed like a zombie. Holding back tears of sympathy, I played out the line, giving him more space, but he stood frozen in place, waiting for direction, which I wouldn't do yet. If he didn't kick, bite, or otherwise threaten my safety, there would be not one directive or harsh word from me.

Heartsick but determined, I focused every thought I had on the imagined vision of him grazing. I picked up a few handfuls and offered it to him and I even asked him to put his head down until his nose brushed the tall grass, hoping the scent and proximity might tempt him. Nothing.

Literally and figuratively at the end of my rope, I folded my legs and sat, my own spirit flagging. Just for something to do, I slowly split strands of grass with my fingernails, stripping them down to hair thin filaments, though my awareness never shifted from him, some ten feet away. I started talking again, desperate for some kind of connection, describing the ranch at home, the deep gully where the creek ran, the swimming hole at the back of the cow/calf pasture, and the sound of wind in the late summer grass at the top of my favorite hill.

Then, blessed purple monkey toes, he lowered his head and took a tentative bite. I stopped talking in shock and he froze, but I stumblingly picked back up where I'd left off, struggling not to whoop with glee when he took a second bite. Slowly, he began to get the idea, chewing longer after each time I went silent, though never longer than a minute. Thus, we occupied ourselves equitably for some timeless while, though I startled when he suddenly flung his head up and stared toward the gate.

Bart approached, back in his riding breeches and half chaps, telling me surer than any clock that I'd burned more time than I thought. He looked more relaxed than I'd ever seen him, though the display was more for Ro's benefit than mine as the horse shifted on his feet, tension bleeding down the lead line. I didn't feel fear or panic, just uncomfortableness, as if he could manage as long as things didn't change, and I immediately worried for his potential as a jousting horse. You could define jousting as condensed organization running headlong toward chaos with open arms; not a good place for anyone, horse or man, that couldn't cope with change.

Crouching beside me, Bart offered a water bottle. "I thought you might be thirsty." An eyebrow arched, though not in its usual sardonic shape, almost as though puzzling me out. I twisted off the cap and guzzled shamelessly at the chilled water, leaving whatever he wondered lost in the silence. "I'm headed out to grab Eros, if you want to wind things up here."

Ah, not an order, not an edged compliment, just a suggestion. Good heavens, what was the world coming to? "Alright. I'll be in shortly."

He straightened to his considerable height, making me feel tiny from my seat on the ground, a foreign feeling that around anyone else would have felt vulnerable. Yet, much like Ro, I trusted him, even if I didn't understand him. Safety felt like part and parcel of both of them. Then he faded away with a grace that I began to realize had always been there, I just hadn't been ready to see it.

I rose from the grass once he departed, standing still for a few minutes so Ro could relax again before turning for the barn. The gusty sigh as I turned to shut the gate gave me an indication he finally felt something, and when I slid the halter from his head and closed the door behind me, he started licking and chewing. The universal sign for a horse in thought, it let me know we were on the right track, and I hurried for the house to get changed. The only known allergy I had was to being late, and I refused to let Sir Clark's trust change that.

Flying into the room at warp speed, Annabelle's screech halted me in my tracks, my eyes widening as I pivoted around and shut the door. Catching her in the middle of undressing hadn't been my intent. "Sorry, sorry!" I stammered, rifling through my clothes to dig out breeches and a sleeved shirt. My shoulders were already pink from the morning outside, and unless I wanted my freckles to merge together, I needed to cover up.

"All clear, Josie, no worries, you just startled me." I turned around cautiously as she sat on the edge of her bed to drag on her hot pink riding pants. By comparison, I appeared to be a boring flower indeed, the sun-faded black breeches in my hand meant strictly for work. There were more at home I could bring if they kept me, and with Ro on my heart, extra incentive conspired to make that happen. "I wonder what we'll be doing today."

"I don't know. Probably something painful." I mused offhandedly, swapping out shirts as we talked.

"Why would you think that? Bart's a nice guy."

Her naiveté floored me sometimes. "Because jousting is going to hurt, Annabelle. He wants to make sure we are tough enough to take the hit before we start running at each other with sticks." The breeches got hung up on my sweaty legs and I did some unflattering dancing to get them up where they belonged, making her giggle. I stuck my tongue out at her in retaliation.

"Well, yeah, falling is going to hurt, but it's not like they actually hit you. It's staged, you know. They flip a coin and decide who gets to win."

I flopped on the bed in disbelief, struck by her ignorance. "Are you serious, Annabelle? Didn't you see the bruises on any of them? Just getting hit causes pain."

"Surely not! The lances are simply made to shatter." The worry in her limpid eyes might have been comical if not for the seriousness of the situation, and she paled when I shook my head in denial. "Why would they do that to each other?"

"Because they're crazy." I tossed out the comment on the off chance she'd be distracted by the attempt at humor, but I didn't hold my breath either.

"But why would *you* want to do it?" Her voice slipped up an octave. "They could really hurt you, Josie."

This time, with all the seriousness I could shove into a sentence, I looked her square in the eye and responded, "Because I'm crazy too." The silence in the room took on a panicked feel, and I moved to her side of the room, placing a hand on her shoulder before she could bolt. "I think you need to go talk to Sir Clark, right now."

"Yes, right now." She mumbled weakly, standing and heading for the door, but I stopped her before she reached it.

"But maybe you should finish doing up your pants first?" She laughed then, a hysterical, brittle edge to it, and shoved her shirt in the waist of her breeches before doing up the zipper and button.

I let her go, not wanting to be there for the conversation that would occur, and finished getting ready. My fingers fumbled uncharacteristically at the laces of my boots, and I stared in amazement when a drop of moisture darkened the fabric of my breeches, rapidly joined by three more. Apparently, there were more chinks than I thought in my well armored heart, and more appearing every day.

I waited until exactly 11:30 to take the path to the barn, chewing my meal bar without really tasting it, a little afraid of what I'd find when I arrived. Stunned, I stopped in the doorway, caught by the sight of Sir Clark hugging Annabelle, the dichotomy of his hardened exterior tough to resolve with that act of tenderness. His eyes flashed up to mine, and he stepped back from her, patting her kindly on the shoulder with a few last muffled words between them. She nodded briefly, much less red in the face than I expected from someone I'd last seen crying, and jogged down the aisle to meet me.

"Hey, Josie. I don't want to make you late for your lesson, but I do want to say goodbye." Before I could respond, she wrapped me in a fierce hug, leaving my arms awkwardly pinned to my sides. I patted her stiffly somewhere in the vicinity of her waist until she let go. "I'll probably be gone by the time you get back, but I wanted to tell you thank you, and to say yes, it is going to hurt. But if any woman alive can do it, it'll be you."

Stunned, I watched her hurry for the house, her booted feet nimble as she dodged the bodies and questions of Cranston and Lee. Before they could reach the barn to ask me those same questions I ducked into the tack room for Ivan's equipment, shaking my head to discourage conversation when I came back out. For once, Cranston kept his mouth shut, and I headed for Ivan's stall, surprised to find it occupied. Looking around, I discovered all of our horses inside, and Bart, standing nonchalantly beside Eros's door. A curt nod was his only reply to the thank you I silently mouthed in his direction.

At 12:30 on the dot, we all filed in the arena behind him, halting when he pivoted Eros toward us. He set us exercises that prevented any chance for conversation, a review of everything we'd covered thus far, and I fulfilled my own early offer to miss every ring in favor of Ro's comfort. Then we did sit ups on horseback, to build our core muscles, and we practiced raising and lowering a jousting lance until my arm burned like I'd shoved it through the fiery gates of hell.

You remember when I first looked at Bart and I knew he would push me to my breaking point? Well, now, I looked him in the eyes, muscles quivering with fatigue, and sweat making my grip slippery, trying not to let the lance touch Ivan's neck.

"Don't drop it, Bowen." He intoned as I raised it back to ready position and Cranston laughed until that deceptively mild gaze flicked over to him with whip like speed. As soon as the silence returned he slowly brought his focus back to me. "You got five more in you?"

"I have ten, if that's what you want." I growled lowly, matching him eyebrow for eyebrow, though I didn't have the energy to return his mocking grin.

"Oh no, ten more is for Wednesday." He responded dryly, absently swatting a fly that landed on Eros's neck as I lowered the lance again, trying to keep it from moving past level while my muscles threatened to quit on me. "Just five today."

I gave him his five, tempted to stick my tongue out at him as he rode away, but two things stopped me. One was the amount of effort it would require, my body begging me to conserve whatever it has left. The other was the suspicion he'd somehow see it, and I'd be doing those ten more raises right away.

I'd love to say the days sped by, or something equally trite, but they actually ran together like watercolors, one bleeding into the next. There were joyful pinks I found in working with Ro, deep reds of hard won victory, painfully hot whites when I woke up in the middle of the night with Charlie horses and the bright blues of defining moments.

Thankfully, the only black in my life was a happy one, as Ivan and I hit our stride working together. He rarely bolted in the lyst anymore, and only occasionally offered to jig at the start of a run. My ring catching became more consistent, and joy of joys, on Friday we were given the chance to level our lance at a target.

When Sir Clark demonstrated a pass at the quintain, a shield shaped target on one end of a rotating arm, he made it look so smooth I actually salivated with envy. Eros knew his job so well that Bart actually dropped the reins before their run started, and Bart's focus became so sharp you could imagine it cutting the air in passing. The lance fetched up against his body, tucked firmly beneath his bicep, and the point never wavered once as he brought it to bear. The thwack of the lance against the shield rang loud, like an axe biting a tree deeply enough to slice it clean through, and the arm of the quintain spun hard, the counterweight hanging on the other end flung horizontal.

As soon as he hit the lance came back to the vertical, and Bart's other hand landed on Eros's neck, barely touching the reins as the horse slowed to a trot, then halted. We were treated to watching Sir Aaron repeat the maneuver, and while his also went smoother than mirror glass, placing his shot so precisely he achieved the same amount of full rotations as his brother, it lacked the same power. No matter who hit you it would to hurt, but I believed Bart would be a force to be reckoned with in the lyst. It probably helped that Eros stayed so in tune with his rider—Byz had a tension about him, as if any movement might turn into a fight.

Cranston got to go first, and impressively managed a hit on his first try. He certainly possessed the upper body strength to aid him in his efforts, while I worked much harder to balance the lance. Thank goodness for the workout routine Sir Clark had recommended before my arrival, or I would have been struggling. It still amazed me how invested he was in our success, pushing each of us just the right amount, but always making sure we mastered the skills to build on before asking for more.

At the call for next I looked over at Lee, who waved me ahead of him with a smile. "Ladies first."

Snorting in a very unladylike fashion and rolling my eyes, I then clucked softly at Ivan, pleased when he stepped forward calmly to receive a lance from the waiting Sir Aaron. Our Captain winked at me, the wealth of good will in his eyes incredibly reassuring. I backed Ivan into the lyst before turning him, the daily drills finally becoming muscle memory.

"Bowen, I want you to sit a little deeper when you ask him to go. That lance is going to pull you back with the force of his departure, and it will help you stabilize the weight." I liked when Sir Clark talked to me like a sensible person, and gave him a tight smile to show my appreciation. The lack of eyebrow conveyed his seriousness, and I focused on business, rolling my shoulders and putting my eyes on the prize.

On an exhale to push my center of gravity as low as it could go, I closed my legs and made a soft kissing noise. Like silk dancing in the wind, Ivan curled up beneath me and unfurled himself more smoothly than ever before, like he knew the importance of the moment. Remember that bright blue I talked about? Yes, that, right there.

The lance came down a little too fast, and I tightened every hard won muscle in my core to keep it from tipping too far, praying momentum wouldn't make it bounce. Unable to focus on the tip like I could on the spear, I looked to my target instead, tightening my arm against my body until the long blur of lance came into the same picture and I waited. It went so fast, yet was the longest stride of my life, afraid to miss, anticipating the impact.

We hit with a hollow thud, the reverberation moving through my body with a delicious hum of satisfaction to accompany it, and my right heel sank down in the stirrup to absorb the impact. Though my hand tingled with the shock, I gripped the lance a little harder and brought it upright, then remembered to breath, relieved when Ivan immediately slowed. At that point my softly uttered whoa became more a formality than a requirement, and a sense of rightness washed over me so hard I almost sobbed with joy. Not that I would yield to such weakness in front of others, but that's what I felt, and I had to at least be honest in my own memories. Instead, I reached down and scratched the top of Ivan's shoulder where he liked it best, along with a cheerfully pitched, "Good boy, buddy."

"Bowen." Sir Clark's voice pulled me back to the real world without yanking me off the high I rode. How could the man make my last name sound just as informal and friendly as my first? I stepped Ivan from the lyst and rode down the arena to return the lance, thrilled with the lightness of the man's posture as I came up to his side. "Three rotations. Pretty good for a first hit."

"How many did you get your first hit?" The question came out before I could check my mouth, and I clamped it shut, his business being none of mine. For a second, his mouth thinned, and I felt sure he would slap the inquiry away like an irritating insect. Then he looked me straight in the eye, challenge and humor soothing the worry in my gut.

"Six." Okay, not surprising, considering the size of him, and the force he brought to bear. "But it took me five passes before I landed it." Oh, how I wanted to laugh, but some things I just didn't want to share with my fellow trainee's, so I pulled the light moment close to my heart and hoarded it. "Now, get your ass back in line."

"Yes, Sir Clark." I answered promptly, cueing Ivan to trot back to our mark. Somehow, even the firmness at the end had felt like approval.

We each made three more passes, and I hit on all but the last one, my arm growing increasingly more tired. Lee and Cranston ran hot and cold, either hitting solidly enough to rock the stanchion or barely tapping it enough to get it moving. In comparison, I couldn't feel bad about my efforts, but it did leave me more determined than ever. As long as I kept improving, I'd be content, and in the long run, I valued the improvements in my partnership with Ivan more than my performance.

As for Ro, well, it was slow going, but I felt satisfied. We'd progressed to my being able to touch him without the pregnant pause, though I still didn't do it more than necessary. You can't force friendship, and that's what I meant to offer him.

After evening chores, I took him back out to the paddock and settled straight on to the grass in an area he had yet to eat down, grateful for a few moments to rest. My successes of the day were proving to be just as exhausting as the actual work, the emotional high tough to come down from. I felt too tired to talk to him, but he caught on after a few minutes, applying himself deliberately to the task of eating. His pattern had become very methodical, which meant I needed to use a different spot every day, because he would mow a straight line, left to right, then take a step and begin again, like a grass-eating typewriter.

Never coming closer than ten feet, he kept his distance, still needing the buffer of space to be comfortable, but I didn't mind. After watching him for a bit I tested my luck and laid back in the tall grass, listening to him pause when he couldn't see me anymore. I mustered the energy to talk to him for a few, stupid stuff about my favorite foods, and how I'd never met a cookie I didn't like, until he resumed the steady tear and chew. I could count heartbeats by it, it became so consistent, and I stayed much longer than normal, content to watch the sky turn shades of pink and purple as the sun went to its well-deserved rest.

As the light faded I noticed something I hadn't before, the few windows along the roof line of the barn catching the reflection of the sunset in them, and I wondered at the two men who lived there. Similar warmth, though in one man it lived a little closer to the surface. Close in height and hair color, but such different eyes. A rock steady solidity to one so deeply seated nothing could shake it, and the other more fluid, like water cutting its way through a canyon, yet able to melt around obstacles. They were good men, men I admired and I flattered myself to consider someday they might call me a sister in arms. Maybe even a friend.

My musings came to a halt at an unexpected warm breath on my knee, and it took a second to remember to breathe around my excitement. I didn't move, so afraid to scare him away, not wanting to shatter the moment. Every cell in my body remained aware of his size compared to me, but I'd seen horses and cows alike around their babies and I knew how careful they could be. That didn't mean I wasn't ready to move if needed, to roll and protect myself, but if he stayed calm I didn't have a reason to worry.

I don't know how long he stood there, not quite touching me, just sharing space and I didn't care. Hell, I'd lay there all night if he wanted. Eventually, he stepped away, but that in no way reduced the golden glow that settled in my heart. Then, like an eighth wonder of the world, he reached the end of the lead, and ever so slightly, he tossed his head in the direction of the barn, and my heart went incandescent. An opinion! A real, live, opinion!

Like the good human I was trying to prove myself to be, I climbed to my feet and fell in beside him, returning him to his stall for the night. You'll forgive me, but I actually skipped back down the aisle with happiness, my joy too much to keep contained.

Saturday became a repeat of the last, though we changed things up a little, with Aaron and John going first. They juggled us candidates around too, leaving me paired with Alex this time. He proved surprisingly friendly, though he was incredibly regimented in his routine, something I could appreciate after scuttling around behind John.

Sir Clark played squire to his brother, at least for the armoring, and I filled in on the field so he could focus on his real job of ramping up the crowd. Trace had explained why the cast was so enthusiastic—not only were they getting into their characters, but many of them wouldn't have the time or energy to come to the jousting field during the actual run of the faire.

After the first show Trace drug me around the faire site a little to meet some of the shop owners he knew, though not all of them were open yet. By next weekend the place would be full to its brim, overflowing with color and sound that would breathe life into the festival grounds. The magic of the faire did not come from its location as much as the people that poured heart and soul into its creation.

I'll admit to being much more relaxed during Sir Drew's joust, knowing he had things well in hand against Trace. While Trace seemed practically unshakeable in the tack his shots were inconsistent, so we didn't have much danger of anyone coming off. It allowed me the chance to watch Sir Clark and Eros more closely, because I had a hell of a crush on their relationship with each other. Not even a real, live wizard could impress me more than those two, going from standstill to gallop, wheeling around with barely any pressure on the reins to sprint the other direction. That he did it all while providing unending commentary that was both entertaining and educational floored me. I rarely could chew gum and walk at the same time, though my ability to multi-task, physically, improved all the time thanks to training. Juggling mentally, I had down pat, as evidenced by my sudden notice of a flopping piece of armor on Alex at the end of the second pass.

"Tape!" I hollered at Steve, and he threw the spool of duct tape high in the air like we were some kind of circus act.

Amazingly, I caught it on the move, throwing in a quick bow toward the audience when the group closest to me clapped. Hillary held J.T. still while I secured the pauldron protecting Alex's shoulder, and I slapped him on the armor covering his thigh to let him know I had finished. They didn't hear very well once the helmets were secure.

Ducking back out of the alley, I basked in the momentary glow of success as Sir Clark rode by at a high stepping trot, favoring me with a rare nod of approval. I wasn't expecting him to yell at the crowd, "Let's hear it for the squires!"

Cheering. For me. Well, for all of us, but triggered by my actions. A rare blush flooded my face and I bowed low toward the crowd as much to conceal it as to acknowledge their attention. The high it brought on I'd love to feel again, and I knew I could become a hopeless addict if encouraged. Jeff slapped me on the back with a grin when I resumed my station mid lyst to gather debris, and the show moved on, moment over but forever ingrained in the fabric of my heart.

♥♥♥

Days end came quickly, the horses settling in for the night, and my nerves were still too wound up from the accumulation of good things clicking into place for me to head inside just yet. I settled on the floor in front of Ro's stall with a smile, tipping my head back against the wood to enjoy the music of the crickets outside, not even shaken when Cranston threw shade my way.

"Hey Bowen, gonna spend the night with the rest of the nags?"

"Their company is infinitely preferable to yours." I answered mildly, not even looking at him until I heard Lee's stifled grunt of laughter.

The black look Cranston leveled on me smacked of enmity so dark I couldn't wrap my brain around it. Why could I trade barbs with anyone else and it was all in fun? Maybe because his comments were purposefully undercutting, but I think in the long run, it came down to lack of real confidence. His lack, that is, because Aaron, Bart and even Trace could take crap and dish it back without getting butt hurt.

Lee tugged on his arm and got him moving, leaving me alone at last. But not really alone, not in the least. The horses knew I lingered, and I flattered myself to think they at least liked my company. Losing Annabelle turned out more difficult than I expected, though I knew it was better for her to move on to someplace where she could thrive. I'd already gotten several texts from her, a couple just to cheer me on, and several going on and on about the resort she was working at, from the hot tub to the hot cowboys.

The door at my back vibrated and I opened my eyes on the miracle of Ro, hanging his head in the aisle. The whole time he'd been here he'd never done it that any of us had seen, even when the other horses went past or raising a ruckus over feeding time. From my unusual vantage I spotted a groove of scar tissue right behind his lip, the hair worn off and the skin thickened from repeated abuse, and my heart twisted again. An individual would have to be very heavy handed indeed to create that sort of scar, made over time by a curb chain on a leverage style bit.

"Hey Ro."

He snorted a soft acknowledgement, and canted his head to the side to train an eye on me as though surprised, but I knew better. Horses, at their most fundamental, survived because they noticed the tiniest changes in their environment, and I'd been pretty stinkin' obvious about sitting down. His ear flicked down toward me, then he looked outside and I laughed.

"Alright, alright."

When I stood, he took a step back, though nothing like his usual retreat. He moved just enough to be polite when I came in the door, waiting patiently for me to buckle on his halter. His skin felt more elastic, more alive under my hand as I adjusted the noseband just so, and I felt energy in the lead as we traveled the well-worn path to the paddock.

I stayed on my feet this time, letting him pick his path, rewarding each soft bump of pressure on the halter with an immediate release, though I certainly wouldn't do the same with any other horse. Ivan, I knew for certain, would happily drag me thither and yon with little concern for my weight on the lead if I offered him the same freedom. Yet, Ro remained painfully polite, requesting each change of direction and waiting for a reply, so I continued as we had been, perfectly at peace.

I ached to touch him, to let my hands flex over the pliant line of his back, but I didn't. That would come in its own time, just as everything else had, and I renewed my commitment to cherish every moment without a sense of urgency.

Morning came before my alarm, and I smiled as I stretched. The potential in the air carried weight, but more like the perfect heft of a blanket on a cool day, making you want to snuggle it closer. Sneaking a quick peek out the window, I saw the light in the barn come on and I slid from the bed, too happy to linger in its comforting embrace.

This time, I pulled on clothes and tidied my hair before venturing outside with a mug of tea, just in time to hear a stall door open. Hoof beats followed, walking at first, and I cleared a row of bushes just in time to see Tuck's red coat glimmering in the early light. He stopped to snatch a few mouthfuls of grass while waiting for the rest of the herd, as I heard the rest of the doors grind open in rapid succession. Then they came on like thunder, J.T. bucking as he rounded the corner, with Eros and Bart bringing up the end.

They were so absorbed in each other I almost felt bad for watching, like some kind of creeper, further torn when Bart spotted me. It shifted his attention away from his horse for only a second, barely a breath, but my guilt swelled regardless. This private moment was not meant for the intrusion of others, no matter how beautiful I found it. That didn't stop me from watching the play of muscles in Eros's haunches as he shifted his weight to head down the hill toward the pasture and the answering change in Bart's position, only trust and a handful of mane keeping him connected to the powerful stallion. Yes, I'd become a stalker fangirl, and now they knew it.

Sighing with self-disgust, I continued toward the barn, intent on taking Ro out for the morning. The morning looked too beautiful to waste and hiding in the house wouldn't change the events of the last several minutes. I found my horse busily munching his breakfast when I walked in, so I leaned on the door and sipped my tea until it was gone. Now, what to do while I waited for him to finish?

The manure rake beckoned me, and I turned to the seemingly Sisyphean task of all horse people, letting the familiar chore quiet my mind. Halfway through my second stall I heard boots in the aisle, and I faked nonchalance until they passed, surprised when I heard the familiar chuff of manure hitting a bushel bucket on the other end of the barn. Alright, we'd just pretend it didn't happen then.

Several stalls later, my arms protested as I lifted the last bucket into the manure spreader, but I rejoiced, because it still felt less achy than last week. A little thing, but I had begun to value the little things a lot more since this adventure started. I hoped even if I didn't get asked to stick around that it would be a lesson I could take with me when I left.

A pinch deep in my chest came at the thought, like my very body rejected the idea of not being here, not living this life. I already loved so much about it, the people, the horses, and the absolute rightness in my bones.

A faint grunt of effort warned me of Bart's approach, and I schooled my face into some semblance of welcome, still choking on my doubts. He tossed the contents of the bucket into the spreader with one arm, muscles rippling with power from wrist to shoulder, then waved in the direction of the barn.

"Thanks."

Uh oh, had we digressed to one word conversations? "No problem. I needed something to do while Ro finished breakfast."

"Going to take him out then?" He inspected the side of the manure spreader for the cleanest spot and leaned against it, hooking his thumbs in his pockets, though he didn't quite look me in the eye yet.

"Yeah. If you are okay with it, I think I'll just turn him loose this time, see how he does." Hopefully that would work as an olive branch, actually seeking his opinion.

"Shouldn't be a problem. I'm glad you are checking in, Jo, but I've watched you with him. I trust you to do the right thing."

Blatant praise. My brain couldn't process it correctly, and I swallowed several times while hunting for a response, my skin on fire with embarrassment. "Thanks." Dammit, now I had been reduced to one-word conversation.

"Bowen, are you blushing or do you just sunburn that fast?"

Moldy yellow teddy bear ears, he could kill me with those sharp teases. I sucked in a deep breath and chuckled weakly. "Maybe a bit of both. Hazard of being so very Welsh a leek looks tan in comparison."

The smile he laid on me should have been registered as a concealed weapon. I didn't think I'd ever seen that many teeth from him before, and it took years off his face, leaving me wondering how old he really was.

"Alright, I'll catch you later. I've got some work to do while you lollygag around today."

I hated that I snorted so often, but sometimes it really got my point across. "Seriously? I strike you as a lollygagger?"

Serious eyes, a little soft with recent humor, finally met mine. "No, not in the least, Bowen, but I'd take advantage if I were you. This week, the real work begins."

"Yes, Sir." I responded just as earnestly. "I'm looking forward to it."

"That's what I like to hear." He straightened from his resting place and headed for the barn, keeping me from getting the last word by his absence, and by the most effective method of all—an offhand compliment.

My day only improved, Ro so happy to go outside he actually stuck his nose in the halter. I sat with him for a little while, but then thirst intruded so I unclipped the lead and turned for the gate. The muted thump of hooves against the grass made me look back, Ro following along as if we were still attached.

"I'll be right back, buddy." Still, he followed, nose close enough to my elbow I could feel a whisker tickling my skin. I stopped, so did he. I walked on and he came with, so I changed directions, laughing when he tossed his head and pivoted to follow. I stopped again and turned to face him, backing slowly toward the gate until it bumped against my back, and he matched me step for step, just beyond the reach of my fingers. "Look, I'm just going to the house, I'll be right back, I promise."

I know, I know, he didn't understand what I said, but with all the talking I'd been doing to him the habit became ingrained. Squeezing out the gate, I started walking to the house, and he stationed himself in the corner, watching intently.

Guilt drove me to jog the rest of the way, and I plucked a couple water bottles from the fridge, rolling those, a sleeve of cookies and an apple in what had become my outside blanket. For good measure I slathered on some more sunscreen, and selected a book from the pile on my nightstand so I wouldn't have to leave him again until dinner. Normal people might call it foolish, but I hadn't been lying to Cranston when I said I preferred their company.

As I hurried back out to the paddock I ducked around the trailer and found him standing just where I left him, but with a marked difference. His nostrils were wide, as if he'd been running, hairs on his neck sticking up with a faint sheen of sweat. That pristine white tail flagged over his back like a nobleman's cape, but the intensity faded, his eye visibly softening the closer I came.

He stepped back, all politeness, allowing me back in the gate without crowding, and followed me to the shade of the single tree available, watching everything I did with a curiosity he'd never shown before. The behavior seemed colt like, as if the whole world was new and fascinating. If that were the case, well then, I'd have liked to pound in the face of whoever deprived him of that innocent joy in the first place.

Once I sprawled out on the blanket he turned back to his grazing as if I never left, and I dug out my phone to take a picture of him. It took a few tries to get just the right shot, since he was still short a bit of muscle and flesh, and I deleted several in the attempt. Eventually, the perfect swish of his tail arced around his hocks, and he peered back at me with an eye and ear. *Click.* Ah, there, just right.

I'd hardly used my phone since arriving at the farm, just to shoot messages back and forth to family, and reassure a few social media friends that I wasn't dead. Of course, Sunday meant calling Mom later, but for now, I just saved his picture as my screensaver. As I was about to shove the phone back in my pocket, it vibrated with an incoming message from Sir Bartholomew Clark, no picture coming up for his contact info. Later, I'd have to snap a picture of Eros.

'Bowen, make sure you are on the Wi-Fi, and download the next message.'

What the heck? I didn't even know he knew how to text, let alone that he might text me. But I did as he asked, my inquiring mind on fire with the need to know what would warrant such familiar contact from him. Even with the wireless connection it took a few minutes to download, and I opened the plastic sleeve of cookies, watching the bar on the phone slowly fill. Two shortbreads later a video came up and I hastily pressed play, rewarded by the moving image of Ro, bucking and wheeling around. The angle was high, and it took me a second to figure out it had come from the window of the apartment, but I kept watching, the snaky neck and supple frame a joy to behold. The horse in the video could do anything, which meant all we had to do was unlock the potential in his heart. I saved the video to my phone and dropped a thank you text back to Bart, complete with a smiley face. He replied quickly.

'He did that the whole time you were gone.'

'He missed me. ;-p' I shot back, grinning over at the horse in question.

'You are spoiling him.'

I screwed my face up at that one, trying to find a tactful way to tell him to stick it in his ear, but luckily he responded before I could find the words.

'Keep it up. ;-)'

Thank you felt insufficient, but I sent it anyway, at a loss for how to say more without sounding like a complete girl. Don't get me wrong, I loved being a woman, but I didn't want to give him the wrong impression. My intent in the next two weeks was to prove how hard I could work, how tough I could be, which would be completely undermined by getting all maudlin. When no response came, I tucked the phone back in my jeans and rolled over on my back to pick up where I'd left my intrepid hero, surrounded by a pack of bloodthirsty hyena android hybrids bent on calling him lunch.

After a while I changed position, rolling on my side, and I came out of the book enough to notice Ro dozing not ten feet away. The lax lower lip and hip shot posture were unattractive, but the scene was one of the most beautiful things I'd ever experienced. For him to sleep around me, even lightly, meant he trusted me to keep the watch, to raise the alarm should something threaten his safety. I couldn't betray that sacred confidence, so I sat up, propping myself against the narrow trunk of the tree firmly enough to feel the bark digging against my shoulder blade. At that point, I skimmed my book a few sentences at a time, caught between the hero's predicament and the incredibly touching display of faith right in front of me.

When he woke it was softly done, a bleary blinking accompanied by a stretch, one hind leg reaching way back as he lifted his head in the air.

"Welcome back, sleepy boy."

He studied me momentarily, then wandered a few feet to begin eating again, and I sprawled on my stomach, flexing my feet until the blood ran back to my legs. Having next to no padding on my butt made sitting on the ground that long a little more taxing than expected. I chewed absently on my apple, trying to focus on my book, but between the reassuring grind of Ro's teeth, the steady hum of insects and the warmth of the day, my eyes grew heavy. Checking to make sure falling asleep would not leave me cooking in the sun, I laid my head down on my folded arms and let Ro keep the watch.

❤❤❤

"Bowen." I swatted lazily at my name, like a fly buzzing around the edge of my consciousness, and snuggled deeper into the crook my arm. "Bowen." At little more insistent, but no louder, so I grunted crankily, hoping it would go away. "Josephine."

A shiver ran down my back at that. A warmth in my name I'd never heard before, and I finally blinked my eyes open, rubbing an itch on my nose before looking up. I could almost touch Ro's foreleg he stood so close, and while it made my stomach tighten with awareness of his size, even more gut clenching was the softness on Bart's face, his usual rigid posture crouched so he could look under Ro's belly.

"You want to call off your watchdog?"

I looked closer at Ro, noticing the readiness in his body to flee at any second from this threat, but he had stood his ground while I slept. His ears flicked and pointed at Bart, then swiveled to me, lingering before aiming at the perceived threat once more.

"Ro, it's okay, I'm awake buddy." His big, dark ears flipped to me and stayed there as he took a step in my direction, still keeping an eye on the stranger. If Bart were a real threat Ro would be gone in a heartbeat, but the fact that he tried so hard to be brave made my heart swell a little. I reached for his neck as I came up on my knees, still muzzy with sleep, brushing the flat of my palm over his coat, letting my fingers briefly comb through his mane before dropping my hand. The gesture came instinctively, absent mindedly, but then he turned and carefully shoved his muzzle against my chest, clearly asking for more.

He froze when I did, having just realized what I'd done, but he didn't leave. No, he stayed, his massive but refined head running nearly the length of my torso, muzzle barely brushing my lap, a whorl of hair on his forehead just in front of my lips, and his ears swiveling in confusion. I bent to look him in the eye, discovering an entire universe of lightness where there last I had seen bleak despair. Crooning softly, I brushed my thumbs gently over his cheeks, the privilege of touch so incredibly precious. A clicking sound drew a sliver of attention away from the magic of the moment, and I caught Bart in the act of taking our picture, my eyes widening with the surprise of it all.

"You know, Bowen, I felt a little weird when you saw me with Eros this morning, but considering the thing of beauty I just witnessed, I think we can call it even." If asked to classify the smile he gave me, I might have labeled it sheepish, but that seemed a strange descriptor to attach to someone so clearly a predator. It was only fair to offer an equal exchange of honesty.

"I caught a glimpse last weekend, and I wanted to see if you'd do it again." My turn to appear chagrined, and when his eyebrow went up I looked away. Ro did me no favors, choosing that moment to turn away, leaving me exposed as he strolled across the paddock for a new patch of grazing.

"Why?"

Such a simple question for such a complicated answer, delivered in the deepest of voices. I chewed on it for a few moments before landing on the simplest explanation, hoping I could manage it without blushing. The pink on my cheeks had become an annoying regularity.

"Call it envy." His brows knitted together, not an expression I had any experience with yet. The only comparison I could think of was what my face did while I worked out a puzzle, so I ventured further explanation. "I like watching you with Eros because it's something I want for myself someday. I've had a really wonderful horse most of my life, but she doesn't want to be that close, keeps herself apart from me."

Understanding dawned, the softness of earlier returning in part, a glimmer of sympathy in his eyes. "It was hard won, Eros and I, but the best explanation is that it's like finding a soulmate. You can ride a hundred horses and do right by them, but when you are with that one, parts of you open up you didn't even realize you were holding back."

"Ugh, then I am probably never going to get it." Disappointment, hot and toothy, chewed on the inside of my ribcage, and I closed my eyes against the sensation. "I can't even manage to be fully invested in my human relationships."

A sharp bark of a laugh made me glare at him, though his smile reduced its vehemence. "Bowen, I can tell you from experience, horses are a damn sight easier than people."

He stretched to his full height, then offered me a hand up, the grip in his callused hands incredibly tactful considering the strength he was capable of. Once I stood up, he reached over and picked a leaf from my hair with all the delicacy of an artist, staring at the leaf with an absent grin before leveling his gaze on me. Before I could get more than a glimpse of the deep green in his eyes, his attention shifted Ro.

"But I'll tell you this, Jo. You are at the start of that road with that horse right there."

He left me there in stunned silence, staring fixedly at the horse who was taking more of my heart each time he offered me more of his.

Monday sucked on a level I could not adequately express. After we finished chores Bart sent us to change into exercise clothes, then set us a workout right in the barn aisle. It gave me a moment's amusement when Cranston's nose wrinkled with distaste. For all his ability to stick to a horse and ride hard, he remained an irritating prat, and it eased my urge to slap him whenever he did something he didn't like. After sweating our way through planks and squats, our sadistic taskmaster brought out an odd set of weights, each of them a solid ball of cast iron with a thick, rounded handle on the top.

"I'd like to introduce you all to the kettlebell." Mild words, but there was a smirk rife with challenge on that scruffy face. "We'll just cover proper form today, but from this point forward, these will live in your room with you. I don't care when you do your workouts, but if you expect to have the core strength to endure a hit, you will do them. Start three days a week, five of each exercise, the full circuit. If you aren't winded and burning, start the circuit again until you are on fire."

Lee looked a little pale, though I didn't know why. His family had him working the farm since he'd grown big enough to string fence, and putting up hay every year had to be worse than what we were being tasked with. With the kettlebell, you could stop when it burned. With the hay harvest, you went until every last bale was put up, leaving your body skirting the edge of hellfire and brimstone. On the other hand, I looked forward to watching Cranston sweat—chances were good all the product in his hair would run into his eyes. The prospect warmed the cockles of my heart.

"What are you grinning about, Bowen?" The inquiring tone did not sound mild. It was ten shades of irritated and two of curious, with just a smidgen of smug. No doubt the last came from catching me out. "You think this is funny?"

"No, Sir Clark." I bit off crisply, just like my Daddy taught me. A glimmer of satisfaction lit up the green in his eyes, but I looked away quickly, not wanting to ruin the response with poor bearing. I never had paid my dues in the military, but I knew how to play the game.

"Then let's get going. I've got better things to do than babysit you lot."

If I didn't live in constant fear of my Grandmother somehow psychically knowing I'd uttered a swear word and showing up to wash my mouth out with a bar of Ivory, I would have cussed a blue streak by the time we finished. Everything, and I mean everything, was on fire. My toes were sweating just as much as my forehead, as well as everything in between.

How I managed to stay on my feet when he called a halt I would consider a miracle of arcane proportions. As it was, I barely stayed upright the few steps to the bench beside the tack room before collapsing like a stringless puppet. But I felt a strange sort of pleasure in the accomplishment, particularly when I noticed Lee and Cranston in similar distress.

After a minute of labored breathing I was able to get some control of my heart rate, allowing me to focus on Bart. Settled cross legged on the hard packed dirt, he looked completely comfortable and ready for another go. He'd done almost as much as us, pausing only to correct our positions, and he was hardly winded, once again raising the bar I hoped to grasp further out of my reach. It took me a second to find a silver lining—the boys were having a harder time recovering than me, still leaning heavily on the walls and panting.

"Get cleaned up, have your lunch, and I'll see you for your riding lesson at one thirty." I looked back toward Bart at the directive, startled to find him staring straight at me. I struggled against the sudden urge to straighten my no doubt wild hair, freezing instead. "Bowen, grab Eros for me when you get Ivan. I imagine you can handle them both." Seemed fair considering his favor last week. Unfolding himself carefully from the floor he headed straight for the apartment, and I closed my eyes for a moment, gathering up the gumption to move.

"Yeah, Bowen, I'm sure you've got lots of practice handling two at once." God almighty, I could hate the oily slick sound of Cranston's voice, but that would imply a level of effort he simply wasn't worth.

"And I'm sure you hardly know what to do with one." I snapped impatiently, looking at him with all the heat I could muster. While his face went purple with rage, he still flinched when our eyes met. "What, exactly is your problem with me?"

Faced with a direct confrontation he flicked a hand in my general direction and headed for the door, leaving something that sounded suspiciously like, "Uppity bitch" floating in his wake. Lee staggered toward me, keeping close to the wall, then dropped on the other end of the bench like a lead brick. The sympathetic grin he offered soothed the ragged edge of my anger.

"Sorry about that."

I wave my hand dismissively at the apology he had no reason to offer. "The douchbaggery isn't yours to apologize for, Lee. And honestly, does he even know what uppity means? If not, he should look in the mirror."

He laughed, his tan face instantly screwing up in discomfort as he clutched at his abs. "Dammit Jo, how can you even think around the thorough ass kicking we were just handed?"

"Mind over matter, Fillmore." Grinning mysteriously, I leveled a bland look at him. "Not that a farm boy like you knows much about using his brains anyway."

More laughter and wincing, accompanied by the shake of his square head. "Jesus Christ, woman, you are going to kill anyone who tries to get close to you with that sharp tongue."

The statement was not meant to be hurtful, I knew. Fillmore didn't have a mean bone in his body. But it bled me a damn sight more than Cranston's jibes did.

By Wednesday, I began to adapt a little, which was a relief of gargantuan proportions considering Sir Clark's plans for our afternoon. We would be fit for armor, then ride in it for the first time, putting us one step closer to the dream we are all there to chase. I would have even been willing to wish Cranston well in his efforts if he would just remove his head from his haunches.

Getting armored became an exercise in discomfort, as Trace and Aaron helped Bart by measuring just about every part of my body. They were polite and clinical, having me hold the tape anytime it involved a no fly zone, but I wasn't really a toucher with most folks, and it still put me off my game.

We were given an arming jacket to wear beneath the suit that wrinkled my nose, the stale smell of old sweat permeating the quilted fabric as I slid it on. I resolved to launder everything in the box it came from at the next available opportunity. Likely, the men couldn't smell it, but the stench lingered despite the soapy scent of detergent trying to mask it.

The armoring itself was too exciting for me to be as bothered, my cheeks aching from restraining my glee. Yes, it was just dress up for big girls, but it felt amazing to reach such a tangible rung on the ladder. The armor hung heavier than I imagined, to one degree, but once they had all the pieces strapped on, the heavily scarred steel didn't feel half as cumbersome as I expected.

Luckily, with my being taller than average, they were able to cobble together something that didn't rub too terribly, and pretty soon I could take a lap around the equipment shop to Bart's satisfaction. Turns out that part of his quarter mastering duties was to fit and fix armor, and I could admit to being a trifle impressed. Clearly, there was very little he wasn't capable of, though I began to wonder why he wasn't one of the working jousters. The skill level and sheer, overwhelming power certainly were his.

All of those thoughts completely disappeared when we headed to the riding arena in the afternoon. We'd been instructed to trudge up the hill on foot and horseless, as Aaron and Bart had specific mounts they wanted us to use, but nothing prepared me for the absolute privilege I would be afforded. Lee was handily mounted on Tuck, who I had seen repeatedly balance himself under his rider, while Cranston settled in on Cappy, who was as reliable as the clock. But when Sir Clark stepped down off Eros and led him to the mounting block for me, my throat closed up and I couldn't speak. Something must have shown on my face, because once I clambered in the tack he walked up to my side and rapped his knuckles on the thigh of my armor to get my attention.

The face turned up to mine looked hard with resolve, but a disconcerting sort of softness lingered just around his eyes. "Trust him, Bowen, like I trust you with him. He'll take care of you."

"Yes Sir." I managed, nodding sharply to disguise my discomfort. Not that Eros made me feel that way. No, he felt so solid and reassuring that I wanted to lose myself in him and never come out. Anything to hide the way I was beginning to look at his master.

I didn't recall having ever been so unbalanced on a horse before, though it must have happened when I was young and uncoordinated. My center of gravity felt so far and away from where I knew it belonged, and it felt foreign, like my body was barely mine to control. It didn't take long to realize that all those exercises we'd been doing weren't just for the hit. I used more of my core to stay in the saddle than I anticipated, and I said a silent prayer of thanks for the torture of the kettlebell, with an internal promise to hit it harder.

Trotting was humiliating, my thighs screaming as I weebled from side to side, feeling hopelessly ridiculous. Eros's trot felt far and gone more balanced than Ivan's and I stayed too busy trying to remain upright to even appreciate it. Thank God for the stallion's sense of balance, because mine was completely screwed. Though some part of my hind brain kept telling me to grab hold of something or we would die, I carefully kept a light hand on the reins. How much worse would it be when they added our helmets next week?

I couldn't have told you how the boys fared, too busy with my own struggle to notice. Bart had us weaving in and out of cones, forcing us to adjust our balance from side to side. Then we were making transitions on command, back and forth from trot to walk, and then, saints preserve me, from trot to halt. The first one threw me up on Eros's neck, but bless his noble heart, he stood while I wiggled myself upright, his typey, sculpted ears swiveling back and forth the whole time. The second was only marginally better, as I remembered to exhale my whoa, dropping my heels deeply to give myself an anchor. The upward transitions were slightly better, though only just, as I was constantly behind the motion.

"Bowen," Barked loud enough to hear over the sound of the armor and my own heart as I rode past him.

I turned my head, wonder and appreciation flooding me on a cellular level when Eros followed my eyes and made the turn toward Sir Clark. We managed an improved halt, as I purposely focused on a tree halfway across the field to keep my spine straight, then I looked down at my instructor, trying not to smile at that simple accomplishment.

"That was better. But for the upward transitions, you need to do the same thing. Look far away. Remember that you'll have your eyes on your opponent for the upward transition, train your eye to go there even when you aren't facing anyone. Quit trying so hard to lift the horse into the change of speed, let him lift you. He knows his job."

"Yes Sir." I nodded again, letting the advice sink into my brain and ingrain itself in my memory. It made absolute sense to me, making it easy to implement immediately as he slapped the calf of my armor and waved me back to the rail to rejoin the others. Balancing became easier after that, actually giving me enough mental breathing room that I noticed the boys getting similar treatment, called in for individual coaching as needed. I just had to be careful. If I focused too long or hard at a point, Eros followed like he was connected to my spine. Yes, riding that horse felt like a mighty privilege indeed.

About the time I started getting sloppy with fatigue, but before I ended up hanging off Eros's shoulder again, Sir Clark called a halt for the day, instructing us to take them on a walk around the perimeter of the property to cool off. Lee led the way, since he and Cranston had gone on that particular ride the day I arrived, and I fell in at the back, content to let Eros amble along on a loose rein.

The blue green hills and lush trees made the ride into something pretty as we traversed a broad swath of turf between the black oak fence that traced the boundary of the farm and the inner pasture fence, made up of wide white webbing. That webbing was deceptively strong, not so much in tensile strength, but in its psychological power. Though the charge of electricity running through it wasn't much, nothing kept a horse from getting tangled up in a fence quite as much as a deep desire to just *not* touch it. But this quiet hack through the countryside proved an exercise in core fitness, as we adjusted our posture and seat to accommodate the changes in terrain. I marveled at the hundreds of thousands of hours that must have gone into Aaron and Bart learning these things so they could share that knowledge with us.

Back at the barn, Trace, Aaron and Bart held our horses for us while we dismounted and I struggled with how to manage it without falling on my face. The armor tried to drag me off the wrong side face first as I leaned over to swing my leg across Eros's broad rump, and my legs were so tired that I got hung up on the cantle of the saddle, having to wiggle rather unattractively to finish the movement. Thankful when no one laughed, I felt twice as grateful when a hand against my back stopped me from toppling as my feet hit the ground. Spreading my legs another couple inches apart, I looked over at my savior, Sir Bart.

"Thanks."

"You'd do the same for anyone else, Bowen." Gruff words, ripe with approval. It felt incredibly good for him to have noticed. He reached for the saddle, but I pushed his arm away.

"No, let me. He more than earned it." I reached under the flap where my leg would usually rest and loosened the buckles of his girth by feel alone, rewarded by a deep sigh of relaxation. Before I could do more, Bart shook his head in denial and led him away, placing a hand companionably on the stallion's neck.

"Go get out of your armor, Bowen. Then you can say your thank you."

We three trainees trucked tiredly toward the armor room, but my feet slowed when I noticed Ro, standing with his head over the stall door, a look of curiosity and worry wrinkling his brow.

"Hey buddy." His ears swiveled madly for a second, as he resolved what he knew of me with this strange, metal shrouded beast before him, and he blew sharply out of his nostrils. "It's just me."

I could read disbelief in the way he raised his head to the full length of his neck, staring down his nose, and I shook my head with humor. The laughter that bubbled up seemed to convince him more than my words, and I reached across the distance to offer my hand for a smell. He used that long, arched neck to tentatively scent me, a quiver of his lips still smacking of worry, but it faded a little once he breathed on me. Carefully, I lowered my hand, not wanting to rattle the armor too much. "Good boy." I soothed before traipsing off to get free of the cumbersome metal.

Amazingly, Cranston behaved decently when I helped unbuckle his pauldrons and returned the favor when I reached the same impasse. Once that layer was shed I turned to Lee and undid his breastplate, frowning at the thin line of blood along his shoulder where it rested.

"You should see Bart about that."

He looked over and down his nose, trying to sight it, and shrugged his shoulders carelessly. "Yeah, I didn't even notice.

I'll talk to him when we get done. And whatever happened to Sir Clark this, Sir Clark that?"

It felt like I bit into a lemon, my face screwed up so hard. "Sorry, I didn't even realize."

Thankfully, he shrugged that away too, and out of gratitude, I finished helping him out of his armor, showing him how to stack it so it fit in the trunk correctly. By the time I tended my own kit nearly twenty minutes had disappeared, and with the arming coat thrown over my arm I shot from the room, not even stopping when I noticed Cranston's sloppy pile of armor left tangled in his trunk. I'd neglected the most important piece of the equation in all this. My horse. Or, Bart's horse, anyway, who I didn't deserve to ride in the first place.

Eros stood hipshot, his eyes closed with pleasure as Bart worked him over with a curry, though he stopped as soon as he heard my hand on the latch. "Don't worry, Fillmore just came by."

I sighed in relief, and fished a brush from the bucket by the door, settling in on Eros's other side to pay my dues. Never had silence between two people been so very equitable, no unnecessary chatter to break the steady rhythm of strokes against the dark coat, the blackness of his hair so absolute as to absorb light rather than reflect it. When I discovered a spot between the muscular haunches that caused Eros to swing his head around and wiggle his lip, I lingered, using my short nails to satisfy the itch. The tiny gesture was the least I could do in the face of his generosity to me. I caught Bart staring bemusedly when I moved back up to brush at the slowly drying saddle mark some more.

"What?"

He remained silent for a moment, and I appreciated that he took the time to consider his answer, unlike me, always so quick to respond. "It's just rare to find someone so comfortable around horses, stallions in particular."

"They're just horses." I shrugged, and tried to follow his example, thinking before I spoke. "Honestly, I'd trust several of the bulls at my Dad's ranch more than most of the momma cows. We've got one, Applesauce, who's almost a pet."

A reflective smile tugged at the corners of his mouth, and he looked away as if he could see a distant memory. "My grand dad, he had a Brahma we could ride. You have no idea the looks we'd get riding him down the trail."

I snorted, and dropped my head against Eros's shoulder to muffle it, imagining how many riders would get bucked off their horses if I rode around a horse show on Applesauce. The mental picture was comical beyond words, and when I looked up, Bart's confusion just made me giggle more. Now it was his turn to say, "What?"

"It's just the thought of taking Applesauce, a one ton Limousin bull, to a hunter jumper show. Girls on imported European warmbloods and custom fit saddles flying through the air like scattered leaves, ruining their three hundred dollar breeches when they hit the dirt."

He shook his head, laughter so low it rumbled in the air like thunder. "You are definitely a rare breed, Jo. It's hard to know what to make of you sometimes. I'd never have pegged you as a jumper princess."

I serioused up in the space of a heartbeat, and leveled a stare at him. "That's the thing, Sir. You keep trying to squeeze me, a square peg, into a round hole. I've never been a princess of anything, ever. All my life, at every faire I've ever attended, I never envied the pretty dresses, the jewels or the crown. I can appreciate the texture of a fine velvet, sure, but I don't think it beats the feeling of a horse's coat thickening with an oncoming winter. I like getting my toenails painted, but see zero point in doing the same to my fingers when they are better served scratching an itchy spot."

I looked away, the solemnity with which he considered me too much to bear as I revealed myself. "I've always been a doer, and with every passing day it becomes clearer that this…" I waved my hand in a circle as if it could encompass everything I'd found here, "This is what I want to do. I wanted it, even before I knew all the hard work that would go into it, and it has only gotten stronger, the more you challenge me."

Swallowing hard, I looked back at him, and this time it he looked away. If made to hazard a guess at what went on in his head, I'd say it looked like I'd dropped him in a well he couldn't see a way out of. Unable to endure any censure, I headed for the door, stopping only briefly to hug Eros's head and drop a kiss on his brow, fleeing not just the imagined recriminations but the sense of utter nakedness now wrapped around my heart.

♥♥♥

We rode in the morning on Friday, back on our own horses as we did a series of kip ups on the move; bringing our lances to bear and back to neutral so often I lost count, though my aching shoulder would like to say it was in the millions.

Saturday morning, up before dawn, few words were spoken in the house, with Cranston and Lee slow to move. In light of the stilted communications with Sir Clark the day before, I prepared a peace offering of coffee again, tossing my day bag in the bed of the truck on my way by. After a quick stroke of Ro's neck, I headed for the feed room, flicking on the light when I discovered it unoccupied. Having never beaten Bart to the barn, I fumbled my way through mixing buckets, reading each horse's ration from the block letters printed so carefully on the chalkboard in front of me. When the door swung open, I didn't even look up, scooping a joint supplement out for Cappy.

"Morning." Judging the grating texture of his voice, I wasn't the only one who hadn't sleep well.

A cranky part of my brain crossed its arms and muttered 'good' under its breath. I pointed at the coffee tumbler in reply, and returned to my task, relieved when I heard him take a sip before heading back out the door to throw hay. Lee arrived just in time to manage doors for me, though I could have handled it on my own. Frankly, that morning, I'd have been perfectly content to be left alone for the duration.

Eros lipped me fondly when I delivered his breakfast, helping me find my first smile of the day, and I finished off in Ro's stall, closing my eyes and pressing my nose against his shoulder just to find my bearings. The change in him was so marked he felt like a whole different animal, peace under his skin now instead of the depthless void of nothingness, and he'd proven perfectly willing to share it with me, thank goodness.

We'd settled into a companionable acceptance of each other, warts and all, spending time after supper in the paddock. I'd groom him slowly while he grazed, and he would always pause and look at me whenever my hands stopped moving as if to ask why I quit. There was bloom to his coat now, the grey shimmering like Damascus steel when the light caught it just right, and thanks to a worming, his goat belly had slimmed. Now, we just needed to work on his lack of muscle.

"Bowen." I wanted to hate the sound of Bart's voice, but with all the admiration I had for him, I couldn't even come close to dislike. Irritation maybe, though it morphed to resignation when I turned my head, leaving my cheek pressed to Ro's shoulder. "Thanks." He raised the coffee, almost like a white flag of surrender. "And I apologize. Of all the people on the planet, I should know better than to assume things. I'll do better."

My smile of acceptance was weak at best, but that was all I had the heart for. "I'll hold you to it." I said, trying for my usual caustic banter and falling appallingly short.

He smiled, leaving my weakness unmarked, but replied to the intent. "I'm sure you will."

He left me alone again, five minutes of peace and I'll admit, relief, charging me up for the chaos of the day ahead.

If I were to be swallowed alive by chaos, there really would be no better place to have it happen than the faire. We rushed to get the horses in and settled so we would all be in place by gate opening, costumes donned and smiles plastered on. But once I slipped my nicest tunic on and belted it securely around my hips, I didn't have to fake the smile anymore. The silvery grey and blue trimmed fabric smacked around my knees as I walked, the front and back split as if for riding, and I looked forward to the day I got to wear it on Ro. It would look amazing with his coat color. Adjusting my broad brimmed flat cap at a jaunty angle I shoved through the gate to the encampment with my hip, almost plowing into Cranston who sneered and grumbled as he pushed past.

"What's his problem?" I asked Lee, glancing back over my shoulder at the departing grumpy pants. Fillmore's shoulders lifted the way I thought a giant's might, like two boulders sliding up and down the side of a mountain. It wasn't his height that gave that impression, as I stood only a few inches shorter, but he just had a sense of solidity about him.

"Damned if I know. He was chatting up a pretty girl over by the horses and Sir Clark walked by. There were words. It's a mystery what they were."

I returned his shrug then and settled in beside him, setting out t-shirts and assorted paraphernalia that would be for sale to the public. I'll admit I had several of their shirts tucked in a dresser drawer at home, though sadly they didn't have any new designs to add to my collection. A shame, as I'd pulled together a fictional marketing campaign for them as one of my finals in college, and gotten exceptional comments from my professor on the quality of the graphics. Maybe I would feel Aaron out and see if he'd be interested? No, they probably already had an experienced professional on retainer.

A face I didn't know slid in the gate to the encampment and I smiled widely as she strolled up to the stand one hip at a time, her leather wench's bodice doing an admirable job of hawking ample wares. I'd be lying if I said I wasn't a little envious. Not only was I as lean as a hunting hound with hips so straight they might make a good drag racing strip, I just wasn't that comfortable flaunting what femininity I possessed. Ex boyfriends had complained that I never dressed up enough, and the memory made my smile falter a little.

"A merry opening day to you, good squires! Do you know where I might find the venerable Sir Clark?" The affected Olde English accent sounded completely overdone, but couldn't be more perfect for the dramatics of a renaissance festival.

"Cassidy!" Sir Clark jogged across the yard toward her, and I fought not to frown when he bent down to hug her petite frame.

She smacked a kiss on his freshly shaven cheek to boot, laughing when he blushed and stepped away.

"Oh Clark, some things never change."

"And some things do." he responded, as if it was an old conversation rehashed a thousand times. "How're the boys?"

The fake accent disappeared, lost in a southern drawl so rich it slid over the ear like warm molasses. "Ah, the little tigers are a danger to man and beast, making their mother and me crazy. But I wouldn't trade it for the world."

"Good. Is Shayla coming by with them later? I've got presents for them." So much warmth in his voice felt foreign, though I'd heard it that way a few times before. I shoved the memories back, not looking too closely before I locked them away.

"If they don't drive her crazy, yes. They'll be thrilled to see you and get to ride the ponies."

He snorted a laugh and rolled his eyes. "Yeah. Ponies."

"Geez, Clark, you should be thrilled they remember riding them at last year. That's a big deal for a five-year-old."

He took her by the elbow with casual familiarity and turned her toward us, a grin still riding the edges of his lips. I'd never seen him that relaxed around anyone except the horses. "Mari Cassidy, this is Fillmore Lee and Josephine Bowen, two of our trainees."

"A pleasure." She tugged her elbow away from him to extend her hand toward me, and the firmness of her grip reassured me. For all her physical attributes a plethora of real cleverness glimmered in her eyes, and I immediately warmed to her. "I've heard you are a promising lot."

"I'd like to hope so, Miss Cassidy. We sure are trying." Her face danced when she smiled, and she flipped her auburn red hair over her shoulder to look knowingly up at Sir Clark. Imagine my confusion when he shifted uncomfortably and looked away from her.

"It's Mari, sweetheart." Then she turned her cunning green eyes on Lee. "And look at you, strapping lad! They must be doing something right where you are from."

Fillmore blazed scarlet red from neckline to hairline, ducking his chin politely. "Nice to meet you, ma'am." Mari's smile grew impossibly broader, and I almost felt sorry for Lee—he'd just proved himself a rich target.

Just then, the opening cannon sounded, and a wave of energy followed the airborne concussion, my whole body atingle with excitement. Game on. We all fell to our stations, and I settled at the gate to answer questions for passersby, immediately enchanted with a host of over excited ten-year-old girls, all dressed in their scout uniforms. They had a hundred questions, several of the girls jotting answers in their notebooks, and sometimes passersby stopped and listened as I tried to answer them all.

"Are those Clydesdales?"

"No, our Clydesdale stayed home today." I grinned at the tallest, skinniest girl when she raised her hand tentatively from the back of the pack, recognizing a bit of myself in her. "Yes, milady, what is your question?"

"Are you a knight?"

"No, not yet, though I am learning to be."

"I thought only boys got to be knights." This from a shorter, sweet faced girl near the front, her nose wrinkled in confusion.

"Girls can do anything boys can do, but sometimes we have to work extra hard for it. When you love it, and you want it badly enough, the effort is worth it." One of the troop leaders smiled and nodded at me, mouthing a quick thank you before she herded them onward.

"Masterfully done, Bowen." Aaron clapped me on the shoulder, and I startled slightly in my seat, paying attention to the people on the road. "Anyone with a little toughness can hit and be hit, but it takes a rare bird to balance the crowd interaction. I think you just earned your first fans. Keep up the good work."

"Yes Sir." Funny how when I said it to him it had a completely different texture in my mouth.

When we paraded to the arena each of us trainees carried a banner, one for each of the knights and one for the company itself, the golden, two headed eagle grasping a broken jousting lance in its talons on a field of blue. It made so much more sense now that I knew Sir Aaron and Sir Clark were brothers. Bart followed along behind that banner, Eros dancing beneath him with huffing breaths like a black dragon about to spit fire, and then came Cranston and I, traveling just before our knights.

We had Trace and Aaron this go round, which made sense in context. Whoever won this one would move on to the third performance to challenge whoever won the second round, which meant Trace would either prove himself ready, or Aaron would go on, giving the audience their money's worth for the final go of the afternoon. For Trace's sake, I hoped he would rise to the challenge. I knew he'd been practicing several mornings a week with Aaron, and now, in front of God and everybody, would put the proof in the pudding.

The King and Queen processed up to the dais, and Sir Clark rode forward to take charge of the Queen's Champion favor, a brilliant white banner embroidered with an ornate crowned heart. I'd loved the sight of the thing every year I'd come, the way it would dance like a living thing on the arm of whoever won it as they gave a victory gallop around the arena, but this year's looked brand new, the threads making the decorations glinting metallically as if it had been crafted in precious metal rather than fabric. He tucked it carefully in his belt and vowed to reward only the worthiest with its keeping.

Then the men fell to their work, keeping us squires on the move with the amount of fragments we chased down. A pile of kindling quickly developed mid-lyst, my grin growing when Trace actually rocked Aaron in the saddle. By points, he didn't win, but it was the best he'd done so far, and he deserved to be proud of that.

As my assigned knight for the day I took Trace's horse after he dismounted, loosening Cappy's girth so he could be comfortable as I followed his rider around the arena, allowing the crowd to pet his massive head. The amount of children asking Trace to sign broken pieces of lance didn't surprise me, but the mothers of said children flirting shamelessly with him made me a little uncomfortable. One woman even asked him to sign her cleavage, her breasts rising like the prow of a ship from the neckline of her bodice. While I'd been immediately against Trace just for his pretty face and foolish behavior, I'd learned over the last several weeks that he was just a sweet kid with a penchant for playing knight. As he tactfully turned down the brazen woman, I discovered a gentleman growing behind that model perfect smile.

Once back at the encampment I got Trace quickly out of his armor, then headed out to check in with Mari, who had manned the camp while we were gone. I found her sitting directly on the counter, swinging her feet like a little kid as she bantered with the passersby.

"Hey lady, do you need something to drink, or a privy break?"

The smile she leveled on me held just as much enthusiasm as the one she had given Bart earlier, further strengthening my like for her. "Oh, no my dear, I am lovely as I am for a bit longer yet. Though would you care if I send you off to procure lunch after the next joust? I'll be perishing by then."

"I can man the booth while you go, if you like." She shook her head at the offer and pivoted a bit closer to me.

"Oh lovey, you're sweet to offer, but it would really be much easier on me if you went." She tugged at the edge of her layered skirts and lifted the hem, revealing the flower printed plastic of a prosthetic sleeve around her calf, her soft Ren faire boots laced on to it. "I'd rather save my walks for when the boys get here. Chances are good that once the four o'clock joust happens, I'll go meander about with them, and five-year-old twins take all my energy."

"Mari, five-year-old twins would take all of anyone's energy." I teased playfully, folding my arms across my chest and purposefully not mentioning what she'd just revealed. If she wanted to tell me more someday, I'd listen, but damned if I wasn't even more impressed with her now. The way she had swaggered into the encampment hadn't betrayed the slightest bit of a limp, and if she hadn't shown me, I never would have known. "I'll come get your order after the next joust."

"Thank you lovey. Just don't forget to take care of yourself too."

Sir John and Sir Alex seemed a little reserved during their joust, simply trading hits like gentleman boxers dancing around a ring, but the crowd still loved it, cheering raucously when the two of them met mid-lyst to hug it out like the brothers in arms they were. Taking J.T. from Alex this time, I quickly learned to keep an eye on him around little kids with food when he grabbed at one little boys cotton candy. I saved it from his grasping, whiskered lips by a hair, grateful when no one seemed to notice, and J.T. flattened his ears in disgust for foiling his rude behavior. When we got back to the encampment, I made it up to him from a stash of sugar cubes John kept in the top of his trunk for Tuck.

Mari sent me on a hunt for roasted corn, and Aaron admonished me to get something for myself too, pressing something a bit like monopoly money in my hands to pay for our lunches. I spent most of my time waiting in line, as everyone always seemed to be hungry at these festivals, but the girl at the counter worked fast, and when I paid with the faire currency she leaned on the counter and grinned.

"You must be new, sweetie. If you are picking things up for yourself or another performer, you go through that gate off to the side and give your order to the kitchen manager. She'll rustle everything up for you right quick."

Armed with the new knowledge, I wound my way back toward camp, arriving to the delighted screams of the two small boys wedged together in Tucker's saddle as Bart led them around the small yard. Mari and a beautiful dark skinned woman I guessed to be Shayla were on either side of Tuck, holding on to their legs and attempting to shush them.

"Again, again, again." They hollered when Bart led them back to the mounting block, and when he looked at Mari and she shook her head, they started to cry. I dropped my delivery on a shelf at the back of the booth, picked up the stuffed dragon puppet resting there and waded in to see if I could help.

"No, no, Percy, I'm sure they are much too busy being brave knights to want to say hello to a dragon." I said just a little too loudly as I walked by, lifting the dragon up to my ear as if listening to him. "I know, I think they look like they would be fun to play with too, but they simply don't have time for us."

Five pairs of astonished eyes fell on me at once, and one of them stared like he didn't know me at all. I swear, they must not have looked over a word of my resume.

"Dragon! We want the dragon, Uncle Bart!" The little boy sitting in front pointed at me imperiously, while the one on the back reached down for his mother, looking me over with shy eyes, while I tried not to blush under the combined stares of the adults. Once both children where off the horse I settled on the bottom step of the block to get down to the level of the boldest boy, who drug Mari closer to me. Bart snuck away while they were distracted, and their mother smiled at his retreat.

"Hello, my name is Jo. What's your name?"

"Jo is a boy's name." the boy said, frowning at me indignantly, his cafe au lait skin smooth despite the expression. "My name is Max."

"Well, my mommy named me Josephine, but that's a lot to say when you are talking, so most people call me Jo." I looked up at the other little boy, his golden hazel eyes widening when I tipped the dragons face up with mine. "And who are you?"

"His name is Mal." His mother answered, smiling again, her teeth white and even like a toothpaste ad. She was the sort of person that instantly made you feel at home, like the scent of homemade pie or the feeling of one of Gran's quilts wrapped around you on the first day of fall. "And I'm Shayla, Mari's wife."

Puzzle pieces clicked together. "Pleased to meet you, Mal. This is Percy. He is shy too." I turned the dragons face against my neck and dropped a kiss on the top of its head as if reassuring it. "He really wanted to meet the newest Knights of the Gallant Company, but he was afraid you might not like him. He said some knights aren't very nice to dragons."

"I'll be your friend, Percy." said Max, only it came out more like Pewcy. It made it incredibly easy to smile at the little boy, and I wiggled the dragon in my lap as if he were excited. Mal didn't want to be left out when Max got to pet Percy's head, and giggled when the dragon kissed his cheek.

Twenty minutes later, I extracted myself and Percy, the boys distracted when Bart returned with the aforementioned presents. In seconds, we were forgotten, as they held a mock battle against their much larger opponent with their new wooden swords. Sure, Bart had looked as me as if he didn't recognize me, but he wasn't the only one looking at someone in a new light. One doesn't expect a bear of a man to roll around in the dirt with a pair of little boys. Of course, one also doesn't expect a bear to have the verbal repartee of a skilled courtier, or the tact to deal with a broken spirited horse either. The surprises never ended.

Aaron startled me again, clearing his throat at my shoulder, and I looked his direction, noticing he'd started armoring already. "Hey Bowen, would you help me finish getting armored? My usual squire is occupied at the moment." He gestured toward Bart tussling with the boys, softening the statement with a grin.

I turned to, falling in at his heels, losing myself in a ritual that was beginning to feel so familiar, like deep in my bones I'd done this before. As we got the chain maile skirting that covered the front of his pelvis settled against his hips, he turned his head in my direction. "You are certainly a source of never ending surprises, Bowen."

"I just do what needs doing, Sir." Embarrassment and pleasure made the back of my neck prickle, but my hands were too busy to rub at it as I work to pull the two halves of his breastplate together, buckling it against his side,

"But you see what needs doing, Bowen. And then you act on it. It's a rare combination." I'd heard similar statements from my professors and teachers, but none felt half as important as hearing it from Aaron. "How is it you are so good with children?"

"I've worked at a kid's camp for the last three summers. Didn't you read my resume I sent?"

He wrinkled his nose in thought as I slid one of his arms on. "I never saw a resume. Bart was the one who sorted the paperwork, I just hashed over things with him after he picked people out." Ah, well, at least that explained Aaron's confusion. "And Bart wasn't feeling so hot when those applications came in, so he might have just misplaced it."

I mused that over for a few minutes, as his arm rested on my shoulder while I attached the pauldrons, the angle more convenient for the tight space my fingers had to work in. The sweaty man-smells hardly bothered me anymore, though I didn't look forward to August, which would turn this room into a hot box. "Speaking of seeing a need, do you think we could get a fan for in here? Summer is just going to get hotter."

"See Bowen, that's exactly what I'm talking about." His blue eyes twinkled, and while I could admire the charm in them, I didn't feel an ounce of attraction to them. The realization was reassuring and unsettling in the same breath, because I couldn't say the same about his brother. In my head at least, I risked a quick dammit.

"Here, sit with me a minute." He perched on the edge of his trunk, the armor keeping him from scooting further back, and I folded myself up on the one across from him. "I want you to know, at least for my part, if you end up not working out as a jouster for any reason, I still want to hire you." I guess I should've been flattered, but my heart rebelled against the idea entirely, my gut burning with bile as I fished for something tactful to say, but then he changed tacks and I lost my footing. "But I really hope you are a jouster, Jo. Something tells me you'd make a hell of an opponent."

"Thank you, Sir" seemed the only reasonable answer and I headed outside to choke down my now cold stew, the contents gluey in my mouth. The stewing in my gut, however, had a full head of steam and didn't feel like it would quiet anytime soon.

Once chores were finished, and Ro took his evening tour of the paddock, I slept like a rock. Sunday morning, though neither Bart nor I were quite so cranky, I still offered him coffee. It just felt right. He rewarded me with a tired looking grin that faded when Cranston finally meandered in at the end of feeding, the line of Bart's jaw going rigid with disappointment.

"I warned you about being late on the first day Cranston. Now I've got to make an example of you. Tonight, you will clean all the stalls on your own."

For all that I disliked him intensely, part of me still sympathized, considering how tired I knew we were all going to be. That sympathy went up in smoke when he turned up his aristocratic nose in defiance. "Sorry, can't do that. I've already obligated myself."

The temperature in the barn instantly dropped ten degrees and I shivered with the coldness in Bart's reply. "Regardless of your plans with Mandy and her cohort of pirate wenches, you will be here, you will clean stalls, and moreover, you will do a good job. If there is enough left of your entitled ass to go fuck around after that, I wish you well. But if you fail in this Cranston, you will find your bags and your car dumped somewhere along the highway out of town. Do we understand each other?"

I'd gulped five times during that short speech and it wasn't even directed at me. Luckily for Cranston, he appeared to recognize his danger, shrinking back like a tiny banty rooster caught crowing in the open by a hawk.

"Yes Sir." he managed to choke out, fading back when Bart stalked past him to head upstairs. "What a fucking killjoy." He bit off once the footsteps on the stairs faded, and before I could stop myself, I moved across the aisle, going nose to nose with him.

"Look, you selfish toad, no one is making you stay." Enough acid filled my voice that my own throat burned. "I'm sure Lee and I would be perfectly content to do your work, if you don't want to be here anymore."

His eyes widened for a moment, but then the snake went back to biting wherever he could find purchase. "Oh, is that so, teacher's pet? Like I'd let a whore like you beat me at anything."

Lee gasped at the insult, but I'd heard worse, and Cranston's manner reminded me too much of the frat boys I had frequently protected my drunk friends from at parties. No, if he wanted to hit below the belt, I was willing to trade blows, so I struck fast and repeatedly.

"Really, Cranston? That's the best you've got? Well, considering how much you've probably had to shell out to get laid over the years, you'd think you'd have a better idea what one of those looks like." My voice dropped another octave. "Would you like to go the lesbian route next? Because while my gate swings straight, I'd bend the hell out of it myself if the only alternative were you. Frigid? No, I'd burn you down like a California forest fire if I had half a mind to. Not that I would touch so much as a hair on your loathsome body."

He gaped like a fish for several seconds, and before I yielded to the temptation to deck him, I spun away and headed outside, desperate to escape the fetid bitterness that surrounded him. My feet carried me to Ro's paddock and I pressed my forehead to the bark of the tree, needing the contact to keep me grounded. I don't know how long I stood there, minutes, hours, but the sound of hoof beats brought me back to myself in a rush. Ro walked toward me, his whole body hesitant as if unsure of his welcome, and I physically shook off the lingering blackness.

When I held out my hand to invite him closer he moved forward willingly, and I looked beyond him to find Bart hanging Ro's halter on the gate. He nodded shortly before walking away, and I took it for the gift it was, trying not to think of anything but the soft feel of Ro's muzzle beneath my hands, his pulse becoming mine. Also, hoping like crazy Bart hadn't heard a single word of that regrettable exchange.

We all piled in one truck for the ride to the faire, having left the diesel and trailer with the working crew of horses last evening. No sense wasting gas, but it left me squished in the front seat between Bart and Aaron, Cranston's eyes boring a hole in the back of my head. Yeah, no doubt adding fuel to that teacher's pet sentiment, but I couldn't imagine him willingly trading places me either. My legs were too long to really be comfortable seated over the hump in the floorboards, but thankfully, Aaron and Bart were both gentlemanly enough not to crowd me.

All the same, I damn near bolted from the vehicle by the end of the short ride, needing some distance from all the touching. Oh hell, if I couldn't be honest in my own head, I really was in trouble. I did it to escape being that close to Bart. I didn't want to think too hard about the warmth still lingering on my skin where our legs and shoulders had bumped against each other.

Byzantine occupied most of my prep time, as he had tipped over the water trough in the paddock he shared with J.T. and rolled in it to good effect. It took some time to chip away at the dried mud, revealing the sculpted muscles beneath. I helped Hillary hose off J.T.'s profuse white feathers, thankful when the cold spray did a good enough job to get us through the day without looking like homeless ragamuffins.

By lunch, Mari was getting restless, and she wrangled Lee into watching the booth after the noon joust, grabbing my elbow and hauling me away by main force. I flung an apologetic look at Bart as we passed the horses and he just grinned at my predicament as she dragged me out the gate. Honestly, I enjoyed hanging out with her, and once we had our food, we meandered through a few shops. I lingered in one of my favorite costume shops, fingering a dark, silvery grey bodice and the silky blue grey chemise that hung behind it with something akin to longing.

"Oh, Josephine, that would look stunning on you." Mari exclaimed before taking another bite of her turkey leg. I shrugged off her encouragement, and turned away to hide my pink cheeks. No doubt I'd look like a sparrow trying to wear peacock feathers in something that fine.

The last performance of the day, Sir John encouraged me to help him with his helm and I climbed the heavy wood block, my fingers clumsy with nervousness, nearly dropping the bolts that secured the last pieces of armor. He stayed my hand for a moment, a kind light in his eyes as I froze and stared at him.

"Slow down, Josephine. You've got this, and Bart knows how to stall with the best of them."

You could see why Caroline loved him so much—armor or no, John Barry was a gentleman of rare vintage indeed. As I slid the visor closed he winked at me, and it eased my heart enough to steady my actions, the buffe that protected his neck and the gridded grand guard that served as a target for the lance falling into place with little effort. I tightened the wing nuts that secured it all, then slapped him on his back to send him on his way.

Before I could move, Bart's familiar call for squire appreciation rang out, leaving me exposed on my tiny stage for the requisite bow. I turned to jump down after the applause faded, and almost fell on my face as he followed it up with a surprising announcement.

"Come back next weekend, my lords and ladies, to see our knight candidates entertain the ladies of the court with a display of gaming. Their speed will astonish, their skill will amaze, and one lucky soul will earn the right to lead the Queen's mount for the final procession."

Come again?

"You alright?" Kory asked as I joined her for what would likely be a rousing round of pick up sticks and knights, considering we had Aaron and John set to go for the finale. I shook off the question with a plastered on grin, trying not to think about something too far away to be relevant.

John did bite it once, on the second pass, though he was fighting to get to his feet before I even reached his side, barely needing my arm for balance when he lurched upright. I still helped him navigate to the mounting block so he could climb back on a long suffering Tuck, breathing a sigh of relief when he remained in the tack for the final two passes. Tuck was a joy to lead around for the crowd, lowering his head over the fence to greet children in strollers, showing no trepidation when a special needs child in a wheelchair poked him in the nose while petting him. He was a love sponge to everyone, but clearly knew his biggest fans were actually his smallest.

After closing cannon everyone switched into high gear, saddles and horses loaded with a speed seldom seen by the laid back crew, but it became pretty clear that some people had plans for the evening, precipitating the rush. Mari threw me an invite to supper with her family, but I begged off for some other night, needing the peace and quiet after the constant press of people. Since Cranston would be cleaning stalls, Lee asked for the night off when Mandy invited him out to the pub with her pirate crew.

Amazingly, Bart just slapped him on the back with a reminder to call if he needed a lift back. Trace had disappeared as soon as his things were packed and Cappy was taken care of, likely with friends he made at last year's faire. Cranky Cranston jumped in the cab of the truck Aaron drove, which suited me just fine, until I realized that left me completely alone with Bart.

I fidgeted with winding up the hose out by the paddocks as I waited, the energy leftover from the day buzzing under my skin like ants at a picnic. By the time he showed up twenty minutes later I had settled on the tailgate of the truck, legs dangling over the end like a little kid, finally content to let the high die down.

"Sorry, wanted to walk Mari out. She looked a little tired." She wasn't the only one, from the looks of him. There wasn't much starch left in his spine, though he could likely dig some out if necessary. I couldn't begrudge him the time, wishing I had noticed, but I'd been too stuck in my own worries. I didn't like

118

how selfish that felt, not in the least. "Hopefully, the boys will be in one of their sweet moods tonight. I hate that she and Shayla are losing their precious time together just because I needed an extra hand."

"Offer to babysit." The words came without thought, and I liked the reflective moments of silence that followed as he leaned against the tailgate, crossing his arms loosely. "I'll offer too, then maybe they can recharge their batteries a little. Those two scamps are enough to drain the energy from a nuclear reactor."

The laugh was tired, but real, and he met my eyes with a grin. "You know, Jo, one day I'll get used to your surprises, but I don't think it's coming anytime soon."

"Thanks, I think."

He offered me no reassuring platitudes, just a wider grin before he straightened from his post. "Come on, let's get home and tend to our boys."

"Yes, let's." I agreed, and we climbed in the truck with equal haste, sharing the drive back in companionable silence, while I tried not to reflect on how much the farm really was starting to feel like home.

♥♥♥

Monday morning, I crawled out of bed at the usual hour, feeling like a dried up husk, even my hair brittle and unhappy. Clearly, the half-gallon of water I sucked down before bed hadn't remedied the all-day neglect of my body. Temptation told me to sneak out and watch the boys head for the pasture again, but practicality said I need to shower before I forced anyone else to look at me. Yesterday, I had charmed small children. This morning, I'd probably make them run screaming.

After a half hour standing under the scalding spray I felt a little closer to human, braiding my hair up while it was damp rather than waiting for it to dry. My oldest jeans felt heavenly against my freshly shaved legs, and I slid into my favorite t-shirt with a groan of pleasure, smoothing the red Welsh dragon down as I tucked it in at the waist.

By the time I pulled on my cowboy boots I almost felt like myself, Josephine Bowen, rancher's daughter, college graduate, marketing major. As I walked up the path to the barn it dawned on me that while those things were still a part of me, I'd grown beyond that. I'd become more myself over the last three weeks than I had the whole time I was at college.

Part of the reason for that stuck his head over the stall door and whinnied loud enough to rouse the dead. I winced at the volume, hoping he wasn't waking Aaron, who I'd never seen out of the apartment before ten unless it was a festival day. But my heart still danced, knowing my special boy was coming out of his shell. Yes, mine, even if only in my heart. It didn't much matter to me whose name was on his papers, he and I belonged to each other.

His breakfast not quite done, I slid in his stall and settled in the corner by the door, content to rest in the thick bed of shavings while he chewed. Non-horse people would never understand how peaceful that sound could be. Heck, I could hardly stand listening to people chew, but if someone made a white noise generator that had barn sounds on it, I'd listen to it every night to get to sleep.

Footsteps on the stairs, just on the other side of the stall wall, made the door at my back vibrate, but I stayed quiet when the door from the apartment opened, not sure who interrupted my solitude. The steps stopped in front of Ro's door, which made me suspect Bart, but when Ro actually moved to greet him I closed my mouth on the good morning that almost shattered the quiet. I put my hand on Ro's dark grey knee as he got close, so he didn't forget the squishy person at his feet, and while he flicked an ear at me, he hung his head over the door.

"Good morning, spoiled pony." Something that sounded suspiciously like a candy wrapper crinkled and Ro crunched happily on whatever it was, while I grinned like an idiot. Yes, big, bad Bartholomew Clark (oh Lord, now I pictured him in a black hat and duster) was a softy. "I hope you are everything she needs."

Forthright words that felt a little like a prayer, and my heart stuttered at the wish in them. No, I couldn't reveal myself now, and I shrunk myself smaller, breathing shallowly until his booted feet carried him out the door to Lord only knows where. Ro took a step back and lowered his head to my bent knees, blowing a minty sweet breath across my face, sharing the secret of his treat with me.

I breezed through cleaning stalls, despite the deeply wet bedding that let me know Cranston hadn't really fulfilled his punishment, but today, just for today, I didn't even want to think of him. I needed this day off, and would be perfectly content to not see an over styled hair on his head. Bart strolled up from the pasture with Buttermilk in tow just as I hauled the first couple bags of shavings in the barn, and I stopped in the wide door to watch his approach, trying not to notice the ripple of his forearm when he patted her on the neck. No, no good at all could come from going down that road.

"Good morning, Sir." I offered genially, though I burned to know why he had the creamy coated mare up from her field. She lived with a few sheep that belonged to one of the neighboring farms when not in the barn. Some might think it kept her from Eros's attentions, but it really was for the safety of the herd itself. Buttermilk had a hate on for Eros that defied logic, and Aaron had told me the last time they tried them all together she had run General into the fence in her zeal. Hard to imagine, when you looked at her big doe eyes and long silky forelock that she could be anything but angelic. Apparently, that only applied to people.

"Morning." A relaxed smile showed true, his shoulders matching it for a change. While he shaved his face for faire days, the scruff coming back in seemed so much more real and I loved it. Like me, he had donned jeans and cowboy boots, though I grinned at his faded t-shirt, the design one of the first I had collected from the company five years ago. "You look in a good mood."

"Well, some semblance thereof, anyway." I quipped nonsensically, picking the rectangular blocks of plastic wrapped wood shavings back up, one in each hand. Turning away to get some distance, I amused myself by doing curls with them as I walked down the aisle, my hands straining with the effort to keep hold of the slippery plastic. I had no plans to work out today, needing the break, but the more I did it, the more my body found ways to keep moving. The plastic yielded quickly to my old pocket knife, and I dumped the contents of the bag in the center of the stall, the second bag meeting a similar fate before I set to spreading it out with a pitchfork.

Nothing disturbed the quiet except for the equitable sounds of Bart rattling around, in the tack room I judged, as the soft thump slide of a saddle being moved traveled through the walls. Halfway through my self-appointed task he called my name, and I automatically responded, my feet on the move before the last vibration of his voice died down. I slewed to a stop in the door of the tack room, lips automatically lifting in a half grin. "You bellowed?"

"I'm not a bull, Bowen." he responded, eyebrow fixed halfway up his forehead like it became stuck there whenever we spoke to each other. Luckily, he didn't appear bothered by the possibility.

"No, more like a bear." I mused, biting my lip when I realized I said it aloud, but it was too late to take it back. The lazier of the two eyebrows joined its brother in arched surprise, and I plowed onward. "Growly, solid and strong."

Consideration, the slow weigh and balance as the scales shifted back and forth, finally coming to a stop before he answered me. "Grrr."

You'll excuse my gaped mouth expression, but Sir Bartholomew Clark just revealed a sense of humor. You'd have done the same in my shoes. I barely repressed my desire to run and hide, not wanting to see this side of him, not wanting to paint him any more attractive than I already found him. This was my teacher, my role model, and the level to which I aspired. It would be like crushing on my marketing research professor, who had certainly been attractive enough, in a tweed and wool slacks kind of way. Charming, kind and refined, every girl I knew, including some very sensible ones, had made comments about how they'd like to do 'extra credit' with him. I had just shook my head and put my nose closer to the grindstone, unwilling to let anything distract me from my goals. The problem was this goal felt ten times more important, weighed against a *much* more potent distraction. I shook my head to clear it, grasping for something to fill the waiting silence.

"I do believe you just made a funny. Alert the presses, Sir Clark has grown a funny bone!"

"Careful, it's new and fragile. You might break it." he responded quickly, the repartee warming me from the inside out as he rubbed at his elbow as if to soothe the delicate new formation in his personality. But maybe it was always there, just buried under layers and layers of armor. "Now, before your quick brain and smart mouth get too far ahead of me, I wanted you to come sit in this saddle."

The piece of tack looked like it hadn't seen saddle soap or oil in a dog's age, but he'd knocked the dust off at least, and the black leather under my fingers felt fine despite the neglect. A diamond in the rough, just like my Ro. In construction, it appeared to be some kind of hybrid between the deep seat of a western saddle and the rounded flaps of the English, the space between my eyes wrinkling as I puzzled over the firm, rounded ears of leather on either side of the pommel.

"It's an Australian saddle. They were developed for chasing cattle in the unforgiving territory of the outback. Those poleys help you keep your seat when you get jolted, but it won't hit you in the belly with the horn like a stock saddle would."

I swung my leg over it and slid into the perfect balance point, the wrinkle on my forehead disappearing as soon as I settled. No other word could describe it other than rightness. My toes instantly found the stirrups, and I tested my weight against them, sighing when I sat back down. This I could get used to. "This is lovely. What's it for?"

He followed the vague question easily. "It's for Ro." He let it sink in for a few seconds, his smile getting broader the longer I remained quiet, it being such a rare occasion. "I think it's about time you two took each other for a test ride."

When I remembered to breath, equal doses of worry and elation came rushing into my chest along with the air. "When?" I squeaked. Seriously. Could I, just once, not live up to my father's pet name for me?

"No time like the present." He answered matter-of-factly, turning away to pluck a bridle from the plethora of available strap goods hanging on the wall as I stepped out of the saddle. The one he offered me had a curb bit, meant for leverage, which I would have no problem with on Abby or another horse, but the memory of Ro's scars lay too thick on my fingertips. The hair would never grow back; the skin would always be knobby with remembered pain.

"No, not that." I didn't elaborate, but something in my eyes must have convinced him, so he wordlessly set it back on its hook. "Can I just ride him in a halter for now? If he's broke, it shouldn't much matter."

"If you feel that's all you need, then that is good enough for me. I just offered you the other since that's what I saw him ridden in at the auction yard."

No, even if Ro could get over it, I didn't know if I ever would. My whole goal with him had become less between us, not more, and my heart clamored for the day where we could be as close as Bart and Eros.

"Thanks." For understanding. For listening and trusting my judgement. For believing. For everything. But I was not ready to share that any more than I was to share Ro's suffering. Bart may have recognized it, but it remained mine to feel. "Is this what they rode him in?" I asked, gesturing at the saddle.

"No, he was in a roping saddle, pushing cows through the pens." Relief flooded my heart. I hadn't wanted to give up the saddle, but I would have for Ro's sake. I wanted this first moment unsullied by phantom hurts.

We fell to the task of grooming our horses, dust flying in brief clouds as the curry combs drew circles on their sleek hides. I took my time, finger picking the tiny overnight snarls from Ro's white tail and ashen mane, loving the way it fell against his neck, growing progressively darker as it moved toward his ears. Those ears, once still as the grave, now danced with a thousand emotions, lively with attentiveness even when still. When I approached him with the saddle his whole body tensed, though not with the intent to flee—he became a frozen statue, refusing to look at me, already turning himself off like a good little robot.

"Ro, hey Ro-ro." I rolled the words out sing song, like trying to cajole a homesick camper out of bed to join her cabin mates for an activity, stopping and waiting for him to come back to me. I had no pride in that moment, uncaring that Bart or anyone else might see my softness. Ro needed me far more than I needed to feed my ego.

I settled in, the saddle against my hip, one leg splayed out like I had all day to be there, truly willing to spend every second of my time off showing him he could trust me. My commitment was rewarded by a side roll of his eye, resting on me momentarily before facing the wall. Still, I waited, murmuring useless words about the adventures we could have, he and I, if he would just try. Finally, he huffed a gigantic breath and turned a worried eye on me, movement returned, though each tick was fueled by nerves.

He didn't like that still place, alone in the dark, he wanted the light. He just hadn't been there in so long it hurt to look at it. I moved to his head then, and his brow bones creased with confusion. In his experience, people didn't do things this way. More likely they simply threw the saddle on and paid no never mind to his feelings on the matter.

I wasn't one for hate, but I came close, thinking of a thousand thoughtless moments that must have passed before this sweet, sensitive boy realized no one cared. They probably thought him dumb, or dull, or, God forbid, stupid, but they had created that deadness. They had taken the artful work of nature and subdued it, like a Monet done in paint by numbers, no feeling or heart in the brushstrokes.

It took him a few minutes to realize I was waiting for him to do something, and then he started hunting for the answer, just as he had for the last two weeks as we became friends. He touched my arm, then withdrew, moving next to bump my shoulder, to snuffle my neck, but I still didn't touch him. When his nose accidentally came into contact with the flap of the saddle I immediately rewarded the effort, stroking the elastic skin on his neck. Then I withdrew and held the saddle out, this time watching the wheels in his head work overtime, his head moving from side to side, trying to reach around the piece of equipment to get to me. When he finally touched his whiskered lips to the leather I immediately stepped closer, scratching the special spot just at his chest where it joined his neck, murmuring a soothing, "Good boy."

The third time I held the saddle out, he touched it without hesitation. So I slid back to his withers and lifted it high, settling it gently on his back. We experienced a frozen moment, but so brief I doubt anyone else would have remarked on it. I left the saddle where it lay and started to stroke his ribs, his belly, easing a soft exhale from him and waiting for the breaths to resume their steady rhythm. Only when they were coming regularly did I slip around to his right side to attach the girth, letting it dangle down his side. The jingle of the buckles made his skin tremble, but I tried to think of that jingling as a joyful thing, something to celebrate, waiting for him to grow soft beneath my hands.

By the time I had the girth securely fastened on both sides it was me trembling, the emotional strain more exhausting than expected. I leaned against the wall, needing to ground myself against something that needed nothing from me, but I kept close enough for him to touch if he wanted. I'd always be there for him, even when I had nothing left of myself to give.

The soft friction of denim reminded me I was not alone and I looked up from the floor to find Bart against the opposite wall, in the perfect position to observe it all. But he wasn't watching me, he was crouched down with his shoulders hunched and his head bowed, a strangely vulnerable position from someone I'd always known to be strong.

"Bart." Oh my. The instant his name hit my lips they tingled, like after taking a sip of too hot cocoa, burning yet sweet. His head snapped up fast, eyes as wide as mine must have been, and the green more vivid and alive than I ever imagined a pair of eyes could be. Say something, Bowen, say anything but what you are thinking. Ro's nose bumped the bare skin of my arm, giving me enough distance to form words. "Are you alright?"

He straightened in a flash, reminding me that while human, he was still the most powerful person I'd ever met. I clung to the sanctity of our teacher/student relationship with desperate fervor, but it felt slippery in my hands, and heavy, just like the bags of shavings had been. He cleared his throat noisily.

"Yeah, sorry, just remembering something similar with Eros. Not the same, but close enough. They have a much stronger capacity for forgiving and forgetting, but I never will."

"No, me neither." I put fire in the words, and this time when we looked at each other it was with perfect understanding. Some things just weren't forgivable.

I took Ro out and let him crop grass while Bart finished saddling Buttermilk, grateful for the space. I should never have said his name aloud, and resolved to not do it again. Such liberties were too close, too familiar a thing to allow myself. Even after the fact, the memory of it felt warm.

We walked up the hill to the arena, and I hurried my steps as if trying to escape him, but it wasn't him I wanted to get away from, and I'd never be fast enough to get away from myself. Halfway up, I remembered the horse on the other end of the reins in my hand, and I found a worried eye studying me. Immediately, I slowed, falling back to his shoulder to reassure him.

"It's okay, buddy, I'm with you all the way."

The trust we'd developed won out over his concern, and he looked ahead, curious about where we were going. At the arena, he seemed not one whit concerned with the ropes of the lyst, or the quintain creaking faintly like some sort of overgrown weather vane. No, he remained too wrapped up in me to pay it any attention all, almost as if afraid I might turn on him at any moment.

I also fought a bit of worry. Not that he would buck me off, not that he would run away, but that he would retreat to the broken place. That what we had would shatter into irreparable pieces because I pushed him too quickly. When I walked him up to the mounting block he looked at it in confusion as if he had never seen such an animal, and if cowboys were using him as a stock horse, that didn't surprise me in the least.

Bart stepped up to hold him, but I shook my head in denial. If our relationship was going to work, Ro needed to let me get on, he had to have a choice. Bart came closer anyway, holding out a peppermint toward me, the white and red striped candy incongruous on his broad palm. I plucked it from him with a smile of thanks though I carefully did not touch his skin. I needed to be there with Ro, not lost in the snarl surrounding my coach.

"Stand." I murmured to Ro firmly once he was positioned beside the block, for a moment pleased by the automatic response to the command. But it felt too close to the unthinking, unfeeling responses I hated, so I stood at his head until a looseness came back to his neck. I tossed the reins over his head, just a simple length of cotton rope with snaps attached to his halter, following them with flat palmed strokes against his neck.

As long as he remained relaxed I slowly migrated toward the steps, never stopping the touching meant to reassure me as much as him. At the top, I paused, sucking in a deep breath. It felt like the time I'd been rock climbing on spring break, and I had done just fine until I realized how high I was and I had to get back down. Too much gravity pulled at me, both physically and emotionally, and my fear had no place on his back.

Gathering the soft rope of the reins in one hand with a silky length of his mane for security, I lifted my foot to the stirrup, my body straining to continue the motion until I was astride, but I waited. Cellular memory screamed at me for the pause, a thousand flexes my muscles had made in the past clamoring to be repeated, but still I waited.

There, so slight as to be negligible, I saw the corner of Ro's long white eyelashes curtaining his soft ebony eyes, as if he too wanted to know what I waited for. I straightened my leg, leaning all my weight on the saddle and he braced against it so I paused. It didn't feel like the brace of before, the anticipation of darkness, the shutting of a door, but more like he was expecting me. Then he really turned his head, looking at me full with one eye, as if to say, 'Come on already'.

At last, I swung my leg over his dappled quarters, the stars on his coat winking with promise, and settled like a feather in the saddle. Both of us exhaled as I came to rest, the perfect click of two souls made more whole.

I could have sat there forever, no future, no past, just the endless moment, but the clearing of a throat reminded me we weren't alone. As my leg closed on Ro's side, unconscious of the action, just of my thought to move, he stepped forward with all the smoothness his conformation had promised. I let him walk, our bodies learning each other, and the more I moved with him, the more of himself he offered, his strides looser, and his ribs more flexible.

By the time I noticed Bart sitting on Buttermilk, we were completely in sync and he followed my eyes to their side without so much as a lifted rein. I'd like to say Bartholomew Clark looked good, sitting on the pretty mare, but I'd be lying. Without Eros beneath him, he seemed reduced, like getting decaf coffee when you were expecting espresso. I shifted my weight and barely lifted my hand from Ro's neck to signal a halt, stopping well outside Buttermilk's personal space bubble. She'd never met him, and I didn't want to risk her ire.

"So?"

The loaded syllable was fraught with a thousand questions, but I couldn't put any of it into words adequately enough to do it justice, so I just smiled, hoping the answer would be clear. His mirrored smile said he read me clear enough and I turned away again, seeking more silent conversation with the horse my heart belonged to.

His trot had a loft to it that the other drafts couldn't match, even nimble Eros, and it took a few tries to not get left behind when he moved into it. There was a push, then air, then fall, making what would usually be a simple one-two beat for me to follow more of a rise-pause-sit-pause. I didn't touch his mouth any more than necessary, only a slight contact to remind him to stay on the rail or to swoop around my leg for a turn like we were working the elastic edge of a round balloon.

Oh, but the joy I found when I shifted one leg back to ask for a canter brought tears to my eyes. Instead of skirting the edge of a balloon we were bouncing along like one caught on the breeze, airy and grounded all at the same time. He rose to the level of my joy, each stride adding an arch to his neck that hadn't been there before, a pride that made him want to give me more, but I reluctantly slowed him. He was not fit enough to give me more yet, no matter how much he wanted to, and I didn't want the silvery glow between us dimmed by sore muscles later. There needed to be no regret in this.

I couldn't even be embarrassed by the tears blurring my vision when we rounded the corner and found Bart waiting for us at the gate. I caught them with my sleeve, cherishing their source too much to dash them away.

"How about a walk?" he asked, and I waved him ahead, following Buttermilk's creamy yellow tail at a safe distance.

Simple thing in theory, a walk, but not so simple in practice. While Ro felt calm, I watched him carefully, looking for the slightest sign of worry or tension. In truth, it really kept me from watching Bart, stopping me from admiring the way his legs hugged the mare like he'd been born astride. Or the sinuous movement of his spine, shifting and flowing with the motion of the round mare's body.

She pretended a spook at a wild hydrangea, the white flowers bright against the all over deep green color that permeated the fabric of Kentucky's landscape. He rode it like a leaf on a gust of wind and chuckled at her bluff, looking back over his shoulder to check on us. My face warmed to be caught watching, but honestly, I'd have done the same with anyone else. I just wouldn't have been mentally drooling while I did it.

Ro asked to stop and look at the bush, curious to know what bothered our companion, and I let him, laughing when he shoved his head in the bush to check if it was edible. Luckily, he pulled away without a bite, snorting a few times as we walked on to clear the pollen from his nostrils. Ivan would have pulled the bush up by the roots and tried to eat it around the bit in his mouth.

Back at the barn I vaulted from Ro's back automatically, just as I would with any other horse, too tempted to linger in the saddle. He deserved a reward for his trust, not a monkey stuck to his back. But while my hands were reaching for the girth he bent his elegant neck around to shove his muzzle under them instead, and I allowed myself the fantasy that he already missed the closeness too.

"We'll do it again, I promise, sweet boy." I pressed a kiss to his forehead, fed him the mint Bart had given me, then gently pushed him away so I could finish untacking. His coat was hardly damp and rather than hosing him off I took him to the paddock to let him roll away the saddle marks, leaning against the tree with a grin nothing could erase.

"Bowen." My head swiveled immediately from my study of Ro, who lay flat on his side, rubbing his face against the velvety turf. Those grass stains would be fun to get out.

"Yes Sir?" From his spot at the gate he shook his head as if amused or disappointed. Distance made hard to tell which.

"You have any plans for the afternoon?"

Yes, me and my busy social calendar. I answered quickly, "No Sir, just grocery shopping."

"Feel game for a run to the feed store? Aaron is hung up on a meeting with one of our clients."

Rather than answer, I shoved away from the tree, dusting my hands on my jeans as I moved toward him. Pleasure and pain wound together, because moments like this made me feel like I was already part of the team, a member of the company. But as we headed into town, alone in the truck again, it began to feel like where I belonged, and in a darker part of my heart I worried how broken it would leave me if I didn't have what it took to be the jouster they wanted. Even if I had the courage to endure a hit from the lance, I didn't know if my heart had enough armor on it to survive a blow as harsh as "Thanks, but no" would be.

The first fall from Eros turned out nothing like I expected, and it didn't come from being hit either. It came from the simplest expedience of a fulcrum, AKA my hips, not knowing how to properly counter the heavy weight now encasing my body from bottom to top.

We'd added helms for the second half of Wednesday's lesson, having mastered or at least not killed ourselves cantering in armor. Well, that extra twenty pounds encasing my brain pan became a piece of shot in a sling, and while I'd managed the depart, feeling Eros rising in front of me like a cresting wave, the halt at the end of the lyst became a travesty. Like, wreck of the Edmund Fitzgerald, only no epic song to go with it. It reminded me of that joke about skydiving without a parachute. It's not the fall that'll kill you, it's the sudden stop at the end.

It knocked the air from me just enough to tick me off, and I sucked in a deep breath, rolling up on my knees by dint of adrenaline alone. The helm and its padding muffled sound, but I still heard laughter, plain as day. Before I could struggle the rest of the way up there were others pulling me to my feet, hands holding my head still as they unclipped the visor. Aaron's face swam into view first, his fine brows puckered with worry and his lips thin with irritation.

"I'm fine." I growled, probably a little louder than warranted, but the laughing had me steaming mad and the helm distorted my sense of proportion. "Where's Eros?"

Laughter, this time from right beside me, and I turned my whole body to face Trace, who quickly went silent under my glare, waving his hands to ward me off. "Sorry, sorry, I just should have known you'd want to know about the horse first."

Scowling, I turned back to Aaron. "Get me back on." The worry vanished like it had never been there, and he smiled, turning me by the shoulders to face the mounting block. Eros waited calmly, but what hit me harder than the fall was Bart standing at his head, decidedly not looking at me. I stomped up the three steps to reach the mounting platform then took a deep breath to calm myself, patting Eros's neck in gratitude. "Sorry big man, my bad."

I stepped in the stirrup and the other leg cleared his back, but the gentle feel of someone guiding the opposite stirrup onto my foot startled me. I looked down to say thank you only to run smack into Bart's green eyes, which felt much like falling off all over again. Not an ounce of worry or doubt shone anywhere on his face, only fierceness, sparking my own urge to fight.

"Shoulders back, Bowen, like you are trying to touch them together."

That was it? Simple concept in theory, but when you were encased in a turtle shell, much harder to implement. My lips thinned and I nodded shortly before straightening my head so Aaron could fit the visor back down, but it was all to distance myself from the fact that Bart's hand hadn't moved. It remained wrapped around the back of my calf, the only part of me not covered in steel.

I refused to mourn the loss as I turned Eros back toward the lyst, immediately focused on the task before us. The laughter would not ring out again, so help me, or I would ring someone's bell and I didn't care whose.

As I backed Eros into the lyst, preparing to make the turn, he snorted heavily, a proud, studly sound I'd never heard from him before. As the quietest stallion I'd ever known, the noise seemed purposeful, a reminder that he was a warrior as much as his master, and I drew strength from his surety. I had everything I needed for success, now I just needed to do it.

Part of me wanted to slow things down, to make it easier to balance, but Eros felt the stronger need for a show of power, to scorch the earth where I had lately fallen. He whipped around the end of the lyst, powerful hind legs digging deeply as he pivoted, pushing me hard into the back of the saddle. The momentum forced me right where I needed to be, and I immediately hunted for the spot my eyes said my opponent should be, my whole world condensed to a thin slit of light and the galloping sound of my heart.

I'd been counting strides in the lyst since the day I started, just as I'd been taught in my jumping lessons, and I counted them backwards now, unable to see the end as he lifted me with each stride. At three, I closed my shoulders together as much as I could and focused hard on exhaling every ounce of oxygen in my lungs in a long breath. I still bounced on his back as he brought his hind legs under him to stop, but this time, I stayed where I belonged.

A whoop of glee pulled my attention, and I angled my head to find Trace jumping up and down with excitement, bringing the Golden Retriever analogy back with a vengeance. I grinned with triumph. No one could see it, but I could feel it, and as I patted Eros's neck and yielded the field so Cranston and Lee could take their turns, it was plenty good enough for me.

We each got three tries, and while I was the only one to definitively eat it, Lee ended up hanging off Cappy's neck, and they had to pull him down to get him resituated. Cranston bounced so hard I winced in sympathy, which said something, since I couldn't have wished his suffering on a better guy.

At the end of it, we were all a mess, and as Trace discovered while helping us get out of our armor, I sported a few colorful additions to my pale skin. Seriously, I hadn't seen that kind of purple on my body since I wore fuchsia in a high school friend's wedding. That didn't stop me from going to see Eros, but now that I knew they were there, the bruises were starting to throb, making me wince as I lifted my arm to brush his back.

"Pick up a couple war wounds, Bowen?" See, if Cranston had said that, I'd have been peeved. Bart said it, and it made me feel like strutting around the yard and crowing about them.

"Yeah. Though something tells me it's just the first of many." I smiled as I spoke, hoping he understood the humor I tried to cut the discomfort with.

"You stay on this path, absolutely." So agreeably said, as he concentrated on brushing Eros's mane flat from where I'd mussed it repeatedly. Girl cooties on the big man's war horse, you know. "You'll see bruises, broken bones, torn muscles, strained tendons and concussions. I've even seen some ugly punctures, from falling on a broken lance."

The hair on the back of my neck rose, an ounce of fear dissolving instantly in the heat of my indignation. "Are you trying to scare me off, Sir?"

He looked at me then, not a sliver of resistance in his eyes, and I almost lost my nerve, the target I thought I was aiming for gone. "That's not my job, Bowen. My job is to teach you how to sit on a horse and get hit with a stick. What you choose to do with that knowledge is completely up to you."

"And you." I bit off lowly, lashing out randomly in hopes I'd make contact. "I get the impression from Aaron that you are just as much in charge of this company as he is. But while he goes out and gets hit with a bloody big stick, you don't. Is that what happened? Did you get hurt?"

Oh crud. I hadn't meant for that question to come out, and thumped my forehead against Eros's side, hiding my flaming cheeks. The silence in the stall burned my ears, and I wanted to melt into a puddle of shame.

"I did."

My head snapped up at the barely audible response, and I found him mimicking my gesture, his forehead pressed against the other side of Eros's back. Only the top of his head remained visible, as he held himself up with a hand hooked over the stallion's wither. No, no, no. Panic welled up, and I fought to keep still. It was only fair that if he was brave enough to answer the question that I be brave enough to stay and hear it.

"Bart." It happened again, the heated response to his name, both on my lips and in his eyes. But the risk of the intimacy was worth pulling him from whatever darkness had found him. "I'm sorry. I didn't mean to ask that, and I don't need an answer."

While an edge of darkness still rode him, his lips shaped a quirked grimace, armor slipping into place. Because of me. Sometimes, I hated myself. "It's okay, Bowen, most wouldn't have been brave enough to ask. I'm not exactly easy to talk to."

"You mean foolish enough? And what are you talking about? You are socially gifted compared to me." There I went, deflecting any vulnerabilities onto myself. I tried for a small smile, hoping to fill the gap I'd just axed into the bridge between us.

"More practice faking it, I think." His eyes shuttered for a moment, and I was swimming in hurt, his and mine. Then they were open, and locked on mine and I drowned in something else entirely. Deep waters I had no business looking at, let alone dipping a toe in. "I'll tell you my story someday, but you need to get in the house and put some ice on those bruises. I'll finish up with Eros and put Ro out for the night."

"No, I've got Ro." I turned for the door, wincing as the bruise on my ribs twinged, freezing when his big hand closed on my arm. I couldn't take much more of this. "Please." It was a plea to escape, to make this disappear, to give me some space.

"Take a deep breath, Jo." All I could manage was a shallow one around the clamoring in my chest, and he turned me toward him. I almost bolted, unable to stay a second longer as a cold sweat broke out between my shoulders, but the concern in his eyes defused me. "Take a deeper one. I need to be sure you haven't broken a rib. Act like you are filling your lungs hard enough to push the bruise out of your skin."

I did as he asked, drawing in more air than I might normally, and while he seemed satisfied with the result, I felt anything but. Less than a foot away from him and one deep breath equated to me heading out the door in a daze, the heady scent of the man ingrained in my brain. I tried to press my nose against Ro, to replace the mouthwatering combination of saddle soap and sweat that made up Bartholomew Clark, but my heart refused to listen, and just clutched it closer.

❤❤❤

Friday, after morning chores, I saddled up Ro and headed for the trail around the property to do some interval training, using the gentle but long hills to put muscle on him. And me, to be honest.

Abby and I had done this sort of thing frequently when I first got her, since we had picked her up while my Dad was stationed in England. Pony Club meant riding English, and while I loathed dressage, and she barely tolerated show jumping, we were fiends on the cross country course. Mud, wind, rain, slick footing or boggy, we didn't care. If it stood still long enough, we'd jump it at the gallop. I'd been called the crazy American, even by the Irish, who were notoriously wild on horseback.

But riding cross country meant being fit, which meant she and I spent hours on long hacks, building muscle and endurance. Jousting had put muscle on me, expressly meant for hitting. I would need endurance too, to take the hits and keep getting back up.

Comparing Ro to Abby would be like putting a Monet next to a Picasso and asking which one was better. Both were beautiful and filled a space in my heart that neither could replace. But Ro felt like joy to me, the way he gave without fighting and looked for more connection every day.

Abby would go from setting her head and plowing into my hand to hollowing her back and running away with me if she could get away with it. No matter what I tried to convince her that it would be more fun if she were having fun, she never believed me. She flat out refused to enjoy herself, unless we were trail riding. That's what had finally softened our relationship, the last four years, me coming home and taking her out for a pressure free ride. It had just taken a while for me to see all those things I thought were fun just weren't as fun for her.

Not Ro. Ro wanted to be with me, wanted to do what I wanted to do, just so I'd call him a good boy. He didn't spook, he never resisted—he became putty in my hands. Unless I corrected him. The first time it happened his body had bowed around my leg so he could get a better look at a rabbit, and I growled softly to remind him of his feet. We went from softly swinging along, to me riding a robot so fast I almost cried with the injustice, all the energy in my body disappearing with his.

Instantly, he slowed down and looked back at me in worry, and I walked him until he relaxed again. It took time to find our equilibrium, for him to learn that a growl was just an attention getter, not a lead up to something more intense. Toward the end, I kept him going after a growl, closing my leg whenever he sucked back. Yet I remained so fair with my hands, and he learned if I sent him forward, he could go there, could move through the contact if he needed to in order to stay balanced.

When we returned to the barn he was sweatier between the ears and eyes than anywhere else, letting me know he'd truly been paying attention. I, on the other hand, was sweaty everywhere, my clothes soaked through from the thick moisture in the air.

I vaulted from his back and offered him a mint, having stocked up on them over the weekend. He plucked it from my palm with a delicacy a surgeon could have been proud of, and rather than chew it right away, sucked it against the roof of his mouth noisily. Laughter bubbled in my chest and lightened my whole body. While this whole relationship had begun for Ro's benefit, I now did it just as much for myself, needing something completely joyful and without agenda in my life. I could save my fierceness up for when I needed it.

After hosing him off and turning him out to graze I headed for the tack room, determined to clean up the saddle Bart had picked out for us. I had cleaned it of dust but ran out of time for much else with the rigorous training schedule. Watching the leather soak up conditioner, and then smoothing saddle soap against it until it caught the light was therapeutic. The metal fittings gleamed with a little bit of buffing from a clean towel and I set it back in its rack with a grin of satisfaction.

Along the cantle of the saddle, a shiny silver nameplate caught my eye, hiding in the deep crease of the leather. Bartholomew Clark. The saddle belonged to him. At every turn, the conflict in my heart spun me around until I was dizzy. He pushed me hard, harder than anyone had ever pushed me, challenging me to work harder, and to fight for what I wanted. On the other hand, in a quiet, non-verbal way, he shared important parts of himself, giving me every chance to succeed. I thought he had given me Eros just because he wanted me on a horse that knew to do his job no matter what stupidness I committed. But it struck me as an incredibly personal thing to do, and not something he would have done for Lee, and certainly not Cranston. He trusted me with these important parts of himself. The realization humbled me.

That afternoon as we assembled in the arena I put my game face on. Nothing would change there; he would be my teacher, and I would be the student, end of sentence, period. We were doing a final practice for the weekend, drilling the games so it became muscle memory, and we would be able to devote some of our attention toward interacting with the crowd. I knew this for the test it was. If we couldn't do it playing games, then it would only get worse once we were jousting.

Ivan seemed a little flat, but to be honest, it wasn't his fault. Hard to live up to the joy Ro brought me or the steady skill of Eros. That didn't make me any less thankful for him. Ivan knew his job and wanted to do it fast and fiercely. It made me focus a little more, deepening my breathing, putting me in my own skin with a vengeance so I could keep him under control. Aaron gave me some pointers for tossing the spear, which we had begun using this week, enabling me to tighten the radius of my shots by a good deal.
Strangely, I wondered if all this hand eye coordination I'd been working on might mean I could finally try roping without embarrassing myself in public.

At lessons end they pulled us together for a quick chat, Bart lounging like a cougar on the top of the mounting block, relaxed but with so much potential power it kept you mindful. Aaron stood beside him, hands clasped behind his back as he stretched his shoulders, the flexing muscles reminding me a little of his brother.

"Pull out your nicest garb and your finest manners, boys and girl." Aaron always spoke with a twitch of a grin at the corner of his mouth. Seriousness could be read in his eyes, if you were looking for it. "You'll be playing for the Queen and her ladies, giving credence to our training program and looking pretty for the public all at once. You win, and you'll be leading the Queen's mount in the final procession of the day, again putting you on display, which means you act and look your best."

Lee raised his hand like a good schoolboy and Bart turned his considerable attentions on him. "Fillmore." I admired the nuance that allowed him to acknowledge and answer in the same word. I tended to throw bad words after good until I hit my mark.

"Sir, I didn't know the Queen rode at all." Confusion wrinkled the guys' brow, and if I didn't feel like he was my younger brother, I might have called it charming. As I did feel like I was his big sister though, I'd have to stick with cute.

"This is new. We're going to put the Queen on Buttermilk, and the King will ride Ivan, since the mare has decided she hates him least." We all chuckled at his deliberate grin and pause. "It'll be the procession after the final joust, taking the royals to the front gate. This helps funnel the crowds toward the exit without having to round them up so much." I nodded at the cleverness of the ploy. Nothing like spectacle to draw the mob, no matter how friendly it may be.

Cranston butted in next, Hawk pinning his ears in irritation when his rider kicked him forward to get the attention of our superiors. It made me wish I had ears to pin at him too. "Wouldn't it make more sense to wear armor? I mean, we'd certainly look the part."

While Bart's expression of disdain said enough for me, apparently, Aaron felt the need to remark on it. "No, Cranston, you haven't earned the right to wear that armor in public." A lengthy pause as he stared the idiot down, which only ended when Cranston looked away. Then he looked at the rest of us and smiled. "Yet. Besides, you really don't want to walk around the faire in a full suit of armor. For now, just wear something nice."

Bart picked up where his brother left off. "If you boys need some help with kitting up a little fancier, we've got a box full of things you can pick from."

Lee looked excited by the prospect. His one tunic was plain, brown and a little rough around the edges, kind of like him. Cranston wrinkled his nose in distaste, likely imagining wearing a hand me down. I wanted to laugh at the image that flashed through my mind of him scrubbing his skin raw to get rid of cooties, but my name fell from Bart's lips next.

"Bowen, the blue grey tunic is plenty nice, but Mari volunteered to let you rifle through her extras if you'd like something else."

Notice he didn't say anything prettier or more feminine. Yeah, to paraphrase Mark Twain, you could put a pig in a dress, but you wasted your time and irritated the pig. But it didn't upset me, it actually made me feel a little more on the same level with the guys, reminding me they weren't keeping me around for decorative purposes. I remained here because I could do the job.

Saturday morning felt fairly relaxed, considering the extra work we had to do. I got up early, just because I didn't want to run around like a headless chicken, but I had packed my bag the night before. At that point, it was quick work to start the coffee maker, nuke the hot water for my tea and chew down a protein bar. Bart and I both hit the aisle way at the same time, and I handed him his tumbler while sipping carefully at my English Breakfast, brewed so strong it might as well have been coffee.

"You don't have to bring me coffee, Jo. I'm a big boy, and know how to make my own." A chuckle shadowed his voice, and it warmed me almost as much as him saying my name.

"I am aware of that, but why risk it?" I slid a grin at him sideways. "Besides, it's becoming part of my ritual for the weekends, and it's worked so far. I hate to mess up a good thing."

He shook his head and turned to greet Eros, while I did the same with Ro, but then like two halves of the same brain we fell in toward the feed room to get a jump on the day. He filled the buckets with grain while I doled out the vitamins and supplements, then he held the stack while I delivered them. I could get used to doing it this way much too easily. We'd gotten everyone fed by the time the others trickled in, and Lee looked around worriedly.

"Don't worry about it, Fillmore." Bart said, relieving the strain in the kid's face immediately. "You can make it up at tonight's feeding, I just wanted to make sure we were on time today, with all the changes."

Just like all the other weekends we were quickly loaded and headed toward the grounds, Cranston in the front passenger seat as if it were a badge of honor. Funny, but while he seemed to take it as his right to be there, he didn't look comfortable at all.

Once we unloaded the horses, Buttermilk, Ivan, Hawk and General got tied to the sides of the trailer with water buckets and plenty of hay and then we fell into the regular rhythm of another day in paradise. It was amazing how quickly it had become part of the fabric of me. If I lost it, it would tear some awfully ragged edges.

The hug Mari threw around my neck seemed natural, and I wondered again at how fast she'd become a friend. I knew that living the way I had been, my world winnowed down to what was vital, had made things like this so precious. In school, I'd been scattered, trying to keep my brain sane under the ever changing workload, absorbing and throwing back details that I might never use again. Add in the mind numbing of TV, which I hadn't watched in weeks now, and the distractions of social media, and I'd been more than a little lost. This life condensed me down into the most essential version of myself, and I liked it.

My stomach tied itself in knots after the first joust as I worried over the performance to come. Bart caught me standing by Eros with my face pressed into his neck, hiding on the side away from the crowds wandering by. I needed the warmth, despite the growing heat of the day, and to borrow some of his strength. My fear of failure felt too great to face alone.

"Everything okay, Bowen?" Both the concern and challenge in that question gave me the confidence to look up. No, I might have my moments of weakness, but where challenge rang I would rise to it.

"Just fine." I scratched Eros's chest, tracing the line where the muscles of his foreleg met pectorals, a silent thank you for letting me borrow his solidity. "I think I need to go get something to eat. I usually eat after the second joust and I won't have time then."

"Good idea. Grab Mari, she needs some adult company, if you don't mind." I nodded shortly, and moved to leave but he grabbed my arm as I passed, and I spun around defensively. Fierce concern blazed hot in his eyes, tilting me off kilter. "And Bowen, you need to eat more. More protein particularly. You are losing too much weight." His thumb traced the muscle in my forearm and I swallowed hard, reaching for some distance as I tugged myself away from that disconcerting touch.

"Yes Sir." I bit off, turning to the safety of our professional roles, grasping at anything other than the warmth lingering on my skin. "I'll pay better attention."

Then I ran away as fast as I could walk, shaking my head as I got close to the booth where Mari was selling a stack of t-shirts to a teenage boy. As she ran his credit card he turned his attention on me with a fervent light in his eye.

"Lady, I heard you are training to be a knight. That must be hard." I acknowledged it to be a good deal of hard work, but he shook his head, stumbling over his words to clarify. "No, I mean, hard for the other knights. If I were a knight, I'd have a tough time hitting a girl, let alone one as pretty as you."

I had to bite my tongue for a moment and gather my thoughts, irritated by the worthless flattery and the assumption that my looks had anything to do with it. "Well, I'm glad to hear you are honorable enough not to strike a woman, but in war at least, it does not matter if you are male or female. We are all honing ourselves into weapons, just as if I were in a karate class. It would be a shame to be limited to only fighting women when the biggest threat to a woman is a man. I have no problem facing an honorable man any more than he should have a problem facing me. I would never want to cross lances with someone less than noble." Cranston's face sprung to mind at the tail end.

"I've been telling my sister about you, she couldn't believe a girl was going to become a knight." he continued, as if my speech had hardly been notable, and I hoped it at least planted a seed.

"I'd be happy to talk to her, if you want to bring her around later." I offered, thinking surely his sister would prove more fertile ground, but his face fell a little.

"She can't come. She's in the hospital." You could see past the brave front he pulled together that the hospital stay was much more serious than he let on.

"Well, I tell you what, can she email? I'll give you my email address and she can contact me there." His eyes lit up with delight as I scribbled my personal information on the back of his receipt, and he faded into the crowd clutching his bag with far more enthusiasm than the t-shirts should have warranted. I had a feeling this little girl's bravery would make mine look sickly in comparison.

Mari turned to me with moisture in her eyes, but no real tears yet. "Jo, give me a second, I need to see Aaron before we go. I figured you'd want to go early, since you've got a show later." She marched off like a woman on a mission and I helped out an older gentleman looking for one of the old t-shirts from a few years ago while I waited.

Lee came to relieve me, and I joined Mari at the gate, heaving a deep sigh in an attempt to relax. She must have gotten a bug put in her ear by Bart as well, because she steered me straight to the steak on a stake vendor, ordering two for me and one for her. She shoved them in my hand with a glimmer in her eye that brooked no argument, and my stomach responded to the scent of the grilled meat with a voracious growl, obviously agreeing with her.

Halfway through the second, she started marching again, the barest edge of a limp showing as she lengthened her stride, and I hurried after her with a wrinkle beginning to form on my brow. If I hadn't known any better, I'd have said she was mad. Just as I dropped my trash in a bin she snatched my wrist, her grip tight enough to ache a little as I followed her into the Pegasus Threads costume shop.

Barely pausing for a breath, she grabbed the bodice and chemise I had admired off the rack and shoving me in a dressing room with them. "Change, Jo, right now. No questions asked, just do it."

Command filled that voice, one that rang familiar to Bart's, and I obeyed without voicing the thousand questions behind my lips. My grandmother had made the tunic I wore, and I carefully folded it, cherishing the familiar bit of home.

The chemise slid on like water, slightly sticking to my damp skin, and I felt bad for sullying it. The bodice was a little more complicated, and halfway through lacing it up, Mari's face peeked through the curtains. "Come here." She got me by the arm again, dragging me out of the tiny cubby and setting to work on the lacing, accomplishing it with all the familiarity I have with putting on a saddle. It fit like a second skin, and I worried a little about breathing in it, but she stopped just shy of limiting motion. "Now fluff."

I tilted my head to the side like a dog that heard a sound no one else could, unsure what she was talking about, and she huffed a laugh. "Reach under your breasts and lift them up. Fluff the girls."

My turn to laugh. "Mari, in case you haven't noticed, I'm not particularly blessed in the chest. Probably all to the good, considering what I'm training to do."

She snorted at my objection. "Jo, even those of us endowed appreciate the effects of a well-made and fit bodice. This is called the boob fairy effect. Trust me, please, and do as I ask."

My face flamed as I turned away to do as she asked, wondering what the hell had inspired all this. When I spun back around she added a few more tugs of the laces, then stepped behind me to pull the rubber band from my braid and undo the strands, settling the waves over my shoulder. When she positioned me before the mirror my mouth fell open in shock.

I hadn't been paying much attention to my appearance lately, but apparently it wasn't just my insides that had been whittled down to the essentials. I was unacquainted with the woman looking back at me; her hazel eyes glowed with life, and contentment rested under her skin. Mari snuck a look around the side of my shoulder, and pressed her cheek to me with a grin, her eyes finding mine in the reflection.

"Here's the deal Josephine. I saw the look on your face when that boy called you pretty, and I could tell you didn't believe it. But you are not just pretty, He doesn't know your heart like the rest of us do. You aren't pretty, Jo. You are beautiful, inside and out." Her hand came to rest over my heart, and while I usually didn't appreciate touching, I folded my hand over hers and sank into the comfort of the embrace for just a moment. "You need to see what the rest of us see, Jo."

Nope, I didn't cry. But I came damn close.

Mari led me back out into the throng, and I shifted uncomfortably, feeling eyes on me that I'd never noticed before. She'd told me arrangements had been made, and the clothes were mine, smacking my hand hard enough to sting when I tried to take them off. I told her I couldn't let her pay for things for me, and she told me I could pay her back someday when I got my knighthood. All I could do was follow the fiery redhead and hope that I got the chance to do so.

We got back to the encampment in time for me to shove my hair under my hat and fall to the task of getting the horses ready, since I didn't have a knight in this particular fight. Hillary did nothing but exclaim over how pretty I looked and it felt like my had skin sun burned from the inside out, the blush became so fierce. Maybe Mari helped me take a step in the right direction, but it would take a while before I believed it.

I led horses to the block, getting John mounted, then headed back for Eros while they got Aaron on. As I led the stallion toward his master it was easy to get lost in the routine, to focus on the job at hand rather than my newly exposed looks. As Bart swung aboard, I moved automatically to slide the stirrup on his foot, my fingers once again landing on the divot in his calf, and I made the mistake of looking up. Pole axed. That's all I could really say to describe what it felt like to meet his eyes, at once reserved and on fire. "Looks good." The words shivered in my ears, somehow more important that Mari's profession of my beauty.

A wolf whistle from Lee made my head snap to the side, and I'd like to say it was my glare that made him pale, but he looked several feet higher than my face as he gulped the rest of the whistle down. Deep down, I was grateful for Lee's intrusion, needing something to make me break away from Eros's side and fall into place at the head of the procession with the company banner. I'd never felt more exposed as I led the men I considered my brothers toward the arena, but even as I faced those eyes, having Bart at my back reassured me. I trusted him there best of all of them, knew I could rely on him to guard it.

After all of that, my afternoon performance felt easier to face, even in my new garb. I'd adjusted to the feeling of people seeing me differently, though I still didn't quite believe it myself. Ivan fed off the energy of the crowd, a little smaller than the ones that attended the joust, and concentrating on him most of the time kept the stares from bothering me.

Cranston rode fast as Hades, Hawk wheeling through the turns like his namesake and flying on a thermal none of the rest of us could ride. But he didn't take the time to aim, and while his crowd interaction was consistent, it came off fake, an act. While this whole festival was one big vaudeville stage a really good actor made you forget you watched a show.

Just before my go Bart strolled by on Eros, pausing beside us for a moment. "Be accurate, Bowen. Fast comes later. And talk to the ladies' court. You at least know them a little, and it'll get you warmed up to the crowd."

148

I gulped hard, and rode forward to be introduced to the women on the dais, letting Ivan's jig happen because it looked more impressive than walking. Bart's voice boomed out of the speakers, surrounding me in the familiarity of his voice, though the words came as a surprise.

"My beautiful Queen and fair ladies of the court, may I introduce one of your own? A beauty known for her bloom as well as her thorns, Lady Josephine Bowen hales from the hardy country of Wales. Her skin is fairer than the palest leek, her spirit fiercer than the war horse she rides. A true warrior princess, here for your entertainment."

All of it burned me with embarrassment, for the truth in it, for the words he had remembered me saying, and for the deliberate prod at the end. I rose to the challenge in the last bit, flashing a grin at his gloating smile before bowing to the women with a sweep of my arm.

"Your Majesty, would that all your ladies prove immune to the flatteries of this noble knight. I am indeed a fierce warrior, but Wales bears no princesses, only taciturn creatures too rough to come before you. I ask Your tolerance as I seek to prove myself worthy of joining this Gallant Company of Knights."

The women all tittered appropriately, and I managed to catch the ubiquitous raised eyebrow on Bart's face before exchanging smiles with the Queen. I'd been introduced briefly at the dress rehearsals, but did not know her as anything other than Her Majesty. She rose gracefully from her throne, a feathered peacock fan in hand, and stepped forward to the rail.

"My dear child, England embraces you, and thanks you for your visit to Our court. Truly, you are fair, as fit to join My ladies as these other worthies." She gestured toward the women behind her with one bejeweled hand, and nodded at me. "Go forth with My and My noble husband, the King's blessing, and show the world what we women already know. Fairer though we may be, weaker is not a hallmark of our sex." The crowd responded with a burst of applause that warmed me to my toes, and I purposely avoided looking at Bart. No distractions, not right now.

I officially had a woman crush on the Queen. She got it. As much as I had given Bart crap for assuming things about me, I'd just been reminded not to judge other women by their looks any more than I allowed others to judge me by mine. I bowed again and turned Ivan for the lyst, grabbing the ring lance from Hillary on the move, grinning when she whooped and gave a little wiggle of glee.

A soft heel had Ivan at the canter and I slid us into the lane without pause, breathing myself deeply into the seat of the saddle, Bart's words ringing in my head. Accuracy I could do. The rings slid onto my lance with a soft snick, all but one of them coming to rest against my hand, the last yielding to gravity when I brushed against it. Casting the lance away, we came to a trot, Ivan chomping noisily on his bit because he knew what this would all lead up to. He steadied with a soft murmur, allowing me to take the spear from Kory, who also shared a grin with me. I didn't just ride for myself. I rode for all of us, and for a moment, I almost faltered under the weight of it. But the challenge loomed before me, and I fell to my task, asking for power from Ivan.

He bucked once in excitement as he launched forward, and I had to adjust my approach on the fly, adding power to my throw so it could close the distance to the hay bales set up as a target. We were past it before I could see where it landed, and I left it behind me.

Hillary waited with the tilting lance, holding it up and out, so I kept Ivan cantering with a half halt to balance him. The lance hit my palm with a slap and I let the sting fold my fingers around it reflexively. The wood kipped up under my arm like it belonged there as we rounded the corner, and while Ivan strained to run, I slowed him to cadence of the word 'accuracy' repeated over and over under my breath. The shield of the quintain waited for my blow like a friend welcoming me to their home and I greeted it with a perfect strike, just inside the top right corner. Then I brought Ivan back down to a trot over the roar of the small crowd gathered to watch, nodding my head to the little girl standing on her dad's lap as she cheered for us. I'd done it! The relief of not choking under pressure almost drown out the giddy butterflies of success dancing in my stomach.

Hillary and I shared a quick fist bump after I yielded the lance back into her hands, then I took my post on the opposite side of the lyst from Cranston. This yielded the field to Lee, who gulped and rode forward to pay his own dues. You'd think he'd have felt pretty good about himself, dressed in a dark green velvet surcoat, but in this case, the garment seemed to wear him rather than the other way around. I sympathized, considering my earlier ugly duckling moment, but I'd gotten past it once I settled to my work. Lee never quite settled, General flicking his ears in confusion as his rider kept leaving him without direction. The rings remained up, except for the last, which traced the same path mine had taken down to the dirt. The spear barely clipped the bottom outside corner of the bale as General veered away, Fillmore correcting too hard, too late. He managed a decent enough hit on the quintain though, giving the crowd something to cheer as Bart asked them to applaud all of our efforts. Then we all rode forward to hear our scores from the Queen.

"My glorious children, would that I could reward you all and gather you close. Lord Cranston, the ladies of the court would like to offer their appreciation for your daring speed and pretty face." All the women rose from their seats and as if choreographed, they blew him a volley of kisses, which he pretended to snatch one by one from the air and press to his heart with a smug smile. I had to give it to him, he knew how to play it up. "Lord Lee, I should like to offer you my appreciation for your heartfelt efforts and courage to try." Now she blew him a kiss, and he colored up like a Christmas tree, the ladies all giggling at his discomfiture.

"Thank you, Your Majesty." he stuttered, making several women in the audience collectively '*aww*'.

"But by dint of her focus and clarity of horsemanship, it would be Lady Josephine Bowen that should accompany myself on the final procession, as an honorary member of My ladies' court. For the Lady, a hip, hip, huzzah!" The crowd echoed her huzzah, and while I blushed just as hard as Fillmore, it stemmed as much from pride as from embarrassment.

Later, after the final joust, Kory and Jeff ran back to grab the horses, and we got the Royalty mounted up while the knights were busy hobnobbing with the crowd. The long walk through the fair behind a large parade of cast members felt disconcerting, though the Queen proved delightful, calling out to people she knew and waving especially at the children. I was simply not used to being watched, or feeling like everyone was talking about me. I felt like a bug under a microscope, though unlike most bugs, I wasn't dead, just getting tired. Once we dropped the royals off, Steve and I snuck the horses through a side gate.

"Steve, do you want to ride back?" I asked him, and he paled as the offer lingered in the air.

"No, no, that's okay, I'll walk. But you can ride back if you want." He was a peach, giving me a leg up onto Ivan's tall back, and I didn't even bother adjusting the stirrups, leaving them swinging freely. I took Buttermilks reins from him, and turned Ivan up the lane that wrapped around the backside of the fair, allowing vendors and cast members to travel the outskirts. The mare made a few nasty faces at first, attempting to menace Ivan, but with a few growls from me she settled. As we swung along in leisurely fashion several people greeted me by name, none of whom I knew, and I nodded to all of them, trying not to squirm under the attention. Apparently, word traveled fast around a faire, and I had become a known entity. Now introduced on stage, I could no longer pretend to be a faceless squire running around in the shadow of the knights.

We meandered into the paddock area and I dropped down from Ivan's back with a sigh. I was alone, and fairly certain they didn't need me in the encampment, so I tied the horses up and got them untacked. In the process, Ivan left a giant stain of sweat on my chemise, trying to rub his head. Honestly, it surprised me that it had lasted that long without getting dirty. Not that I looked forward to doing laundry, but filth was the price you paid when you played with horses.

The closing cannon sounded right at six, just as I finished with chores, all the water troughs in the paddocks full and hay already distributed. John came through the gate first with Tuck in tow, and he looked back over his shoulder and hollered, "Found her!" When he turned back to me with a broad grin I tilted my head in inquiry. "Oh, we were contemplating sending a search party, is all."

"Didn't Steve tell you I was riding back?"

"No, we haven't seen him yet either, but his daughter works at the place that sells wooden mugs, so maybe he stopped to chat." You had to love that John saw the good in everyone. "Should have known you were back here working while the rest of us sat on our butts and talked about you behind your back." Teasingly said, of course, but it made me wonder what they said while I wasn't there. "All good, of course. You're the sweetheart of the fair it would seem."

Alex came next with J.T., trailing in at the end of the conversation and picking up where John left off. "Yes, it would seem no one recognized you as our girl squire of the last few weeks. Our little caterpillar is a butterfly now." I rolled my eyes as obviously as possible and stuck my tongue out at him, prompting a laugh, but his eyes were serious. "I mean it Jo. We knew you were hiding under there somewhere."

"Oh please, you guys. I'm not some decorative toy to trot out for the amusement of others." So much for being on equal footing. I would be back in the tunic tomorrow, so help me.

Aaron and Bart came through the gate side by side, Byz trying to bully Eros with wrinkled lips and laid back ears. All I had to do was point behind them and Bart stepped between them to break it up, not even slowing down.

"Jo, don't discount being a pretty face. It sure works well for Trace." Aaron remarked, and I swear, both Bart and I wrinkled our noses at the same time.

"Bowen is not a pretty face." My gut clenched hard and everyone froze in place, looking right at Bart in surprise, including me. He didn't stop moving, headed for the paddock to turn Eros loose even as he talked, as if he didn't know we all

153

hung on every word. "It's not to say that she isn't lovely to look at, any idiot can see that. But a masterwork sword is beautiful as well. That doesn't mean you hang it on a wall and look at it. You admire its balance and edge and character by using it."

Then they weren't looking at him. They were looking at me. I'd never felt more exposed in my life, and the only thing worse would have been the nightmare of finding yourself naked in public. All I could do was raise my chin and head for the encampment to finish helping with cleanup, throwing a parting shot over my shoulder. "And this sword is going to go shovel some horse manure now, while you all pull your heads out of your asses."

Smart words, considering I found myself wedged in between Bart and Aaron on the way home again. Bart's jaw looked tight enough to crack a molar, and it felt like sitting next to a granite cliff. Aaron just shrugged and looked away when I mouthed 'what's wrong?'

There were no horses to take care of except Ro, so I headed straight for his paddock with a bucket of feed, happy to let him stay outside for the night. As I sat under the tree while he ate the light in the sky faded quickly, and I reveled in the quiet. The boys wouldn't be done showering for a while, and if I wanted any hot water I'd have to give it time. Contemplating the changes made in me today, I poked carefully at the newness like you would with a sore tooth, distracted when the light in the big window over the paddock flicked on.

It cast a shadow that could only be Bart's through the curtains, a breadth and intensity of movement to the shape that Aaron could not match. It was too close and too far away at the same time, and I was not brave enough to stay and torture myself over someone too old and too far out of my class, so I headed to the house after giving Ro a quick kiss. While the pint of mocha ripple gelato I ate as I did my laundry didn't do much to appease my appetite, it went a long way toward soothing my raw heart.

Sunday, Cranston beat me out by three points, and I yielded the honor of leading the Queen with whatever grace I could scrape together while the idjit preened like a peacock. Ivan had gotten cranky about being held back, fighting contact all the way. To be honest, he probably fed off my edginess. I had no reason to feel that way, nothing I could share with anyone anyway, but Mari seemed to know something was up.

Add in ninety percent humidity and eighty-seven degree temperatures, and I wilted like nobody's business as we headed back to the farm with a full trailer. We settled everyone in for the night and I headed into the house with a headache that felt like a draft horse was leaning on me from both sides.

The boys headed out to meet friends and I felt incredibly grateful to get the house to myself. After a cool shower, some ibuprofen and a gallon of water I felt vaguely more human, but no matter how I angled the fan on my body, I could not get comfortable enough to sleep.

After trying to read for a few hours I gave up on sleep entirely, wading up my blanket and another water to go sit with Ro. Assisted by the flashlight on my phone, I snuck around the side of the barn, trying not to rouse anyone inside. When I undid the chain on the gate and slipped through, Ro's whiskered nose touched my cheek, and I choked down a girly scream. He stayed right in step with me as I padded toward the tree, politely watched me lay out on the ground, and then trustingly folded his legs under him to do the same less than ten feet away. Maybe tomorrow I could talk to Bart about integrating him with another horse. While that would leave him without his friend on the weekends it seemed selfish to limit his herd to a screwed up two-legger the rest of the time.

Speaking of Bart, my eyes automatically went up to his window, and the faint glow peeking between the curtains. As I tried to wrap my brain around what might keep him up at one AM, just to keep from thinking about what went on in my own head, the soft sounds of snoring intruded. Yes, apparently Ro snored. I had to giggle at the ridiculousness of it, but the way his nose pressed to the ground as he lay recumbent pinched things off just enough to cause a faint grunty snore with every exhale.

Pretty soon I ended up on my back, staring at the stars as they made their way across the sky. Between the slow inevitability of the earth turning on its axis, and the memory of doing something similar on the family ranch, I too yielded to sleep.

I don't know what woke me but I came awake all at once, sitting up so fast my head spun. From forty feet away, Ro startled in response, snorting and looking around for the threat, and I immediately felt guilty. Again, he really did need more than a two legger on the verge of a nervous breakdown. The sun was just coming up, which made it about five thirty, and I fished my phone out of the tangled blanket to double check. Yup, that would mean almost time for Bart to feed. Rubbing at my eyes, and the lingering remnants of my headache, I considered my options. Sneak back in the house now, and risk getting caught wandering around barefoot in my PJ's again, or wait until he let the herd out to pasture. That would certainly give me plenty of time to get inside unnoticed.

Just then, I caught movement out the corner of my eye and swiveled my head around to find the curtains on Bart's window falling closed. Well, son of a tea biscuit. Already well aware of my status as a socially awkward idiot with no life outside of the barn, he now he knew I had nothing better to do than have a sleepover with my horse. In cartoon pajamas no less. Yes, let's point out exactly how young I was, even if I didn't usually act my age. Screw it. I flopped back on the blanket in disgust and wondered how long it would take my grandmother to get here and wash my mouth out if I just swore like I wanted to. If ever a situation called for cursing, this one did.

The snick and slide of stall doors being opened interrupted my pity party, followed by the rumble of feet marking the mass exodus of draft horses, moving fast. I started to gather the blanket in my lap, and hunted for the energy to head inside, but I froze immediately when a body rounded the corner of the barn. Every square inch of my skin heated as Bart got closer, and I fought with the urge to pull the blanket over my head when he let himself in the gate.

Ro hardly flicked an ear at him, probably hoping for a mint, but otherwise ignored us in favor of the breakfast that Bart set down in front of him. I felt like a rabbit, frozen with fear and hoping the big bad predator wouldn't turn and look at me. But he did turn, barely smiling as he drew closer. I supposed I should be grateful he smiled at me at all considering Saturday's fiasco and the distance I had maintained since. I hadn't even brought him coffee yesterday, and while he hadn't remarked on it, the cup in his hands told me he noticed. He crouched just outside of my reach and held out the tumbler I gave him coffee in on Saturday.

"Come on Bowen, no sense letting perfectly good tea go to waste." A hint of tease, and I reached for the cup. I almost felt ashamed he could punch my buttons so easily, but I was also flattered he knew me so well. "Drink up before it gets cold."

I sipped gingerly at first, then took a larger draw when the elixir hit my taste buds. It reminded me of the tea my Gran made, dark as sin with two lumps and dollop of milk. It tasted like home. My eyes closed for a moment before I could manage the nerve to meet his eyes. They held a wealth of patience, but an edge of impatience all at the same time. Green like a new leaf right around the pupil, they were circled by a deeper shade that reminded me of the forests in Snowdonia. Seriously, I would run out of adjectives to describe them long before I tired of looking at them.

"Thank you."

"It seemed an appropriate peace offering, considering how often you've plied me with caffeine."

"How did you know I drank tea?"

"I could smell it in the truck on Saturday." Oh the cleverness of you, to have noticed, I thought. I couldn't smell anything past the press of bodies. "I hope you take it with sugar and cream."

Rather than answer, I drew another swallow and smiled. He smiled back just a little more than before. "You didn't ride Eros down?" That's right, Jo, deflect, deflect.

"No, there was a *tylwyth teg* outside my window. I thought I ought to make peace with her before she made mischief for me." Oh, no, he did not just call me one of the fairy folk of Wales. Was it really fair for him to be cunning enough to know my heritage so well, when he was already handsome, and strong, and admirable. Charming even, when he had half a mind to it.

"No fairy folk would dare the wrath of our cousin England." I quipped, keeping my tone conversational.

"Nay, lassie, cousin England only in part." I'll admit, the brogue that rolled off his tongue, while affected for humors sake, left me effected in a way that felt anything but funny. "The rest is Scottish thistle, prickly and unwelcoming."

"Ah, but it is also hardy and impossible to eradicate." Yes indeed, and rooting itself deeper all the time. It also had a certain rugged handsomeness to it, but I'd rather have eaten my blanket than let that slip. "And this particular thistle seems to make a particularly good cuppa." There you go, take another sip, Jo, before you say something incredibly stupid.

"You're welcome." He shifted from side to side as if to relieve stiffness and my brows pulled together, remembering the feel of his leg under my hand. An old injury, and I had kept him crouched down like a gargoyle.

"You are welcome to sit and share the peace." I offered, waving my hand to encompass the quiet surroundings.

"No, I'd best take Buttermilk down to her wooly companions and go close the gate behind the herd before they notice it's still open." He straightened, the muscles in his thighs bunching beneath the worn denim of his wranglers, and looked down at with me mischief. "And, by the by, nice jammies."

He made it half way to the gate before I could fish up a reply to throw at his back. "Nice of you to notice."

Swiveling on his heel, he walked backward for a few steps, his eyes locked on mine. "I notice everything." It took five minutes for the goosebumps to fade from my skin at the intensity of his stare, and whatever hidden depths there were in that parting shot. But I didn't think anything would make the image of his denim clad butt ever fade from my memory.

♥♥♥

That afternoon, Ro and I went for another ride around the property, taking a different turn than last time, and we ended up skirting the edge of the pasture the herd lived in. He looked at them with curiosity but no real longing, and selfishly, I felt grateful for it. I still needed him too much.

When we cantered up a long hill I stood up in my stirrups, letting him unfurl underneath me for a few strides. His was not the same speed Abby would give, not even on her worst day. She could blister my hands with her mane when she had a full head of steam. But it held a power she couldn't touch, not just over the ground, but over my heart. It felt perfect.

If they decided to keep me I'd bring my English saddle back and see if it fit him. While Abby tended toward greyhound lean and Ro was decidedly not as aerodynamic, they both owned a good wither for holding the saddle in place and well sprung ribs that filled up my leg, so it was possible. Though I would definitely need a new girth. He'd put on near a hundred and fifty pounds already, and once fully muscled he would be thick.

There was also the question of adding a bit. I'd been tempted today, but I'd needed a peaceful ride far more than he needed a bridle. Someday, I wanted to ride him bareback as well. Abby had always gotten in a snit over it, I think because we were too close, touching too much, but I didn't think that would be a problem with Ro.

Thinking of Bart's admonition to eat more protein, I headed into town for dinner, hunting for a decent steak. At home, that would have meant the freezer, and for a second, my stomach lurched around a knot of homesickness. A huge sign proclaiming hometown cooking in vivid technicolor seemed promising enough, so I pulled off the highway and parked, digging out my phone to call home before heading inside.

"Jo!" was my father's jovial greeting straight out of the gate. "How's my little girl?"

"Hungry, bruised, and tired." I shot back with a smile. "But loving every second of it. You wouldn't believe what they've got us doing, Daddy."

He grilled me for several minutes, concerned for my safety, but once I mentioned Ro he shifted his focus. "Are you sure that's smart, baby? You get attached to this horse and they don't keep you, that's not very fair to either of you."

"I couldn't have helped myself if I wanted to Daddy. Besides, that's one of the things driving me so hard. I don't want to leave him." Or the rest of the herd, come to think of it. Or the men I thought of as brothers. Or the one I definitely did not think of like a brother. I picked nervously at a hang nail just thinking the last bit. "You really should come down and meet everyone. They have us riding in an afternoon show, just games really, but it is fun. Do you think Momma and you could spare some time?"

"I think your Momma would slap me silly if we didn't make the time, sweetie. Which day would be better to come down?"

"Well, Saturday nights we don't have barn chores, so if that's okay with you?"

"That sounds grand. How about we bring down a cooler full of steaks and grill our dinner? We'll bring enough for your friends, of course."

"Let me check with Sir Aaron, but I think that might be alright." Chewing on my thumbnail to quell the growling of my stomach, I considered the likely outcome. Mom would probably go overboard with making food, but I didn't think anyone would complain after a full day at the fair. "I'll let you know tomorrow and get a headcount. And Daddy, these people are like family, so be nice."

"When am I not nice?" he asked, mock affront in his voice.

"When your little girl is essentially sharing a house with all of them." I remarked dryly, knowing his silence for as good as a confession. "They are good people." Well, all except Cranston, but every family tree grew a few bad apples. I probably should just be grateful we only had the one. "Now, I need to go get a steak before my stomach eats my spleen in protest, so tell Momma I love her when she gets back from book club."

"You mean drink wine and complain about your husband club?" He laughed at the old joke, knowing full well my mother hated wine and would never complain about her husband. Except to his face. I did love that about their relationship. If they had a problem with each other they addressed it. "I love you, baby girl, and we will see you next weekend."

"Love you too, Daddy." The words and the feeling behind them left a pleasant taste in my mouth that went particularly well with the medium rare ribeye I enjoyed for dinner.

Aaron was as excited as a little kid about the prospect of having people visit. On Tuesday, I found him puttering in the equipment shed with a lawn mower, determined to get the overgrown backyard of the house ready for company. Apparently, we had a big back porch and a barbeque back there that I'd never even paid attention to, though it currently resembled the thicket surrounding sleeping beauty's castle. By the time I got back from chores he had the old walk behind running, if roughly.

"Wow, Aaron, I never would have taken you for mechanically inclined." I teased, handing him a rag and pointing at his chin so he could get the grease off of it. He must have yielded to the urge to scratch an itch that overcomes us all when our hands are dirty. "More than just a pretty face then."

His laughter vibrated with sincerity, and I reflected once more how odd it was that, for all intents and purposes, he was a handsomer man than his brother, and I felt not an ounce of attraction for him. He had become an older, trusted brother that I knew would have my back, but that was all.

"You aren't the first to say it and you won't be the last. People are always surprised when they find me changing the oil, let alone dropping a transmission. You'd think it would be Bart, but he's more of a techie and Renaissance man. Ask him to debug your computer or build you a house or train a horse. But engines turn him into a confused monkey."

Computer techie. Maybe that explained the light in the window Sunday night. I'd sunbathed in a similar light at all hours of the night over the last four years of school. "You two are full of surprises." I admitted with a grin. "But I hate being bored, so that is all to the good as far as I am concerned."

"Ah, that would explain the incessant need to be doing something. So help me, if you stick around Jo, you and Bart together could take over the world by sheer volume of effort alone." He shook his head with a rueful grin. "I can do nothing and be perfectly happy, and it took a long time for the two of us to be able to share a roof without wanting to kill each other."

Holy cheesy crackers, he was just a veritable font of information this morning, and I certainly didn't want to fish. Frankly, it made me feel like I was spying on Bart, even though I hadn't solicited anything. "Well, I'll leave you to it, boss. I've got to grab some lunch before we have to get suited up."

"Sounds good, Bowen. We'll see you in the arena. And Bart is right, you do need to eat more. You are working too hard to survive on protein bars and frozen food. It eats muscle when you do that." A gimlet stare convinced me of his seriousness.

"Tell Bart I'm the one who's supposed to be the mother hen." He grinned at that, hinting there would be some crap given to his brother for that statement. I grinned back, unrepentant. "And I'm all properly stocked up now, lots of meat and veggies and even some protein powder for smoothies, so you two can rest your worried minds on that count."

"Glad to hear it, Jo. We all want you to succeed. Even Alex and John noticed."

"Oh heavens, if Trace suddenly starts taking an interest in my food consumption, I'm going to be vexed." He started guiltily and I fixed him with a hard stare. "Aaron Drew, you are not my keeper."

The indignation in my voice had an odd effect, part mischief and part guilt in his eyes. "Look, it's not like we actually did it, we just considered it. And you've been working non-stop, even on your days off, taking care of everything but yourself."

"We?" My eyes narrowed and I put my hands to my hips, but it didn't have the desired effect at all as he burst into laughter.

"Yes, we." From behind me, the deeper voice shivered in my ear. Yet, I clung too closely to my pride to yield to my enjoyment in it, and I turned to pin Bart down.

"Well, before I know it, you two will be sitting over coffee discussing my feed schedule like I'm one of the horses. 'Oh, you know, we might want to start giving Jo some extra beet pulp at supper, she's looking a little poorly. Can't have her ribby for the next show.' What the hell!" The eyebrow went up about the same time I realized I just swore out loud, and I threw my hands in the air in disgust. "Look, now you've driven me to curse, and I'll be expecting my Gran to show up sometime this afternoon to swat my knuckles with her wooden spoon and wash my mouth out."

"Actually, there was note in your file about that, I think." Oh, that growly tease in his voice almost took the starch out of me. "Aaron, I'll get her arms, if you'll get the soap."

Out the corner of my eye, I saw Aaron headed for the sink, and I took a step back, crossing my arms over my chest. "You wouldn't dare." Bart's only response to my narrow eyed gaze was to lift the other eyebrow to match its neighbor, begging me to test that theory. Oh yes, he certainly would. I talked fast. "Well if you force feed me soap, then that'll ruin my appetite, and all your plans for me to eat more will go right out the window."

"Might be worth it, the once." mused Aaron, and I whipped toward him, eyes going immediately to the green bar of shop soap in his hand.

I stepped backward, angling for the door and away from them both. Bart made as if to close the distance and I held out my hand to stay him, shocked and a little disappointed when he stopped. The foolish portion of my brain had been looking forward to a possible scuffle, for some excuse to tangle with him.

"Just remember, Aaron, at some point I get to hit you with a big stick, and I'm going to enjoy it." I growled darkly. Aaron crossed his arms and grinned, obviously unimpressed, but then I leveled another glare at Bart. "You, on the other hand, I might just hit for fun." Then I broke out the shop door and headed for the relative safety of the house, Aaron's roar of laughter accompanying me.

Oh, prophetic words. I had to eat them later that day, as we rode up the hill to find all the knights waiting for us. Aaron was suited up and mounted on Byz, grinning at me like an idiot. Bart's grin looked a little more restrained, but only just. After practicing some solo passes with kip ups, we were declared ready to hit something. Well over their earlier teasing, I chose to focus on our instructions.

"He's just here for you to hit today. If this goes well, next week, we'll be hitting you. Treat this just like you are riding to the quintain, aiming for the upper right corner of the grand guard. Let your horse do the work of applying force, your only job is to aim." Only job, right. For once, Cranston's snort of derision matched my sentiments, and I had to fight an internal conflict. It felt too strange to agree with him in anything.

Bart had dug out a slightly thicker arming jacket for me to use under my armor, after the depth of my bruises last week. I'd argued that no amount of bubble wrap would keep me from getting hurt. He'd fired back with he was only trying to protect his investment of time, and it had stung a little. It took me a few minutes to realize I should be thankful for the comment. Anything to put distance between us. Now, I could focus on the business at hand. Even if my heart felt bruised.

That extra thickness proved frustrating, bunching under my armpit when I leveled my lance, resulting in three near misses.

I'd be so close to catching the edge and then it was close, but no cigar. As I came to a halt on one end of the lyst, growling with frustration, Alex rapped his knuckles on my leg to get my attention. I tipped my head down as far as it could go and tried to focus past the blood pounding in my ears.

"Jo, you are trying way too hard. Focus just a little further inside where you've been putting your eyes. And pretend you are bending the lance around your ribs, it'll feel more secure."

I nodded as best I could and tapped the butt of the lance against my leg to signal I heard him. Then he stepped back and lifted his arm to signal the other end of the lyst. Muffled words, telling me to come about, but I focused on his hand, waiting for the circular motion.

As much as the helm limited so much of your vision, it felt like the difference between standard sights on a rifle and a scope. The scope made it easier to concentrate your focus, to ignore the visual white noise usually present. Eros coiled up under me like a snake and launched us forward, so sure of his job, and it gave me an extra edge of confidence. My eyes landed where I had practiced, and I slid them just a few inches inside that mark, bringing my lance to bear with hardly a fumble. The closer he got, the more I tightened my gaze, until all I could see was the one-inch square where I wanted my lance to go. A jolt came that made my palm tingle, followed by a rush of confusion as I came to a halt, Eros roaching his back under me in a way he never had before when my hand closed on the reins. Did I do something wrong?

But then Trace jumped up and down like a hyperactive terrier, and Bart stood far enough back that I could see his grin. He nodded once and suddenly, I felt light as a feather. I'd done it. I looked up at my lance, and while I'd been hoping to see it in pieces, it remained intact. Logically, I knew a broken lance was too much to ask for on my first hit, but the disappointment fueled my desire to go again. Breaking a lance was the next rung on my ladder, and I wanted it something fierce.

I rode to the mounting block slightly miffed, wanting to go again right away, but to be fair, everyone needed to get in at least one shot for the afternoon. John met me there, and pulled off the helm, offering me a drink of water as we watched Lee take his turn. The first pass made me wince with worry, flying too far inside and sliding across Aaron's body until he carried the lance away with him. Lee almost tipped off himself before letting go, saving it by a hair at the last second as Cappy threw his neck up to catch him. The lance bounced on Byz's neck for a couple strides until Aaron could get a hand on it enough to shove it off. Luckily, no one was hurt, but a long conversation with Bart waited for Fillmore at the end of the lyst.

I averted my eyes, not wanting him to have an audience and John caught my eye instead. "You know, that was pretty impressive, Jo."

The compliment caught me off guard, and I knitted my brows together, testing it for truth. "You mean, for a girl?"

"No, I mean for anyone. Usually, it goes more like Fillmore. I was a hopeless mess my first few practices, not just the first passes." He shrugged his shoulders and smiled. "But I was also a less competent horseman than you, so perhaps that is the difference."

"I don't know, John. I don't feel like that good a horseman when I'm wearing armor. It's like an out of body experience." My lips quirked crookedly at the admission of fault.

"Well, let me put it another way. Bart has never, and I mean never, let anyone but himself or Aaron ride Eros in the lyst. He sat the whole time Bart was away, and no one but Bart has ridden him since. Except you. You move like he does in the saddle, unconscious of your balance and at the same time completely aware. And for Bart to put you on his stallion smacks of a compliment far more than words can say."

The compliment warmed me, but my brain took off like a shot at the new information. Bart went away? When? Why? It took a few minutes of silence to chew on all those questions, my gloved fingers dragging gratefully through Eros's mane as we watched Lee go again. There was a pass where he cast the lance away as soon as it bobbled, nearly bouncing off Cappy's neck, and another where it seemed like it came together, then missed within one stride of the canter, bounced high and to the outside. Just a guess but he looked too scared of making his first mistake again, not wanting to risk hurting anyone. Being afraid wouldn't fly.

"I'd ride against you, Jo, right now, as you stand." I looked back to John sharply, the sincerity in his blue eyes completely humbling. "I'd not worry for my safety or Tucks. And that is the best compliment *I* can give." At that point, I did the only thing I could in the face of such trust. I said thank you like the polite girl my parents raised me to be and asked for another drink of water.

My second go landed me two hits out of four, but by the fourth my shoulder and arm burned with fatigue. I needed to start doing my lance practice in armor to accommodate the extra weight. As soon as John took my helm off I dismounted to tend Eros, rubbing his prominent brow bones and fine muzzle in thanks. John scooted over on the block to give me room to sit once I'd loosened the stallion's girth, and Eros stood beside me with his head inches from my knee, watching the goings on with as much interest as I was.

Cranston landed the largest number of hits, though I got the impression he was trying to punch in at the last minute rather than letting the horse carry the shot. The blows skipped off once they landed, twice twisting the lance across his body, though he saved it much better than Fillmore.

"One more thing Jo, just so you know I'm not blowing smoke up your skirt," John started and I interjected quickly.

"John Barry, does your wife know you are blowing smoke up anyone's skirt but hers?" He flushed hard and his eyes darted away, swallowing several times before he could meet my eye again.

"Caroline would have my guts for garter straps if she ever heard me talking about another woman's skirt." I chuckled at the truth of it. Sweet Caroline Barry was just as fierce as her husband in the right circumstances, and I wouldn't want to cross her. Apparently, she was a champion fencer and archer in her own right. "But back to what I was trying to say. The best compliment you could have received, you got."

167

I raised my eyebrows when he pointed at Eros with a smile. "That stud is a pussy cat in the lyst, generally. Except when Bart rode him to joust, he used to make the ugliest faces at the other horses, like being with Bart made him fiercer." I'd seen how they were together, so this held no surprise for me. "The thing is, I haven't seen that face in years. Until today, with you."

It began to feel like some of the biggest hits I would endure were going to have nothing to do with the lance. Because at that moment, you could have knocked me over with a feather.

That night also put me on my figurative butt, but in an even more emotional fashion. I was checking my email, expecting something from my father on a prospective buyer for Abby, but just below my father's message sat one addressed to Lady Josephine from an address I didn't recognize.

'Hi Lady Josephine,

You have a really pretty name, and my brother showed me pictures of you at the fair. I love your long hair. I used to have long hair, but it fell out. Mommy said it will grow back even prettier once my cancer goes away. I wish I could come see you, for real, but the doctors said I shouldn't go to places with that many people, because my immune system can't fight regular sicknesses right now. Maybe next year I can come see you joust! Until then, I'm going to wear the t-shirt Seth bought me at the faire, so I can remember to be a fighter while I get my chemo. I hope you are kicking boy's butts, and that you write back. Mom said you might be too busy, so I won't be mad if you don't.

With Hope,

Marley'

She included a picture, and it took twenty minutes before I could look at it without tears burning my eyes. Her head was covered in a bright purple cap, and her eyes popped from the screen a vivid blue, but it couldn't cover the fact that the body wearing our t-shirt was too thin, worn from her struggle. Her skin was pale and thin, and the bruises under her eyes broke my heart even more. Yes, indeed, my struggles were a weak and piteous thing in comparison to hers.

My brain kept trying to function around the pain in my chest, looking for an angle to work, anything I could do to help, but I couldn't see past it. In frustration and guilt, I slammed my laptop closed and stalked outside, seeking the only refuge I had. Ro. It didn't even seem fair that I could go outside and find some solace when Marley was stuck in a hospital, fighting for her life.

Ro lay curled up under the tree where we usually snoozed together, and he lifted his head, but didn't move to get up. Despite the tension in my chest, I relaxed my body to reassure him, incredibly touched when he allowed me to come to his side without getting up. A truer profession of his trust I could not have received. That's where Bart found me, curled up against Ro's side like his bulk could protect me from my own heartache. I didn't move when I heard the gate, barely turned my head when he folded his legs and sat in the grass, letting the silence get heavier and heavier.

"You alright, Bowen?"

I'd like to say the dam broke and I spilled my aching guts right away, but it took a lot of stops and starts to tell him everything I knew. Bless his heart, he just listened, nodding to let me know he was paying attention. Silence with Bart had two flavors: the peppery bite of censure or the soothing reassurance of consideration, and he employed the second to great effect that night. Wedged between Ro and him, I dug past the emotions to something I could actually do.

"I'd like to go see her, under the company's banner." He nodded for me to continue, and my heart eased a little more, now that my heart no longer spun in circles. "Maybe take her a t-shirt, a piece of lance signed by everybody."

"Good ideas, but I think we can improve on that." His smile felt warm in the darkness, barely visible, but still a potent thing to experience. In fact, if anything, the darkness added an intimacy I wouldn't have expected. "We could take your armor."

"Who's this we, white boy?" Throwing his words back at him made me smile, a real one that I could feel in my heart, warming me at last.

A brief chuckle. "I remember something about not being able to unsee something. Well, in this case, I can't unhear it. And if you take your armor, you are going to want help getting in and out of it."

My turn to nod and smile. "Thank you. Maybe now I can go in and write her back without crying."

"You remember what I said that first day with Ro? It applies here too. Your tears won't help her and will only hurt you. You are doing something for her Jo, doing what you can to help her do what she has to do. Give her an extra bit of fight, but realize you can't fight it for her any more than you could for Ro."

Silence again, settling comfortably between us like an old blanket, and somehow, the dark intimacy made my brain run out my mouth. "I wish it could be like this always. Just being able to talk to you makes everything make sense. I hate when we aren't speaking to each other."

I couldn't even hear him breathe and I shrunk against Ro's side, afraid to have broken the bridge again. Then he split the silence with words I hadn't been expecting. "Me too, Jo. You and I could be good friends. But for now, we'll just have to dance around each other until we know if you are staying or going. Aaron said he told you there was work for you whether you jousted or not, but you seemed upset by the offer."

It took a minute to cobble together an answer around the maelstrom of emotions threatening my sanity. "I don't think I could stay if I couldn't joust. My heart is in the lyst now, and it would be like slowly starving to death standing outside the finest restaurant in the world." I shook my head against the threat of tears, not willing to yield to the weakness twice in one night.

"I understand, better than most." A bone deep ache lay in that admission, but he pushed past it. "But this is family, and I know *all* of us want you to be part of it."

171

I couldn't see his eyes in the darkness, but I could feel them like a physical touch, closing the distance between us. "I don't know, Bart. I went to college, got a degree so I could make something out of myself, not be a glorified horse groom. I'm willing to table that to joust, but I can't commit to less than that."

"I understand." Acceptance. It felt incredibly freeing to have it from him, but it hurt just the same when I went to bed that night, the darkness feeling closer than ever.

❤❤❤

We arranged to visit Marley on Friday morning. Aaron helped load my armor trunk in the truck and sent us on our way with not just a t-shirt, but a few signed photos and a stuffed horse that reminded me of Eros a little. Her parents had sounded thrilled with the visit, though her brother was upset to miss it because of swim team practice. Bart packed an extra gift for him, since I never would have heard from her if not for his chat with me. The drive into Louisville was relatively painless, since most folks were already at their day jobs, and we pulled into the children's hospital with plenty of time to spare.

We received no shortage of odd looks from people as he helped me armor right there in the parking lot so we wouldn't have to drag the trunk in. Those looks doubled as I clanked through the lobby and got directions to the oncology unit, one of their aides guiding us up so we wouldn't be stopped. The scent of antiseptic burned my nostrils after spending weeks practically living with the horses, though they were trying to cover it up with floral scents that were anything but natural. The nurse in charge met us at the floor desk and asked a few pointed questions about our health history, just to make sure we weren't carrying anything in. Once we checked out she pointed us down the hall, but half way there Bart tugged me to a stop.

"What?" Being there had me edgy. Kids were supposed to be running around causing trouble, not attached to machines and tubes, trying to survive the betrayal of their own bodies.

"Your hair, she said something about your hair. You should let it down."

I reached for my braid, but the armor limited my range of motion, and I couldn't grab hold of it. Bart stilled me by the shoulders and took matters in his own hands, my cheeks slowly flushing as he pulled out the rubber brand and carefully undid the plait. To make matters worse, he stepped around my side and his hand moved under the heavy mass of waves to settle it over one shoulder. I almost bolted when his fingers brushed the back of my neck, but kept myself still by the simple expedient of not breathing.

"Better?" I finally growled, hiding my reaction in impatience.

"Perfect." He really needed to stop saying things like that. But the distraction got me to the door, and then he rapped his knuckles on the frame, leaning in to announce me, his face instantly softening. "Milady Marley, Lady Josephine Bowen requests an audience."

Her squeal of glee pulled me in the door, and there she sat, a feeding tube in her nose, and various lines running under the edges of her Gallant Company t-shirt. Absolutely, radiantly beautiful. She looked alive in a way I couldn't describe, as if fighting for that life made her more of this earth than the rest of us mortals.

"Lady Josephine, I can't believe you really came." Her mother squeezed her thin shoulders before stepping away to let me closer. Marley held a hand out for me and I folded it carefully in mine, grateful I'd left off the gloves so I could lend her some of my warmth. Being encased in steel didn't leave you much room for softness, so I gave what I could.

"Of course I came. The Gallant Company of Knights prides itself on keeping our word, and I needed to bring you some gifts from everyone."

Her forehead shifted up, eyebrows gone due to the chemo, and her chapped lips folded into a perfect bow. "You didn't have to do that. This is already way more than I thought. Maybe I could share some presents with the other kids here? Not everyone gets special visitors like this."

Bart cleared his throat and Marley and I both looked over at him. The man wore his best, the same split surcoat I'd first admired, over tall black boots, with a wide metal studded belt. I couldn't blame the girl her faint blush—I'd have been twitter pated at her age too. Oh, who was I kidding? I was twitter pated now. "I've actually brought some things you can share with the other children, at the behest of our Captain, Sir Aaron Drew. Should you require more, we will provide them."

We showed her photos of the horses and I told her stories about training. Bart nodded along and agreed in all the right places, standing just on the other side of her bed as I held her hand. I imagined us standing guard for her against the wretched disease until she could stand on her own again. Marley's mom took photos, a flinch in her eyes that would make me more tolerant the next time my mother wanted to take my picture. I unloaded items from the leather satchel Bart had brought, and Marley was more excited over the horse than any of the rest of it, immediately endearing her even more to me.

We invited her to come to the farm and visit all the horses when she felt better, if her parents were okay with it, and she lit up like a crystal chandelier I once saw in a castle, making shadows of the rest of us in her excitement. She flagged fast after that, and I signed her t-shirt with a sharpie Bart had in his belt, blazoning '*Fight like a girl*' in huge letters. Leaving her with a kiss on her hand, I promised to come back after I won my knighthood and she wished me luck, though I wished she would keep all that luck for herself.

I'd never been around anyone but Bart who could make silence seem as loud as conversation or as quiet as peace. Anyone but the horses that is, though theirs usually didn't carry so much intensity. The whole experience left me a little numb, which made touching him a little easier as he helped me out of my armor. Yet, those little touches, as impersonal as they were, no different from anyone else who had ever helped me, felt meaningful. They anchored me back in the real world, pulled me back from the edge of the rabbit hole one warm knuckle or fingertip at a time.

"So, what now, Lady Bowen?" he asked, once we were back in the truck and rattling down the road. "We've got two hours before we have to be back at the farm for the afternoon lesson."

"Ice cream. I need ice cream." My inner child was crying right now, scared for this little girl that was already so precious to me. He didn't say a word, just aimed us for the nearest 29 Scoops, and quietly enjoyed a double scoop of fudge ripple while I dammed up my aching heart with cookie dream and mocha brownie. We sat on the edge of the tailgate, soaking up the sunshine, and in no hurry. Yeah, we could be friends alright. If only there were enough ice cream in the world to make that feel like enough. But then my butt would be too big to fit in armor, and where would I be then?

Saturday. I began to love weekends, really embracing the insanity of it all. Knowing Marley was fighting her disease had lit a new fire under me that would have been tough to snuff out. Her mother had emailed to thank us for coming, and apparently, the hospital wanted to have us out again with a couple more knights to visit more children. One and all, the idea had met with enthusiasm, except for maybe Cranston, but I couldn't see him doing anything charitable unless he would get publicity. Ooh, publicity! My marketing brain latched onto that and worried it like a hound as we fed the horses. It would be good for the Company and for the hospital. I'd need to contact the hospital PR people, but the possibilities were exciting.

Aaron gave me tickets to leave at the gate for my parents, and with the cooler temperatures and cloud cover, I enjoyed the walk. I caught Mari coming in on the way back, so we chatted on the move as she filled me in on Max and Mal's antics the night before. They had apparently staged a dinosaur battle royale under the kitchen table that had spilled into the bathtub when it was time to get ready for bed. It would probably take a week for the baseboards in the bathroom to dry.

Later, as I helped Aaron get armored he kept looking at me with an indecipherable furrow in his brow. I tried to ignore it, but by the time I was buckling his breastplate together it got on my nerves. "What?"

"Nothing, Bowen, just trying to put a puzzle together in my head." He shook that head, his over long locks brushing against the joints in his armor. Those strands were at that annoying stage between short enough to ignore and not long enough to tie back. They made me want a pair of scissors.

"Well, stop looking at me like I'm one of the pieces and you don't know what to do with it." I groused as I got his pauldrons on. "I've got better things to do than worry about the mess in your pretty head."

He laughed, and the cloud over his head cleared, at least enough to get us through the joust. Surprisingly, Trace beat him out by a point, Aaron's last lance unscathed while Trace's well-nigh exploded. A good deal of back slapping happened before we could settle down enough to greet the crowd, and a larger throng than his normal set of groupie's clamored for Sir Trace's attention. But as I followed along beside Aaron, managing Byz's crowd interactions, a familiar voice broke over the crowd.

"Jo!"

Immediately, I scanned the crowd for my Dad, thankful for the height I got from him. His straw cowboy hat gave my eyes an easy target, and I waved him closer, trying not to squeak with excitement. See, I did have *some* self-control. As the crowd in front of Aaron thinned Mom appeared just in front of me and flung her arms around my neck, making Byz snort with dismay and take a step back. I hugged her with one arm, keeping my hand soft on the reins as I pulled him forward again.

"Josie, you look stunning, baby!" Mom had been calling me pretty since infanthood, but my cheeks colored anyway, recognizing the sincerity of her praise. I had a feeling I'd be hitting the costume vendors with her later to do some shopping, as she loved dressing me up and I'd been resistant to the bodice idea before. She would love Mari, for sure.

Mom looked pretty stunning herself in a burgundy renaissance dress, the waist nipped in tight with long, flowy sleeves. Neither her nor Dad were slouches, and kept pretty trim figures just from staying so active on the farm, and she blushed prettily when Aaron took her hand and kissed it.

"Mistress Bowen, might I commend you on cutting a ravishing figure and raising an amazing daughter?"

Dad pretended to glower at Aaron for a second, the laced front shirt he wore his only concession to the surroundings, and it stretched tight across his shoulders when he crossed his arms. But then Mom tucked herself against his side and he scooped up her hand and brushed his lips over her knuckles, making her titter when his mustache tickled her skin. Yeah, my parents were *those* parents, the ones that embarrassed their child in public. She hooked her fingers in the belt loops of his wranglers and hugged him close before releasing him so he could greet me.

"Seriously, you two are incorrigible." I mumbled as he tugged me against his chest, the rail of the arena cutting into my stomach for a second. But I loved it just the same and hugged him back twice as tight. As soon as he let me go I made our excuses, the crowds now quiet enough to cross the road to the encampment, and we all marched back over, accompanied by Steve's warning cries.

"Horses coming through, war horses coming through."

Once I finished my work with Aaron, and made sure of Byz's comfort as well, I let my parents in the gate to introduce them to everyone. Well, all but Cranston, who had disappeared with a few guys from the Celtic drum band as soon as he took care of Trace. I tried not to let it sully my mood. I mean, I took breaks too, but Cranston disappeared at every available second. It felt like he didn't even want to be here anymore.

"Mari, this is Elaine and David Bowen." Mari slid off her usual perch on the counter, where she could prop up her artificial limb, and immediately hugged my mother. Yes, they would be thick as thieves by days' end, I knew it. Then she turned to my Dad with a more serious look in her eyes, firmly shaking his hand.

"Sir, I'd guess you for a military man, an officer if I'm any judge." Dad looked to me and I raised my hands in the universe gesture of 'it wasn't me'. Mari grabbed his attention again quickly. "No, Jo doesn't have anything to do with it, you just have an air about you that rang familiar."

"Did you serve Miss?" Dad asked, measuring Mari with his eyes. I breathed carefully so I didn't miss the answer, hoping to add more pieces to the puzzle I've been worrying at.

"Yes sir, First Sergeant Marilyn Cassidy at your service. Now, just plain old Mari, wife, mother to twin boys and friend to your daughter. Though once a Marine, always a Marine." Her eyes flicked to me, the bright green warm with affection, but then she looked past me with a widening grin.

"What, Mari, we're not friends anymore?" rumbled over my left ear, and I tried not to flush at how close he felt. Bart slid past me to move in next to Mari. "You've thrown over one of your oldest friends for the new and shiny?"

"Well, she is much prettier than you, and she lets me dress her up." Mari teased, poking him in the ribs with her elbow. Well, more like his waist, anyway. She was petite and he definitely was not.

"I won't argue the prettier part." Yes, I flushed then, fanning myself with my hat as if against the growing heat of the day. "And I'm sure she looks much better in a dress than me."

He chuckled before offering his hand to my mother, pulling it up just like Aaron had. At the last second, he pressed his forehead to the back of her hand instead, a gesture of fealty that touched me more than I'd like to admit. Then he straightened, his height a match for my father's I noticed.

"Mistress Elaine, I owe you a debt of gratitude, for raising such a lovely daughter, and no doubt for much of her strength of character."

"She's a treasure, for sure." My mom agreed, smiling brightly before her eyes flicked from him to me with a curiosity I didn't care for at all. "This is my husband, David. And you are?"

He turned to my Dad and they clasped hands with a manly slap of palms, their forearms flexing as they tested each other. "My apologies, I'm Sir Bartholomew Clark, also lately of the Marines."

Dad's grip immediately relaxed, and a smile lifted the edge of his mustache. I, on the other hand, only grew more tense. Seriously, a Marine? Did he have to keep adding layers to his already considerable appeal? Stuck somewhere between heaven and hell, I clung desperately to my conviction that he was too old for me. Wasn't he? The argument began to weaken and I didn't know how long I'd last before it crumbled under the weight of my attraction. Not that he'd ever see me as anything other than a sister in arms, of course.

"Glad to meet you both." Dad said, nodding to both Bart and Mari. "I've been out for five years now, after retiring from the Air Force. Nothing quite as tough as what you've no doubt experienced, but I was following in a long line of family tradition."

"It's always a pleasure to meet someone else who was called to serve, sir. Mari and I aren't hung up on branches, we all have the same roots and grow from the same tree." Stop being so charming, Bart, you are killing me. Slowly. With splinters and shards that I doubted I'd ever dislodge.

"True enough. Now what's this I hear you've been leaving my daughter beat up by days' end?" Dad spoke playfully enough, but thankfully, Bart caught the serious light in my parent's eyes.

"Well, I've given her all the tools and skills she needs to hit and be hit. Thus far, we've only had her hitting things, and she's proved adept, as you'll see this afternoon. The real bruising is coming this week when Aaron starts hitting back."

Mom paled, and I stepped forward to take her hand. "It's alright, Mom. Sir Clark has me in the best armor, and I'm riding his very own horse, so I'm as prepared as I can be."

I steered her over to the horses, introducing her and my Dad to Eros first, and being horse people at heart, the distraction worked. Hillary got folded into my Mom's arms instantly, and one by one, the members of the troupe succumbed to her warmth. Yeah, Mom had never met a stranger. Even in foreign countries where we didn't know the language, her smile and congeniality won people over.

I let myself be dragged out for lunch when Aaron reminded me to get something to eat before the noon joust, and Mom wasted no time, immediately heading for a turkey leg. It used to be we had to share one, but with my workload, I asked for my own, and picked the bones clean.

"Are you getting enough to eat, sweetie?" she asked as we lounged in the shade near a stage, listening to a trio of musicians play a Celtic reel. "You feel thinner."

"Just a little, but I'm working on it." I groused, not liking the scrutiny. But then Marley's mom came to mind, and I softened. "I'm just having to learn to eat enough for my workload is all. Ten-hour work days are not sustainable on the same food I ate in school."

"Alright. Well, we'll feed you all up tonight, and you'll have plenty of leftovers to keep you going for a bit." She set her turkey leg down on a piece of wax paper, and cleaned her fingers off with a wet nap pulled from her purse, eyeing me critically. "I don't want to see you worn down to a nub."

Truthfully, I really liked my body right then, though there wasn't much soft about it anymore. Muscle had developed where a layer of baby fat had once been, and while I wasn't cut like some sort of sports model, that lack of definition actually lent me a bit of femininity. My waist had toned, leaving me slightly curvy where I'd never been before, and I hadn't really paid it any attention until Mari laced me into the bodice.

I settled for something more diplomatic in answer. "I'm taking care of it, I promise. But all this hard work is necessary, Mom. I can't tell you how hard it is to just keep yourself upright in armor."

She insisted on going to the shoppe my bodice had come from, and I yielded to the temptation of a second one, mainly to keep me from having to wash my costume every Saturday night. One less bit of work would be worth every penny pulled from my savings, and it would be lovely to have something new to wear tomorrow. This one shone a deep blue, which would go with the chemise I already had, but in the interest of laundry, I purchased another, opting for white. It would be easier to get stains out of, and cool on hot days, though I knew it would end up being a dirt magnet.

Mom bought several items, and I caught her in whispered conference with the pixie haired girl at the front of the booth that made me think I'd be seeing a gift later in the day. She really did like to surprise me, even if subtlety wasn't her strong suit.

For the second joust my parents headed over early to pick good seats, leaving me alone with the crew. I threw myself into getting John armored while Lee assisted Alex, needing something to do with the extra energy coursing through me. Bart walked in just as I latched John's gorget, the collar that protected his neck.

"I've got it now, Bowen." He stepped forward to lift the chain maile skirting that came next, but I covered the short step between us and closed my hands over it as well.

"No, I like herding this particular cat, you go stand around and look pretty." John busted up in giggles immediately, pointing at Bart briefly before turning away to stifle the laughter against his knuckles. Bartholomew Clark, baddest of the bad, hiding the biggest softy I'd ever met, actually blushed, albeit faintly.

I lowered my voice slightly, trying to soften his embarrassment at the hands of my smart mouth. "Seriously, one masterwork blade to another, let me do this. I need to be busy or nerves will eat me alive."

Understanding lightened his eyes, and he nodded sharply, yielding the heavy chain fabric to my grasp. I turned back to John, who was busy wiping his eyes, raising my eyebrow in silent censure. It flew right over John's head, close enough to shave him bald, but too far away for him to grasp around his amusement. "Seriously, Josephine, calling Bart pretty? I've never heard anything funnier."

Biting my lip against a reply, I managed to get John kitted out without yielding to the temptation to crack him on his thick pate. While Bart had a certain rugged handsomeness and intensity that made him appealing, I began to understand that his heart had truly made him beautiful to me.

I tried my best to keep my attention on the joust, despite my parents cheering from the front row, and the temptation to watch Bart enliven the crowd. Alex and John gave as good a show as I'd ever seen, as if there was something extra in the air driving them on. They'd gotten the crowd good and rowdy, cheering back and forth over who had the better supporters, and taunting each other with insults before donning their helms. All I could hope was that they wouldn't freak my parents out in the process. The first pass yielded just a soft click of lances on targets, but a sharpness still flavored the air, and the next pass made use of that razor's edge.

None of the times I'd ever attended a fair left me prepared for the collision that came to pass, the sharp crack of wood like lightening striking, my ears burning as they landed their shots in perfect synchronicity. Both rocked back in their saddles, and my abs ached in sympathy as they tried to right themselves. Still, gravity proved too much for John almost immediately, and he slid sideways from Tuck's back, landing with a thunk that shook the dirt beneath my feet, taking out a stanchion in the process.

I was on the move immediately, though my eyes were still fixed on Alex as J.T. shambled toward the end. Momentum conspired to tip him off his horse's shoulder as they came to a stop, and I winced before giving my full attention to John. Again, Aaron met me at his side, but this time, as we helped John to his feet, a groan of pain came from inside the helm. I quickly raised the visor, revealing a forced grin that he leveled on Aaron.

"You pulled a double, John. It was textbook. You okay to continue?"

The grin broadened, though his skin looked paler than normal, and his breaths came shallow. "Get me back in the saddle. I can fake it through two more passes." My skin suddenly felt clammy, but worry for my friend overrode any fear that might have been creeping in.

Clearly, he favored his right arm, keeping it close to his body, but once back in the saddle, he waved to the crowd. They cheered like wild things as the two men nodded to each other and

182

returned to the lyst, John using his lance hand to steer Tuck into place. The sweet Belgian knew his job, and he waited with no hand upon the reins as John received his lance. Truly, the next two passes were nothing but display for the crowd, Alex barely tapping John's grand guard both times and John only managing one touch. But that didn't stop them from meeting in front of the crowd to exchange a victorious fist bump.

After Alex was declared the winner John muddled through greeting his fans, though he bowed out of signing anything after the first attempt. As a left hander, the pain was simply too great, though he told the kids his pen ran out of ink. Immediately, I stepped forward, informing the gathered people that Tuck needed to go back to the barn to get a drink, and John rewarded my cover with a weak smile, falling in beside us for the short walk.

A quiet, waiting energy shrouded the encampment as we arrived, and Hillary took Tuck from me so I could help get John out of armor. Even with Aaron and Bart helping, John looked close to fainting when we slid his arm out of the steel that had protected him from greater harm. We sat him down immediately, and he sucked on a bottle of water as we removed the rest of the pieces like a high speed NASCAR pit crew. At last, Bart inspected his arm, then rose to grab a radio to contact the first aid crew. As I headed out the door Caroline burst through the back gate, her eyes gimlet hard as she hunted for her husband.

"In here, Lady." I said, pointing back the way I had come, and moving out of her path as she aimed herself in the door, her skirts smacking my legs with the force of her passing. As much as John was a treasure, he had a match to beat all matches in his wife.

Knowing I had nothing else to do, I headed for the back gate to get Ivan ready, grateful for something to distract me from worthless worrying. He greeted me with a hopeful snuffle, and I considered the idea of getting myself a belt pouch to keep goodies in. While I'd never been one to believe in spoiling horses with treats, I didn't mind doling them out if the horse asked politely. Ivan had learned quickly that if I said no, I meant no, and it had made him much more mannerly in all our interactions. I'd groomed him earlier, and as I threw on his saddle, I paused for a moment to press my nose against his neck to steady myself.

While John likely had no more than a broken wrist or arm, it would keep him from jousting the remainder of the faire. Besides John being my friend, his accident gave credence to Bart's earlier warnings about injuries. I remembered Bart's admission to being hurt, which kept him from jousting even now, leading me to believe his injury must have been much worse. Flames curled along my spine to think of him wounded, giving me even more sympathy for the worry Caroline must be enduring.

Unable to hide in my work any longer, I untied the big black from the trailer and headed for the gate, my feet picking up speed when John emerged, Caroline on his heels. His arm was splinted heavily, but his face had a lot more color, and I sighed in relief.

"Josephine, come here, dear." he called, and Caroline's smile assured me of a welcome as he hugged my waist with his good arm. The smile lines around his eyes were deeper, making me wonder how much pain they masked, but I wasn't going to draw attention to it. "I wanted to say thank you for your help today. An injury on the field isn't easy to deal with, but you handled it like a champ."

"I get it, John. The show must go on." Caroline's faint grimace disagreed, but that was only her love for him showing through.

"And that, as much as your hard work and horsemanship, tells me you are meant for this, Miss Josie." Yeah, I blushed a little. If you hadn't noticed by now, compliments made me uncomfortable. "I'm thinking we won't be making it to the barbeque tonight, once the ER gets me straightened out, so give your parents my regrets."

"They'll be sad to miss you both, but I just want you to heal fast. You told me you'd dance with me as I stood, and once you are declared fit to compete, I'm going to hold you to it." The grin he answered me with looked much more himself, and that alone reassured me.

"Dancing?" Caroline interjected, a delicate arch in her fine ebony brows as she stared expectantly at her husband.

"Now, darling, you know you are the only woman I'd ever waltz across the floor." He took her hand and pulled it to his cheek momentarily, a comfortable sort of gesture that reminded me of my parents and how much they adored each other.

"Oh, stop you flatterer. I'm going to go get the car, you stay here and reassure Josephine." She kissed his cheek and gave me a brief hug. "Don't let this stop you, Jo. The whole ladies court is rooting for you, and he'll be back next weekend, even if it's just to ground crew." Then she hustled off as quickly as her velvet skirts allowed, and John reached for my hand.

"I want you to promise me, Josephine, that you'll keep fighting." Worry creased his forehead and his pale eyes were icy hot on mine. "Fight for what is in your heart, whatever that may be, and today, I want you to fight for yourself."

"I wouldn't know how not to fight John." I smiled ruefully, squeezing his fingers, heartened by the strength of his grip.

"You are wonderful, Jo, and no matter what, I'll be back to watch you take the field for the first time. You've kept me together too many times for me not to return the favor." He kissed my cheek briefly as a car pulled close, and I tugged Ivan out of the road to make room. Then he slid into the vehicle and was gone, leaving me to gather my scattered thoughts and head back into the fray.

As I waited by the fence for Cranston and Lee to get their own mounts ready, I stayed busy, answering questions for passersby. Mom and Mari were indeed, thick as thieves, their heads bent together like little girls on a playground, and Dad had fallen into helping Kory and Jeff with tearing apart the broken lances for parts. Aaron and Bart were making me nervous, in low voiced conference by the armor room, their jaws so hard you could probably drive nails with them.

Once the ten-minute call came the three of us mounted up and followed Bart across the busy road, and I took a few minutes to warm up, losing myself in schooling Ivan. I had sensitive, cranky Abby to thank for that lesson. She had always taken exception to my moods, resenting the extra baggage when there was work to do.

Once Bart made a greeting to the Queen and set Lee loose on the course, he eased Eros up beside me to watch, but I could feel questions behind his silent observation.

"You okay, Sir?" I'd never call him Bart, not in front of God and everyone. Someone might ferret out the truth of my affections, and I couldn't afford the risk.

I'd say he startled, but it didn't show as a jump or a flinch. Only an increase in tension, as he stared so hard after Lee that

Eros started to sidle in anticipation. The instant the stallion side stepped, the horseman I knew came to the fore, and bled all the excess physical tightness away. "I'm fine, Bowen." I wanted to call him a liar, particular when he met my eyes, an overabundance of worry in his gaze. "Are you?"

That's what the anxiety stemmed from? They were worried about me? I watched Lee deliver a solid throw of the spear, and clapped appropriately as he passed, returning his grin before looking back to Bart. Weighing my words with all due seriousness, I told him the truth. "I'm ready to ride."

While the haze of clouds remained overhead the ones in his eyes cleared immediately. Truly, it was such a comfort to have one person who really got me. I didn't have to explain, didn't have to convince him. If I told him something was so, he knew it was, no clarification needed.

"Good." His gruff voice couldn't cover his relief. "You are going last, so put on a show. We need something to cheer about." Just like I didn't have to explain, neither did he. He wasn't talking about the crowd, or the cast members, or my parents. He meant we, as in the team, and I'd never felt more a part of the crew as I did right then.

We applauded Lee as he managed a bit of showmanship for the crowd, whooping it up when the girls from the bawdy wenches show shimmied their hips for him. Folks at a renaissance faire tended to consider just about every of form sexual harassment law as less of a rule, more of a guideline, and then jumped on the wrong side of that line with both feet and bells on. Lee was obviously reaping the benefits, both in attention and the confidence it lent him.

As Bart rode forward to herald in Cranston, I truly was happy for Fillmore. He was young, sowing some oats, and since I knew him to be respectful, even somewhat shy, I wasn't worried about the girls he hung out with. If I even considered Cranston doing the same, my skin crawled with revulsion. No matter how charming, how handsome, he lay like a snake in the grass just waiting to strike.

Then there was me. I didn't sow oats, didn't dally with men without being in a serious long term relationship. A total of two guys, in my almost twenty-three years, and even with that kind of devotion to them, to myself, it didn't last. I wanted what my parents had, if I went down that road, and I usually ran men off on the first date with my, ahem, 'forceful' personality. Never girly enough, too goal oriented, and too intense. Mostly, I didn't let it bother me, staying focused on my objectives, and right now that didn't include indulging in groupies like Lee and Cranston were enjoying.

Hawk was on his game today, his bullishness channeled toward the job at hand as they ran the lyst, his rider garnering two rings. Nothing if not consistent in his need to showboat, Cranston almost missed his spear throw entirely when he spun it overhead in a flair maneuver that the crowd loved. But his quintain pass would to be tough to beat, a full five revolutions that the crowd counted out loud until it came to a stop. Once he made his gallop around the arena to their enthusiastic cheers and received his volley of kisses from the ladies' court, I moved to meet Bart in front of the dais.

"Your Majesty, Lady Bowen comes to defend her reputation for accuracy and heart, her own family here to witness the attempt. Would You give Your blessing for her success?" Bart looked right at me as he said accuracy, and I nodded shortly, a tiny grin creeping over my lips. Yes, I knew, I hadn't forgotten.

"Lady Bowen, We would have you display your skill with horse and arms, so that you might accompany Us on Our afternoon sojourn. You have Our blessing for luck, as Lord Cranston has laid down a fine score already."

"My thanks, Your Majesty, would that God and providence allow me to entertain sufficiently, for I too hope to walk the streets of this grand festival in Your shadow." Dad had to be grinning like a mad man. He'd coached me through a long spate during high school where I had anxiety speaking in public, and you couldn't get more public than this.

Ivan turned with a leg against his side, already rolling the bit against his tongue with excitement, and I knew he would take some tactful riding. But if I could manage him through the first two goals, I'd be able to let him run for the quintain—that might be the only way I could win. Cranston had me beat for body weight, and I'd need speed to counterbalance that.

Breathing deeply, I stopped to take the ring lance from Hillary, thankful to see her there, as she had less flinch factor than Kory. If I rode past her at the canter, she would hold steady. Ivan walked to the end of the lyst, though his back was curled up with impatience, and I backed him in just as if we were setting up to take a pass, asking him for calm. He jigged sideways with the drumroll from the musicians in the Queen's gallery, but I couldn't begrudge it for the dramatic effect, as the crowd waited with hushed breaths. The pause was barely more than a few, but the deep bass vibration of the drums made it seem like an eternity, a lifetime between heartbeats.

Adjusting the length of my rein, I stroked his neck with my knuckles, then cued him with my right leg. Ivan slewed around the corner like a truck going too fast on a dirt road, momentarily losing traction until he gained purchase on the straight away. It slid me a hair off center, but with the strong core I'd developed over the last several weeks, I helped us both balance. Three rings skittered down my lance, and I watched the fourth fall as it had every time I'd done this, pushing aside my irritation to toss the lance and steadied my horse for the next turn. Shifting my weight further back caused Ivan to focus more, driving his legs deeply beneath him as I leaned out to grab the spear from Kory, trying not to scare her into stepping back. It landed in my hand perfectly, needing no adjustment as I rode down on the hay bales and loosed it at the target. Our rate of travel was collected enough that I saw it land dead center, and then I put all my focus on my last chance. I needed a matching five to beat him, and I intended to give everything Ivan and I had to make it happen.

The tilting lance slapped into my palm like shaking hands with an enthusiastic old friend, and Ivan immediately threw in a crow hop to express his impatience. I'd never really let him run at it before, and he expected me to hold him back. When I pressed my heels to his ribs it slowed him momentarily, his ears flicking back to make sure he understood me correctly. I closed them again, kissing my lips noisily, and he took me in earnest, flattening and lengthening in one stride.

Taking bead on my target, I focused on a bit of chipped paint right where I wanted my strike to land, and let the winged creature beneath me take me there. The jolt of impact traveled up the lance, my whole arm tingling at the concussion, but most of my focus went toward getting Ivan reeled back in as he screamed around the corner at Mach one. It took a few breaths to convince him he wasn't a thoroughbred, and once more I had Abby to thank for my ability to ride with subtlety, allowing me to get him collected.

We came to a halt on the other side of the arena from the quintain, Bart counting the rotations out loud, the audience chanting "Go, go, go!" as the arm swung around. "Two." The counterweight still had some speed, moving flat and smooth. "Three." The momentum slowed, and I counted the seconds with Ivan's heaving breaths as this rotation took much longer to complete. "Four." Come on baby, just one more. I almost wanted to blow some air toward it, to give it a little push, but it wobbled. The crowd gave a universal 'aww' of disappointment when it stopped just shy of the mark. A tie. What did we do with a tie?

"Ladies and Lords, I beg your patience, as we seem to have a tie!" Bart's voice rang out, and he spun Eros toward where Aaron waited by the gate. After a moment of whispered consultation, he cantered back to his spot in front of the dais. "Your Majesty, as this competition is meant to be for the pleasure of Your court, we leave this decision in Your capable hands. Bowen, Cranston, come forward."

We fell in on either side of Eros and waited the Queen's judgement, but she proved her wisdom once more. "My people, in cases such as this, I believe the choice should fall to you." Her eyes took in the whole crowd, this slightly larger than the one last week. "Your accolades shall declare a winner. Should We favor Cranston?" The applause and hollers that went up were sizeable, no shortage of people jumping to their feet to make themselves heard, and my heart fell. The Queen lifted her hands to quiet the crowd, then looked right at me with a knowing grin as she shouted, "And what of the House of Bowen?"

The unexpected wave of noise landed as physically as a slap, and I flinched, Ivan flicking his ears nervously as it increased in volume. She quieted them, and tested both our names once more, but the volume made clear by a fair margin that I had won, not just for the Queen, but for the crowd. No doubt, my parents had been screaming themselves hoarse to encourage the people around them, but as I took my lap of victory the flush on my cheeks didn't all come from Ivan's speed. Neither did the tears trying to leak from my eyes.

After the last joust, which was significantly more dialed down from its usual intensity, Dad stayed at the encampment to help put away armor. Mom got sucked into the cast parade by the gal from the costume shop, and I once more accompanied the Queen through the streets of our make believe town. At the end, I sent Steve off to visit with his daughter, and Mom and I walked back to the encampment, stopping occasionally to allow the horses to grab a mouthful of grass. By the time we got there, Buttercup had my Mom completely under her spell, one glance from her doe eyes resulting in kisses and cuddles.

Lee had gotten the paddocks ready for their evening occupation and he waved at us as we tied the horses to the trailer. Closing cannon rang out, and the horses were in their pens within minutes, rolling enthusiastically as we all gathered around the truck, laughing at their grunts of pleasure.

While Aaron gave me the go ahead to ride back to the farm with my parents, I chose to stay with the team, wanting to be close to those who were becoming a family of another stripe. I won't lie, I also wanted to sit next to Bart, even if just for the fifteen-minute ride. We hadn't spoken since the games, and as dumb as it may sound, I missed him. As we made to spill from the truck Aaron cleared his throat, and we all froze, Lee hanging halfway out the door.

"Good job, today, all of you. I know it's hard to come back from seeing an injury happen, and I appreciate your commitment to the team. You have my thanks." Nods of acceptance moved all

191

of our heads, and I could feel Bart's approval at my back. "Now, go get cleaned up, Jo's parents will be here shortly for dinner."

I bolted for the house, barely getting the bedroom door closed before yanking off my shirt and cranking up the shower to full blast. No way would I let the guys beat me to the hot water, particularly since I knew Mom would put me to work as soon as she arrived. As sweet and loving as anyone could ask for, she was also as much a taskmaster as Dad. Even though I rushed through washing up, I still emerged from the bathroom to find her perched on the side of my bed, looking over the pile of books I had been working through. She'd changed into jeans and her favorite light brown cowboy boots, the decorative stitching on the toes a vivid purple that matched her flowy shirt.

"Hi, sweetie." Her smile made me suspicious even before she picked up the bag at her feet and held it out to me. "I know you probably think it's silly, but I bought you a little something today. And I brought you a few things from home. While it's clear you are one of the boys here, sometimes it's good to remind them they have a woman on their hands."

Oh heavens, exactly what I'd been hoping to avoid. I only cared about one of them looking at me as a female, but now wasn't the time to point out the obvious differences. Just like Mom to shove me right out of my comfort zone with a boot to my rear. I sighed and took the bag, my hand coming into contact with a silk that slithered against my fingers, even as rough as they had grown with all the recent work. Pulling out the blouse, I gasped, the deep charcoal grey so rich I just wanted to stare at it. It seemed a shame to wear it, but my mother would never let me out of the room without it on. Further digging revealed my nicest jeans, a small makeup kit and my dressiest cowboy boots, the black leather buffed to a soft shine. Likely Dad's work, as I'd thrown them in my closet without cleaning them just before heading here.

Frowning slightly, I turned back to Mom. "You know, this isn't going to make them take me seriously. I don't want them to see me as decorative."

"Josie, I'm not asking you to wear a dress, God forbid." She rolled her eyes and smiled, trying to tease me out of arguing. Tempting as it was, I tried again.

"This is too nice to wear to help you cook dinner."

"Well, it's a good thing you don't have to help at all." She ticked off my objections on her fingers one at a time. "Dad is already getting the grill hot, corn will go on with the steaks, and then it's just a matter of heating up the beans. Potato salad is done, and I brought carrot cake for dessert."

My stomach growled, and I yielded the moral high ground with a sigh. It had been an inevitability anyway, as I couldn't stand to disappoint her, but the mention of carrot cake obliterated my token resistance. "You really don't fight fair." I groused, stomping back toward the bathroom with the bag in hand.

"Where do you think you got it from, sweetie?" she threw after me, laughing as she let herself out of the room. I couldn't even object, because it was completely true. When I emerged from the bedroom I found Mom alone in the kitchen, and she looked up with a grin of triumph. "I knew it would be perfect! Now, here, take these steaks out to your dad."

Picking up the platter, I waded outside like a soldier into a war zone, never expecting I would be shot down first. I lost all forward motion as I caught sight of Bart. Standing between Aaron and my Dad, he wore a pair of Wranglers so dark an indigo as to be brand new, a crease ironed into them. The dark teal button up tucked into his jeans had the sleeves rolled up above his elbows, the color deepening his tan, and a trophy buckle caught the light at his waist. I'd have stood and studied him longer, but then his eyes flicked up to mine and the bottom dropped out of my world for a second. If green could be said to smolder it certainly managed to do so, leaving me flushed and uncomfortable. Thankfully, Dad noticed me standing there and took the platter of T-bones from my hands, dropping a kiss on my cheek in thanks.

"I see your Momma managed to talk you around to prettying up, Josie." He grinned at me with a tease in his eyes, and I flung a half smile back, looking anywhere but at Bart. I could still feel him watching me, and I didn't need to yield to the temptation to stare again. "You look lovely."

"Thanks, Daddy. You know she could talk a Bedouin into building a sandbox." He barked a laugh and I'd swear so did Bart, though Aaron looked at me like I had grown another head. I didn't think my joke had much to do with it though, as he couldn't seem to fathom the change in my wardrobe. "Aaron, have we heard from John or Caroline?"

Blue eyes finally met mine, a wrinkle forming between his dark brows as he processed the question. "Yes, sorry, compound fracture of his ulna, just above the wrist. He'll be going to the orthopedist in the morning to talk details, it might need surgery." His lips twisted hard at that, and I could only imagine how this would change the season for him, being a man down.

"We'll be alright," Bart rumbled, and I forced myself to meet his eyes then, just to prove I could. "Everyone will joust twice a day is all." The heat lay banked now, enough to warm my cheeks, but not enough to burn, and I smiled faintly when he looked away first. "Mr. Bowen, sir, would you like a beer? Aaron and I brought a cooler of cold ones over. Grilled meat always comes out better if the cook has a beverage in hand."

Dad nodded at this universal man truth and I rolled my eyes. "Josie, would you check with your Momma and make sure she's okay driving home?"

"Yes, David, you can have a beer. Silly male bonding ritual aside, it really is the best thing at the end of a long day." Mom answered, coming out the back door with a bowl in her hands, headed for the picnic table I didn't even know we had. Judging from the pale newness of the wood, I'd have put money on the guys cobbling it together just for the occasion.

Trace and Lee peeked out the backdoor next, grinning like idiots when Bart offered them a beer as well, and leaving me a little peeved that no one offered me one. I decided to make an object lesson out of it, stalking across the porch to snatch one from the cooler before Bart could close it. His eyebrows shot up in surprise and I smiled sweetly, but before he could offer me the opener I turned toward the picnic table and used the edge to pop the top off. "I'm going to go check on Ro while you guys burn cow flesh. Have fun."

My parents frowned at me as I pushed past them, but I kept going, not wanting to be chastised. So much for being treated like a girl. Now the guys would be even more confused about how to treat me, and I'd gone from fun to bitchy in record time, pushing them further away. I left the beer sitting on the wheel well of the trailer, not even wanting it after the first bubbly swig. Ro didn't care though, he came straight to the fence with a nicker of welcome, snuffling my hair with his whiskery lips. I scratched his cheeks, not caring if I got hair all over my pretty new shirt. My insides were a mess and a half, my mind whirling with confusion. I hadn't wanted to be looked at like a girl, and the instant they didn't treat me like one, I acted like a spoiled brat. What the hell was wrong with me? My phone buzzed in my back pocket, and I found Eros's photo filling the screen, telling me I had a message from Bart.

'Don't want to wait until Monday to talk. It'll make Sunday miserable. You okay?'

Oh, yeah, I'm just peachy. I've got the hots for you, you're too old for me, and probably think I'm a petulant child. What could be wrong? But, not wanting to rock the boat, I settled for something more diplomatic. *'Just needed some time to decompress.'*

The phone volleyed back a response quickly. *'Take your time. Be more fun with you though. Need some Jo perspective, before we die of testosterone poisoning.'* I snorted impolitely at his attempt to lighten my mood, truly laughing when Ro looked at me askance for the very horse like noise.

'Giving Ro his bucket, then I'll be in. You'll all have to live without me until then.'

Then I made truth out of the statement, heading in the barn to mix grain, hardly needing to flick on a light to find my way. The barn, the feed room were all so familiar now, so much a part of my home, and I walked back down the aisle in minutes, the full bucket swinging in my hand. Ro settled in to munch his dinner with gusto, and I snatched up the beer bottle on my way back to the house, finally smiling again.

That smile became harder to maintain as Cranston let himself out the front door, his standard frat boy uniform of polo shirt and khaki shorts stirring unpleasant memories of friends saved from date rape. His hair was back to its over styled glory, fake highlights combed just so, and I felt the urge to muss it, but that would mean touching him.

"Hey, goody goody, you headed back in to Mommy and Daddy?" I could barely see his face in the yellow light of the porch, but I could hear the sneer just the same.

"I am. You not sticking around for dinner?" See, I could be polite, even when I'd rather not. "They brought plenty."

"No, you hillbillies are welcome to your fun, I've got classier company to keep." Then he shoved past me, jamming his shoulder into mine hard enough that I dropped my beer, the glass shattering on the brick pavers. I stared after him in consternation, until he turned back long enough to throw a parting shot. "Don't worry, little whore, I know you're just playing it up so everyone likes you. The truth will win out in the end, and everyone will know what a loser you really are."

Confusion laid heavily on me as I wondered what had brought him to hate so very much. I let him go without so much as a word of censure, finally understanding that no matter what I did or said, he would be determined in his dislike. Mom came looking for me just as I swept up the last of the glass from the front walk, worry darkening her eyes.

"Josie, baby, is everything okay?"

"I'm fine Mom, just cleaning up my mess." I faked a smile that seemed to allay her concern, and fell in arm and arm with her after disposing of the glass. Dad speared the last steak off the grill as we entered the yard, and we all squeezed around the picnic table, shoulders bumping and elbows smacking each other as food got passed around. Hunger drove out any other worry, and I fell on my steak with a vengeance, barely managing to be mannerly about it.

Trace looked queasy when most of us cut into our rare meat, but rather than complaining, he just stared pointedly at his own plate, determined to ignore us. Fillmore noticed though, and gave him crap about it, then the ribbing started in earnest. The whole evening passed in a comfortable haze, the overwhelming sense of family filling my heart with peace. Well, mostly. There were still moments when Bart looked at me and I shifted in my seat, not sure if I should run or throw myself on his mercy.

Later, as we carried dishes in the house to start cleaning up, Bart caught me picking crumbs off the carrot cake platter, and I feigned wide eyed innocence until he laughed. The boys set to doing the dishes, leaving my parents at loose ends, so I drug them out to meet Ro. In this, my heart remained absolutely clear, and I wanted their approval of him, though it wouldn't have changed a thing. Love was love.

As we stood around Ro, my Dad admiring his angles and my Mom kissing on his face, he still watched me, reading my moods with ease. His ears never stopped following me, even when he could barely see around the arms Mom wrapped around his face. "He's such a sweetie, Josie! I really hope you get to stay, if only because of him."

I couldn't disagree with her, as my heart would indeed be broken to leave him, though he wouldn't be the only one I'd hate to see in my rear view mirror. Tracing the shape of tree branches along the marking on Ro's shoulder, I smiled through the ache in my chest. "I hope so too, Mom. I was worried you'd be set to drag me out of here trussed and tied after John got hurt."

Dad pulled me roughly under his arm and squeezed. "Well, my girl, we can't say we aren't worried, but honestly, this is no less crazy than the jumping you've done with Abby. You are putting in the sweat equity, according to Aaron and Bart, so you are as safe as you can be in this situation." I wrapped my arm around his waist and hugged him back.

"Thanks Daddy. You too Momma. I've never wanted something as much as this." The truth of it made my shoulders shake with barely contained emotion. Jousting had become so fiercely a part of me, in ways I never expected, and I didn't think my attraction for my coach had a darn thing to do with it. In fact, you could pull him entirely from the situation, and I'd still be chasing it with every cell in my body. I just wouldn't have as much to lose if I failed.

After goodbyes were passed around, manly handshakes for my father and careful hugs for Mom, the guys all headed for their respective beds, leaving me alone with my Mother. Dad had gone off to warm up the truck and adjust the seat for her, and she hugged me hard, as if she felt me struggling to keep the pieces together.

"Baby, you know I want you to do well, and I look forward to coming back and seeing you joust, but I want you to guard your heart in case it doesn't work out." A tremble shook her voice as she clutched my arms, then she headed after my Dad with an "I love you" lingering in the air.

Too late Momma. You raised a woman who knew the only way to win at anything would be to do it with her whole heart, even if it meant it would break.

The heat felt oppressive on Sunday, and the horses became sluggish as the day rolled on, my new bodice soaked through with sweat from me and the horses both. Aaron installed a fan in the armor room at least, and there were arming jackets draped over every available surface in hopes they might be dry by the end of the day.

Cranston was completely off his game, and I'd lay a good bet that he sported a killer hangover, making his performance for the day less than impressive. General proved to be the least bothered by the heat, by dint of his lighter color and bonier frame, and put in a heck of a run for Lee, resulting in his winning the games. I might have gotten a little lax with my own aim once he put that run down, but don't you tell him. He needed that walk of pride far more than I did.

They pawned off leading the King to Cranston, I'd suspect because he's become more decorative than useful in his current state, and I settled into loading the trailer with a vengeance. Mari wandered out the gate and found me climbing in the tack room with a saddle under each arm.

"Jo, are you hiding from me?"

I laughed, and once the saddles were stowed on their racks, I leaned in the doorway with a grin. "I'm too exhausted and hot to put effort into hiding from anyone, Mari." She crossed her arms under her breasts in a posture more habitual than belligerent and returned my smile, her petite size almost comical from my higher vantage. I stepped down and settled myself on the running board so she didn't have to crane her neck. "What can I do for you?"

"You'd mentioned being willing to babysit last week, and I was wondering if you are available tonight? I've got a reservation for Shayla and I at eight, and our sitter backed out."

A grin split my chapped lips. "Of course! Give me your address, and I'll head straight there when we get back to the farm." Surely Bart would excuse me from evening chores, in light of the circumstances.

"Actually, do you want to just come home with me? I cleared it with Bart, and he said he'd come pick you up whenever you need." The hopeful light in her eyes shone too brightly to be dimmed and I agreed, hopping up to finish the needed work before closing cannon. She headed back to the booth to gather up her own things, and I moved toward the stalls to collect the last saddle, slowing at the sight of Bart sitting in Eros's hay manger, the stallion's big head pressed against his chest.

As I attempted to pick up the saddle without disturbing them, he looked up and smiled a welcome, never shifting from his precarious position. His thumbs rubbed slow circles on the tips of Eros's ears, a delicate bit of work from such strong hands. "I'm guessing you said yes. I'd have volunteered to watch the little stinkers instead, but she thinks I'll ramp them up too much."

"No, I'm glad to do it, though I heard you are going to be my escape route when all is said and done." I hitched the saddle against my non-existent hip, smiling when Eros groaned happily as Bart started scratching his forehead.

"Oh, believe me, once those boys work you over, you are going to be happy to have a chauffeur. It'll be my honor to get you home safe, Miss Josephine Bowen." The cowboy gentleman in his voice made me like my name. Not Jo, not Josie. Josephine. The way he said it sounded strong and beautiful all at once, as if he knew all the parts of my heart and liked them just the way they were.

I sketched a playful curtsy that prompted a larger smile, noticing one slightly crooked incisor that seemed incredibly human in its defiance of the rest of his well-ordered appearance. "Well, thank you kindly, Bartholomew Clark. I'll be pleased to inform the women of the world that chivalry is not dead, just in hiding at the renaissance faire." He laughed then and shook his head as if to deny it, but I knew the truth.

After finishing the packing, I took a moment to change clothes, my sweaty skin grateful for the chance to breath as I traded my bodice for a t-shirt. Once the horses were loaded I fell in beside Mari for the long walk to the cast parking lot, waving at people I'd come to know over the last several weeks with easy familiarity. Randall the Rat Catcher, the Pirates of the Maiden Voyage, and even a few of the shop owners called my name, each of them adding color to the expansive palette of family this had all become. Then Mari looped her arm through mine, lending a sisterly air I cherished.

As Mari wound her car into the suburbs of Louisville, I closed my eyes and rested my head against the seat back, charging my batteries against what would be a long night. I'd brought Percy with me, certain I'd need all the resources at my disposal to keep the twins from running me ragged. I wasn't wrong, because as soon as we pulled in the driveway of their cozy brick bungalow the two boys shot out the front door like baby jack rabbits.

"Mama, mama." This from Mal, who glommed onto Mari's neck right away, and a high pitched "Josie!" that sounded more like a war cry from Max as he flung himself at my lap before I could climb out of the car. Shayla stood in the doorway looking like she'd just survived the battle of her life, and judging from the two little boys that looked to be freshly bathed, I didn't doubt it. I gathered Max in my arms for a quick hug, then enlisted his help carrying my bag inside, letting him hold one of the straps while I carried the weight on the other.

Before Shayla could say a word I hugged her first, whispering in her ear. "Go, get your own bath and cleaned up. I've got them." She flashed me a look of gratitude that looked one step from tears and I decided then and there if I was still around after the end of the fair, I'd do this a lot more. Mari and she needed time for themselves and there simply wasn't any available when you had two ruffians like the boys on your hands.

Mal released his hold on Mari as soon as I slid Percy from my bag, shouts of "Pewcy, Pewcy" echoing off the high ceilings, the boy's bare feet thundering along the wood floors as we made our way into the living room where their toys were scattered. We spent a half hour as the boys built a crazy castle tower out of blocks that they wanted Percy to knock down. Percy, being a nice dragon, didn't want to hurt anyone, and they promised to evacuate all the people before he attacked. The cheers when Percy flapped his wings and dove down on the precarious building, scattering blocks everywhere, were just as enthusiastic as any I'd ever received from the crowd at the faire.

Then they rebuilt it, because Percy didn't want people to be without their home. When Mari and Shayla peeked around the corner with cautious smiles, I waved them in, the boys proudly displaying their creation before their Moms said goodbye. Though Mal's eyes looked suspiciously damp, both boys seemed content to stay with me when the women let themselves out. A text came a few minutes later from Mari's number, just as I got the boys settled on the sofa with a Mike the Knight DVD.

'Thanks again, there are cookies on the counter for dessert, they should be in bed by no later than eight, you can read them up to three stories, but then it is definitely sleepy time. Max will turn on Mal's night light, their PJ's are on the beds. There's a twenty by the phone if you want to order a pizza once they are in bed. Call or text if you have any questions, we'll be home around ten or so.'

Smiling at Mal and Max, who were sitting side by side on the couch holding Percy in their laps, I snapped a photo and sent it to Mari with a return text. *'Take your time. The company is charming. :-) Don't have anywhere else to be. Text when you are on your way and I'll let Bart know I'm ready to go.'*

'Aww, so cute. Thanks sweetie, Shayla and I owe you one.'

I shook my head as I typed another reply. *'Friends don't owe friends.'*

We were a half hour into the video, Mike and his friends on an adventure, when I finally got another text. *'I'll hold you to that when you try to repay me for the bodice.'*

Chuckling lightly at myself, I had to admit I'd walked right into that. We ate our cookies sitting at the kitchen table, and I yielded to their pleas for a glass of milk, rolling my eyes when I had to clean up the resulting mess after a dunking contest ensued. Mal turned out to be a strategist, quiet and thoughtful, as he carefully held his cookie in the milk to soak. Max tended to throw himself after things with enthusiasm. He'd shoved his whole cookie and hand into the cup, milk immediately overflowing across the beaten stainless steel to drip all over the floor.

Then came the usual objections on the way upstairs to bed, dragging feet and whining as I got them to brush their teeth. By the time they were in their jammies my phone showed a quarter after eight, but I remained patient with them. Horses taught you if you got in a hurry, you would lose by default, and years at camp had proven kids to be much the same, particularly the younger ones.

I settled on the floor between their two beds, and they picked out three books, one for each of them and one they both agreed on. After Percy read them the first story, being a dragon whose treasure was books, I curled the dragon in a cozy nest of blankets and tucked him in just as I did the boys. Max was already yawning, though Mal remained wide awake, his brain still going a mile a minute even as I tucked the blankets around him. My phone buzzed halfway through the second book, but I ignored it, focusing on the story of the little bunny who didn't want to go to bed.

Before the end of the third, both boys were completely asleep, lashes heavy on their soft little cheeks. They didn't even move when I climbed to my feet and let myself out, leaving the door open a crack so I could hear them if they called. Creeping down the stairs, I picked up a couple toys as I went, intent on taking them to the toy box in the living room, when my phone buzzed again. It was Bart, checking in.

'You still alive Bowen?'

'If I don't hear from you in ten, I'm sending a team to extract you.'

I had to muffle a giggle as I entered the kitchen, not wanting to wake the boys. I found the money pinned to the note board by the house phone along with a flyer from the local pizza place. My stomach growled, reminding me lunch had been a long time ago. Before I could dial them my cell phone lit up with an incoming call from Bart and I accepted it quickly before the noise could wake the boys.

"I'll admit, I was tempted to wait just to see what sort of rescue you were planning, but it might wake the sleeping dragonet's." I answered, rewarded by a warm chuckle. "Seriously, though, we're all fine here. I'm about to order some pizza and work on picking up the house a little."

"You know, they didn't ask you to do housework, Bowen. You've already had a long day. They've got cable, go sit on the sofa and watch a chick flick or something." Concern laced his voice, along with a hint of a tease. He wouldn't be able to sit still either, and I knew it.

"If I sit still I'll stiffen up, which is already a going concern after sitting on the floor for story time. Don't worry about me, I'll call you when the ladies are headed home, and you can fuss at me then. And stop assuming you know what I'd like. I'm as likely to watch a John Wayne film as a romantic comedy."

"Shayla keeps the painkillers in the cupboard over the fridge so the boys can't reach them." Sore shoulders twinged just then, and I turned to do as he suggested. "And someone has to fuss after you. You take care of yourself last."

It took a lot of restraint not to snort when I laughed at him. "And there is one of the worst cases known to man of the pot calling the kettle black. But thanks for worrying. I'll call you later." I'll admit a twinge of regret over ending the call mixed in with the satisfaction of stopping any further objections, as I'd been enjoying talking to him.

My stomach distracted me, and I dialed the pizza place next. They assured me the pizza would be there in twenty minutes, so I turned toward the living room to pick up toys, and tidy the surrounding rooms. I didn't have much work to do, honestly, as the house was already clean. Things were just a little out of sorts, probably a constant state with twin whirlwinds in occupation. I turned toward a soft rap at the door, grateful for the restraint as I'd forgotten to ask the delivery person to be quiet, but my thank you stuttered to a halt when I swung the door open.

"Don't be mad, I waited for the guy to bring it and gave him a hefty tip. Didn't think you'd want him using the doorbell." said Bart, holding the pizza in front of him like a peace offering. Or a shield. So completely disarmed by the careful smile, and the caution in his eyes, I dug my fingernails into my palms to stop myself from grabbing him by the sleeve to drag him in the door.

"Well, since you had to check on my safety personally, not trusting me when I told you I was okay, there will be a fine." I stepped back, waving him toward the kitchen, thinking I should get a medal for not staring at his butt. I'm no saint, I looked, the leather Wrangler patch drawing my eye like a magnet, but I didn't linger, a feat of herculean proportions. "You'll be helping me with the dishes."

He looked toward the small pile in the sink and raised an eyebrow. "That's all it'll cost me? I'd say that's a bargain. I thought you might say I had to clean the boy's bathroom."

"Ah, now there is a worthy punishment, Sir Clark." I grinned mischievously and tapped my chin as he looked at me in mock disbelief. "Males of any age are indeed animals when it comes to their bathroom habits, and it would be much more fitting to send you in to wage war on their toilet. It is not a task fit for a lady."

The playfulness in his eyes looked tempered by something darker. "Are you a lady, Josephine? Or are you a knight?"

"Who says I can't be both?" I threw the riposte quickly, turning away from the questions to fish plates from a cabinet. "They are not exclusive of each other, last I heard. Or is there some kind of rule I don't know about?"

The growling of my stomach silenced his opportunity to answer when I lifted the lid from the pizza, melted cheese, grilled chicken and basil hitting my nose with a one-two punch of hunger. I dragged a slice straight from the box and folded it over, blowing on it a few times before taking a bite. It didn't occur to me to even look at him as I chewed, my eyes closed to better savor the rich taste.

"Jo." My eyes flew open and found his as I swallowed down a still too hot bite, pressing a hand to my chest as it worked its way down my throat. "You've got a little something there." He pointed at his own chin, and I found myself studying the scar there before turning away in self-defense. Under the guise of grabbing a paper towel, I swallowed a second time, forcing down a lump that had nothing to do with the pizza as I cleaned my chin.

"Better?" I asked nonchalantly, turning back and lifting my chin for inspection. He studied me thoughtfully before nodding, and I took a deep breath of relief when he turned his attention to his own pizza. Desperate for something to distract me from being alone with him, I turned to the one thing that was neutral ground. "So, tomorrow, I'm thinking of introducing Ro to the gaming. Any suggestions?"

We traded ideas back and forth like we were playing go fish, one of mine matching his and being tabled before he returned the favor. This, more than anything, made me feel closer to him, this shared wavelength. Nothing felt impossible if we came at it together, no task too great, and no challenge insurmountable. Having been so strong on my own for so long, it felt odd, but also so comfortable, like I'd always had these conversations with him. Mom, Dad and Grandma were the only other people on the planet I could talk like this with, knowing even if we disagreed on a fundamental level, it would draw us closer together in the end.

Mari and Shayla came in the door at ten after ten, making slow progress toward the kitchen, whispering quietly as Bart and I finished the last of the dishes. I pulled the plug on the wash water while he dried the last plate as they walked in, mutual confusion knitting them together.

"You guys, you didn't have to clean up." Shayla said softly, taking in the freshly scrubbed table and countertops. "This is way too much."

I dried my hands on the towel Bart handed me, and moved forward to hug her. "Nonsense. I wouldn't know how to sit still if my life depended on it, ask Mari." Shayla's arms trembled as she accepted my embrace, and I held out my other hand for Mari, squeezing her fingers. "It really was our pleasure to help you both out, considering how much Mari has helped us at the faire."

I didn't miss the moisture in Mari's eyes, or the questioning look she threw Bart, but Shayla hugged me too tightly to allow me to look at him.

"They weren't too much trouble, were they?" Mari asked, hiding whatever she thought in eyes that were just a bit too wide to be believable. "Mal doesn't fall asleep so easily, poor boy still has a hard time feeling safe."

My brows closed in on each other, and I fought a frown. "He did great, though Max was definitely out first. Why wouldn't Mal feel safe though?"

Shayla covered a soft gasp with her hand, sharing a quick glance with her partner. "We never told you, I'm so sorry Jo. It just feels like we've known you forever."

The confession warmed my cheeks, the sentiment completely reciprocated, each of them already so entwined in my heart. "I love you all too, but please don't feel like you have to tell me anything you don't want to."

"Oh, no, sweetie," Mari took my hand and met my eyes, so much remembered pain in hers I had to blink to keep from crying. "Max and Mal are adopted. Their mom was a druggie, their dad her dealer, and the first three years of their lives were pretty chaotic. Max seems determined to move past all of those old, scary memories. But Malcom is a watcher, and I think he remembers more than he lets on. He sometimes has nightmares, and can be scared of strangers, afraid someone is going to come take him away from us."

Nope, there were the tears, salt stinging my eyes as they welled in the corners. "I'm so glad he has a loving family now. Everyone needs to have people to call home."

"Aptly put, sweetheart," Mari responded, a smile tugging her lips as she looked past me. "And I'm glad to add you to our people."

"You couldn't shake me if you tried." I grinned, pushing the tears away with humor.

We said our goodnights, hugs all around and I turned down their attempts to pay me, feeling more than rewarded by the experience itself. As I tipped my head against the window of the farm truck on the way home, Bart's comfortable silence filling the space between us, I contemplated what family meant to me. Considering everything that had happened since my arrival in Kentucky, I'd say my definition was changing too fast to peg down, but I couldn't find it anywhere in me to regret it.

Monday morning, Bart kept Eros in when he let the rest out to pasture, and I found him currying the well-muscled stallion when curiosity pulled me toward the barn. No worry shone on his face, easing the tightness in my gut, as I'd been concerned something might be wrong.

"What's keeping the big guy in?" I asked, as I crossed the aisle to greet my own horse. Ro nodded his head at me enthusiastically as I closed the distance, stilling the instant we touched so I could reach his favorite spot between the cheeks of his jaw.

Seriously, I was beginning to crave that lifted corner of Bart's mouth that signaled a possible smile. "Well, I thought we might try giving your boy some company after you have your ride."

I managed not to squeak—see, I was getting better. "That would be wonderful. Are you going to ride with us?"

"I suppose we could keep you company in the arena, no work though. He deserves the day off if he's going to teach you how to take a hit this week." A sliver of apprehension became completely eclipsed by a thrill of excitement, and I concentrated to keep my touch relaxed on Ro's cheek as he leaned into the pressure. "But that's not for now, that's for later. Today, you just need to enjoy your horse."

Hard not to think about, since it would be a sink or swim moment, but I focused on the task at hand instead, pulling Ro out to start grooming him. Concentrating on the circular *shush-shush* of the curry, the *swish-flick* of the stiff brush, I brought my heart back to the moment. No future, no past, no agenda, just breathing and existing in the same space as my friends. Thinking about how the stallion and his master were now important to me, I looked toward them, smiling at the sight of Bart with his arms draped over the stallion's back. Eros looked back at him with one eye as Bart murmured nonsense I couldn't hear, reinforcing my opinion of him as a horseman. Skill, Bart owned in spades, but that would be a pale accomplishment without the heart he put into his horse. I resolved to be brave enough to ask him why he didn't joust anymore…but maybe not today. Today, I just needed the peace.

When I started throwing tack on Ro, Bart stayed right where he was, barely shifting on his booted feet to watch me. The regard made my neck feel warm, but I took extra time with my saddle, *his* saddle, settling it just so along Ro's back and smoothing the hair flat beneath it before buckling the girth. When I turned us both toward the mounting block outside the barn, Bart surprised me, vaulting from the ground straight onto Eros's broad, bare back, only a lead rope to control the powerful horse. They fell in beside us and I snuck surreptitious glances at them, studying the easy sway of their bodies, as if they shared the same skin whenever they touched. The halter Eros wore looked different as well, his normal leather strapping replaced with a knotted rope that laid over his face like a whisper.

"What's with the halter?" I asked, as our horses carried us up the hill, and Bart slid the smooth yacht rope of the lead through his fingers before answering.

"This is for having fun, for being close. He knows if I put this on, we are playing together, and that we might be learning something new." He softly made contact with Eros's face, and as soon as the stallion flicked an ear back at him, Bart shifted his left leg forward of the girth line. The stallion responded by lifting his left leg to match, bringing it near horizontal to his body, his hoof stretched far in front of him. A few steps later, they repeat the maneuver on the other side. I'd seen something similar, from the stallions of the Spanish Riding School in Vienna, and never expected to witness it coming from a one ton Percheron.

"So, there is more to Eros and you than meets the eye." I said, letting well deserved admiration creep into my voice.

The look Bart cast my direction appeared dark along the edges, though the tease came through clearly enough. "Something about trying to put square pegs in round holes comes to mind, Bowen."

I laughed weakly, taking the chastisement as deserved. "Touché, Sir. Do not judge lest ye first be judged, as my Grandma likes to say."

Nothing but hoof beats sounded out as we topped the hill and entered the arena, not even the grind of bit chewing to intrude, since both horses wore halters. Eros and Bart made themselves comfortable mid arena, content to watch Ro and I warm up. The ritual would be boring to the casual observer, the serpentines and circles limbering up our muscles, getting Ro stepping further forward with his hind legs, but it fascinated me. Each foot fall had purpose, readying us for the next movement, a building symphony of motion. When I asked for the canter he gave me a crisp depart, lifting his wither up in front of me in a perfect dolphin arc that I had only felt in dreams. Whoever had caused him to shut down, the loss truly belonged to them, to have missed this soft power, this malleable intensity. Selfishly, I felt grateful. If not for their ignorance I might never have known him, never discovered this version of myself. I'd have given it up in an instant if it would have saved him an ounce of suffering, but I chose to rejoice in where we were now instead.

We'd been practicing passes in the lyst for the last week, just a few quiet ones at a time to ingrain the habit in him, and he backed into the lane like a champ. His turn felt eager, seeking, and I let him have a few strides of power before bringing him to a stop at the other end and repeating on the other side. Then I moved to add the ring lance, riding up to the weapons rack while

210

patting his neck. But the instant the wooden pole left its resting place, he shied hard, taking several steps sideways. The movement almost unseated me, since I had leaned over to reach for the pole. Thank goodness I didn't drop it as he would have learned it was an effective evasion. At the same time, his trembling frame and rolling eye almost made me wish I had. Murmuring nonsense as was our habit, I stroked the knuckles of my rein hand back and forth over his neck. Having taught him to have an opinion I would need to prove my commitment to that path.

While the tension remained spooled under his skin like a tightly wound bobbin, the instant he exhaled a big breath I cued him to move back to the weapons rack. His nostrils flared hard on approach, but he stepped close, and I set the lance back down. When he remained standing there, even around his fear, I loosened the reins and we rode away, his unease dissipating with each step. Taking the long way around, we approached again, only this time I applied a firm leg to keep him still, a soft voice to ease his worry.

"There's my brave boy, what a lovely strong man, so good." The litany continued, until he relaxed and licked his lips, then I reached for the lance again. His whole body went rigid, like water frozen into a sculpture, but my free hand just kept rubbing his neck, willing the knot of muscles to unravel. I waited again, my arm outstretched, thankfully much stronger since we first held such discussions. It was a long game to play, moving closer each time he made an effort to settle, stopping the instant the tension returned. I'd known many people who would have just pushed through, and I could have done the same. He would have let me force the issue, but I'd have lost every ounce of trust we had gained, and I refused to go there.

I tipped his nose slightly toward the rack, so he could see it coming, and lifted the lance carefully, letting it make noise so it came as no surprise. His eye rolled and his nostril trembled, but he kept breathing, so I brought the butt of the lance to rest on my toe and cued him to walk. He shambled away, the least graceful thing he'd ever done, but I made a big deal out of it just the same. "What a big boy, so clever, so smart."

Then we moved on to giving his feet something to do, treating it just as if there were no lance in my hand at all. It took a few circuits of the arena to connect his brain to his body, to really help him change perspective. We trotted figure eights, using Bart and Eros as the marker for our changes of direction, their presence a comfort to us both. Herd animals learned a lot from their friends, for good or ill, and Eros could influence Ro's reactions just by remaining calm in the face of Ro's worries. It would be even better if they became friends this afternoon, but I wouldn't count my chickens before the hen had a chance to lay the eggs, let alone hatch them. When Ro had fully invested in listening to me, I rode him right up to the rack and asked for a halt, stilling my body so he could do the same. He loaded his weight to the rear and dropped right into a square stop just as I finished breathing out the word whoa, and I made more fuss. "What a love, my darling boy, what a clever lad."

Tipping his nose this last time revealed a much softer eye, his nostril dilated from effort not stress, and I sighed in relief as I reached out to put the lance back. There was a slight hitch in his breath but no indication of the urge to flee he had previously expressed, so as soon as the lance was secure I vaulted from his back. Pulling his head against the front of my tank top, I scratched the sweaty spots beneath the straps of the halter and murmured sweet nothings for his bravery. "Oh, *fy annwyl*, you did so well, I'm so proud, lovely, handsome boy." My lips tipped up at the affectionate Welsh moniker, straight from Grandma's mouth to mine. She'd called me *fy annwyl*, or my darling, all my life.

Our audience of two made a slow approach once I loosened the tack and pulled the reins over Ro's head. "Tactfully done, Jo." The praise and the sound of my name were what I imagined it would feel like to do a shot of whiskey, a warm burn in my gut and lightness to my head I could not afford, either from the man or the liquor.

"Thank you. Clearly, we have a long way to go." They fell in beside us as we traipsed back down the hill, but my nerves made a mess of the silence until I had to fill it with words. "I'm worried he will never joust, if the fear is that deep. I'd like to think we can overcome it, but it feels so wrong. He's not meant to be scared like this, he's a naturally curious and trusting boy."

"Don't sell your efforts short, or his heart. He's trying for you, and I don't think he'd be doing as well for any of the rest of us." The words felt right, though my ego didn't exactly clamor for them. I'd rather this had never happened to Ro. As for Bart, I could reach out and put my hand on his knee he rode so close and I clenched my fingers against the urge, joints aching with the force of my grip.

At the barn, I quickly stripped Ro of his tack and hosed him down, not minding the faint breeze that carried some of the spray onto me. Were I alone, I wouldn't have thought twice about turning the stream directly onto my head, but I really didn't want to engage in a wet t-shirt contest. After scraping the excess water from his coat so he would dry faster, I turned for his paddock, finding it already occupied by Eros.

Bart lay draped across his back as the stallion grazed, his booted feet crossed at the ankles and resting on Eros's neck, while the broad rump served as a pillow for Bart's equally broad shoulders. Just as I hunted for my phone to snap a picture Eros noticed us, lifting his head from the grass to stare at Ro. Pulling himself upright by the strength of his abs alone, Bart kicked a leg over the stallion's neck and dropped to the ground with cat like grace that countered his bulk. I'd be lying if I said it wasn't one of the sexiest things I'd ever seen a man do.

"Come on in. Eros is a nice guy, he's usually the first horse we put anybody new with. Then they have a friend when we move them out to the herd." I moved closer, allowing Ro a little room on his lead so he could sniff noses with the stud, trying to keep breathing as worry burned in my chest. While Ro was graceful and athletic, the stallion would totally win if it came down to power, and I knew from experience how quickly he could move.

213

Bart let Eros step closer as well, the inside of the stallion's nostril showing deep red as it flared to take in the newcomer's scent. A forceful exhale vibrated all around us, and Ro lowered his head, mouthing the air like a colt. While we had guessed his age at around six, the submissive baby face made me wonder if he was younger. Most horses stopped such behavior around three. Thankfully, the stallion immediately softened his approach, a soft, playful squeal inviting Ro to be brave, and I looked to Bart for confirmation.

"It's as safe as we can make it, Jo. They'll be alright, I feel it in my gut." Trust for both man and horse steadied my hands as I slipped the halter from Ro's head, and Bart did the same, the two of us immediately retreating to the gate.

After some more posturing and squealing, Eros lifted his impressive bulk into a rear and spun away, inviting Ro to run, and my concern faded exponentially. In fact, I smiled hard enough to make my cheeks ache as I used my phone to snap some pictures. They were at it for a good five minutes, even in the heat, spinning and wheeling together like birds in flight. Once they settled down to graze in earnest I felt so happy it became borderline uncomfortable, and I shifted on my feet, needing to bleed off energy. I looked to Bart, catching a glimmer of a pleased smile.

"So, how about those stalls?" I asked.

He nodded and we turned away together, as matched a maneuver as any our horses just accomplished. As we did chores, comfortable in the routine, I began to wonder if I could walk away from this all. I could be happy like this, content, free of the stress of working for a large company. Maybe Aaron's offer was worth considering. After all, could I really walk away from Ro just because *my* plans didn't work out?

Pulling my phone out to look at the pictures I just took, I discovered several messages that came in while it was set to silent, all of them from Bart. I leaned against the manure rake and opened the files, my breath catching when I found a slew of photos from my ride this morning. The only photos I had of the two of us, together. We looked so balanced, so well matched, his grace elevating my own and my confidence lent to him in turn.

As my heart softened to the idea of staying, if only for him, it also yielded a little more toward the man who took the pictures. Brotherhood of knights remained my end goal, and all I could afford to chase right now, but once that question had an answer perhaps I'd have the leisure to consider pursuing more with the man I found more and more to admire about.

♥♥♥

Tuesday morning, Bart rapped his knuckles on the front door of the house, and I looked up from my book with surprise, tugging a throw blanket over my too white legs. I'd only pulled on shorts under my PJ shirt before coming out to have my tea, which left me feeling exposed. It was not lost on me that I wouldn't have cared in front of anyone else, but he made me self-conscious.

He peeked his head in the screen door, looking at me and then around the room, a frown pulling his eyes into a faint squint. Business brought him here, not my company, and I sharpened my attention. No one would ever be able to accuse me of my girly side interfering with my work.

"I'm the only one up." I offered, pointing down the hall. "There's been no movement from that camp yet."

He strode down the hall before the sentence ended, and now that I knew where it came from, I recognized the military efficiency in his gait. Places to go, things to do, no time for nonsense. Pounding issued from the darkness, Bart's fist heavy on their hollow wood door, and groggy mumbling made a response. The grind and swivel of the doorknob was followed by a growled command. "Get some clothes on, and meet me in the living room. We've got to make some schedule changes."

Then he came back, filling the room with an intensity I wished I could help relieve. It felt like sharing a cage with a tiger as he prowled the room with a restlessness that made my skin itch, never looking at me, but completely aware of every move I made. At any moment, that edginess could become violence, like a sword just beginning to leave its sheath in threat. Anything I could say or do would seem far too familiar, and the last thing I needed was to expose myself like that. Thankfully, Fillmore and Cranston were quick, and the instant they joined us Bart's tension leveled down a notch, allowing me to draw a full breath again.

"Sit." He pointed to the sofa and loveseat, and Lee claimed the smaller of the two with a negligent man sprawl that told me he really wasn't awake yet. Otherwise, he never would have let Cranston join me on the sofa. Luckily, the mutual dislike proved useful, and Cranston took the furthest edge away from me as he could.

I didn't know if Bart could read the murky tension filling the air but my own discomfort made me straighten, unfolding my legs so my feet rested on the floor. The blanket slipped from my lap as I scooted to the edge of the cushion so I could face my coach. Bart's eyes flicked to my bare legs, then away again so fast it was like being stung by a whip and I grimaced, freezing against the urge to cover myself. Too late now.

He stared fixedly at Cranston as he spoke. "Today and Thursday, you will be taking your first hits. As it will be easier to manage you one at a time, rather than as a group, your lessons will be private. I don't care if you come watch your fellows, but there will be no laughter, no teasing, or catcalls. You will respect each other, because if you don't, the resulting Karma will not be gentle. Trace will help you armor, Steve is coming out to help me in the lyst, and Aaron will be delivering blows. Expect that you will hit the ground. Expect it to hurt, to get the wind knocked out of you. When we scoop you up, we expect you to get back on unless you are headed for the hospital."

None of it came a surprise to me, though Lee looked a little wild eyed with apprehension. Physically, he should have been able to manage this best, but I began to wonder at his mental aptitude. The possibility of getting hurt bothered him more than it should. Aaron had made sure to explain the realities of this job when Annabelle had left, so that no one would be surprised in the future, but now it became incredibly real.

Bart's voice cut into my musings, "Lee, you are going at one, Cranston at two, and Bowen at three. If you haven't shopped for the week yet, get it done this morning. Put muscle cream, ice and anti-inflammatories on your shopping list because you are going to need them."

I lifted my hand, a random thought chasing its way across my brain, speaking the instant Bart nodded at me. "How about Arnica? For healing the bruising faster? We keep it on the ranch for healing up that sort of thing."

"Smart idea, though I don't know if the stores you are going to are going to stock it." Gruffly, he turned to Lee next, making sure he'd looked at us all. "Get lots of protein for your supper, and green veggies, you'll likely be craving them after your body takes a beating. All I expect of you today is to take the hit and get back on, take another. Tomorrow, you'll be expected for chores in the morning, then to free school your gaming horse at some point. Evening chores will be light, as the horses will go back out after you ride them. Thursday, you prove to me you've got the heart to have another go at it, when you are sore, aching and unhappy. You do that, then we'll move on to trading hits next week, ramping up for final weekend. You'll be paired with one of the guys to joust in front of the crowd, to truly prove you are ready to play the game. We aren't looking for you to win, that'll come in time, but we are definitely looking for who can smile through the discomfort. Be good sports, support each other, and you'll see your knighthood in two weeks, with an invitation to join the company for a season. Any questions?"

Cranston sat forward, his beady eyes calculating like a vulture hunched over roadkill. "Has anyone ever not fallen off?"

"No." The answer came flat and cold, an icy slap of reality. "Aaron, who jousted theatrically well before he started heavy armor, still fell off his first day. I fell off twice. The only saving grace was we both already had the skill to fall safely." Well, there was a hard truth to swallow. If this bear of a man had yielded to gravity, who were we mere mortals to defy it?

Trace stumbled into the kitchen, his shirt and jeans a crumpled mess, like he slept in them. On the way to the fridge for his usual energy drink, he interjected his two cents. "Hey, I fell off seven out of eight passes in the beginning. On the upside, I got them out of the way early and hardly ever fall off now."

Bart huffed a laugh, and I grinned, appreciating Trace's candid honesty. Indeed, you could hardly rock him in the saddle anymore, but my Daddy always said the best way to learn how to stay on was to fall off a couple times. Cranston flopped back in his chair sullenly.

"Alright people, get your stuff done. I expect you on time for everything, no excuses short of equipment or horse issues, as that is all that should ever keep you from starting a show on time. Prove to me you've got what it takes to play this game." Then he turned sharply enough that he should have left a hole in the carpet, quitting the room without a backward glance, creating a vacuum of power that stole the air for a moment.

After a second to recover, I looked around the room, even at Cranston. "Good luck, gentlemen. I think we are all going to need it." Then I got up, and headed to my room, needing to get ready to face what looked like one of the most challenging days of my life.

♥♥♥

While Lee had his lesson after lunch I took Ro out for a quick ride around the property line, just letting him trot on a loose rein. After the mental work of the day before, I wanted him to remember we could just have fun. Rising in my stirrups for each long hill, I felt his back come up as well, his ribs filling my leg. However much I had lamented my height and lack of chest as a teen, it had always made it much easier to sit a horse, allowing me to come to grips with my body much sooner than my peers. Bart had been right about me being a masterwork sword. While there might be a few feminine flourishes here and there, my body was meant for function over form.

We walked the last quarter of our route so he could come in cool, but Ro's stride still covered a lot of ground, so we made good time. After settling him back in his stall, I turned to get Eros ready, and the stallion bumped me excitedly with his nose as if he knew what lay ahead. Likely, he was just picking up on my nerves, but he'd played this game enough to feel the change in the air.

I helped Trace get Lee out of his armor, wincing every time the poor kid flinched. When we slid off his arming coat the thin t-shirt he wore rode up, revealing a bruised line just above his hip. Further movement uncovered a grouping of bruises on his left shoulder, kinetic energy leaving several radiating imprints of the lance tip. Lee looked right at me when I bit my lip, mistaking my concern for him as apprehension for myself.

"You don't have to do this, Josie. I've got more where those came from. There's no need for you to go up there and get hurt."

Smiling at the foolish statement, I shook my head. "Fillmore, you are sweet to think of me, but that face was worry for you, not for me. I've sported bruises before, I'll wear them again, and I can think of no better reason to add to my collection than to chase my heart."

Now he shook his head, looking away from my sympathetic expression. "Annabelle said you were crazy enough to want this, and it shouldn't surprise me after all this time, honestly. It's just so hard to think of a girl *wanting* to get hit."

My edgy laughter made both young men freeze and stare. "That's where you've got it wrong, my friend. I don't want to get hit. I want to hit someone else, and it's only fair to let them take a shot back at me. I want to test my limits, to never stop testing them. I want to look my fear in the eye and laugh. This was *never* about getting hit."

Trace dropped the leg harness of Lee's armor in a trunk and turned back to look me in the eye. "Then, Jo Bowen, you are more knight than me." Gone was the Golden Retriever, the eerie light of a wolf in its stead. "In fact, I'd say I've only seen the like of your heart in two others, and we call them Captain and Quartermaster. And in two weeks, whether you ever unhorse a single soul, I'll be proud to shake the hand of a sister in arms."

Swallowing down a lump in my throat, I clapped Trace on the shoulder. "And I'll proudly call you brother."

"See, Jo, you do shit like this, and you scare the crap out of me." Fillmore's smile seemed forced, but I cut him some slack after his recent ordeal. "I'd be more scared to trade blows with you than Aaron."

"Aw, poor farm boy, I think it'll be some time before they let us greenies run at each other, so you'll be safe for a while." I accompanied the tease with a companionable squeeze of his shoulder, only remembering his bruises when he hissed a breath. "Sorry, so sorry. But seriously, go get yourself a shower and grab an ice pack before Cranston gets back and steals all the hot water."

When he laughed, he clutched his ribs, and winced, a sheen in his eyes when he looked up at me one last time. "I dunno what's more dangerous Jo; facing you in the lyst or shielding against the sharpness of your humor." Then he heaved his bedrock solid body to its feet and made for the door, leaving me alone with Trace.

"Alright, my friend, let's get this done. I've got a date with destiny." He gave me a funny look, but as soon as I fastened my arming jacket, he set to work. Before long, I sat astride Eros, my heart whirring in my chest like a humming bird about to take off. I took my helm from Trace and pointed the stallion up the hill, eager to wear the bruises like the badges they would be. Don't mistake me, I knew they would hurt like the blazes, particularly after they stiffened up, but I'd own that part too.

I nodded at Cranston as he came out the gate, and his mouth wrinkled with distaste, the bit of exhilaration that made me like his face for a moment disappearing like it never happened. "Take your licking, bitch. I'm sure you'll be doing some of your own later."

His hate still confused me so much I could only recoil from the verbal blow, unable to even look over my shoulder at him as he dropped down the hill. Luckily, I had better things to do with my energy, and I latched onto the sight of Aaron and Bart waiting together, Eros carrying me steadily forward. Byz was taking a well-deserved break, sucking down a long drink while Aaron sat on the edge of the mounting block, his generally untidy hair slicked to his head with sweat. His face looked flushed and I didn't like the paleness around his lips, but with Bart fanning him and the long draws he took on his own water, he'd probably be fine.

"Are you okay, Sir? I don't want you overdoing for my sake." Eros came to a halt the instant I began to tighten my hand, and I ran my gloved fingers through his mane in thanks.

All fox in the hen house, Aaron grinned up at me. "Trying to get out of this, Bowen?"

"Hell no." I growled, my eyes widening in alarm at the easy curse. They'd driven me to cursing. Next thing you knew I'd be a foul mouthed dissolute.

"Did you remember the soap? I think her Mom said Ivory was best." Aaron asked his brother before they both turned mischievous smiles on me.

"Settle for getting your far too charming ass in the saddle and hitting me." I groused, though I didn't mind the teasing. Brotherhood, indeed, complete with the requisite dishing of crap.

"Bart, I do believe we've corrupted her! I don't know if it would be in the best interest of the company to keep around such an unrepentant, ribald shrew." The solemn delivery, so completely dead pan, had me hoping he was teasing, but anxiety chewed on the corner of my confidence with sharp teeth.

Bart's placid response, thank goodness, eased the sting of its bite. "Aaron, I think you'd best do as the lady says. You get her much more ramped up and I'm going to hand her a lance so she can hit back."

Aaron looked to his brother with wide eyes before turning toward me with a wink. "Don't worry, Jo, I'm just giving you a hard time, to take your mind off things. I get squirrely when I land this many hits, the adrenaline makes me mouthy."

"I'm not worried." I winked back, just so he knew I was returning the favor. "I meant every word. Put up or shut up."

Aaron laughed and stood up to shake his armor back into place before turning to climb the mounting block. "Ooo, I like it when you get mean, Bowen. Keep it up, and I might believe you."

Steve checked Byz's girth and positioned the dark grey gelding alongside the platform, Aaron swinging in the saddle with more ease than I would have expected for as much work as he'd already done. Oh, yes, Sir Aaron Drew still felt fresh and full of run, and I was about to face him down in the lyst. Shit. Sorry, Grandma, sometimes only a curse word will do.

Once Aaron was helmed up again, he rode away, and I asked Eros to step up to the now empty spot, grinning indulgently when he took a moment to bump Bart with his nose. Bart snuck in a quick stroke of his forehead before guiding him closer by the cheek of his bridle. "Move up, you big dog." Then he stood right beside me, a breath away as he took the helm from under my arm, the relaxation on his face steadying my eager nerves. "You ready for this, Bowen?"

A little stung that he would doubt me this far into the game, I bit my lip to suppress a frown. "Don't tell me you're worried about me too. I've already gotten the spiel of 'you don't have to do this, delicate flower' from Trace and Lee."

The grin he laid on me had not an ounce of worry in it, and plenty of tease. "The flower I know has thorns to spare her from attack, should she wish it. No, Bowen, you're just the right kind of crazy for this, or I'd have sent you down the road with Brantley." He pressed the closely fitted helm over the crown of my skull, my ears folded flat for a moment until it slid into position. Before closing the visor, he leaned a little closer so I could hear him. "Look at him just like you have a weapon, bring your lance arm up just as if you are loaded for bear. It'll help, I promise."

Then darkness descended, my eyes adjusting to the close confines and the slit that helped me focus. I turned Eros away from the comfort found beside his master and guided him into the lyst, letting routine erase the last of my nerves. A strange calm infused me, nothing left that I could do to prepare and all my training having led me to this. The weighty serenity felt familiar, from years in the start box waiting for cross country, only now wasn't the countdown. Now was Bart lifting an arm to gain my attention, and I nodded my readiness. Now was him twirling his arm in the air, signaling us to come about. Now, I just needed to ride.

Adrenaline flooded my veins as we turned to face our opponent, and I let go of the reins, trusting Eros to do his job. Mid-lyst was seven strides, so I turned my countdown there, hitching my right arm against my side as though set to deliver a blow of my own. Aaron came into focus quickly, Byz moving like a freight train, and at the last second the motion of his lance pulled my eye away from my own target. The blow felt similar to the day a young steer hammered me in the chest with both hind feet, knocking me back enough to make my heart rate spike. By will alone I hauled myself upright, breathing hard when I finally found the reins and asked Eros to stop. Taking a second to remind my chest to expand and contract, Steve ran forward to check in with me, but I straightened with determination, wondering if Aaron had pulled that blow. If he had, would I be able to endure a real one?

The answer came quickly, Steve signaling Aaron's readiness for another go, and I didn't even take time to think. Eros followed my train of thought as much as the cues I gave, launching us both toward the coming blow. This time my eyes bored a hole in the center of the grid on Aaron's shoulder, and I flexed my arm against my body as if steadying the weighty length of a phantom lance. The hit came fast, so fast my body didn't have the slightest chance to argue with gravity, the strike, the fall, and the collision with the ground all taking up the space of a single heartbeat. Nothing registered for a second or two, everything dark, no sense of up or down. Then light filled my visor, bright enough for me to wince against as someone rolled me to my back, my equilibrium returning in a dizzying rush. Worse still was the sudden flood of sunlight as my visor rose, two faces swimming into view, and I blinked rapidly to bring them into focus.

Steve and Bart manifested, silhouetted against the achingly blue sky, both with a pucker of worry on their foreheads. "I'm fine." I spat out crankily and held up my arms. "Help me up?" This I said a little softer, my failure to stay on not really a surprise. We'd been pretty much promised it would happen. Strong hands gripped mine, and together, we heaved me to my feet. I'd have turned straight for the block if not for Bart grabbing my elbow and stepping in front of me to look in my eyes, concern still laced across his features. "What?" That came out a little crankier, annoyance with myself coloring my response. "I'm fine, Bart, seriously."

The eyebrow went up half a tick, and I shook my head, realizing I'd just used his given name in public. It shouldn't matter, as I already addressed the rest of them by name, but it felt significant somehow. "I'm just making sure he didn't ring your bell too hard. You're stubborn enough to keep going even if you were hurt."

Adrenaline and impatience joined forces, narrowing my eyes and raising my chin. "Pot."

Anyone else might not have caught it, but Bart snatched the tiny word I threw at him with martial precision, worry taking a back seat to his grudging amusement. "Kettle."

Sighing, he turned me around and lifted the lyst rope so I could duck under. Steve, who I hadn't even seen leave, already waited for me with Eros, the stallion pawing his eagerness despite the calming strokes of the squire.

"Hey, big fella." I ran my fingers along his neck to find the reins, Eros calming with the touch of my voice and hand. Swinging back on, I quickly adjusted the skirt of chainmail that protected my pelvis so it rested in front of the saddle pommel and turned to look at Bart so he could secure my helm. The instant the pin scraped into its slot, I adjusted my grip on the reins and moved off, ignoring the twinge of my body. There would be plenty of time to catalog my bruises later, when I had received all of them.

The next pass had the same speed, but this time when the hit landed my whole body strained against it, all those core muscles I'd been working on screaming under the load. Without Eros, I might not have managed it, but the left leg I curled against his body to keep him under me actually served to move him under my hips, and we jostled to an ungainly stop at the end of the lyst with me still on his back. A small part of my brain ran circles and threw its hands in the air with happiness, my unseen grin hurting my cheeks, though my ego wasn't so large as to assume I'd achieved this on my own. While I could hardly see his tippy ears, I still scratched beneath Eros's mane for a second, grateful that he had saved my bacon. Movement in my limited scope of vision pulled my attention back to the task at hand, and I nodded at the shape of Steve, cueing Eros around the turn before I could overthink the last of my blows.

The stallion felt careful, his strides slower and loftier for the first few, and I relaxed into it, bringing my arm into position as if that alone would allow me to defend myself. The effort was futile, logically, but I couldn't just sit there and take it. The instant I lasered in on my target, Eros flattened out, as if he too wanted to hit back.

You'd think being hit while wearing a metal suit would sound like a car wreck, but it came off as more of a dull tink and the deep bass reverb of your whole body absorbing the concussion. It drove me back on my right hip, and I tried to take the weight in my joints, but once out of center the armor dragged me off with excruciating slowness. This time I hit the ground on my side, and immediately rolled to my back, pounding my fists in the dirt once, just to hit *something*. Only Bart that blocked the light as I thrust my arms up, my heart a little thrilled by how easily he gripped my hands and got me on my feet. When he pulled the pins on my helm he removed the whole thing at once, and answered my grin readily.

"You're crazy, Bowen."

"Then I'm in good company, don't you think?" I asked, smiling harder, not caring that my hair was probably awful from the helm and sweat. "Where's Eros?"

Bart rooted in the pocket of his jeans and came up with a mint, trading me the manfair that protected my hand for the plastic wrapped sweet. Then he pointed behind me, to Eros waiting patiently for his reward. My hand almost disappeared in his mouth in his enthusiasm, but he very carefully didn't touch my skin with his teeth. I accepted his reins from Steve with a thank you for his work, and turned at the sound of Aaron's voice.

"Bowen." He approached still astride, then dismounted, Steve stepping forward to take the horse for a moment. He held his open hand out and I reached to shake it, but he latched onto my forearm instead, a Roman variant that made the blood rush to my head. The grip felt like an induction into a secret society and I returned it as best I could around our armor. "Well done. Never doubted you, but well done just the same. I look forward to facing you in truth."

Then he turned away, and I stood in stunned silence for a moment, numb from the surfeit of emotions. Eros brought me back to reality with a well-timed bump of his nose, and I ruffled his forelock before heading down the hill to the barn. By the time I got out of armor and Eros had been cared for the bruises were beginning to set up. Though wincing at every movement of my torso, and with my shoulder sporting a purple circle testifying to the tightness of Aaron's shots, danged if I wasn't proud of each colorful mark. Little did I know, so much more went into earning a knighthood than the ability to hit and be hit in the lyst. There were some hits to endure to my heart that would hurt a lot more than the lance.

Getting up Wednesday morning was among one of the hardest things I'd ever done. I mean, I wanted to get up, I really did, but everything hurt, even the roots of my hair. My left pinky toe ached like one of the horses had trod on it, even the blood felt sluggish in my veins. But, being a practical girl, I knew very well that made it even more important that I got up and moved. In fact, the sooner the better, as every second I lay there my skin and muscles were screaming at me that death would feel preferable to that agony. They were lying of course, so I rolled onto my feet with a sigh and dragged myself into the shower first.

As I stood under the stinging spray of hot water I remained grateful for my tendency to rise early, as I had the hot water all to myself. Every bruise felt on fire at the first touch of the spray, but I just breathed my way through the pain until everything settled into a state of numb reprieve. Turned out I bore a palm sized bruise on the front of my hip from the edge of my armor, another on the shoulder I had fallen on, a faint one along my collarbone on the right, and of course, the tag marks on my left shoulder. It hurt to lift my arms and shampoo my hair, but I made myself do it, making each movement a purposeful stretch. By the time I wrapped a towel around my limp frame, the ache had settled into more of a dull roar, and I dressed myself without dying a slow, agonizing death.

After several cups of tea, two pieces of toast and some scrambled eggs, I let myself out of the house an hour later than I normally would have. Down the hall, a bunch of whining and grunting began, so I wanted to get out before they really started in with the complaints. People talked about girls being delicate, but seriously, I wasn't impressed with the pain tolerance these guys were exhibiting.

Ro and Eros both looked up from their buckets when I got to the gate, and judging by the busy chewing sounds, Bart had only recently delivered them. I turned away so they could finish, sighing as I walked down the barn aisle. In a perfect universe, I wanted to ride both Ro and Ivan today, but judging by the soreness, I didn't want to risk not accomplishing my assignment. So I grabbed Ivan's halter and began the long trudge down to the field to fetch the big Percheron.

It shouldn't have surprised me to bump into Bart, standing in a large puddle of mud around the water tank. Everywhere I went, there he appeared, either physically, or just in my thoughts. "Fancy meeting you here, stranger. What brings you to this dusty watering hole in this no-where town?" I asked, leaning heavily on the gate as he turned my direction.

"J.T. being himself." He sighed and pointed to the trough, drawing my attention to the giant crack in the side. "Everything is a toy to him, and apparently he thought last night would be a good time to soak his feet and splash around. Looks like I'll be headed into town to buy a new one. What I want to know is what a stubborn mare like you is doing out of bed at this hour. You'd think after yesterday's beating you'd have finally slept in."

"It's like you don't even know me." I teased, grinning unrepentantly when he tried to give me a stern glare. "Seriously, the choices were lay there and wallow, or get up and distract myself. This seemed the better choice. At least if I move the muscles will warm up eventually."

"True enough." He grinned back finally, chipping away at my resistance to him even more.

I let myself in the gate and meandered toward the herd without much agenda, actually stopping a few times to stretch. The horses barely flicked an ear at me, but as soon as I closed on Ivan he gave me his attention, something in his expression telling me he might be in a mood. The kind of mood that would make it hard to catch him. But I knew his kryptonite, and I crinkled the granola bar in my pocket, laughing softly when he trotted the twenty feet toward me, his lips already reaching for the goody.

After giving him a little bite, I slipped the halter on his roman nose and headed back to the gate, the other horses falling in behind us in hopes they'd get something too. A slight ruckus to the rear made me sharpen up and pay attention. As much as I acted pretty casual around the horses, awareness kept me from getting hurt, and I didn't want to get run over by any horse, let alone these one-ton puppy dogs. They wouldn't mean to hurt me, but they could without trying. A squeal and the quick thunk of a hoof connecting with muscle made me pivot on my heel, finding Tuck and Byz arguing over their places in line.

"Boys!" I bit off, parade ground loud and drill instructor sharp. "Knock it off!"

Both stopped in their tracks, Byz splay legged and ungainly looking as he had been going in for another bite when I yelled. It was hard not to laugh, but I bit my tongue on the humor. "Good boys. I'll bring you something later."

Bart stood at the gate, holding it open for us to pass through, and stepping into the gap to shoo the peanut gallery off to their grazing. The three of us trudged back up the hill, and I tried not to wince as my breaths deepened from the exertion, letting the discomfort serve as a reminder of my accomplishments thus far. I loved the speaking silence that surrounded us though, even as my muscles complained about their current state. It gave me something else to think about other than my physical discomfort, though I felt more awkward with my emotional conundrum. "So, two more weeks. What then, fearless leader?"

It's dumb, but I loved that he snorted too. We both used them like the horses did, little exclamations of nervousness, excitement or humor. "Then you go home, whether we sign you or not. We have a couple weeks off, the horses and the humans, before the real madness begins."

"Madness?"

"Yes, we'll be getting packed up to go on the road, which means getting the horses ready, restocking supplies and doing vehicle maintenance. We'll check over all the armor suits, resupply the first aid kits, and a thousand other things."

"Ah, so like somewhere between TDY and PCS." He looked at me hard, as if not quite sure I was real. "I did spend seventeen years of my life following my Dad around the world, Bart. We weren't the stateside kind of family, so I know what it means to have to pack everything you need and nothing you don't."

"Sorry, you just keep surprising me. No one here speaks in military vernacular but me, and I've all but phased it out of my vocabulary at this point." He looked up the hill, as if he could see beyond the horizon line, like at some distant memory.

"So how long are you on the road for?" I asked, trying to pull him back to the present, waiting patiently for his answer as we entered the barn. He didn't say anything until I had Ivan tied and was walking to the tack room for my grooming tools.

"Three weeks, then home for two, a single and then home. After that, we have a two weekend run, home, then a final show. Once Thanksgiving hits, it'll be mostly quiet until the New Year." He grunted something like a laugh and rubbed his stubbly jaw. "I, for one, am rooting for you to be jousting, Jo."

While the humor went over my head, the faith in those words warmed me from the inside. "Well, me too, but what are your reasons? I have a feeling from that laugh that they probably aren't the same as mine." I started currying Ivan's dense black coat, letting the circular motions loosen the muscles in my shoulders.

"Because if you don't, I think you'll be competition for my job." I looked at him sharply, softening at the quirk of amusement on his lips.

"As if." I threw in an eye roll for good measure and returned to the smooth rhythm of strokes. Ivan grunted in appreciation when I scrubbed the underside of his belly, and I lingered until he relaxed, trying to show my appreciation for him in that little gesture. Bart's next words were completely unexpected, making my hands slow as I worked up the side of Ivan's neck.

"If I weren't part owner, I'd be deadly serious. If I weren't family, I'd feel damn threatened anyway."

I chewed on the words for a minute, finally stopping to turn toward Bart, and leaned against Ivan's side for support. "You can't be serious? I don't possess half the knowledge you do. Or the skill to teach it to anyone else."

"But you've got a knack, Jo. And you will learn all those things. I'm just a washed up jouster who needs something to do that will keep me close to the action. Living vicariously through the people I call my team mates." There wasn't even a blink to accompany that statement, telling me he believed every bit of it, and not an ounce of self-pity to dull the edge. God, it stabbed me in the heart. How could this strong, capable man not understand his value? "I said I'd tell you about my injury, and now is a better time than any other, since the boys likely won't be out until after lunch. You feel like riding into town with me to get that trough?"

One day I would blurt out something dumb, like 'I'd follow you anywhere'. Which I would, even if I didn't have the completely unreasonable hots for him, because I knew him to be a good man, worthy of my trust. Thankfully, my sense remained intact enough to keep the words behind my teeth. "I don't mind going, but what about Ivan?"

He grinned and headed for the feed room. "I think if we feed him, he won't give us a moment's thought." I laughed, because he was right.

Settled in the truck, ball cap pulled low against the sun, I watched Bart from the corner of my eye, his hands gripping the steering wheel like he might tear it off at any moment. It took him fifteen minutes to relax, but we had another thirty miles to town, so I didn't hurry him. Whatever he wanted to say, it bothered him enough that it showed, a strange thing to see on his normally calm face. I closed my eyes and pressed my head against the edge of the door, letting the thick breeze wash my face, content to wait. Like Ro, I felt he'd prove worth the effort.

"It wasn't jousting." He paused, and I caught the darted glance he threw my way. I nodded to let him know I heard him, and waited some more, my own jaw aching in sympathy for the tension in his. "I was on my second tour in Afghanistan, two weeks from getting to go home. We were on a routine convoy to another location, and a roadside bomb took out the side of the five ton I was in."

A slow blink was the only tell, as if he didn't want to close his eyes and see those memories. My body grew tense, holding myself achingly still, or I might have reached across the truck and touched him. Neither of us could afford that intimacy.

"That's how I know Mari Cassidy. She was my lead NCO, though in that instance, I had to take charge of her. I didn't notice my own wound until after I had her stabilized, adrenaline accelerating my blood loss, and I passed out shortly after the medics started working on me."

My fingers tingled with the remembered feel of his calf, and my eyes watered at the knowledge of Mari's injury. "She showed me, you know."

Again, that furtive flick of his eyes, though his concentration on the road never wavered. You had to love that military prioritization, that ability to distract yourself from things by the simple expedience of focusing on the job at hand. He acknowledged my words with a short nod, a degree of tension leaving his shoulders.

"Anyway, turns out aside from the injury to my leg, which I think you know about…" A pause to look over at me for confirmation, and damned if I didn't blush hard enough to burn. Damn him, he actually cracked a tiny smile, which made the embarrassment worth it. "I woke up in the hospital after twelve hours of being non-responsive, swelling in my skull impairing my ability to function normally. Not only had the concussion of the bomb affected me, it was helped along by the piece of shrapnel that struck my helmet. An eighth of an inch more would have killed me."

Curling my fingernails into my palm, I hoped the physical discomfort would distract me from the pain in my heart. I'd never wanted to cry so badly, nor been more convinced that I shouldn't. He wouldn't understand that anger and frustration and fear for him prompted the tears. I wouldn't allow him to think I pitied him, or that I was scared of what he was talking about. Rather, I felt proud to know him, and he probably wouldn't accept that either.

"Anyway, it took about a month to regain all my motor function, two to let my leg heal, and then I was in therapy for a while, both physical and otherwise." Notice the skip over talking about his feelings? Yeah, me too. "Mari and I leaned on each other all through the process, and I stuck around to help her adapt. Having someone to take care of gave me something to focus on, kept me living. But when she didn't need me anymore, I slid back down the rabbit hole."

Now *that* took some courage to admit. "But you crawled back out." I made a statement of it, because the answer sat beside me in the truck, baring his secrets. Bravest thing I'd ever witnessed.

The short laugh felt like the dark side of the moon, cold and without remorse. "Well, Aaron came and pulled me out by the scruff of my neck. Literally drove to Virginia, threw me in the truck with a duffel of my clothes, and made me detox on the drive back here. It was ugly."

Heavy quiet, unlike our normal comfortable silence, pressed against my skin, making me claustrophobic. I hunted for words to clear the air. "My bruises are pretty ugly. Mari's leg, and maybe even yours, are likely a little ugly. But those things are the past, not now. Now is you, riding Eros bareback into the dawn light like some sort of centaur from the Greek tales. Now is Mari, a mother, a wife, a friend. Now is me, finding myself."

Gusting a big sigh as he pulled into the parking lot of the feed store and shifted the truck into park, I turned to face him. Denial sat just behind his lips, and I threw more words at it to stop it from manifesting. "Now is me, lucky enough to call you my friend, and I don't let my friends talk badly about themselves. And in a couple weeks, you'll be my brother. Family. You fall down that well again, then I'll be right there with Aaron, dragging your sorry ass out."

The curse did it, I think, a glimmer of humor flashing past the memories. I smiled, trying to encourage it to a brighter flame, unthinkingly tapping him lightly on the shoulder with my fist. Even delivering that soft concussion hurt like fire, but the brief flare settled quickly back to ache. He still noticed, and turned toward me. "You sure you are okay, Jo?"

"I'm going to be." Smiling again, I popped the door and slid down to the ground, putting distance between us. Crossing my arms, I added firmly, "And so will you."

His nod of acceptance reassured me as much as the easy way we fell in beside each other as we headed for the equipment yard to hunt up a replacement water trough. We made it through the afternoon with few words, him in the shed hammering away at a bent piece of armor, and me riding both my horses. With anyone else, the unsaid words would feel too heavy to bear, but for him, I happily carried them around.

Thursday, God, Thursday morning burned, my joints throbbing against the abuse inflicted on my body. But just like the day before, I dragged myself upright and forced myself to move. The horses had been out overnight so there were no stalls to clean, but I meant to beat Bart out to the barn, to feed breakfast to our boys. *Our. Boys.* Completely, irrationally stupid to be so tickled about our heart horses getting along so well, but the thought still pushed a smile across my face as I started scooping feed.

As soon as the grain hit the bucket, I heard Ro's little whinny, shortly followed by Eros's more guttural plea to hurry me along. Yeah, pain seemed a little less important in the face of their care, and once they had their buckets I folded myself under the tree to watch them eat. Absorbed in the peace, I closed my eyes, tipping my head back against the trunk to think. College seemed so far away, those four years a blink of time compared to the impact the last six weeks had on me. The hammer of adversity had pounded me against the anvil of routine, forming me into a shape I hardly recognized. Bits of the old me were still folded in amongst the stronger steel. They added texture and character, all of it together making me beautiful, even to my own eyes. I didn't even mean physically, though I still marveled at the changes in my body, but internally, I truly admired who I had become.

Later that day, the temper of my steel resolve was tested sorely. Sorely being the operative word. I'd stretched everything, iced and ibuprofened, arnica'd and massaged, but just the armor touching my waist where the bruise lay hurt enough to make my eyes water. Once at the arena I trotted Eros around, trying to loosen my hips, to soften my body to his movement, but the armor thumped against every purple inflammation with no mercy. I felt marginally better at the canter, thank goodness, enough that I could face Bart to get my helm on with dry eyes. His gaze narrowed as he studied me, but I clenched my jaw bullishly, staring without flinching until he slid my visor in place.

I got to go first, meaning Aaron looked totally fresh and ready to rumble, and just the thought made me cranky. All of this would be so much more endurable if I could even *try* to hit him back. My heart rebelled against the idea of laying myself open to harm without even fighting. Still, I sucked back my frustration and blew it out in a hot breath against the close confines of the helm, setting Eros up in the lyst for our run. The turn around the end had a comforting sort of familiarity, and while I brought my arm up into lance position, I relaxed with the knowledge of the inevitable hit.

Aaron didn't miss, a fact as universal as the rising and setting of the sun. He didn't miss this time either, but the relaxed posture of my body somehow absorbed the shock, even as my shoulder burned enough to make my eyes sting. My left hand found the thin strap of the reins, knotted against Eros's neck, and I pressed my knuckles against him as we came to a stop. Sucking in deep breaths, I pressed them out just as forcefully, not wanting to actually cry since I could not wipe my eyes with the helm on. Nodding to signal my readiness for another pass, I watched for the upraised arm, and we were in the lane again, testing my new found relaxation.

Apparently, when you had nothing left, there was nothing left to lose, and the hit felt about the same, pressing me more deeply into the saddle as it skipped off my grand guard with a faint crack I hadn't heard before. As we stopped in front of Bart, he stepped forward, waving me to lean down a little. The position pressed the armor against the bruise at my waist, but I endured with a couple deep breaths as he popped my visor. The wide grin on his face when I could see him clearly made it worth it.

"He just broke a lance on you."

My eyes widened in disbelief and I straightened in the saddle, trying to turn and look. "Seriously?"

His knuckles rapped my thigh, bringing my attention back to him. "Seriously. I'll grab you a souvenir later. But since you stayed rock solid, we were wondering if you were ready to hit back."

Apparently, all the recent falls had muffled my cognitive function, because it took me a second to comprehend what he said. For all the delayed reaction, my enthusiasm was hard to tamp down, so I pressed it into service as an overly dramatic smile, batting my eyelashes like an innocent schoolgirl as I answered. "Who, me? Want to hit someone? Well, I never."

Then I slapped the visor back down and bent so he could secure it, teeth aching with the growl I held in. Even through the helm, I could hear the deep bass rumble of his chuckle, and as soon as I held out my hand he lifted a lance up for me to fold my fingers around. Testing its weight for a second, I made sure of my grip, reveling briefly in the soreness that let me know the muscles were engaging. Then I lifted the lance to signal my readiness, sliding into the narrow pocket of quiet preceding the charge.

Eros's ribcage expanded into my legs, and I relaxed into the exhale that followed, matching our breaths for just that moment. The raised arm twirled briefly as I set my heel into the stallion's side, and my eyes found Aaron without effort. Everything felt so slow for a moment, I probably could have counted the rivets on his shoulder, but I was concerned with nothing except a one inch square of scarred steel peeking from between the grid marks. The lance came down like the extension of my body it was meant to be, and I waited. Three. Two. One.

The shock of impact struck both sides of my body near simultaneously, but my focus on the hit had turned my torso just enough that I could absorb it into my core. The next pass came much the same, and while I didn't break a lance, I satisfied myself that Aaron hadn't broken another on me either. Steve took the lance from me, and I rode to meet Aaron, a euphoric grin still hidden behind my helm. But judging by the enthusiasm of his grip when we clasped arms, he didn't need to see it to know it was there.

After Bart helped me get the helm removed, he too clasped my arm, acknowledging me as his brother had. As I rode back down to the barn everything in me wanted to gallop back up the hill and go again. Sucking on the marrow of excitement, and savoring the flavor of success, I admitted, if only to myself, that I was becoming a junky.

Though I sported some new bruises under my lance arm come Friday, the rest of them settled to a tedious annoyance. No lessons were planned, though I still hopped up on Ro for a long trot around the property, stretching out the remaining aches in the process. Aaron found me in the armor room in the afternoon and settled in beside me as I tidied my trunk. Yesterday, despite my excitement, I'd been tired, making me negligent with my things.

"So, tell me what's on your agenda when all this is over?"

Taking a few extra moments to inspect the holes in the leather straps that secured my pauldron, I mulled over my answer. "Truthfully, I'll be winging it if you don't keep me. This came on suddenly, and I lost my placement at the summer camp. I'll probably just go home and start job hunting." One of my college friends had sent me a job listing for the firm they were at, and it had crossed my mind to apply. But the thought of moving to

Chicago when I'd grown so content in the countryside irked me. "Or maybe I'll just take a year off and work the ranch with Dad. He always needs hands."

Aaron sat uncharacteristically quiet, a stillness foreign to his body, the coiled consideration something that looked better on his brother. "Well, barring anything ridiculous, the three of you are on track for acceptance. I don't know if the guys will sign, they would be more on a contractual basis, for the occasional gig. But after a little talking with Bart, I think we'd prefer you to be around full time, on the road and off."

Even as tired as I felt, flames roared to life on the fuel of hope that had built in my chest, and I struggled to keep my emotions in check. "I'd prefer that as well." I answered carefully, allowing a small smile that barely showed a glimmer of my happiness.

"That's settled then. Now, to get through the next week with everyone intact." He sighed dramatically and shoved himself up with his hands on his thighs, leaving me sitting in a cloud of contentment. Yet, in the back of those clouds, thunder threatened—everything could be ruined in one reckless breath if I couldn't get control of my feelings for his brother.

Evening rolled in on heavy clouds, quickly darkening the sky with a promise of thunderstorms. On my way up to the barn to check with Bart about bringing the horses in, the first crack of lightning resounded in the distance, hurrying my feet. The men met me half way up the path, their eyes dark with worry and a slew of halters strung along their forearms as the wind began to kick up. Heading toward the pasture moved us closer to the storm, but thankfully the horses were waiting at the gate in a milling throng.

Their massive bodies trembled and flinched with agitation, and my heart thumped hard when Bart let himself in among them. My worries were quickly allayed when he moved out the other side and started catching up the ones on the outskirts. Tuck and General quickly came to hand, and he waved me in to take them, making it my turn to move through the smaller press of bodies, running hands over taut skin as I went by. Then he went after J.T and Cappy, though Cappy lifted his head at the slightest noise and darted away several times when the wind flattened the grass. Aaron appeared beside me, taking the two geldings from his brother, though all of us jumped in unison when the lightning flashed just over the hill. Byz took off like the hounds of hell were giving chase, tucking his hind end under him as he ran a lap around us all and I started murmuring, not only to reassure the horses but myself.

Hawk rolled his eyes and snorted when Bart approached him, trying to press his body through the gate to escape his fear. I swallowed hard when one feathered hind foot sliced backward to warn Bart away, but he dodged it easily. Not that I doubted him with a single horse, but my growing feelings put worry where there shouldn't be. A heavy growl from Bart, barely audible over the racing storm, grabbed the gelding's attention enough that he turned to face the man. Instantly, Bart's shoulders softened to reduce the threat he presented, and he lifted a hand in invitation. Hawk, seeking any port he could find, stepped forward to have the halter slid over his ears.

Thankfully, Byz had expended most of his usual orneriness in his race around the field, and he trotted to a stop at the garbled words Bart murmured into the wind. Everyone secure, we swung the gate open and fastened it so it wouldn't be torn off by a random gust, walking hurriedly up the hill toward the barn. Inside, we tossed them in their stalls, not even bothering to remove halters as we latched their doors closed, and Bart and I hurried out to grab our last two. Buttermilk was probably hiding in the barn she shared with the sheep, warmed by wet wooly bodies pressed together for reassurance.

Eros stood at the gate expectantly, waiting for rescue, yet Ro appeared anything but calm. He tried to stay close to his friend, but each fresh roll of thunder increased the shaking of his body, and he paced off his nerves with rolling eyes. Once Bart caught Eros, I moved into the paddock, my shoulders tightened with the instinct for self-preservation when the lightning fell mere seconds after the thunder. Struggling to remain calm, I pretended we had all day to catch him, when my brain knew we had mere minutes before the storm caught up with us.

"Ro, Ro, my sweet boy, I'm here. We're going to get you inside." He pivoted toward me, seeking the comfort I could usually offer, but an unexpected jagged sword of light cracked behind him. Leaping forward to escape it, he had no concept of my presence beyond his panic, and even as I calmly stepped aside to keep from being run over, my throat closed with fear and tears.

"Ro!" I nearly screamed into the thickening gale, leaves torn from trees now pelting my face. Thankfully, at the desperate plea, he turned, his eyes flicking past me to the storm and back again. I hurried forward and buckled on his halter, turning to follow Bart and Eros's shapes toward the barn as the rain finally sheeted down. Aaron slid the barn door closed as soon as we cleared the threshold, and we dripped our way down the aisle to tuck our horses in, the sound of the rain muffled with the apartment overhead.

Poor Ro was too keyed up to settle into his hay like the rest of the herd, and despite my soaked clothes, I folded myself into his manger. Every time he stopped pacing to check in, I offered him a bite of the hay, both of us shaking. Mine came from the quick chilling of my jeans, his from lingering fear, though we both jumped at a cascade of lightning outside his window. As the storm slowly began to level out, he spent longer pauses with his head nearly in my lap, nibbling furtively at his supper as I stroked his forelock. Exhausted and now cold, I became drowsy, my hands falling to my lap to be warmed by Ro's steadying breaths as my eyelids grew heavy.

On the cusp of dozing off, I startled upright at the sound of the stall door opening, relaxing marginally when Bart let himself in with a pile of fabric in his arms. My arms caught the bundle reflexively when he set it on my lap, my fingers curling in the plush wool as he took the top blanket off and turned to lay it over Ro's back. His soft drone soothed my worried boy as he unfolded it, revealing it to be a cooler that buckled around the chest and belly. It would keep the gelding from catching a chill and help dry his coat much faster, hopefully aiding in slowing the muscle tremors. Bart's voice soothed my own heart as well, though it did nothing to dispel the chill that shivered over my own skin, making me clutch the remaining blanket closer.

I almost fell off the hay rack when the heat of his palm met my cold cheek, wanting to curl closer yet frightened of the familiar contact. Eyes wide, I studied his, a softness in them that helped unstring my nerves, his lips moving, though I couldn't hear anything around the sound of my heartbeat and the storm. Leaning away from the tempting warmth, I shook my head. "What?"

"I said you need to get out of those wet things. Aaron invited you upstairs, since the storm is going to hang around for a while but I figured you'd want to stay with your pony. There are some dry things in the blanket, I'll close the stall door and you can get changed."

Nodding slowly, I slid down from my perch, my tired legs biffing the landing. I might have hit my knees if not for Bart's arm around my waist, hitching me against his side. While I'd like to say I was thrilled to be there for very girlie reasons, it was his heat I wanted to curl into more than anything. In a moment of weakness, I actually turned my cheek against his still damp shoulder and leaned in, shivering once. "How are you so warm? So not fair."

His chuckle, vibrating through both of us, now that absolutely woke me up. I straightened, trying not to blush, immediately regretting the loss of heat. "Well, Bowen, I think if I'd gotten beat up repeatedly this week, and worked myself ragged on top of it, I'd be cold too. Now get changed, and I'll be back in fifteen with some tea and toast." Then he left, and I had to stifle a whimper of longing against the blanket in my arms. Why, oh why, did he have to be so likeable?

Ro hardly looked up from his hay as I shucked my wet things and rolled them into a bundle to take to the house later. The dry clothes helped me feel a little more human, though as I rolled the ankles of the sweats up to keep from stepping on them, it dawned on me they must be Bart's. Aaron and I were closer in height, slighter of build, and the Marine Corps hoodie I wiggled into confirmed it. These things were definitely Bart's and the

241

knowledge warmed me all the way through. Always giving me what was his, though this was perhaps the most physically close of all those gifts. He'd worn these, against his skin, and now they were touching mine. I wrapped the blanket around my shoulders and hopped back into the hay rack, allowing Ro to inspect me briefly as my cheeks cooled. No matter how much I wanted to get closer to Bart I still lived in limbo. Student, not quite friend, and still too young, no matter how I looked at it.

To be fair, I'd always been considered an old soul, more comfortable with people older than my peer group. Partly from the company of my parents, partly from an overactive brain that thought beyond the usual sphere, and thanks to the military, partly from exposure to the world. Each had engendered a sense of responsibility for myself and how I interacted with people around me. Bart felt like an echo of that sense, like when I was around him, I fit. Neither too young in years nor too old in experience, he made me feel just right.

Warm now, my body began to relax, but my brain spun too fast to follow. I slowed my breaths, watching rain slither over the glass of the high window at the back of Ro's stall, finding a sense of rightness on my own. By the time Bart returned I was curled like a cat, deep in the corner of the hay manger, and I had to unfold myself to reach for the proffered tea. I met his tentative smile with one of my own as the heat of the mug seeped into my hands, the ache in my lance hand quieting. "Thank you."

"No, thank you." He set a folded paper towel on my knee, and sipped from his own mug. "That would have taken much longer without you. I wouldn't have wanted to trust Cranston or Lee the same way."

"Oh, either of them would have been fine." I shrugged away the praise, not wanting to be singled out just yet. Cranston still considered me a threat, in his desperate need to be the best, and I didn't need anything exceptional to come to his attention. "Lee's strong, and Cranston knows how to deal with polo ponies, which make these tigers look like kittens."

"How do you know he plays polo?" Bart's eyes sharpened quite obvious, compared to the usual subtle nuances I had to decipher. "You two buddying up now?"

I'd never say out loud how much I loathed the frat boy, but I pressed a singular eyebrow high enough to furrow my forehead, and flattened my tone when I replied. "I'd sooner bathe in sheep dip." That startled him enough that his coffee sloshed, a splash of it quickly spreading across the chest of the dry shirt he had changed into. "But honestly, Cranston's favorite thing in the world is himself, and he does like to brag. There's a lot to be learned when you keep quiet. I know all about the string of ponies, the Argentinian coach, and the brand new trailer his daddy just bought him."

Bart nodded, hiding a smile behind his coffee cup, and watched as I pulled a slice of toast from the bundle on my lap, the real butter slathered on it making my stomach growl. I swear, exhaustion gave food a flavor that couldn't be found any other way. Nothing bottled or boxed could replicate the excitement of one's taste buds when you needed the nourishment most.

Chewing slowly, I giggled when Ro came to check out what I had, and I peeled off a bit of crust to offer him. While he took it in his mouth and rolled it around, his ears swiveling as his brain worked, ultimately, he spit it out and returned to his hay. So far, hay, grain, grass and peppermints were it for him, but I intended to encourage every bit of curiosity he offered.

Clearing his throat, Bart pushed himself away from the wall. "Alright, I'll be upstairs. This is supposed to push through in an hour, I left an umbrella by the tack room door so you can get back to the house without getting soaked." A flicker of tension marred his features, so brief I could have imagined it, but then he stepped closer and held his cup out to me. Confused, but trusting him, I took it, squeaking when he flipped back the edge of the blanket covering me.

"What do you think you are doing?"

He pulled a pair of thick socks from his back pocket, and gathered one up in his hands, holding it open for me. Carefully, I unfolded myself, touched by the gesture but conflicted about his manner. When I pointed my foot he slid the heavy knit over my still chilly toes, only the faintest of knuckle grazes registering against my skin. We repeated the same cautious maneuver with the other sock, then he plucked his coffee cup from my grasp and retreated to the door like his tail was on fire. Certainly, it felt like my cheeks were.

"Goodnight, Jo."

"Goodnight, Bart."

Simple, everyday words, really. But when it came to Bartholomew Clark, it was the simple, everyday things that were working their way into my heart.

The weekend turned into a kaleidoscope of mud and sunshine, sweat and surprises. I slept like a rock, falling straight asleep to the sound of the rain and the warmth of Bart's sweatshirt. Morning aches became bearable with a shower and ibuprofen, and when I arrived at the feed room Bart and I exchanged travel tumblers. Midnight black coffee for him, and tea for me, marginally less dark, but not by much. The two lump sweet and barest hint of milk calmed my self-consciousness about yesterday, content in the knowledge our friendship remained intact.

Mari brought me finger paintings from the boys, Mal's a remarkably recognizable dragon holding a book, and Max's a slightly less recognizable blob of a horse with a big smile. With Aaron's permission, I tacked them up inside the door to the armor room, the wild colors making everyone grin. Well, except Cranston, but as I'd never seen him smile over anything that didn't directly benefit him, it didn't surprise me.

The faire had come through the deluge in better shape than expected. In fact, it gave everything new life aside from a few spots on the road that were a bit washed out. Every color on the shop fronts looked brighter, the grass had thickened into a living carpet, and the people themselves appeared refreshed.

For Celtic weekend the whole grounds resounded with bagpipes and drums, Eros dancing even more animatedly to the rhythm and wail. Kilts were everywhere, and my vivid imagination kept wondering what Bart would look like wearing one. At one point, I almost walked into a post and forced myself to shake off the mental image while Mari laughed at my near miss. It really wouldn't do to put a divot in my forehead because I couldn't keep my mind on business.

The guys were all a little cautious in the lyst, though I doubted anyone could tell from the audience side. They still whooped it up, and cantered around like normal, but the wet spots in the footing made them pay attention and rate their horses. John came out to the arena with us, arm in a sling, but smiling, helping us pick up broken lance bits and such. Turns out the break hadn't needed surgery, but it would still be a long time healing.

"Aw, poor Tuck, he'll miss getting to joust with you." I teased, knowing full well the butterball Belgian wouldn't mind the vacation in the least.

"Oh, I know he's still got Lee, at least until next week." John's wink and grin lightened his whole face, deepening the lines around his eyes and mouth. "And I trust you'll make sure he stays well spoiled until I'm ready to get back in the saddle."

"More likely you'll come back and find we have to let his girth out a few holes. You know he's just going to stuff his face the whole time you are out."

John laughed as we darted in to clear the lyst. Once back at our station, he clapped me on the shoulder with his good hand. "Honestly Jo, the holidays will be during my healing period, and it's just as likely I'll have to let my own girth out a bit. Caroline loves to feed people, me in particular."

"Grandma likes to say feeding people is like hugging them from the inside." I answered, a slight pang of homesickness tugging at my heart. It would be good to go home, even if only for a few weeks. Then once I settled into the company I would have a little more freedom to visit, since two hours really wasn't that far in the greater scheme of things.

"I'll have to tell Caroline that one, she'll probably have a needlework sample of it done before the weekend is out and have it hung in the kitchen by Monday." His cheeky grin erased the last of the worry I'd been harboring about his injury, and as the joust ended, he rejoined his wife with a promise to come watch me ride later.

Turned out, Hawk hated working in the mud, an unusual trait among the rest of the herd. Recalcitrant in the lyst that afternoon, he balked at every puddle, and while Cranston rode him through it they gave a poor showing. General and Ivan both proved nearly giddy to splash through the wet with their plate sized feet, and Lee actually laughed several times, losing his usual shyness in the process. I honestly couldn't have cared who won at that point, just seeing him having a good time, but I edged him out just enough on the quintain to see myself back in the Queen's company. As we waited for the parade to move out so we could fall in at the end, she leaned down and touched my shoulder.

"Lady Josephine, I have heard rumor that we are to raise you and your compatriots to the office of knighthood the weekend next."

"That is our hope, Your Majesty." I answered cautiously.

Her clever mind seemed awhirl in her eyes, and she smiled secretively. "Then I beg you consider joining me in a bit of planning for such eventuality. And please, when we are not here before the crowd, I would be flattered should you address me as your familiar. I am Lynn when not wearing the crown of state."

Taking her hand from my shoulder, I shook it carefully. "It would be a privilege, my Queen. Those I call friend refer to me as Jo, if you like."

"Then you and I shall hatch a plan to set the crowd on fire and light a flame in their hearts they won't soon forget, dear Jo." Her wink held mischief of the best kind, and as we fell in at the tail of the procession, I found myself with another friend.

❤❤❤

Sunday turned into a muggy mess, all of us sweaty and cranky even before the gates opened. Thankfully, we were all professionals, or some facsimile thereof, and pulled on our smiles with our costumes. The drumming and pipes made my head throb in time to the music, and I drank water like a fish, but still I soldiered on. As I suited up Alex in preparation for the mid-day joust, he stopped me before I could secure his cuirass, worry in his eyes.

"You doing alright, Bowen? You look a little flushed."

Pride straightened my spine, and I wrinkled my nose at the idea of having a weakness. Not a chance I'd admit to it. "I'll be okay, let me get you kitted out and I'll go get some more to drink. Everyone else is in the same boat."

"To an extent, but you aren't normally so miserable looking around the eyes."

"Ah, and insulting my looks is going to make me feel so much better." I teased, trying to downplay my condition. We couldn't afford for any of us to have problems.

"Well, I'd tell you I thought you looked fetching today, but I have a feeling it might get me a beating." His grinned at his own cleverness, and just for fun I threw a light punch at his shoulder. When he pretended to be hurt by it, we both chuckled, and settled back to work, me ignoring the fact that just laughing had made me lightheaded.

I adhered to my word though, and got another bottle of water out of the huge cooler full of ice that lived in the souvenir booth. Chugging it too quickly left me in the breathless grip of a brain freeze, Bart eyeballing me with concern from across the yard, but I smiled as it eased and waved away his worry.

Once the knights were mounted I walked around each of the horses, spraying them with repellent to ward off the mutantly aggressive fly population that had quadrupled overnight. General sported a collection of bites that proved him incredibly sensitive, but all of the horses had garnered a few welts overnight. Unfortunately, the combined scent of sweat, the heavy chemicals in the spray and the sunscreen melting off my skin made me a little nauseous. Still, I swallowed it back and fell into place in front of J.T. for our jaunt to the arena.

Once there, under the oppressive sun, I wilted again, but Hillary pressed another water bottle on me with a sympathetic grimace. "I get it, I do, but don't be proud, Jo. We need you fit to ride this afternoon."

Wrinkling my nose to be caught out again, I took a swallow of water before responding. "Thanks, Hill, I'll try. But you know how it is. There's so much that needs doing."

"And you are only one person, Jo. Spectacular, to my mind, but still human. You can't do it all. Would you trust me to tack up Ivan for you later? I'd like to help."

Had I really pushed that hard that she felt like I'd say no? Goodness, I would have to work on that. Just because I wanted to be a knight didn't mean I felt myself better than anyone else. I touched her elbow to get her attention before time came to helm Alex. "Thanks, Hillary, I'd really appreciate that. And of course I trust you. I'd like to think in a couple years you'll be ready to join me in knighthood."

Her eyes went round, and her mouth moved without noise, but I couldn't wait for her reply as Alex approached. I left her to hold J.T., climbing the block to pick up the blued steel helm from under the towel I'd covered it with. Even with that protection, the metal felt warm to the touch, and I wondered at Alex's choice to darken his rig. Days like this, it would be like wearing an oven. Once secured I slapped him on the back to send him on his way and sat on the edge of the platform to watch. Cranston and Kory were clearing the lyst, Lee and Jeff handing up lances, while Steve and Aaron were running their respective ends. For once, it left me little to do but study the knights, and in moments of weakness, Bart.

I began to develop a radar where he was concerned, so that even when not looking directly at him I could feel a warmth from his general direction. Having a sense of knowing so singular, particularly since it came so naturally, felt comforting and alarming by turns. Actually, to be perfectly honest, it scared the crap out of me. The harder I tried to look at him as just a coach and a brother, the more my heart rebelled against my good sense.

As I watched Alex sight in on Trace, I picked up a slight difference in his aim than what I'd been taught. He appeared to sweep the lance in rather than bringing it straight down to bear, and when those hits landed, it rocked Trace hard. Once, the younger knight lost a stirrup and nearly fell, likely only his slightly lower center of gravity saving him from a dirt nap. Trace on the other hand, his hits came straight on. The difference showed as a waver in the tip, as if it took him a second longer to sight in.

They ended with Alex the winner by a narrow margin, but Trace would be coming back to face Aaron later, since Alex had already ridden in the morning joust. The schedule ended up being pretty do-able, though I'd had my doubts at first. At least this way, Trace consistently got to make more passes, which equated to more practice. With luck, he'd develop a little more feel for the game in the process. I mean, not that I had any room to criticize. I was greener than the grass surrounding the arena. But that's what my eye saw, and I wanted the whole team to be good, not just me.

Some of my light headedness returned once we were back in camp, the hot box of the armor room making my head swim, and I went seeking shelter at the booth. Mari turned as I approached, her eyebrows drawing down so hard her eyes nearly disappeared. The expression was a full on mom glare that I wished I had the energy to laugh at. I couldn't even manage a weak protest when she shoved me in a chair.

"You stubborn idiot. If you get any more like Bart, I'm going to swear you were separated at birth." She grumbled and shoved another water bottle in my hand before turning back to the ice chest. My eyes widened in alarm when she spun around with both hands cupping a sizable scoop of ice. "Pull your bodice out away from your body."

I covered my shallow cleavage with both hands, shaking my head. "No way, Mari, it's not happening."

Her dark eyes narrowed dangerously. "Josephine, so help me, if you don't do as I tell you, I will call in reinforcements, and you will not like the results."

Being a moderately intelligent individual, I took the red head at her word and turned my head away from the oncoming shock as I pulled the front of my bodice away from my chest. The ice hit my overly hot skin, breath hissing from my lungs, adrenaline and relief mixing together like oil and water. My skin felt on fire, but that faded quickly as my veins dispelled the freezing cold through my overheated head, the fog lifting from my brain. Closing my eyes, I let it melt, tipping my head back against the shelves at the rear of the booth and sipping slowly on my water.

"Better?" Mari asked after a few minutes. I made sure to meet her eyes when I nodded emphatically. "You were on the fast track for a trip to the hospital for heat stroke. Don't let it happen again Jo. I expected you to have more sense than a certain young marine I once knew."

"Yes ma'am, I'll keep it in mind." She turned away to help a few customers and I closed my eyes again, grateful when a breeze cropped up for a moment. When I heard the people leave, I looked back up at her with a grin. "What's this I hear you've had to rescue someone we both know from something similar?" She looked at me speculatively, as if unsure she should say anything, and I leveled a more serious look at her. "He told me you served and were injured together. I'm not fishing for information to hurt him with. I respect him too much."

She sighed as if coming out from under a heavy weight and shook her head. "A miracle enough, right there. He doesn't tell many people what happened. But this particular idiocy occurred early in his first tour, about five years ago. I think he was probably about your age, actually, which is another disturbing similarity. Apparently, all twenty-two-year-old martyrs forget to take care of themselves, still too young to realize they are mortal. He had run out of water early on, and completely underestimated the desert heat. By the time I caught on to him, I had to send him to the medics for an overnight stay and IV fluids."

"Thank you for saving me that, at least." I shivered for effect. "I'm not very fond of needles."

Once the ice melted I got up to check on Ivan, but Hillary, bless her, already had him tacked and waiting. "Hills, thank you." I grinned as I checked her work, not because I doubted her, but because my Daddy taught me well. It wouldn't do to let something small like a wrinkle in the saddle pad or a twist in a billet to come between me and my goals. "You did great."

Her Irish fair skin, cousin to my own, flushed around the edges of her sunburned cheeks. "Thanks, Jo. I'm not ever going to be a knight, but I can make sure you have every chance to be one."

As I shared a granola bar with Ivan, I studied her, taking in the athletic frame and sense of capability she wore. "Why not? I mean, if I can, you can."

"Well, my parents can't afford riding lessons. I'm saving for college, so I can't either. I have to settle for going to visit my cousin in order to ride. The most contact I get with horses is the summers working here. Aaron hired me last year to squire, after I'd spent a couple years working the booth and pitching in after hours."

"Yeah, I can see that being a problem." I chewed on the problem as I worked on another bite of granola, swallowing an idea before I could give it voice. "Do you have a car?"

"Yeah." The pride in her eyes made me think Miss Hillary probably scrimped and saved to make that happen, confirming my admiration of her work ethic, and solidifying my idea. I needed to put a bug in Aaron's ear. Likely, he was too busy to notice the potential growing right under his nose, and she probably didn't want to be a bother. I'd been there myself at her age. Amazing the difference five years could make.

My afternoon ride ended up a little wobbly in places, after all I'd put my body through the week before, but I didn't embarrass myself too much. Cranston edged me out by two points, and I couldn't begrudge him the long walk around the faire, settling into packing the trailer as we waited for closing cannon.

Unfortunately, when I took a minute to rest in between trips to the trailer, a cannon of a whole different kind went off in my brain. Mari had said five years. Only five years ago, when he was my age. The shot hit its mark, obliterating the largest bulwark that had been holding out against the idea of

252

Bartholomew Clark. My brain grabbed at the tattered bits of my defenses while my heart danced a jig on the remains.

It went against my practical nature, but Sunday night when I washed the clothes Bart had lent me, I mourned their loss for a moment. I wanted so badly to curl myself up in that sweatshirt again, surrounded in its well-worn embrace and the memory of his warmth. But it seemed far safer to give it back than to yield to the sentimentality I'd already attached to it. Another week of forcing distance, seven days until he would no longer be my official coach, though I'd be picking his brain for a long time to come. What I didn't count on was how working with the horses just seemed to bring us closer.

♥♥♥

Monday morning fell to the same routine we always kept, with me wandering in after he'd let the horses out, then turning to the mundane task of manure moving. As we dumped the last of our efforts in the spreader and headed back inside I closed my eyes against the play of muscle in his arms and shoulders. Needing a distraction, I turned to the tack room, on a mission to hunt up a bridle for Ro. The sense of his presence behind me came before a single noise hit my ears, and I spared him a glance as he leaned casually in the doorway.

"Can I help you with something?" He responded to the forced casualness in my voice with a shadow of a grin, hooking his thumbs in his pockets.

"No, just checking in to see what was on your agenda for the day. Can't have you overdoing it when you've got such a big week ahead."

"Now who's the mother hen?" I teased, turning my attention to the tangle of strap goods covering an entire wall. Some of the things I ran my hands over were familiar: European leather, or well-oiled Western latigo supple with care and time, but some defied the scope of my horsemanship. Things I'd only ever seen in photos. A tasseled Bedouin bridle rested over the thicker buffalo leather of a US Cavalry marked headstall, while a white bridle complete with blinder cups hung beside a wide surcingle that sported heavy duty handles. Each of them prompted curiosity, but I was too focused on my goal to linger. "Do you have anything super mild? Maybe even a rubber mouthpiece?"

Closing the distance between us so quickly my mouth went a little dry, he bent to open a trunk next to the one I knelt on. The inside contained a heavy puzzle of metal, shanks of curb bits poking through the loose rings of snaffles, a mechanical hackamore half buried under a side pull and a mullen mouthed liverpool. He shifted them aside easily, clearly hunting for something specific, his focused expression clearing when his fist closed on something I couldn't see. The bit he offered me was a straight bar of whitish plastic with an oval copper roller in the middle. When I closed my hands over the material I noticed how quickly it warmed with contact, and how soft the plastic felt. The roller would give Ro something to fiddle with, keeping his mouth soft, and the plastic would present no real threat of harm. Perfect.

"Thanks, this is lovely."

"My pleasure. Have to keep you two moving forward if we are going to make jousters out of you both. Now how about a bridle so you can keep it in his mouth?" All of it said so lightly, as if that's all we were to him, a job. It stung more than I'd like to admit, but it accomplished something I'd been fighting with all morning. Distance. When he handed me a basic black headstall and some rope reins that matched, I turned away to put it together, needing some physical distance as well.

When he didn't leave right away, I tried for my own nonchalance. "Left your clothes in a bag just inside your door. Thanks for that too."

"Yes, I saw them. I appreciate that. Not that I doubted you, but I know whatever I loan you will be well taken care of."

"I'd do the same for anyone." See, completely truthful, but it still felt dishonest. I'd always value what he lent me far more than I probably should. "You've been terribly kind. I wouldn't have made it this far without your help."

"I'd do the same for anyone." That echo stung my heart, made me glad I had my back to him so he couldn't see the flinch around my eyes. His sigh sounded heavy, then his boots were clunking toward the door. "Have a good ride, Bowen."

"I will, Sir. Thank you."

Footsteps carried him overhead, and a heavy thud made me think he must have sat down, leaving me alone with my thoughts, none of which I liked. Ro happily played distraction, and he surprised me by actually reaching for the bit when I offered it. I rewarded the effort with a peppermint, trying not to think of Bart in the process and failing miserably.

Wishing Mari had never shared her story, I dragged my feet out to the mounting block. Hoping I could turn off my overactive brain and aching heart, I tightened the girth. Praying I could find some peace with Ro, I heaved a deep breath and pushed my feelings away, sliding into the one place guaranteed to make me feel at home.

On Ro's back, I felt complete, whole, and utterly in the moment, leaving me overwhelmed with gratitude as we picked our way up the hill around a few wash outs. My breathing quickly evened out as we walked laps around the arena, barely needing the bit to steer him, a whisper of contact all that he required. I didn't even think his responsiveness was something anyone taught him before, but he was just so grateful to be listened to he wanted to do the right thing. Forcing him into anything would likely see the return of the robot formerly known as Roscoe, and to me, nothing would be worth that price.

Amazingly, he let me pick up the lance with only a moments tension, and I found another thing to be grateful for. Apparently, Ro was a one lesson wonder. There would be no repeating as long as he continued to trust me. His first canter down the lyst with it leveled at the rings felt a trifle stilted, but I made a big deal out of him and gave him a mint, waiting until he finished it to try the other side. Too focused on him to pay the rings their proper due, I only landed one out of the four, forcing me to the ground to retrieve the ones I'd lost. As I pulled myself back into the saddle and adjusted my feel on the reins, motion pulled my eyes toward the gate. Bart and Eros crested the hill, my heart soaring and plummeting in the same beat.

Forcing myself to turn away, I used Ro's added height to put the rings back on the stanchions so we could try again. Now that he grasped his job, it would be easier to focus on the target. In truth, fixating on the target helped him as well, now that he understood our objective. He couldn't very well put a full effort in until he knew what I was trying to accomplish. We came away with three out of four on our next try, which is what I ended up with half the time, so I counted it a win. More than anything, Ro just wanted the good boys at the end, though mints were always welcome.

Of course, the mints made me mindful of our audience and I contemplated my next course of action as I reset the rings. Confrontation or retreat? They took the choice from me as Eros headed in our direction, and Ro gave a tiny nicker of welcome. Slouching in forced relaxation, I feigned a grin, confused by the shadow in Bart's eyes. "Gentlemen, what brings you up here on your day off?"

"Eros was staring up the hill after you both, but for my part, it's guilt." I straightened slowly in the tack, giving him my full attention. "I feel like I did something wrong."

"No, I wouldn't say that," I dissembled. "You've been nothing but helpful."

"I thought we were friends, Jo." Oh, there he went, using my name. Yanking away whatever high ground I stood on. "But what happened down there did not feel friendly."

"No, it didn't." Honesty, I'd give him, but I wouldn't give over my feelings that easily. Everything was still too much of a grey area for me to risk showing my hand. Coming even remotely close to how I really felt might see me booted straight out the door for making a pass at the owner, and no way did I want anyone to think romantic feelings had an ounce to do with my acceptance to the troupe. I wouldn't be able to live with myself.

"I'm sorry if I was short. While I'm really enjoying watching you work with Ro, it's bringing up some raw memories of when I first got Eros." The memories that played behind his eyes hurt to see, not wanting to think of either of them in pain. "Sometimes it cuts a little deeper than others."

"No, it's okay. I can only imagine if it was anything like Ro, I wouldn't want to be reminded either. But you two have a marvelous relationship to celebrate now, surely that counts for something."

"It was worse. So much worse. But you are right. We've come a long way together, and he's returned the favor, digging me out of my own dark places." A smile of pride and the predatory gleam of victory pulled the weight from his shoulders. "Thank you, for being my friend, and his, to see that so clearly. To accept it. I really do appreciate it, even when I'm distancing myself."

Distance, to save himself pain. Yes, that I could completely understand. "That's what friends are for. To hold up a mirror when we need one, for good or ill. Once I'm not your student anymore, expect I'll probably call you out for the not so pleasant stuff more often. Then you might have to reevaluate being friends with me." I meant it to be a tease, but he responded to the truth in it.

"Expect the same treatment, Jo. Though I promise you now, there isn't much I expect you are capable of that might make me regret the arrangement."

Swallowing my heart, I plastered on another smile, and pointed toward the gate. "Then how about a quiet ride, my friend? Something relaxing before the toughest week of my life begins."

He nodded and sent me ahead, but once we were headed up the driveway toward the trail, he moved Eros abreast. The stallion stretched his steps longer to accommodate the difference in leg length between him and Ro, no words marring the peaceful breeze *shushing* through the treetops. We could have ridden that way for hours, I think, and it would have felt just as comfortable as conversation. Which is why I started slightly at the sound of his voice, a little lost in basking in the warmth of the moment.

"I think your pony needs a proper warhorse name. Something to convey strength and resiliency, with a little beauty thrown in for good measure. What do you think? I can't very well announce him as Ro in the arena."

"Hmm, that will bear some thought. His former name wasn't very warhorse like either. More like a good cowboy name." My brow puckered as I watched Ro's ears, flickering this way and that as he took in the world around him. This innate curiosity was his true nature, but he'd shown a strong survival mechanism in the beginning, protecting himself the only way he could. He didn't have much fight in him, but surviving, well, that he managed abundantly well. "It needs to be something that speaks to his ability to endure, to stay so beautiful despite adversity."

"When I bought Eros, for a mere three hundred and fifty dollars at an auction, he was listed as Demon. And he sure fought like one, sending one of the two guys who led him through the ring to the hospital with a broken shoulder. Aaron thought I bought him just to put him out of his misery, since he was so wild and in such rough shape." His sigh held all the weight of a colossus. "I think I even told myself that, to justify spending the money, but I had met him in the back lot, with no one else around. They had him in a tiny pen he couldn't even turn around in, and while he acted scared at first once I started scratching his neck, he melted against the rails trying to get closer." His fingers found the stallions neck, making the memory part of the present as he drew firm circles on the dark coat. "I told Aaron we'd feed him up for a month, just so he could know a little kindness before we put him down. Every feeding, I'd hold his bucket just over the stall door, not wanting to risk injury going in with him. I'd scratch his neck a little, but the instant I tried more he'd lash out with his teeth. I'd handle him just enough to take him out to clean his stall, but otherwise, left him to himself. He hated the geldings, and the mere scent of a mare made him wild. Turns out that's all they ever did with him, kept him in a stall and pulled him out to breed. Nothing to do but obsess about the girls, since that was his job."

Trying for a little humor, I chuckled softly. "So many people think being a stallion must be the best thing ever, having women lined up for you to breed and such. Funny thing is, every stud I've ever seen who had to live with those mares was hen pecked and beaten up regularly. It's not all it's cracked up to be."

"See, I knew that from being around my Grandad's stud horses. I'll have to show you sometime, but those pampered beauties, as coddled as they were, also got to live as a herd. Five stallions, living peacefully, able to work together. You've never known such well-adjusted horses of any sex." Those memories took years off his face, lightening the weathered lines by his eyes and mouth that must have come from his time in the deserts of the Middle East. "Anyway, I told Aaron I'd let him go after my next drill weekend, since I wanted time to cope with the aftermath. But when I came back he called out when he heard my voice, and I had to give him another month. I kept saying I'd give him one more month, and Aaron just let me keep lying about it. It took six months to finally achieve total breakthrough, as I had to leave for my two-week drill in the summer. I guess he hardly ate and paced most of the time, not trusting Aaron to hold his bucket. He shoved me with his head, hard, making me spill his morning bucket, and I didn't even think about it, just went in the stall with him. When I realized what I'd done, I froze, but he just stood there. I scratched his shoulder and he leaned in for more. I moved to his cheek and you could see the wheels turn in his head, where he had to make the choice to accept me or not. But he did."

Goosebumps moved over the entirety of my body, and I closed my eyes for a moment, smoothing Ro's mane with blind fingers. "When they are that damaged, it risks so much more of our hearts to love them." I murmured around the thickness in my throat.

"I think that's love in general, Jo. Real love, anyway. You can't give part of yourself to the endeavor, it has to be all or it might as well be nothing. But the risk of pain can be worth the reward, in the end."

That bit pummeled me hard, knowing with the two boys I'd thought I loved I'd always kept a part of myself away, saving it from the possibility of being hurt. I shook it away with determination, not wanting to repeat my mistakes. All or nothing. "True enough, my friend. Now, how about we make some new memories with our partners? Care for a canter?"

His reply came in the shift of Eros's weight as they lifted into a gentle rocking gait. We were barely a stride behind as I cued Ro for the same, and he quickly brought us level again. One day, I'd like to race Bart, to see whose horse proved faster, to see who did the chasing and who did the running. But that day, watching him sit the stallion with nothing between them but their relationship, felt like more than enough.

When the trail headed uphill again we slowed by mutual design, our horses on a loose rein as they leaned into their work. My heart trilled a little at the sight of a large branch fallen across the path ahead, and I looked over at my companion. "Will Eros be alright if we go on ahead?" Bart nodded, the line of his faintly stubbled chin tight with questions I felt too impatient to answer. "If this kills me, tell my parents I died happy, okay?"

Then I closed my legs, kissing faintly when Ro seemed reluctant to leave his friend. Three quiet strides into the canter I lifted into a half seat, hovering just over the leather so his back could stay soft. Thirty feet out, Ro's ears radared in on the branch ahead, and he hesitated; it didn't feel unwilling, just questioning. 'Do you see it there? Is that what you want?' I closed my legs again, softening my hand so he knew I wanted him to go.

Go he did. Nothing like Abby's pell-mell power, flinging us to the other side so we could gallop again, Ro condensed himself just enough to clear the obstacle before continuing on. We flew, like a bird soaring from branch to branch. No effort went into it, on my part or his, we just flowed together like water. Sure, the obstacle probably didn't stand more than two feet high, but it made something in my heart click into place with all the finality of gravity.

I never even realized how much I had fought for everything with Abby, and the bitter knowledge brought me to tears as surely as my happiness. I never, ever wanted to fight that selfishly again. To fight for myself, to fight for others, sure, but to go so completely against the nature of another for the sake of myself—it made my stomach roll. Ro came to a stop of his own accord, confused at the emotional human on his back, and looked at me out of one worried eye.

Bart pulled up just as I dashed my tears away, the concern on his face fading marginally when I tossed him a smile. "Sorry, don't mean to be a hyper emotional girl. Just had one of those painful moments of self-realization at the hands of one of the most beautiful moments in my life. It kind of stung."

The humor I'd been going for barely chipped away at the tension in his shoulders. "It's alright to get emotional sometimes. I mean, that was beautiful from where I was sitting. I can't imagine how it must have felt."

Eros resumed his place beside us as I cued Ro to move on. I let Bart see me looking him over, and the way my eyes included the stallion as part and parcel. "Oh, I've got a feeling you know exactly how that felt."

He smiled then, sweetness a foreign expression on his lips, but one I'd like to see more often. "Fair enough."

We rode the rest of our route lost in our own thoughts, though my thoughts didn't have much to do with my brain and everything to do with my heart. The armor I'd put around it was coming off a piece at a time, and it wouldn't be long until I had nothing left to protect me.

The next morning started rough, through no fault of my own. I got up at my usual hour, hoping for a little quiet time, but a ruckus down the hall became the opening salvo to a rather unpleasant exchange. I'd barely finished my first cup of tea when Cranston stalked in the room and polluted the peace with his mood. Ignoring his pique proved ineffective, as he began shoving things around in the fridge and cabinets, throwing a skillet on the stove with a clatter. Sighing, I tucked my book under my arm and headed for my room, hoping a closed door would at least block out the worst of his temper tantrum.

"Where are you going, teacher's pet? Long ride yesterday wear you out?"

I swiveled on my bare feet to face him, the darkness permeating his expression making my skin prickle. "What crawled up your butt and died Cranston? I rode my second horse, and got some coaching. I'm sure you could have done the same if you weren't sleeping off a drunk binge."

"Coaching? Is that what they call it these days? Is that like all the sorority girls doing 'extra credit' in college?" He negligently tossed a carton of eggs on the counter, and I heard at least one of them break from the impact. No doubt that would help his mood.

"I'll pass. I don't need to suck up to the teacher to make the grade."

"Well, Cranston, if you actually showed some initiative and work ethic maybe you wouldn't feel so threatened by everyone." I bit off carefully, trying to keep my anger in check.

"Don't think I didn't notice you sneaking back from the barn the other night wearing someone else's clothes. What happened, Bowen, did you make a mess of yours in your enthusiasm?

Before the vitriol continued, I closed the distance between us, stepping close enough that he could feel my anger. A flinch tugged at his skin, otherwise I might have just walked away, not wanting to risk a fight. "My enthusiasm to bring horses in from the storm, including *yours*?" I growled, low enough that my voice wouldn't carry through the rest of the house. "My enthusiasm to save them from being struck by lightning? If that is the enthusiasm you are referring to, then yes. Otherwise, I strongly suggest you pull your mind from the gutter, Mr. Cranston. That is conduct unbecoming of a member of this company, and I refuse to let you sully it with your crass accusations. The next time you see fit to attempt to insult me, I'll be bringing this to the attention of the entire troupe."

His angry flush quickly bled white with alarm, and before I succumbed to the urge to slap him I headed for my room. It took thirty minutes in the shower before I felt clean enough to get out, the ugliness of those moments still vivid in my memory. I peeked from the room before opening the door fully, making sure the coast had cleared, and took myself straight out to the barn. I'd have cleaned a thousand stalls to appease the churning of my gut, but I settled for currying Ro until he gleamed.

By the time his silky coat caught the light my shoulders were tired from the endless circles I'd drawn on his body. I picked his tail apart, hair by hair, until the full skirt belled at the bottom. Running a brush through his feathers also proved therapeutic, allowing me to focus on the texture of his skin and the soft cascade of white beneath my fingers. Even then, I still felt agitated, and I turned to Eros, treating him to the same thorough grooming. Thankfully, the stud played willing victim, pointedly asking for more scratches as I went over his body with the curry and brush. No friction was too rough, and he grunted and groaned appreciatively through the whole experience. Once finished, I headed back to the tack room to drop off the grooming kit, but I nearly head butted Aaron in the process as I plowed through the door. He grabbed me by the shoulders to keep both of us from toppling.

"Hey there, Jo, what's the rush?"

"Nothing, just wondering what the plan was for the day." Hmm, my acting skills must have been improving. Aaron actually looked like he believed me, though I wouldn't want to try it on Bart. He was remarkably observant. "We're getting close to lunch, didn't want to miss anything."

"Ah, well, that's where I'm headed now." Flashing his best charmer smile, he let me go and stepped back. "We've paired you off for next weekend. Alex is coming here this afternoon to practice some passes with Toby, Lee will run against me tomorrow, and you'll get Trace on Thursday. Everyone will be off Friday so we are fresh for the weekend. You can ride your other horse or horses in your case, but otherwise, your time is your own until Thursday. I suggest you take advantage of it."

"Yes Sir." I nodded sharply and slid past him to put the grooming kit back where it belonged. "Do you need any help running lyst or armoring? I'll go crazy with so little to do."

"I think we're okay, but if you really want to help, maybe you could get horses ready? I mean, don't feel obligated, but your horse's care is going to be the responsibility of a squire over the weekend, might as well do the same now."

"Yes Sir, thank you." Something I could do to stay busy, be helpful and keep away from Cranston as much as possible. The perfect assignment. He headed for the house as we parted ways, and I plucked up Cappy and J.T.'s halters to head for the field. Might as well get the big lugs while I was on a roll and have them clean before lunch.

I felt quite proud of myself that afternoon as Cranston mounted his horse, managing to get his foot in the stirrup without touching him in the slightest. Alex gave me a worried scowl, but I blew it off with a smile and a good luck as I watched them head up the hill.

Excitement plucked at me, thinking of facing a new opponent on Thursday, but at the rate we were going I would crawl out of my skin before then. Too much tension weighted the air for me to get out from under it and I decided to clean tack until everyone returned. They were back in less than an hour, Cranston the picture of cocky pleasure and Alex scowling even more deeply.

Aaron, Trace and Bart were on their heels, a bit of shadow in their eyes as well, but we were too busy getting the horses taken care of for me to ask what happened. By the time the boys were hosed off and cool Cranston had already flounced out of the barn, but Alex at least stopped by to give J.T. a carrot for his efforts. When Cappy made with the puppy eyes, he gave one to him too.

I knew, in my heart, that the horses didn't mean the same to everyone as they did to me, but at least they understood and were kind to them. Never once had Cranston rewarded a horse, his ignorant negligence all they could hope for if they did the right thing. Some people on this earth, I could get by with just ignoring, live and let live. Yet, with the frat boy, I began to actively dislike him and wish him gone. Anywhere but where he might dirty the Gallant Knights by association.

"Hey Bowen."

My head snapped around so fast my neck popped as Bart approached in a hurry. "Yes, Sir?"

"Can you ride bareback?"

"Sort of. Not as well as I'd like." Truthfully, I wanted to ask him for some tips, but the coiled rattler impression he gave off said now was not the time.

"You want to ride Cappy down to the field and lead J.T.? It'll save you a little time. I would go down too, but Aaron has an online meeting scheduled with our West coast faire, and I want to be in on it." By this time, he stood right beside me, tying Cappy's lead into a makeshift rein. "I'll give you a leg up if you want."

I didn't say a word, just turned my body toward the big gelding and grabbed a handful of mane, lifting my left leg for Bart to grasp. The feel of his broad palms on my shin and knee felt like a brand, each fingertip burning a lasting impression, but I managed my end of the deal, springing up on my other leg and hauling on my fistful of mane as he tossed me in the air. I'd never been more aware of our differences in that moment, his strength incredibly clear in the way he lifted me up as if I really was a delicate flower.

Once I settled, my thighs complaining at the width of Cappy's back, he patted me lightly on the knee. "Don't worry, Capstan is a teddy bear, and they are both going to be glad to head back out. We'll see you in the morning."

A breath later, he left; It was still a bit disconcerting, how quickly he moved when the muse came upon him. No effort wasted should be inked on his arm. Which led my brain down a far different path as Cappy let me steer him toward the pasture. Did Bart have tattoos? Marines seemed to be notorious for them, and I'd already caught one peeking out the edge of Mari's sleeve.

I mean, not that my stupid brain needed any more fodder to fantasize about, but turning the idea loose once I had ahold of it proved impossible. If I'd thought the same of any of my past relationships, I'd have been incredibly put off, but in the great mystery of Bart, it held appeal. Memories and meaning chronicled on his skin would be fascinating, though I doubted there would ever be anything about him I couldn't like.

When we reached the gate I shook the thought away and slithered from Cappy to turn the geldings loose. Hiking back up the hill, I swung the halters against my leg and considered the possibility of getting a tattoo myself. Maybe someday something would mean enough to me to warrant carrying it the rest of my life, but not yet. As I hung up the halters my phone buzzed.

'Meeting is boring, on internet looking for names for Ro. How about Robin, like Robin Hood?'

I grinned down at my phone as I headed for the paddock, wanting to sit under the tree and watch the sun go down in the most pleasant company I could conceive of. *'No, he's not even close to being an outlaw, even when his cause was just.'*

'Insightful of you. OK then, Roderick?'

From my seat against the tree, I fired back a response. *'A little Slavic sounding for a horse of English decent, I think. Of course, you do call a French Percheron by Ivan.'*

The sun just touched the tree tops when I got another text. *'Picky, picky. And he came with that name. Rohan?'*

'As much as I had a total crush on Eomyr in LOTR, I have to say no. I was neither blonde enough to identify with Eowyn, nor lady like enough, and that name made the rounds on the show circuits. Too done, thanks to pop culture.'

'Lord, woman, must you be so fussy? ;-)'

'You wouldn't find me half as entertaining if I weren't. ;-p' I shot back, wondering what sort of response that would garner.

Barely a sliver of light still streaked the sky and my stomach was rolled with nerves by the time he answered. *'Probably so. I've been told I'm a glutton for punishment. Alright, how about Roman?'*

'Hmm, promising. A centurion would have to endure the trials and tribulations of his service and come out the stronger. But I don't really see him looking good in a toga and sandals.' I giggled when I sent it, breaking into outright laughter when he responded.

'You're dangerous, I almost spit my coffee out on the computer screen. Aaron thought I was choking, though I couldn't tell him why.' It made me irrationally happy that he used the correct form of you're in his texts. Phones had keyboards, and there was no cause to be lazy. Chalk up another point for the man, not that his score didn't already assure a total victory. *'What about Romeo? I know you love him.'*

Good intentions and his knowledge of my feelings kept me from snorting in derision. *'You want me to name him after a kid who was so broken hearted after he thought his lover was dead that he poisoned himself? That is not really the kind of survivor I was going for.'*

'Ugh, too true. My list is getting short though. Ronin? The masterless samurai?'

Chewing my lip for a moment, I rolled it over in my mind. The idea held some appeal, as I tried not to be all absolute power when I worked with Ro, but a samurai should be happiest in service. No, still not quite right. I went with more humor when I said no again. *'Why do I have a feeling you have all the movies Toshiro Mifune was ever in? And I'll pass on that one too. Sushi kind of grosses me out.'*

'You're killing me, Jo. I'm going to have a hernia from trying not to laugh. And you are not wrong, though I prefer Ken Watanabe.'

I almost didn't want him to come up with anything that worked, just so we could keep bantering like this. On the other hand, I didn't want him to miss out on the meeting, no matter how dull. *'I hope I'm not getting you in trouble. Not the impression I want to give the captain, that I'm disruptive.'*

'No, my part in this is over. Just had to make sure we had our equipment needs met. Aaron isn't so good at those sort of details. I'm just lingering in the background. Now, for my last offering of the night, and the one I should have opened with. But this was too much fun to miss.' The text split off there, giving me a moment to digest the fact that he'd enjoyed this as much as I had. I was a goner. *'How about Rowan? Sacred tree to my people and yours, rare, beautiful, known to grow in inhospitable ground.'*

That one I let roll off my tongue right away, enjoying the texture of it more than any of the others. I'd seen those trees while dad was stationed at Lakenheath, on numerous trips through the countryside, and the white flowers reminded me of the star pattern in Ro's dapples. Looking out at where he grazed, dark veins of color of his right shoulder reminded me a bit of a tree, branching out from the trunk of his foreleg. Yes, indeed. My beautiful survivor. *'It's perfect. Thank you for thinking of us, even if we were just a distraction from the tedium.'*

Rising from my spot, I moved to Ro's side by the light from the apartment window and traced the lines on his shoulder.

"Rowan, my lovely boy. Keep growing." He lifted his nose from the grass long enough to touch my hand, his warm heart shining in his eyes. I pressed a quick kiss to his forehead then turned toward the house, hoping I'd have the kitchen to myself.

I'd pre-cooked chicken for the week, and had a nice salad thrown together after a few minutes, heading for the bedroom to eat. I didn't want to be caught alone with Cranston again, both to avoid the ugly words and keep away from the temptation to punch him. As I settled on the bed with pillows at my back, the phone buzzed one more time.

'Jo, one of my fondest hopes for you joining this team is that you continue to break up the tedium. Be clever. Use big words. Hit hard. Don't ever change. We like you.'

Smiling, I wondered who the 'we' referred to. Aaron and him? The whole team? Or maybe Eros and him? Regardless, I crafted a well thought out reply. *'No fear there. I change for no one but myself. And we like you too. Goodnight, Bart.'*

'Goodnight' came back quickly, and after a long chew on my dinner I took another shower. I never could stand putting a dirty me between clean sheets. A few chapters of my sci-fi book helped me wind down, but that night when I dreamed it was all about tattoos and tartans.

My passes against Trace ended up better and worse than I hoped for. Due to Trace's hesitation while targeting, I found if I asked Eros for a bit more speed it gave my opponent less time to sight in. That made his shots inconsistent, mostly skipping off, though he started to adjust by the sixth pass, so I still got a good feel for his capabilities. What I hadn't accounted for was his sturdiness. Hitting him felt like tilting against a brick wall, he felt that solid. I'd guessed, of course, but feeling it myself was incredibly humbling.

As I prepared for our final pass I had to shake my lance hand to alleviate the prickling sting that had built up, rolling my fingers around on my thigh for good measure. The ice pack would be gettin a work out later. Then I held out my hand for the lance, letting it rest on my thigh until I saw my signal. Eros moved even before I put my leg against him, reminding me once again that he knew this game far better than I ever would.

Trace's grand guard was freshly painted, the grid marks vivid red around the background of scarred steel, which made it that much easier to sight in. I came to level quickly and waited like I'd been taught, but apparently, Trace had finished taking his measure of me. We both struck hard, and I experienced an unpleasant struggle with gravity, tossing the lance away to free myself of it.

The idea of falling on it brought up the thought of the puncture wounds Bart once mentioned, and while I could endure any number of bruises and broken bones, I had a problem with being stabbed. Thankfully, though I almost ended up on Eros's neck when I over corrected, I remained on my horse, and when we came to a stop I couldn't resist a quick fist pump toward the sky. Another rung on the ladder achieved, in the greater scheme, which felt incredibly satisfying.

A rap against my leg made me bend down so my helm could be pulled, and though sweaty and breathing a little heavy, I returned Aaron's grin.

"Good job, Jo! You broke your lance for the first time!"

Forgive the moment of foolishness, but I actually shimmied a little in the saddle with happiness. Aaron laughed, but I didn't feel slighted in the least. Honestly, a girl happy dancing in armor had to be odd looking. "Can you grab me a piece of it? It's dumb, but I've already got some of the first one broken on me. Apparently, I'm starting a collection."

"Sure thing, I'll take it down to the barn for you. Now go shake Trace's hand. I think you made him work much harder than he thought he would, and his ego probably needs salving." His wink before he swaggered away just made me smile more, and I trotted the length of the arena to meet Trace at the block.

He held his hand out as soon as he saw me, grinning like a mad man. "Holy hell, dude, that was awesome!"

See, we were all crazy. We liked getting hit, in a strange way. I clasped our gloved hands together, regretting it briefly when he squeezed the bones together a trifle too enthusiastically. He didn't even notice, just let me go, but I caught the concern in Bart's eyes as he unbolted the buffe and grand guard.

"Yeah, thanks for letting me break my first lance on you. You're a freaking brick." I shoved his shoulder playfully, but even that hardly moved him the saddle.

Trace preened like a peacock at that, his baby blue eyes sparkling with humor. "See, Bart, you guys give me crap for being a pretty face. I can be useful too."

"Pretty is as pretty does, you idjit." Bart grumbled good naturedly, slapping him on the back—now *that* rocked the kid a little bit. Trace might be a wall, but my gut said Bart was a sledgehammer when he wanted to be. "Now clear the way so the lady can have her turn."

I leg yielded Eros within reach as soon as Trace moved away, clenching and releasing my fist so the hand didn't stiffen up while Bart worked. "Hand okay?" he murmured, voice so close it startled me from my post joust reverie.

"Just a little sore. He really is incredibly solid to hit, and it stings."

"After we get you out of armor, I'll show you some things that will help, if you aren't too tired." See, I might have bowed out and just gone back to the house to ice if it weren't for the little challenge at the end. It left me little choice but to accept his offer, really.

"Thank you, I'd appreciate that. Knowing I've got to face him this weekend is a little daunting the way things stand right now."

"Oh, you're ready. Aaron is almost giddy with excitement over this." He huffed a chuckle then patted me on the shoulder. "I'll see you at the barn, just chuck Eros in the stall, and I'll take care of him."

"Actually, I'm going to walk. He's carted me around plenty, and my legs work just fine." Bart quickly jumped down and put his hand on Eros's bridle, making room for me to dismount. After I heaved myself off I reached for the stallion myself, but Bart was already turning away. I fell in beside them, grateful for the courtesy that kept them from hurrying ahead.

We went our separate ways, temporarily, me to the armor room so Lee could help shell me out of my steel casing, and them to the stall to divest the stallion of his tack. Once free of the metal I ducked into the tack room, bracing my foot against the door so I could change into a dry shirt without being disturbed. While I didn't mind being sweaty, the sopping fabric sticking to me felt unbearable, like my skin couldn't breathe.

Afterward, I found Bart in Eros's stall, clearly waiting for my arrival. He held out the requisite peppermint so casually, like we'd done it a thousand times, and truthfully, that was the way it felt. Like we'd always known each other, and always would. Damn, I hoped so. I fed the stallion his peppermint, and giggled uncharacteristically loudly as he wiggled his lips against my cheek when I pressed a kiss to the tiny arrow of white just above his left nostril.

"It's good to hear you laugh, Jo. You should do it more often."

I threw a quick glance at him, my brow wrinkling when he didn't meet my eyes. "You make me laugh all the time, but it's not always a good time to indulge." I admitted, hoping that would get a reaction. "I imagine, the longer I'm around, the more you will hear it."

Sometimes, you get what you wish for. His eyes came up, the intense dark green threatening to steal my breath. "Well, hopefully you'll be around a long time."

"I'll be here until you all get tired of me." I managed it with a bit of a chuckle to disguise how seriously the words were meant, quelling my nerves by scratching along Eros's cresty neck. "You guys are a family I didn't know I was looking for. I could have jousted with anyone, but it's the people I can't walk away from now." Including you, my heart wanted to add, but I swallowed the words. "Now, what can we do to make sure I get through the weekend with my hand intact?"

Once Eros went back outside with Ro, Bart led me to the armor room again, cracking open one trunk I'd never seen opened before. The armor inside glimmered softly in the low light, any scars buffed to mute their appearance, etching along

the edges blackened in the grooving to make the Celtic knot
work stand out more. My gut twisted when I realized it must be
his, unworn the last several years, and waiting patiently for his
return. He pulled a fabric bandage from the little tray off to one
side, and hastily dropped the lid to sit on it, beckoning me closer.
I perched myself just across from him in attentive posture,
unsure of what we were doing.

"Give me your hand." Gruffly said, with a hint of reluctance
that my body echoed, my shoulders tightening even as I held out
my hand, palm up. Don't mistake me. I wanted him to touch me,
but a tiny part of my brain screamed against the idea, knowing I
would want more. This obliterated the distance I needed in order
to keep myself safe. "We're going to wrap your hand so that
when you grip the lance it'll support the structure of your hand,
keep everything where it belongs. It'll affect your feel as well,
but if you do a little practice with the lance tomorrow, I think
you'll learn to accommodate pretty quickly. It'll be worth it."

He didn't look up at me for the entirety of that little speech,
his thick fingers grasping my wrist so he could turn my hand
over. At first, he studied it, as if he could look beneath the skin
to the weaknesses we were trying to compensate for. But I didn't
see whatever he was seeing, not once I noticed how small he
made my hand look. I'd always been a little embarrassed by the
way my hands were of a size with a man's, leery of holding
hands because I hated the similarities. I loved my hands for their
strength, their capacity to get things done, but they never once
felt feminine until just that moment.

My internal reflection shattered as he brought his other hand
up as well, cradling the back of my hand against his fingers and
using his thumbs to apply pressure to my palm. Those callused
thumbs thoroughly explored my palm, hunting for the sore spots,
but that didn't stop my knees from going to jelly. I forced myself
to speak, purely out of self-defense. "As much as I'd be happy to
endure that for another hour or so, the soreness is mostly on the
outside."

Those expressive eyebrows knitted closer together, his mouth
tightening as he turned my hand over, but this position was even

worse. Now his fingertips were against my palm, the sensitive skin tingling with the rougher texture of his. It felt too much like having my hand held, too intimate, and I was frozen between the urge to escape and the temptation to torture myself more. In the end I stayed, as his thumbs found the bones supporting my pointer and middle fingers, a hiss of pain escaping my lips as my fingers curled in. "Yup, right there." I squeaked, not caring how silly it sounded. He soothed over the spot for a few strokes, a tic appearing briefly in his cheek.

"Sorry, at least we know they aren't broken now. I was a little worried."

"I'm glad to hear it. But what can I do to keep them from getting broken?" I asked shortly, pulling my hand away so I could breathe properly. He'd have given the same thorough exam to anyone else's hand, but I highly doubted anyone else harbored the hots for him. The mixed emotions swirling in my chest were tough to keep in check when he touched me.

"I'm going to wrap my hand so you can watch, see it from the right perspective first. Then I'll wrap your hand so you can see how it is supposed to feel. You'll take the bandage so you can practice, but this weekend when you compete, I'll wrap it for you if you want. It'll give you one less thing to worry about."

I nodded brusquely. "Thank you. I don't know that I'd trust myself to do it right after just learning how, particularly with my blood up."

My whole body tightened up as he moved to the trunk beside me, excited and scared to have him even closer, but then he held his hand out in front of him so I could see it clearly. "Alright, first, you run your thumb through the loop, and draw it across the back of your hand."

Concentrating on his instructions, the smooth motions of the bandage as it covered his knuckles, I easily found some emotional distance. He'd always be my teacher, in some respects, even if I ever worked up the nerve to try for more. A well of knowledge was meant to be drunk from, as my Dad liked to say. Once he had the bandaging complete he held it out for my inspection, tightening his fist so I could see how the fabric became firm under tension.

"And that, Bowen, is what will save you a broken hand. No guarantees, of course, it could still happen at some point, but this will reduce the likelihood of injury."

"Exactly what I need." As he unwound the bandage from his broad palm, I fiddled with the zipper tab on my half chaps, my brow puckered. "I'm not scared of being hurt, you know. I'm just an impatient patient, and would hate to sit out while everyone else got to play."

"You don't say?" That freaking mild tone would make me crazy one day, I felt sure of it. "Don't worry, you are in good company. None of us like recovery. Alex jousted through a tournament weekend with a slipped disk, a couple years ago. Aaron blew out his knee and kept riding last summer, didn't get it fixed until after Faire was over."

"Exactly. I rode cross country once with a sprained ankle, just taped the heck out of it. Mom was livid when she found out." A measure of respect in his nod of understanding knit him even closer to my heart. Then he wrapped my hand, and I marveled at the relief given by the extra support, able to flex my hand with only a mild twinge of discomfort. "That's perfect. Thank you."

"You are welcome. Don't use the kettlebell for a few days, save your grip for when you need it. Now, get yourself inside and ice it before it swells any more. I'll feed the boys their supper."

"Yes, Sir." I got up to leave, but something prompted me to turn back for a moment. Still sitting on the trunk, his disciplined posture held a little too much tension, and I touched his shoulder briefly. "I really do appreciate everything you've taught me, Bart. About jousting, about horsemanship, and about friendship. It means a lot to me."

The wary edge in his eyes eased, and he laid his hand over mine, lightly squeezing. Like I was standing in a swath of sunshine, my whole body warmed, wanting to tip closer to the source like a flower. "It's truly been my pleasure, Jo. Student of a lifetime, and hopefully, the friend of a lifetime."

"I hope so too." I murmured, pulling away to head for the door before I could do anything ridiculously dramatic. After swinging past the paddock to give Rowan a few minutes of scritches, I retreated to my room with my constant sidekick, the ice pack, to keep me company. Tired, and more than a bit overwhelmed, I went to bed early, but spent several hours staring at the ceiling before succumbing to sleep.

An ulcer sprung up overnight on Friday that made dinner unpleasant, but I slogged through it with some antacids. I couldn't afford to miss a meal; it would have been too big a risk with so much going on over the weekend. No weakness could go unanswered right then. Breakfast on Saturday went down a trifle easier, some oatmeal and a protein shake to keep me well fueled. Mom and Dad were driving down on Sunday to watch me joust, but I had Saturday to get through first.

Cranston was so cordial to everyone it made me itch, like an allergic reaction to his bull pucky or something. As much as I had mixed feelings about going home, wanting to stay here, and needing some time with family, there were zero mixed feelings at all about needing to get away from the frat boy.

"Bowen, would you like help loading your armor?" he asked, trotting up to me as I pulled the trunk down the aisle on a dolly. I managed not to gag on my revulsion and accepted the help with every sign of outward graciousness.

"Thanks, Cranston. Good luck this weekend." Though the sentiment was honest, as I didn't have it in me to wish him ill, I still didn't like his false cheer.

"You too."

We shook hands like professionals and I headed back to the barn to gather Eros up. Bart chose to ride Ivan this weekend, both to give the sensitive gelding some exposure to the crowds and to spare Eros for the jousting. Since Cranston and Trace needed to share Cappy we had split his workload, meaning Cranston would go first with Alex, then Trace would go last with me. But aside from that, the rest of the crew would get off light, just one go a day, and it made the trailer seem a little empty to not be loading up the gaming horses.

At the grounds we all set to work like it was just another day in paradise, and I tried to cling to that impression so I wouldn't overthink. Eros just about glittered obsidian, I'd groomed him so thoroughly, the smoky quality of his coat making it appear faintly translucent when the sun hit him. After checking my tack and armor trunk several times, I walked back outside, my eyes darting around the yard for something to do.

"Josephine Bowen!" Mari's familiar bark made me smile. "Get over here, I need an adult to talk to!"

Doing as she bid, I strode over to the booth and hitched a hip on the counter opposite her seat. "You bellowed, my friend?"

"Oh, don't you act all superior, Miss Soon To Be A Knight." She teased, crossing her arms under her breasts. "I'm doing this as much for your good as mine. A wee Scottish birdy informed me you might need a distraction."

Slumping dramatically against a post, I casted a sideways look at her. "Yes ma'am, I do. But honestly, calling Bart wee is like calling a war horse a pony."

"Do I detect a hint of admiration for your brother in arms?" She leaned closer and lowered her voice while I worked up the nerve to lie, profusely and creatively. "Something beyond the ken of knightly brotherhood?" Sadly, my blush gave me away, even as I glared at her. She sat back like a cat in the cream, and I expected her to preen over the morsel of information, but her face softened. "Oh honey, I was just teasing. I suspected as much, mind you."

"Don't you say a word, Mari." I growled it out like an injured animal, thumping my forehead against the post in frustration. "Swear it, dammit."

Her hand at my shoulder startled me straight, and I almost knocked her over in the process. The close confines of the booth gave us plenty to grab onto, and we righted ourselves, but then she got right back in my face. "I swear, Jo. I didn't mean to scare you; I'm just trying to keep your mind off the day ahead."

My lip trembled slightly at the depth of dismay in her eyes, and I faked a weak chuckle. "Well, it worked. But seriously, not a single word more. I have to survive this weekend before I can think about anything else." She mimicked locking her lips and tossing the key over her shoulder, and it tempted a slightly easier giggle from me. "Now, how about you tell me all about the actually wee rascals that run your life?"

"Well, they want to know when Lady Jo is coming back with Pewcy, but aside from that, it's chaos as usual." Her warm smile as she resumed her perch and arranged her skirts eased my worried heart. "Malcom learned how to tie his own shoes, but Max is having a hard time. It resulted in him flinging all his laced shoes on the front lawn in frustration."

Settling myself on the opposite counter, I let my legs swing to soothe the last of my raw nerves. I trusted Mari with the secret, I just thought I'd kept it better hidden than that. "Oh, the poor sweetie! I can't imagine how rough that has to be for him. I mean, your identical twin being able to do something you can't."

"There are tradeoffs, of course. Max can already ride his bike without training wheels, but Mal will probably have them for another six months." Shrugging her shoulders against the helplessness of it all, she smiled. "But no matter what, they love each other, and we love them. The rest of it will work itself out with time. Your situation is no different."

I shook my head, needing to deny the possibility of loving someone I hadn't even fully admitted I liked. There was no way I could go there, not in seven weeks. It had taken me eight months or longer to allow myself to love in my previous relationships. I couldn't love him, particularly when he might not feel a damn thing for me aside from friendship. Right?

"Stop overthinking so much, Jo." Firm, no-nonsense Mom tone pulled my gaze back to hers. "They'll be calling in the fire brigade to douse the flames on your brain if you keep this up."

Giggling slightly hysterically, I conceded her point, rising from my perch. "More than likely. Anyway, it's about time for me to help everyone get ready. Figure out what you want for lunch and I'll be back after a while."

Thank goodness for the busy work, as I helped Alex into his kit, dancing around the other people in the close confines of the armor room. I scurried to get him suited up after the alarming events of the morning, which kept me from dwelling on the steady beat of my heart, incessantly hammering out the word love.

The joust went off without a hitch, Ivan keeping his dramatics to a minimum, though he did try a brief runaway during one of the cantered rounds of the arena. I had to grin at the disappointment that wilted his ears when Bart brought him around in a tight circle to stop him. Cranston was announced as a Knight-Initiate, then offered a rose to one of the ladies in the crowd. He and Alex each broke a single lance amongst their multiple touches, my eye starting to notice a faint difference in Cranston's position. Almost as if he stood in his stirrups until just before the hit, then sat down, which lowered his grand guard by a couple inches.

No wonder Alex had looked frustrated—having to compensate for that shifting target could go horribly wrong, sending the lance down along the cuirass to strike the hip or groin area. The prospect made me a little squeamish, honestly, and I didn't even have such sensitive pelvic equipment to worry about. At the end, the King offered him congratulations, and invited him back the next day to defend his worthiness to the office of knighthood. The crowd ate it up with a spoon.

For lunch, I forced down a bread bowl with chicken soup in it, hoping the starch would keep my stomach from revolting too much. I'd popped antacids like tic tac's all morning, and needed to slow down before I ran out. While we could have eaten after the noon joust I didn't want to risk my performance on an unhappy tummy. As we were on our way back, one of the shop owners hollered my name, and while I didn't have much time, I ducked in to see what he wanted.

"Sir Bart came in here this morning. He thought if you were giving out favors this weekend a fella might not be keen on flowers." The bearded gentleman pulled a couple short wooden daggers from behind his counter and held them out for me. They were as finely wrought as any he had for sale, though the length of the blade bore elegant script with the name of the shop. The other side revealed a similar treatment with the Gallant Company of Knights, and my heart squeezed to know I'd soon join their ranks. I also thought of Marley. She'd love one of these, an outward symbol of her inward struggle, something she could figuratively fight her leukemia with.

"Thank you so much, good gentle. You've made a pleasure out of a task I hadn't been thrilled with."

The man's eyes twinkled with merry humor and when I offered him my hand in thanks he lifted it to his lips for a chaste kiss. "No, Lady, the pleasure is mine, to be part of the ascension of a knight, particularly one so favored in our fair Shire. Go in good health and come back again next year. I'm sure we can strike some sort of arrangement."

Mari and I hurried back to the encampment then, as fast as her prosthetic allowed. We arrive to relative quiet, disconcerting in light of the time, but trouble made itself known by the retching coming from the armor room. Half kitted in his armor, Fillmore was bent double with his head between his knees, spewing his nerves into a bucket. While Bart sat beside Lee with a cold cloth on the back of the kid's neck, and Aaron hung outside away from the stench, I braved the smell. Trading out the soiled bucket for a clean one, I handed Bart a bottle of water, and headed out back to rinse the offensive contents down a drainage grate. This sort of problem I could handle.

It took a few minutes for Lee to get back on his feet, and then I set to helping Bart finish getting him in armor. Our captain enjoyed Alex's capable assistance, though it didn't escape me that Cranston was nowhere to be seen. Entitled brat was no doubt run off by the messiness of real life, though judging by his drinking habits, he could be no stranger to vomit.

The joust went about how I expected it to, Lee freezing up a little here and there. Oh, he tried like the dickens, but his movements were stilted. When he leaned over to hand off his rose to a pretty blonde I breathed a prayer of gratitude that we'd gotten him to take some mints. The girl colored quite nicely when he spoke to her, and he firmed up a bit after that, the boost to his ego strengthening his nerve.

Bless his broad Belgian booty, Tuck babysat him admirably, halting at the ends with little assistance from his rider as he wobbled to a stop the first few passes. Happily, the last pass redeemed him, barely a tremor in his lance as he leveled it on Aaron, a harsh crack of the wood following as it broke. From a point perspective it wouldn't make a difference, as Aaron had already broken two on him and touched the rest of the time, but it would shore up his confidence. To me, that was all that mattered.

When they dismounted to greet the crowd I took Tuck and gently steered Fillmore toward the rail where his admirer waited. He did a good job signing lances and shaking hands, though he kept looking at the girl like a beacon in the darkness. Hey, whatever gets you through, I say, and when the crowd thinned I shoved a bit of paper in his hands.

"Give her your number, goof ball." I murmured lowly, then walked away with Tuck to greet a little boy confined to a wheelchair.

After seeing everyone settled back at camp I headed back to the booth where Mari proved able distraction. We played gin rummy for candied almonds, though I ate most of my coinage while we laughed at each other's poor hands, the chewing keeping my nerves under control.

At the half hour mark I headed for the armor room, swallowing down the last of the almonds with a few swigs of water. Aaron waited for me with my arming jacket in hand and I shucked my tunic to expose a tank top. I'd forgone the bodice so it would be easier to change, and the jacket slid on quickly. Focusing on my breaths, in through the nose, out through the mouth, I kept them slow and even as we got everything buckled in place. Just a few feet away, Alex helped Trace with his armor, each piece going on at a pace with mine. As the last pauldron got buckled on Trace reached across the space between us and offered me his hand. I shook it quickly and smiled. "You ready to rumble, pretty boy?"

"You tell me, lady. Am I to go easy on you?"

The tease did what it needed to, narrowing my eyes and putting a growl in my voice. "Only if you want me to kick your ass around this encampment when we get done."

Aaron laughed and clapped us both on the shoulders. "Now, now, save it for the field."

With fifteen minutes to spare I perched on the mounting block that currently enjoyed shade from an overhanging oak. Eyes closed, I visualized sighting in on the red hash marks of Traces grand guard over and over.

"Did you forget something, Bowen?"

I startled just a bit, having not seen Bart much today outside of the arena. Perhaps it had been for the best, but as he approached with the rolled bandage in his hand my heart started its ridiculous litany again. It got stronger as he studied my face, the green eyes rich enough to have ingrained themselves on my memory. "Sorry, it's not routine yet. I'll remember tomorrow."

A corner of his mouth kicked up in amusement. "Hmm, too bad, I was looking forward to giving you crap about something for a change. You don't give me much to call you on."

I held out my hand and grinned back. "Well then, far be it from me to deprive you. I'll be sure to forget tomorrow too."

"See that you do." He grumbled, flipping my hand so he could secure the thumb loop. All his concentration went to the task, giving me a minute to study him without interruption. His features were so familiar to me, though I didn't often indulge in looking, the thick brows, broad jaw and full lower lip a book meant for reading over and over. "This is just like practice, Jo.

Once the helm goes on, shut the crowd from your mind. It'll just be Eros and you, a lance in hand, a target to hit."

While I focused on the words for their content, a soothing surety to the way he said them salved my frayed nerves. I clung to that, closing my eyes again to imagine the lance coming down once more, and the impact. Just the imagining made my hand twitch in his, and he tightened his grip, making me open my eyes.

"Sorry, was thinking about the hit." I didn't have to explain myself any more than that, he simply nodded his understanding. "I'll be fine once I get there, Bart, I just tend to overthink beforehand. I always did it before my cross country ride too. It's totally normal."

"Okay." I loved how he just took me at my word. Dammit, that word again, only it had snuck into my inner monologue. His thumbs brushed over the bandage, checking his work, then he let me go. "I'm going to go get your horse, it's almost time."

He was gone before I could say thank you and back before I could work myself into a tizzy over anything. Eros bumped me with his nose, this a little harder than normal, as if to say *'It's game time'*, and I clapped him on the neck in answer.

"You ready to rock and roll, big man?" I asked as I climbed up on his back. Bart's hand lingered on my calf as it had several times before, and this time I looked at him, setting my bandaged fingers on his shoulder just to touch him. "Thank you, Bart. Getting to ride Eros is the best gift anyone has ever given me, and I know I wouldn't be this far along without him. I really appreciate it."

He cleared his throat and looked away, stroking the stallion's shoulder. "No one else I'd have trusted him to. Now, ride him like you stole him."

"Yes, Sir." I bit it off just like I always did, hoping he could feel the respect in it, and squeezed my fingers into a fist when he walked away. I didn't have time to think about the hazy future; now I only needed to get through this moment and the next.

I cleared the block when Hillary walked up with Cappy, sharing a secret smile with her as she went by. Today, I needed to ride for all the Hillary's, all the Marley's, all the little girls who wanted to be so much more than a princess. Those girls perfectly capable of making friends with dragons and saving themselves from the petty evils of this world. And most of all, for the girls who couldn't save themselves but wished they could.

We formed up behind our banners, Trace heralded by a sleeping golden wolf on a field of blue that was surrounded by a white border. I grinned when Aaron unfurled mine. Someone had dug up the Welsh flag, the red dragon of Cadwaladr on a split field of white and green. My face flushed as red as the dragon by the time we reached the arena, so many people wished me luck, and the embarrassment was only beginning.

"Your Majesties, we, the Gallant Company of Knights, bring before you another knight-initiate, known to you these past weeks as Lady Josephine Bowen of Pembrokeshire." Bart's voice rang sharp and clear, even with the tinny echo that came from the sound system. "She seeks to prove her right to the rank of knight through skill at arms against our youngest brother, Sir Trace Davies of Montrose. Do you give us leave to test her?"

The King rose from his throne, offering his hand to the Queen before coming to the edge of the dais. "Indeed, Sir Clark, though it seems a shame to waste so fair a beauty to the art of war. Dear lady, would you not prefer a place amongst the flowers that live in the Queen's court?"

The pretty speech left me flat footed, and I needed to channel my frustration toward something tactful. Thankfully, the Queen nodded a blessing, likely guessing the words clamoring behind my teeth.

"My King, Your wife and I have conversed at length, and She has given me Her blessing to prove that women are more than blossoms to pretty a garden." My voice kept increasing in power, throwing the words out where everyone could hear them. "They are also swords to be wielded in the name of justice and shields to protect the noble ideals Your kingdom is founded upon. No, Your Majesty, I am far more than my petals. I am also my thorns, and I intend to cut my opponent with them."

The faint drone of the crowd erupted in applause when I finished, and while the sound hummed in my veins, I kept my eyes on the King, unsure of the reception my words would receive. His wink of amusement told me I'd done my part perfectly, and after raising his hands to ask for quiet, he addressed me as well as the crowd. "Nobly said, Lady Bowen. Let us now see if your deeds may prove as worthy of nobility as your words."

"Thank you, your Majesties, I endeavor to serve Your will." With that, I bowed myself out, not even looking at Bart. I could scarcely afford the distraction on a quiet day, but particularly not at that moment. Instead, I listened to his voice, clinging to the familiarity as I held out my hand to take the small dagger from Hillary.

"And now, our combatants shall choose a Lord or Lady to carry their favor as they do battle. Lady Josephine, as custom dictates, ladies first." I rode the fence for a moment, hunting for some adorable little boy to catch my eye, but none jumped out at me. Half way around the arena a ten-year-old girl dressed as an archer met my eye and waved excitedly. She was what I imagined Marley would be like when she was whole and healthy, and when I leaned down to hand her the dagger she took it as if I were handing over a solemn relic.

"Fight like a girl?" I asked her seriously, and her face split in a wide grin, braces glinting in the sunlight.

"Fight like a girl!" She hollered, loud enough that everyone in the general area heard her as she thrust the dagger toward the sky. The chant was quickly taken up, and I gave her a grin before riding away to get my helm. By the time Aaron slid it on, grinning just as hard as me, I was glad to see the visor close. Sixteen-gauge steel was the only thing that could disguise my blush of pride.

Once the helm snicked closed everything condensed down, reducing the crowd to white noise. Guiding Eros into place for the first pass, the only thing I could hear was my own heartbeat, my own breaths in the close confines of the steel. Like clockwork, the lance met my palm, and I firmed my grip around it. One waving arm spurred me on and I closed my legs, riding the raw power of the stallion like an eagle in a storm. Eros didn't hold back, flattening himself out to meet our opponent with every muscle at his disposal and as I brought my lance to bear, he found another gear. The clash of mutual hits made my heart thrill, my hand taking the shock with much less complaint as my seat deepened in the saddle to keep me upright.

We repeated it, just as if it had been rehearsed, the dance of impact tingling against both sides of my body once more. The third felt much the same as we rounded the corner, and I sighted in, asking Eros for more, wanting to leave an impression. Yet, the extra speed on my part not only aided my strike, but his as well. I didn't know if it was my own lance or his that shoved me off center, but the armor pulled me the rest of the way over, my slim view of the world canting sideways and picking up speed.

As I slid through the air, a victim to gravity and inertia, it wasn't my whole life that flashed before my eyes, just the last six months. Among them were seven weeks of the hardest work I'd ever done, all leading up to this breathless moment, as more than a hundred pounds of armor dragged me toward the ground, my leg scraping across the saddle as Eros continued galloping. A few seconds of raw adrenaline slowed everything to a crawl, my brain flashing back to springtime.

Are we all on the same page now? Good, because here is where it all starts to pick up speed, and I don't want to lose you. Much like jousting, once you let go of the reins, you are at the mercy of your horse—such as it is with this story.

I hit the ground like a plummeting comet, no doubt leaving a divot they could plant crops in if they were so inclined. For a moment, I couldn't breathe, my lungs burning with deprivation as my heart thumped faster to compensate. Then the vise on my chest eased and I sucked in air like a bellows, becoming faintly aware of my limbs again. Blinking revealed light, giving me perspective, and I wiggled my fingers and toes to make sure everything worked before shoving against the ground to get myself up. A couple someone's levered me to my feet, Steve coming into focus when he lifted my visor.

"You alright, Jo?" At my quick nod, he flashed a grim smile and pulled off my helm entirely. "Good. Now, raise your arms high so the crowd knows you are okay." I did as he said, the faint ringing in my ears intensifying when the audience cheered. Still, Steve's manner had me worried, and I turned to the other end of the lyst. A bomb dropped in my gut at the sight of Trace on the ground, Bart and Aaron kneeling on either side of him. Before I could take a step Steve stopped me by gripping the edge of my armor. "No, you can't help right now. Let's just get you back to the block just in case."

Numb with the surfeit of adrenaline and no small measure of horror, I let Steve lead me away, reaching for Eros as soon as Hillary brought him to my side. EMT's vaulted the arena fence with quiet intensity as I anchored my hands on the stallion's muscular shoulder and prayed for Trace to be okay. I don't know how long we stood there, but eventually, one armored arm lifted past the pile of humanity surrounding him to give us all a thumbs up. The tears of relief that ran down my face had no shame in them as I cheered with the crowd, my throat raw by the time they had him on his feet. He leaned on Aaron as Bart stepped forward to face the dais.

"Your Majesties, by dint of double unhorsing, we would like to call this joust a draw. Let us tend our warriors and return tomorrow to find a clear victor to satisfy the crowd and Your noble sensibilities."

The King gave him a half bow I could hardly see through my burning eyes. "Indeed, Sir Clark, we look forward to your return on the morrow. Good people of the Shire, let us hear three cheers for the Gallant Company of Knights, for their bravery and skill. Hip, hip…"

"Huzzah," Rang out like a rolling wave of sound, and I closed my eyes against the throbbing that it started between my ears, pressing my forehead to Eros's warm shoulder as they shouted it twice more. Then Hillary turned me away from him, and guided me through the gate to the comforting familiarity of Steve clearing the path, a vague sense of other horses and people following in our wake. I yielded Eros to Hillary when we reached the yard, briefly catching sight of Trace as Aaron and Bart helped him through the back gate, the flashing lights of the ambulance making my head throb again.

Steve and Lee helped strip me of armor, as I unwound the bandage Bart had set on my hand less than an hour ago. Once clear, I found myself alone, and I rerolled the bandage while sipping slowly on the water I'd left on a shelf. The dim light helped my headache and I fiddled with the label on the bottle as I tried to think.

Trace shouldn't have fallen, particularly not to me. Not the brick wall that had hurt my hand the last time I faced him, not the pretty boy whose hard head rivaled mine. Aaron could hardly unhorse him, and his skill level was astronomically better than mine.

Closing cannon spooked me, as time had escaped my notice, and I headed out to see what needed doing. Bart and Aaron were bent together in conference at the back of the yard and I left them to it, gathering up Eros and Ivan to put them out for the evening. Having another injured jouster had to stink, and I didn't begrudge them the mess it must leave them with. By the time I got the boys settled with supper and full water tank Cranston and Lee had also brought out their charges, and I pushed back through the gate to get Byz, his worried whinny making my head twinge again. I knew if I stopped moving I'd lose momentum, and since we are already a man down, I didn't want to be the weak link.

Once Byz settled in with Cappy, I noticed everyone waiting by the truck and hurried over to meet them so we could get home. I'd never needed to lean on Ro more, and tears were already making tracks down my face as I squeezed in the back seat next to Lee. The whole ride remained silent, but not with the tired and satisfied feeling I'd come to appreciate. No, this nipped and gnawed at my heart like the desperate claws of a panicked wild thing. When Bart shut off the engine we all stayed just as we were, waiting.

"Everyone inside. We need to have a meeting." This from Aaron who seemed to have his wits about him a little more than the rest of us. As a body, we exit the truck and move down the path, while my heart screams *'no, no, no'*. I shook my head against the clamoring, and kept walking, hoping to go curl myself around my horse soon.

I fell into the recliner and slumped against the back, too tired to care what anyone thought of my gracelessness. Bart and Aaron found kitchen chairs again, their postures too rigid, as if the world would shatter with one wrong move. Hunched as if expecting a blow, Lee perched on the edge of the sofa, while Cranston lounged on the arm of the loveseat.

He still made my skin crawl, because while his brow reflected worry, his posture reflected an indolence far too casual considering the results of the day. Mind you, he had done the best out of all of us, so maybe that was just his usual cockiness coming through.

A big sigh pulls my eyes back to Aaron, though they are slow about getting there. "Alright, here's what we know. Trace is stable, they are doing an MRI to make sure he doesn't have any swelling that might cause complications. More than likely, it's just a hell of a concussion, and he'll be fine in a couple weeks." My heart squeezed in weak relief, but his next words froze it solid. "What we also discovered while untacking his horse is that his right stirrup had been cut. The only reason Jo unhorsed him was equipment malfunction."

"Cut? Not just broken, but cut?" This came from Lee, voicing the questions that rattled around in my tired brain.

"Yes, cut. It was far too clean a break to be natural." Bart said darkly, as I struggled upright.

"Thank goodness." I mumbled, freezing like a bunny in the open when every eye in the room fell on me. "No, no, not like that. I mean, I was thinking there was no way he should have fallen off. I can't hit that hard. I've never so much as rocked anyone, let alone Trace, who is a freaking beast to hit."

A snort of derision from across the room pulled everyone's attention from me. "Are you kidding me? Bowen, you probably did it." While my gaze was slow to get there, the sticky pollution of Cranston's accusations sharpened me right up. "I mean, there's no way a girl would ever be able to unhorse any of us without cheating. She was probably trying to show off for her little fan club."

My mouth turned into the Sahara as the seconds ticked by and no one refuted him. Lee looked at me like he wasn't sure of me anymore, and I couldn't bear to look at Bart and find censure. It felt like an eternity with those foul words picking up speed in the silence, but I finally shoved to my feet. "Fine, if that's what you all believe of me, then I'll take the blame. But if you can think that, after all the time we have spent together, as friends and as my brothers in arms, then this company is not near so gallant as I came to believe it was."

I couldn't even stalk properly, picking my steps across the floor carefully, fixing my eyes past Cranston to the beckoning dark of the bedroom door. The vibration of a chair being shoved across the kitchen floor barely registered on my consciousness.

"Jo, no one said you did it."

Swiveling slowly toward Aaron, I tried to keep the tears burning my eyes from making an appearance on my cheeks. He held out a placating hand to restrain Bart, who stood beside him like a dark cloud, his hands clenched into fists.

"No one here had the balls to say I didn't either." I growled, my throat burning with bile. "I trusted you guys to have my back, and at the first sign of trouble, you drop me like a hot rock." I pointedly didn't meet Bart's eyes for that part. Out of all of them, I really thought he'd be there for me, and the betrayal slices deepest coming from him.

Aaron had the good grace to look chastised. "We'll get to the bottom of this. Please, don't walk away, we really do want you here as part of the team."

"No, Aaron, you'll find someone else willing to bust their ass for the love of the game." Bart startled hard at that, like I slapped him, but I steeled my heart even more. "This is just what I needed, so I could walk into a corporate job with a clear head. This made it abundantly clear where my priorities should be. For that, at least, I can say thank you."

A hand on my arm stopped me before I got more than three steps, the familiar weight and breadth telling me without looking that it belongs to Bart. Cranston's snake eyes land coldly on mine before I turn to face this last appeal.

"You can't leave, Bowen." So we were back to last names, were we? His throat sounded as raw as mine felt, and I clamped down on the sympathy that welled up. "Ro needs you." Ah, a nice below the belt hit that made my stomach heave, from the one who knew me best. But was it enough to make me fight the doubt in Lee? Was it enough to risk my heart being broken because the men I thought my friends didn't trust me anymore.

"Oh, this is bullshit." I swallowed nausea at the naked hate in Cranston's voice as we all turned toward him. On his feet now, his fists clenched as his face turns scarlet. "This fucking goody two shoes has you all wrapped around her finger. Or maybe it's just your cocks in her mouth, because there is no way in hell she's made it this far on her own."

The shocked silence in the room solidified behind me, like a bulwark against the rage coming off Cranston in waves, and when Bart started to shift forward I reflexively held up a hand to stay him. The coiled power stayed on its toes, but didn't move, reinforcing my faith in him again. "Cranston, you might want to watch what you say right now. I've had a horribly long day, and it wouldn't take much to pull my trigger."

"What are you going to do, whore? Call your little lesbo friends to come kick my ass? Or is the chemo brat going to do your dirty work for you? Ooo, maybe that troop of girl scouts that worships at your feet?"

I'd warned him, and my Daddy had raised me to be fair like that, but the instant he started talking badly about my friends, I felt nothing but a righteous sense of justice burning a path from my heart to my fist. There was no forethought to it, but the weeks of training my aim had me sighting in on the corner of his flapping lips, and my fist just followed through with weeks of pent up frustration behind it. He hit his ass with a grunt of surprise, reaching up to dab at the blood dribbling down his chin with an injured whine.

"Cranston. You can say whatever you like about me, but nobody gets to talk shit about my friends." For a second, his image wavers, splitting into two and coming back together as my gut rolls. A giddy laugh escaped as I considered my suddenly prolific swearing, but I had a feeling, in this case, Grandma would give me a pass. "Now, if you all will pardon me, I'm going to my room."

I made it another three steps before my knees gave out and I threw up my toenails, everything going fuzzy as a pair of arms closed around me.

I didn't pass out, but as they carried me to bed and settled me against the pillows, my head swam. Trembling with the rush of adrenaline from throwing up and the confrontation itself, I squeezed my eyes shut and willed my body to calm. The after effects fade quickly when a cold cloth comes to rest on my forehead, and I murmured a thank you once I took a sip from the water glass pressed into my hand.

Thank God they left the lights off, a large shadow moving around in the faint light from the bathroom making me wonder who kept me company. As they pressed some ibuprofen into my other hand, I knew it was Bart. Seriously, no matter how out of it I may be, I would always know his hands now. I closed my fingers around his to keep him still for a moment, sighing when the edge of the bed sinks with his weight.

"We need to take you to the hospital, Jo. I'm just waiting for Aaron to get back from dealing with Cranston."

"No." I murmured, turning my head so I could find his eyes. They glimmered softly in the dimness, a world of apology swimming in them. I closed my eyes again, fighting more tears. "No, I'll be fine. I probably hit my head a little, but I think most of it was just everything else stacked on top of it. I was so worried about Trace, and then I thought you guys were accusing me. I didn't eat or drink enough either."

"Stubborn much?" he grunted, though I detected a faint air of humor.

"Pot." I fired back, the giggle that followed making me wince again.

"Kettle." He pulled the cloth off my forehead and fanned it in the air to refresh the coolness, carefully replacing it. The headache receded again and I relaxed into the pillows. "You think you can handle me looking at your eyes with a flashlight? If you can hack it, and your pupils look good, I'll let you skip the hospital."

"I can handle it. Probably won't enjoy it, per say, but I can handle it."

"Alright, keep yourself awake, and I'll be right back." The bed sprang back into shape as he rose, pulling his fingers from mine. I curled on my side after finishing the glass of water, carefully checking my head for any sore spots while I waited for his return. My whole world was a soft flannel grey by the time he walked back in, but I pulled back from the comforting promise of sleep with a will. "You still with me, Jo?"

"Not going anywhere, Sir." Really, I wouldn't. If I wasn't in love with him before I was getting there fast now. He'd had my back, when push came to shove, and let me fight my own battles in the same breath. "Is Cranston gone yet?"

A heavy sigh as he resumed his seat. "He's gone. Aaron followed him all the way to the highway to make sure. Lee told us this isn't the first time he's gone after you. I wish you'd have said something."

I shook my head, relieved when it didn't hurt as much, then realized he probably couldn't see me. "*Dywed yn dda am dy gyfaill, am dy elyn dywed ddim.*" I mumbled absently, wrinkling my nose to have one of Gran's proverbs come so easily to my lips.

He slouched down to catch my eye, alarm writ all over his thinning lips as he studied me in the light from the bathroom. "Wow, if you are speaking in gibberish, maybe I really should take you to the hospital."

Managing a rusty chuckle, I waved his concern away. "Sorry, my Gran has a Welsh proverb for everything. This one basically meant speak well of your friend, of your enemy say nothing."

The damned eyebrow went up, his lips echoing its posture of grudging amusement. "I still wish you had come to me with it. You can trust me."

"No, I trust you. But I kept hoping he'd get over it. I endured worse during college, so I didn't feel threatened. Just irritated as hell."

"Look at you, turning into a regular potty mouth." His chuckle rippled over me, and I just wanted to wrap myself in it.

Rough fingers close on my chin and tip my face toward him. "This isn't going to be pleasant, Bowen."

He hadn't lied. After the welcoming dimness of the room, the bright pen light stabbed me in the brain for the first few seconds, and I hissed in a breath. But after that, it simply felt irritating, leaving me blind for a minute when he turned it back off. "So, Doc, am I going to live?" I quipped as he moved away again, this time stopping to lean against the door frame.

"Yeah, I think you just might live to irritate me another day." Let me irritate you forever, please? "I'm going to go fill Aaron in. Do you think you can manage getting into your sleep clothes? I'm going to come back and keep you awake all night, but there's no reason you can't be comfortable while I irritate you for a change."

"Hmm, comfortable and irritated at the same time. It's that an oxymoron?" The off the cuff reply got another laugh.

"Yeah, you're going to be just fine if you are still being clever. Get changed, I'll be back in twenty. Pop the door open when you are ready for company."

"Yes Sir." I struggled upright as the door closed, and swung my legs over the edge of the bed with a grimace. My body was one giant ache, and I'd never felt dirtier, certainly nothing I wanted to slide my pajamas onto. Thank goodness my phone was on the bedside table, and while it took a little squinting to type a legible message, I managed.

'Give me thirty. Need a shower. So gross.'

As I slithered out of my filthy clothes he answered. *'Text me when done. You like mac-n-cheese?'*

'Are the Welsh mostly non-conformists? (FYI, the answer is yes)'

After a hot shower to strip away a layer of my skin and getting my hair wound up in a towel, I drug on some sweat pants and my unicorn sleep shirt. Not like he hadn't seen it once before, and I was rapidly losing my give a shit to exhaustion. Just as I picked up the phone to text the all clear, a rap of knuckles sounds on my door. Thinking it must be him, I flicked on the bedside lamp and shoved my legs under the covers to get comfortable. "Come in."

No, not Bart. Lee's sheepish face peeked around the edge of my doorframe. "Jo? You okay?"

My reply came out chilly and measured. "I will be."

He stepped just inside, crossing one arm over his torso to pick at the opposite shirt sleeve, looking a breath away from rabbiting out the door. The skin of my cheeks tightened with the memory of his face when I stood accused, and I had to look away for a second.

"I'm sorry." While the sentiment was appreciated, and I did believe him, it still hurt. Lee was not lion hearted, but I'd hoped at least for loyalty.

"For what, Lee? There's the rub, you know. I'm sorry isn't going to change the fact that when I needed support you didn't say a word. And the way you looked at me. I can't believe, with all you'd seen happen before, that you would believe that snake."

"I should have had your back, I know. You've always had mine." I had to study him after that last bit, surprised he even noticed. "I can't change a moment of weakness, but I can promise you it won't happen again. I'd just shared space with him all these weeks, and I guess some of his shit wormed its way into my brain."

I yielded a little to that last fact. I'd known plenty of people talked around to stupidity with enough exposure. Grinning very faintly, I slung a fond insult his way. "Well, farm boy, considering your thick skull, I'm surprised anything was able to penetrate at all."

He clutched his chest in mock pain, managing a half smile, though the worried wrinkle over his eyes remained. "Ah, well struck, lady. I'm going to yield the field before you decorate it with my remains."

I winged another one at him just for fun. "Hmm, all that pretty speech making for a crowd is giving you a vocabulary, Fillmore. Whoduthunkit? You're gonna be the fanciest talking plow boy at the local honky tonk."

More of the wrinkle disappeared as he pretended to fall against the doorframe. "Jesus, Jo, you're killing me here. But it's a small price to pay if you can still call me a friend."

I leaned forward over my legs so he could see me better, clutching a pillow against my chest for support. While the moments of weakness were dissipating, I didn't want to risk it. "I've always been your friend, Fillmore. And soon, you'll be my brother. Family means forgiveness, according to my Grandma, so I think you're in the clear." For a second, I was afraid he'd collapse, relief taking the steel out of his spine. It made the tiredness riding him more obvious, and I reflected on how long one day can feel when your world shakes apart. "Now, get out of here, I need my rest, and so do you if we're going to be knighted."

He brightened a little at that. "Thanks Jo. See you in the morning. And feel better."

The instant he left I fell back on the pillows again, pulling the other over my face to block out the light. Focusing on him took the stuffing out of me, and while my head no longer throbbed with the effort, it still tired me.

"I know you've had a rough day, but smothering yourself might be a little mellow dramatic." How could one man's voice be so rough, so humorous and so comforting at the same time? I let the pillow fall and drink the sight of him in, looming beside the bed like a stone guardian, slightly softened by the sweatpants and worn t-shirt he changed into. A stone guardian holding out a bowl of cheesy deliciousness, which only served to make him more attractive.

"Hey, maybe I was using the pillow to muffle all the curse words I want to say?" I took the bowl from him and he sat on the opposite bed, crossing his legs to set his own bowl in his lap.

"Your Grandma would be appalled, I'm sure." He answered dryly, pulling two water bottles from under his arm and setting them on the table between us. "Now, no more talking until you eat. Then I'll check your eyes again."

"Yes Sir."

I'm not at all ashamed to say I fell on the pasta like a ravenous creature, though I managed to keep my mouth closed while I chewed. It wasn't fancy food, just the stuff straight from the blue box, but considering my earlier nausea, it's exactly perfect. Mild and starchy to quiet whatever rolling my gut may attempt. However, remembering my earlier collapse reminded me I'd thrown up, and I swallowed my last mouthful down a throat tight with embarrassment. At least I had enough class to wait for Bart to finish eating before voicing my worry.

"So, earlier. Um, please tell me you didn't clean up my vomit?" I asked, staring up at the ceiling to hide my blush.

His faint chuckle eased my heart just a smidge. "No, I didn't. Lee did. He said it seemed fair after you cleaned up after him this morning." Surprise had my eyebrow arched in disbelief. "But I'd have done it without blinking, you know. Too much time with my Marine brothers has made me a little more familiar than I'd like to be with the contents of someone stomach."

"Ugh, please. I have a feeling Marines can handle their liquor better than Airmen can. I've dodged more inebriated lieutenants outside of the officer's club than I'd care to remember." I shivered for effect, the remembered smell making my stomach clench, and I pressed my hand against it in objection. "Okay, change of subject, or I might be revisiting dinner."

"Let's not have that. Alright, drink some water and I'll do the talking for a few."

A few smart-aleky comments crossed my mind, but I swallowed them with a gulp of water, genuinely happy just to listen to him. After a few anecdotes about his reserve unit, involving juvenile antics that reminded me a good deal of working at summer camp, I relaxed and was able to smile again. Between one blink and the next, he'd crossed the room to kneel beside the bed and grasp my chin. "Jo, you can't go to sleep."

"Not sleeping, just resting my eyes. Promise." I tugged his hand down off my chin and squeezed it carefully, sighing when he pulled it away. Why did he always have to be so warm? "Sorry. How is my Ro tonight?"

"He's fine, but I can tell he's looking for you. Every few bites of his dinner he'd look toward the barn as if you might appear."

"Such a sweet boy." A sigh escaped me and I squeezed my eyes shut, fighting tears again. "Sorry again. This tired, I get a little emotional."

"Stop apologizing. You've done nothing wrong. I'd be more worried if you were being stoic." My eyes flew open when his hand landed on the fist I had clenched in the blanket, and I was immediately drawn into the depth of his, so incredibly vivid this close. "I need to apologize though. You'll get an official one from Aaron tomorrow, but tonight, this is your friend saying he's sorry."

The wound was too close, too fresh, and I looked away in self-defense, though I left my hand where it lay. An anchor of warmth to keep me from getting lost in the hurt, if you will. In fact, I studied his hand covering mine as if it held all the answers I searched for. "It only hurt because I actually care what you guys think of me. What *you* think of me. Rationally, I can understand the impartial study of the situation. Personally, though…"

"Believe me, I wanted to jump to your defense. You'd sooner cut your own stirrup than harm someone else." The vehemence in his tone made me brave and I looked at him again. Conviction blazed as brightly in his eyes as it had in his words, warming me in a sense of hope.

"Well, clearly, that wasn't the case, considering I punched the Frat Boy." I offered, trying to be light about such a heavy subject.

"That wasn't selfish though. I know why you punched him. He could have hammered on you all night, and you'd have answered with your wit. But you couldn't allow him to hurt someone else." The mirror he held up to my actions was so true it hurts and heals at the same time, and I pulled my hand away to press both of them against my eyes. They were too late to stop the tears though, and I choked back a sob. I couldn't stop the next one though, as his hand slipped away and his warmth moved back.

One whimper later, his weight sank the mattress, a thigh laying along the length of mine. His fingers wrapped around my wrist and tugged my hand down to press a tissue into it. That just made me cry more, my shoulders hunching in around the pain in my chest. "How can I help Jo? What do you need?" Worry, distress and softness all thread those questions together and I gulped down the next sob so I could answer.

"Unless you can bring me my Mother or Ro for a proper hug, I think I'm just going to have to ride it out." My chest spasmed with the suppressed tears, stars dancing behind my closed eyelids.

"I know I'm just your friend, but would I make a good substitute?"

The offer was so completely unexpected, and I froze, which prompted a hiccup of objection. I couldn't speak, afraid my heart would pour right out of my mouth, so I risked a nod of acquiescence. He was so careful, pulling us slowly together with one arm around my shoulders, and as my cheek met his shoulder, I melted. No one would be able to resist his warmth, I warrant, and looking back, I ought to get an accolade for not climbing right in his lap like a scared puppy. The tears faded quickly, contentment shoving them aside, and I wound an arm around his back, careful not to cling. My hiccups took a bit longer to subside, particularly when he chuckled at one of the higher pitched vocalizations.

"It's not funny." I objected weakly, though I was smiling against his shirt. Each inhale pulled him a little deeper into my heart, the scent of soap and horse as soothing as the sound of his heartbeat. I could imagine him giving Ro scritches as the gelding ate his grain, giving me a little of the man and a little of the horse in the same breath. Once the hiccups dissipated, I shifted away reluctantly, not wanting to come off desperate. "Thank you."

"My honor." A soft smile then, rare and treasured, affects a slight dimple in his right cheek. "Now, is it safe to move? My leg is going to sleep sitting like this."

I chuckled faintly and waved him off, horrified to have made him uncomfortable. He squeezed the hand in my lap briefly before wobbling to his feet, completely contrary to his usual controlled power. Wincing, he bounced on his toes a few times, likely to get the blood moving, then moved over to the other bed. I slid out of my own and headed for the bathroom to refill my water bottle, allowing him a few minutes to get comfortable, and me a few minutes to calm down. It was a complete dichotomy, how he made me feel so peaceful and so restless at the same time.

"You know, you don't have to sit up with me." I offered as I flicked off the lamp, my still stinging eyes exhausted by the brightness. His bulk shifted in the faint light coming from the bathroom, and I retreated to the safe embrace of my blanket while my body complained about it being a poor substitute.

"Sure I do." In the dimness, his voice felt so close, and I wrapped my arms around a pillow just to have something to hold. "Even if we weren't friends, you're still my responsibility until tomorrow."

"Ugh, tomorrow." I closed my eyes for a moment as the weight of the future pressed close. "I can hardly wait, but I imagine jousting on no sleep is going be awful."

His silence was full of consideration, and I could practically hear his brain deliberating on his next words. "You can't joust tomorrow."

Forgive my reaction, but I shot up in bed and stared hard in his general direction. "The hell I can't."

The groan of the mattress and a shifting shadow told me he was sitting up again. "You have a head injury. I cannot, in good conscience, allow you to joust."

Angry now, I flicked the light back on, both of us wincing against the glare. "Sir, my parents are coming. I have a knighthood to earn."

He ground his teeth before meeting my eyes, a flare of impatience in his. "Dammit, Jo, your health is more important than your pride."

"You can't do this to me!" Tears were welling again, and he plucked another tissue for me, but I batted it away. Angry tears wouldn't be stopped by the small kindness. "Don't let Cranston take this from me, Sir. I can't have him win."

Grinding the heels of his hands against his eyes, he groaned. "And what if you get hurt again, Jo? Will it be worth it when you're lying in a hospital bed, unable to speak or feed yourself?"

Oh. His memories then, making the possibility incredibly vivid in his imagination. That was much harder to combat. "Don't go there, Bart." Anger and hurt filled the eyes that met mine, and it's my turn to cross the room, sitting beside him. No touching, except for the wide hand I folded between my two smaller ones. That would never get old, I swear. "It won't help me, and will only hurt you."

He chuckled faintly and bumped our shoulders together. "Why do you have to be so clever, Jo? Why can't you just let people take care of you?"

"Because I wouldn't like myself if I did." I answered honestly, squeezing his fingers for a moment. "But seriously, let me joust Aaron. We can go half speed, and he can place his shots like a freaking world class surgeon. Four passes and I'm done. I promise I'll be good and rest after that. Please?"

"Hmm, now who is selling sand boxes to the Bedouin?" The look he slanted me still looked frustrated, but at least he wasn't swimming in old recollections anymore.

"Trees, apples not falling far from them and all that." I teased, unthinkingly dropping a kiss on his cheek before scurrying back to my side of the room in dismay. Turning the light back off so I didn't have to face what I just did, I curled back under the blanket and tried to chew away the warmth lingering on my lips. It only made it worse though. The silence stretched on so long that a panic attack became a real possibility, but I didn't know what to say to break the quiet. I heard him settle on the bed again, the sound of a fist against a pillow, a blanket shifting. Another tear threatened, and I dashed it away, angry at myself. One unthinking moment just cost me a good friend.

"Did you know the national animal of Scotland is the unicorn?" The complete randomness made me giggle, and I stifled it against a pillow to disguise my relieved hysteria. "Your shirt reminded me."

Flopping on my back to stare at the ceiling, I fished for something equally as random. "Did you know the Welsh consider the daffodil as much a national symbol as the leek?"

Jesus, how could I go from the depths of despair to the heights of happiness in one day? I closed my eyes and hoarded the feeling close to my heart as our conversations wound their way from one end of the spectrum to the other. Turns out my intrepid hero hated mayonnaise and secretly liked black and white movies like *Casablanca*.

Somewhere around three AM, he asked me why I didn't call him by name more often, and in my bleary eyed exhaustion, I told him about the pirate image that had popped up in the beginning. I experienced a giggle fit fueled by the hour and his brief chuckle, my ribs aching enough that I got up for more ibuprofen.

By dawn, I knew we had both dozed off occasionally, but never for very long. I didn't wait for my alarm when I woke up and found him flat asleep, and I snuck from the room to start the coffee and make my tea. About the time both were ready he emerged from the room, sleep rumpled, and regardless of the bruised circles under his eyes that likely match mine, every inch of my skin woke up. Struggling not to blush, I recalled kissing his cheek, the faint stubble scraping my lips. Remembered every little touch that had provided comfort and distraction. I was in so much trouble. But the half shy, half bold look he leveled at me made me brave enough to face whatever was ahead.

For today, I was going to love the friend that stayed with me during the roughest night of my life. Starting with handing him the blackest cup of coffee I had ever made.

Aaron offered me a sincere apology, just as Bart had said, coming up just short of begging me to stay, and I resorted to a quick hug to shut him up. My heart was there, and unless that changed, they had me forever. Mari mother henned me through the morning, fussing over my insistence to help armor. Lee and Alex went in the morning, and I cheered when the sweet blonde from the day before showed up ringside again. Her appearance had a bracing effect on Fillmore, adding a little pop to his shots and flair to his speeches.

Mom and Dad showed up at the same time as their last visit, and while Mom gave me a worried frown, Dad was all smiles and hugs. Back at camp, I gave them an abbreviated version of the previous day, omitting the nastiness at the end and Bart's sleep over, because I didn't think that would go over well. We endured a riot of questions. Once an officer, always an officer, and my Dad had no shame grilling both Bart and I like guilty school children. It was easy to face the inquisition though, with Bart just behind my shoulder, a quiet bastion of encouragement. By the time we mollified him, my stomach was growling, and Mom volunteered to go get me lunch. I yielded with good grace, needing a few minutes quiet to calm myself.

Eros, at least, remained a source of peace. Ro had been so worried this morning, snuffling me all over to check me out. He paced the fence when I had to leave, and guilt tore a hole in my heart. The stud though, he'd seen the dark side, and come out the other side wiser for it. I got my usual nose bump, though maybe a trifle more careful, as if he was aware of my bruised body. I sported a riot of color along my side, where impact had driven the armor into my skin, some of the purple and blue already going green along the edges. But the aches only served to add to my determination to see this finished, to claim the title I earned through blood, sweat and now tears. Thankfully, after the drama of yesterday, my nerves were too tired to overthink, and all I could do was exist. Eros was perfectly content to chew his hay and let me wrap my arms around him, not even caring that I preferred to be leaning on his master.

"Penny for your thoughts?" I smiled against Eros's shoulder at the sound of Bart's voice, as if thinking of him summoned him. Neat trick. Looking over the stallion's neck put us almost eye to eye, as he leaned on the horse's broad back.

"No thinking. Just being today." I sighed and fought the urge to move my arm a few inches, wanting to touch him, but too aware of the careful line we were still walking. A cautious part of my heart still warned this might all be one sided, but I squelched it without much effort.

"Good plan." A smile that felt like a gift skated across his face, before hiding behind a façade of responsibility. "Don't forget to come see me before you get armored so we can take care of your hand."

"Yes Sir." I answered, though my grin probably ruined the quick reply.

My appetite had returned with a vengeance, and while Mom brought me two steaks on a stake, I still ended up finishing her turkey leg while she looked on in amazement. Likely, I would be at least a week recovering from the day before, but on the other side of the ugliness I wouldn't trade it. It amazed me how much more peaceful the encampment felt without Cranston's smoggy temperament to sully it. I dutifully tracked Bart to Mari's booth when the time came, and bore up under her knowing gaze with minimal blushing while he wrapped my hand.

Trace ambled in as Alex helped me armor, a small bandage perched rakishly over one eye. "Hey there, Jo! What's this I hear you pack a mean right hook?" Relief at his condition and panic at his big mouth had me mentally scrambling. Thankfully, Lee punched him in the shoulder to redirect him and saved me just in time as Mom came in to take pictures of me getting kitted out.

Once mounted on Eros some of the excitement started to shimmy along my nerves, and I closed my eyes to fully absorb the moment. The hundreds of voices raised in celebration all around me, instruments vying for attention, and the giggles of children in the nearby maze. Air so humid it had a silky feel, even under the weight of my armor. Floral candles and soaps wafted faintly across the familiar scents of sweat and manure, barely noticeable over the fly spray the horses wore. Eros's mane brushing my knuckles, his ribs rising and falling in calm breaths. My own body, so much stronger than I ever would have guessed, enduring its injuries with nothing more than a few aches to mark them. This is home, among friends and family I hadn't understood the value of less than two months ago. A hand fell on my knee, pulling me away from the internal reflection.

"Promise me you are going to play it safe." The narrowness of Bart's eyes told me he suspected I might argue, but I wouldn't be there if it weren't for him. Thanks to him, I had hundreds more jousts ahead to push the envelope.

"I promise."

His face relaxed, and he smiled, patting Eros on the neck before going to grab Ivan. My parents waved as they let themselves out the gate to get their seats at the arena. Hillary ran into the booth, emerging with the wooden dagger I would be needing soon. Aaron pulled up beside me on Byz and tapped me lightly on the arm with his gauntleted fist. "You ready to rock and roll, Jojo?"

I rolled my eyes at my least favorite nickname in the history of ever. "Don't call me that, or so help me, I'll flatten you." I muttered darkly, only half kidding. "Makes me sound like someone's purse dog."

Mischief lit his blue eyes and dimpled his cheeks. "Hmm, I'll have to save it for special occasions then. I'm under orders to play nice today."

"Me too. Lucky you." Wrinkling my nose, I stuck my tongue out at him. Yeah, brother in arms, indeed. "But I'll hold a big hit on account for you, okay?"

He sighed dramatically and sagged as best his armor allowed. "Promises, promises. That's all I ever get from you, Bowen."

"Better hope she never has to make good on them, Captain." This from Trace who came up on my other side, the Cymru flag already unfurled. "She's like a freaking lightning bolt, she hits so fast."

Then the gate opened, and we fell into line, walking quietly to the arena. There, the calm became a memory as John waved at me from his seat beside Caroline, and the Girl Scouts from my first weekend scream my name as I trotted by. I paid my respects to the King and Queen after they inquire about my readiness to compete, and handed out my favor, picking a fresh faced little girl in a princess dress who was rocking a well-worn pair of riding boots underneath. Strength could be hidden under satins and sequins more effectively than any place else, and I didn't want to forget that, thanks to the Queen.

Our joust was a dance so subtle I doubt many caught on to the absolute farce. I went through all the motions, setting up Eros properly, waiting for my signal, and sighting in just as I had any other day. But we went half speed, slowly enough that even Eros grew antsy, tossing his head to express his confusion. He and I were meant to run; didn't I know? To fall on our opponents like the hammer of a Norse god, all thunder and power.

All I could do is pat him, and repeat my promise to play it safe under my breath. Each of Aaron's blows felt like it struck the same square inch all four times, barely tinking off the edge of my grand guard, hardly remarkable. I managed three touches myself, the ache in my ribs and shoulder too great to maintain my aim by the last pass. Yet, as my helm came off at Alex's hands, the cheers of the crowd sounded just as loud as they had ever been. It didn't keep my efforts from tasting like sawdust in my mouth, a lie perpetrated with my compliance. May I never have to keep a promise like that again, I prayed as I dismounted to greet the eager throng.

It took my parents an oddly long time to show their faces again, still not back once I was out of armor. I'd actually dug my phone out of my trunk so I could check on them when they slid through the gate, a garment bag folded over Mom's arm. My heart plummeted at the sight, not wanting to fight with her over whatever gilding she wanted to drape me in, but when Mari joined her, all I could do is cross my arms and wait. Whatever it was, I'd be saying yes, it was simply a matter of how much I wanted to object first.

Mom delivered the opening salvo, smoothing a hand nervously over the burden she carried. "Don't look like that, Josie. It's not like it's a princess dress, for heaven's sake."

Mari took her shot while Mom reloaded. "Don't you trust me? I haven't steered you wrong yet, kiddo."

They didn't even give me a chance to return fire, each grabbing an elbow to steer me toward the gate. At that point, I was too tired to drag my heels, and close to tears by the time they shoved me in the tack room of the trailer. A washcloth and clean bucket of water waited for me, as well as a clean chemise, the high collar trimmed in tasteful lace. A lone tear escaped as I picked up a single daffodil from the built in seat along the wall, running my finger over the butter yellow petals. Bart. Dammit. Stock up on the soap Grandma. I was beginning to think the cursing might become my vice of choice.

After a few minutes to clean up and collect myself, Mari's fist pounds on the door. "Stop hiding, Jo. You won't like the results if I have to bring my crippled butt in there after you!"

I popped the door open and stood hip shot, raising an eyebrow at her. "If you are a cripple, then I am an idiot."

I swear you could see the horns sprouting from her curly red hair as she traded me glares. "Well, that still is under question."

While I rolled my eyes, she snatched my wrist and pulled me down to their level.

Mom tsk'd "Girls, girls, be nice," even as she opened the plastic to reveal charcoal grey leather so buttery soft it hardly warranted the title of leather at all. I was all set to drool with avarice at it until she peeled back the cover, revealing a full-fledged rose appliqued in burgundy across the left breast of the tunic. My mouth went dry at the level of detail, the thorns on the stem looking sharp enough to cut and a single drop of blood falling from the largest of them. Longing to touch it, but not quite sure I was worthy, I just stared. "Your daddy and I thought this up. We were shopping the last time we visited, and bought this tunic, but it needed something more. You can thank Grandma Pearl for doing the stitch work."

My eyes started leaking again, and Mari stepped up to keep me from using my sleeve. No, it wouldn't do to muss the clean shirt with tears, would it? "I don't even know what to say. This is going to look so good on Rowan!"

Mom laughed. "Honey, leave it to you to think of how it will look on a horse. It's going to look perfect on *you*."

She was right, at least I thought so, because it felt amazing. The tunic had a high mandarin collar that the lace of the chemise framed perfectly, then fell down to a modest neckline where the lacing began just above my breasts. That lacing, and some fitted lines along my ribs, gave me a waist, the remaining length falling softly to just below my knees. The split front, back and sides were full enough to give some femininity, but nothing that would hinder movement, and while I enjoyed the bodices now, this was so much more *me*. Mari finger combed my hair again, this time gathering the sides back so it cascaded between my shoulders and wouldn't obscure my vision.

"Now there is a woman fit to be named knight." Mari proclaimed, after studying me. She looked at the pocket watch hanging in her skirts and grabbed my elbow. "With that, ladies, we are out of time. Let's go."

"Wait!" I yelped, throwing myself back toward the trailer to grab the daffodil. While Mom gave me a curious look, Mari just smiled, confirming my suspicion that she'd been in on it all.

On the other side of the gate, everyone waited, already mounted and ready to go. "Figures, Bowen, early for everything but your own knighting." Aaron teased as I hurried forward to tuck the daffodil in Eros's browband.

I scrambled in the saddle with a quick thank you to Hillary and caught Bart's eye. He had his business face on, all noble and firm of expression, but I thought I knew him well enough to confirm the tiniest glimmer of a smile before he turned Ivan away. The parade he led us on was quite the spectacle, with Fillmore and I falling in behind Aaron and Alex. They were going to give the crowd their joust before knighting us, and I was grateful to know that the final show would at least be genuine.

"I feel overdressed." Lee grumbled as we made our way toward the waiting throng, tugging at the bottom of the velvet Elizabethan doublet he wore. "It's not fair. At least you look knightly."

A glimmer of fair hair along the arena rail had me grinning and slapping at his hand. "Shut up and smile, Lee. Your sweet admirer sure seems to like it." He sat up straighter to find her, and as soon as I pointed her out his whole face softened. Yeah, serious puppy love going on there.

He and I ended up stationed on opposite corners of the arena where we were least likely to block the view, and I tried not to fidget as the rest of the crew ran around working. Sitting still while everyone else was busy just wasn't my nature. It wasn't even in my nature when everyone else *wasn't* working.

I spotted Mari sitting next to my parents, thrilled that they had let her shut down if only for this. She'd become family, just as surely as the rest of the crew, and it felt right to have her there. Aaron and Alex proved themselves more than capable of satisfying the mob, Bart egging the crowd on to let them have more passes after the first four were satisfied.

"Look at these unused lances, good people! Should we let them go to waste, like swords that will never know battle or

should we use them as they were made to be used?" It took me
back to the moment John had stood up from his fall to encourage
the crowd to greater cheers. The resulting rain of broken lances
looked ridiculously like confetti on the ground by the time they
were done, Aaron taking the last unbroken lance and shattering it
against Alex to the baying of the mob. I didn't know if they
would calm enough for the next bit, but amazingly, when the
King motioned for quiet, they complied.

"Good people, please join me in welcoming our knight-
initiates, Lord Phillip Lee of Shropshire and Lady Josephine
Bowen of Pembrokeshire." Enthusiastic applause, from both
patrons and cast, lightened my heart as we rode forward to
dismount. Hillary took Eros from me and I strode through the
small gate to take my place on the dais, kneeling at the feet of
the King and Queen. There were no nerves, surprisingly,
particularly when Bart and Aaron fell in behind us, guarding our
backs.

"Is it still your intent to the office of knighthood?" The King
asked, his tone that of a fond patron, nodding wisely when we
both answered yes. "Do you swear to serve your liege lord in
valor and faith? To protect the weak and defenseless? To never
refuse a challenge from an equal nor to turn your back upon a
foe? To guard the honor of your fellow knights and to live by
truth and for glory for all the days you have on this earth? So
thee swear, and be named knight."

A pretty speech I'd be playing over and over in my heart for a
long time, and I answered with a resounding "So I swear," that
widened the good King's eyes and prompted a smile from his
Queen. Lee's was equally as firm, though perhaps not as loud.

"Then We shall offer you your last unanswered blows and
dub thee knight."

Just as the Queen and I had discussed, as the King stepped in
front of Lee and carefully slapped his cheek, she stepped before
me fit to repeat the same gesture. As her hand flew toward me, I
lifted my arm to block the blow and raised my chin in defiance,
her smile widening.

"Do you mean to offer Us insult, daughter?" she asked, while everyone else gasped and whispered, the two men at my back shifting restlessly. They hadn't been in on this part.

"Nay, my Queen, but as one of the fairer sex, I know you would not want one blow against any of your daughters to go unanswered. Thus, I shall defend even the least of us from this offense, as I have defended myself."

She dropped her hand and smiled wide enough for even those in the back of the audience to see. "It is as you say, dear child. Thus, your last unanswered blow shall be this instead." Bending forward, she cupped my cheeks and tipped my head up, pressing a soft kiss to my forehead.

Applause again, around the hum of whispering voices, likely passing the story around as she turned to the man who played her husband for seven weekends a year. "Husband, would you grant me leave to call Dame Josephine Bowen the first of my own knights?"

The confusion on his face quickly cleared and he grinned at us both, pressing a kiss to her knuckles with his whiskered lips. "Of course, My lovely, may she serve You in good health, all the years God may bless You with."

Lee rose as a Knight just before me, and I wobbled slightly as I joined him, only to have the Queen press a folded white cloth into my hands, leaning closer so her words were for me alone. "For winning the hearts of the crowd and myself, I pray you will wear my champions favor until you choose to yield it to another."

I let the fabric slide in my fingers, the tail falling open to reveal the crowned entwined hearts I'd admired for years, a breeze cropping up like a blessing to make it dance. Bart stepped forward then, and tugged it from my hand to knot it around my elbow like the badge of honor it was. I barely felt Aaron kneel down to place the ceremonial spurs on my boots, Bart's fingertips searing my skin as he helped me balance. Surreal was the best adjective I could come up with for the remaining hour, as a thousand faces offered me congratulations while we rode to the gate as guards for Their Majesties.

Nothing felt real until later that night, long after a celebratory dinner with the whole crew and some of the other cast members. I couldn't sleep, despite the almost forty-eight hours I had been awake, the room too empty and the dark too heavy. Gathering up my blanket and a pillow I headed for Ro's paddock, fumbling the chain in the darkness to let myself in. There in the thick grass, under the arms of the lone oak, even with the horses peacefully resting close by, I still tossed and turned. But then the chain rang against the gate, and footsteps approached, too quiet to be anyone but Bart. He propped himself against the trunk of the tree to keep the watch, a blanket for a cushion, and my muscles finally grew lax. I was safe, with the horse of my heart on one side and the friend, maybe something more, of my heart on the other. Now, I was home. Now, I could sleep.

Epilogue

Years in the Marines had prepared me for guard duty, but never did I bear the chore more gladly than on Sunday night. Jo's trust was something I thought I had lost, for ten of the worst minutes of my life, and her acceptance of my presence reassured me more than words that I had it again. She hardly moved from midnight until dawn, just a few soft noises I couldn't decipher whenever one of the horses grunted. Even in her sleep, she worried about others, never taking enough care of herself.

Part of that long night, as I stared sightlessly up at the stars, I fought with anger darker than any I had wrestled with in years. While I couldn't regret a single moment I spent taking care of her the night before, my fists still tightened with the urge to pummel Toby Cranston until he needed a plastic surgeon. Which his parents could no doubt afford. Not that I would have allowed myself that, as it would have created more problems that it fixed, but the fantasy remained. He deserved it, for his hollow accusations and the trouble he had been inflicting on Jo for the last couple months. Even knowing Aaron had bodily shoved the kid in his car after Trace had wadded all his belongings in the back seat of his shiny little Porsche didn't help. I wanted blood for her pain.

Then I worked through anger with myself. To have stood by as Jo took those accusations still made my stomach roll.

Rationally, I had needed to stand back, as half owner of the company and as her trainer. Playing favorites never went over well. Which only pointed out what a tangle getting involved with her would be, not that it wouldn't be worth it to me. Everyone in the troupe knew she had earned her place, on her own merits, and the decision to hire her had been met with unanimous agreement. But would it be worth it to her?

Pre-dawn light began to fill the sky and I took a few minutes to study her face as I had never been able to awake. Despite the faint bruising beneath her eyes and a bit of hollowness to her cheeks, she was so beautiful it made my chest ache. Day one I'd thought her pretty, but with every day since she had become that once in a lifetime sort of gorgeous. I wanted to brush my fingers through the thick tangles in her dark hair, to trace the constellation of freckles that graced her cheeks and run my thumbs over her stubborn jaw.

Once the sun actually cracked the edge of the trees I shook her shoulder, waking her enough to send her inside. It tested my self-control to do it though, because all I wanted was to pull her into my arms and hold her. She was too stubborn to let me protect her during the day, even from herself, which made it hard to let her go.

After a cool shower to wake up, I slogged downstairs to feed, the silence that once seemed so pleasant when I had the barn to myself now no longer a comfort. She certainly needed the sleep, but I missed all the little noises that had marked her presence. Then I took another shower to get clean and a black hole of a nap on the sofa, Aaron for once in his life not bothering me with incessant questions or his need for social interaction. I didn't see her again until supper, walking in on her bent over as she fished for the crumbs on the bottom of the oat bin. It was difficult not to stare at her slim hips encased in denim, her long legs, strong and supple. I kept expecting a memory full message to pop up behind my eyes, I'd memorized her so many times, but where she was concerned, I apparently saved everything to the cloud.

"Bowen, what do you think you are doing?" I barked, just to watch her jump a little. The flush on her cheeks when she righted herself was too charming to properly describe, all I knew was I lived to see it every day. From day one, she'd impressed me, the horses attracted to her instinctively and her courage beyond compare as she stared Aaron down. Trace's pretty face had mattered not one iota to her, and neither had Cranston's money and false charm, her admiration only won by actions.

Her lips bowed lopsidedly with humor and she set a hand on her hip before replying. "Doing your job, apparently. I was told I had Mondays off, but these two horses professed your neglect, and I had to remedy it immediately." She had guts to spare, standing up to me and anyone else without flinching, never yielding until the work was done.

I crossed my arms and leaned against the doorframe as she turned to add supplements to the buckets at her feet, waiting for her to finish. "I'm sure they were starving to death, to have achieved your sympathy." I loved her quick mind, and that I never had to pull my verbal punches. Hell, I'd started digging deeper into my own vocabulary just to keep up with her.

"Of course." She brushed past, forcing me to yield the doorway if I wanted to keep my feet and I fell in beside her, taking Eros's bucket from her fingers. We leaned against the gate while the boys ate, a silence between us that had always felt familiar. I could feel a change in the quiet, slight, ephemeral, but I breathed a prayer of hope at it. "I'm leaving tomorrow afternoon. Mom wants me home so she can feed me up and trot me around to her friends. More than likely she'll be taking along video and pictures, so she can sell me properly."

The wrinkle on the top of her nose told me she was being funny, but a twist in her lips said she was not comfortable with the idea. No, I doubt she would be able to sit through the praise she deserved without squirming in her chair. The faintest compliment always made her spooky, like she couldn't believe the good in herself.

An idea springs unbidden to my brain, and I chew on it for a few before voicing it. "Want to take the boys for a ride? There's a state park just a few miles down the road, we could go exploring for a while."

It never took her long to answer me, instinctively going with her gut, not the overthinking of everything I said that had plagued my past relationships. "That actually sounds perfect. A good night's sleep, and I'll be up early. Breakfast in a cup?"

I didn't even have to ask what she meant, grinning at all the mornings we had traded cups, her original offering of coffee to mollify me on a cranky morning. She hadn't known about my leg then, still didn't know about the random cramps and nerve issues that could crop up without warning. But she'd waved a white flag anyway, trying to fix a problem that had nothing to do with her. Thankfully, she'd accepted my apology of Earl Grey with a lump and a quick splash of cream, just the way my Mom taught me to make it. Amazingly, she even seemed to like it.

"Sure. Time to grab lunch when we are done?" I asked, feeling out how much more time I had left with her.

"You pick. I have yet to try all the local cuisine." She sighed, another sound I was learning to read, but this one defied attempts to categorize it. "I'll just make sure to have my bags packed before we go, so I can leave right after we get back." Bumping her shoulder against mine, she chuckled, a warm, live thing that made me greedy for more. "If I didn't have things to pick up, a birthday fete to attend, and respects to pay to Grandma, I'd just stay. I'm more at home here, now."

"Oh, we aren't going anywhere." I assured her, though my heart clutched at those innocently said words with both its insubstantial hands. The farm would feel a whole lot less like home the instant she left. Before I could say as much, she stepped into the paddock to pick up the now empty buckets, pausing to press a kiss to her horse's nose. For good measure, she gave Eros one too, a content heaviness to her lashes that hid her hazel eyes. "Ro's going to miss you something fierce though."

Her eyes widen and flash straight up to meet mine, the amber in the middle disappearing into the wider band of olive green with the pinning of her pupil. "I'm going to miss him too."

I found myself hoping she meant those words to encompass more than the big grey snuffling her cheek like a puppy. She shoved him off with a laugh, her whole torso vibrating with the sincerity of it, and I closed my eyes for a moment to store that snapshot away with the rest.

Tuesday morning, we met in the aisle and exchanged travel tumblers, her giggling like a little girl when she looked over at me. I'd dug up a bit of leather from the scrap bin to fashion an eye patch after her two AM confession about why she couldn't say my name in the beginning.

"Oh my, your funny bone must have grown a size. You might want to get that looked at."

"Arrgh, me matey, what is this bone of funny you speak of." She leaned against the wall to support herself, bending over her knees with laughter. It left me with another warm memory to cling to, when she wouldn't be close enough to make more with, and further determined to do whatever it took to keep her smiling.

We rode for two glorious hours that I didn't have to share with a singular other soul, just my favorite horse, and my favorite girl, out in the sunshine as we topped the hills, and back in cooler shadow as we traveled through the treed valleys.

At first, I watched her for signs of discomfort. I hadn't seen her bruises, but I'd worn enough of them myself to know where they probably were. She'd moved carefully as we loaded the horses, but the longer we rode, the more her movement smoothed out. Once sure she was doing alright I studied her in every light, from every angle, letting her lead when we couldn't share the trail, just so I could watch her hips match her horse's, stride for stride. God, the day she had ridden him over that little jump, it had been goose bump inducing, like joy given a shape as they both momentarily laughed at gravity. I could imagine the antics she and my grandfather could get up to if they ever met, her fearless heart and clever brain more than a match for his.

When Ro startled at a rabbit shooting between his feet she floated with him like a cloud on a breath of wind and laughed at the gelding's surprise. I marveled again at her courage. So many women could ride, but she didn't fear the fall, like she knew the risks and considered it a worthwhile price to pay. It didn't matter

319

if she was in or out of armor, the horses were part of her, would always be part of her, just like they would always be a part of me. She'd understood, instinctively, when the big Shire had needed to move, needed to be still, needed soothing or pushing. It had been a treat to watch her heart and his come together.

Speaking of her heart horse, I had a lot to thank Ro for, as without him, I might never have seen beneath her bravery and work ethic to the soft heart of a woman. I'd gone from simple admiration of her as a person to an avid observer in the space of a breath, the day she first laid eyes on him. Whatever had caused the gelding pain, I'd been glad to give him someplace to heal. I just hadn't known she would heal more than his heart in the process.

We parked at the local drive in, the boys content to wait in the trailer with their full hay nets as we settled on a picnic bench. The carhop brought us a tray covered in wax paper and we shared the monster pile of chili cheese fries, arguing casually over where the dividing line was so neither of us got more than the other. She snatched the cherry off of my milkshake and popped it in her mouth with an unrepentant grin, unaware I was restraining myself from kissing her silly.

It amazed me to think that so much softness and so much strength could exist in one person. Jo was the bright white of innocence, the red of passion, the blue of compassion. She was the sunshine yellow of laughter, or the purple badge of courage, or the soft green of healing. Sometimes, she was all of them at once. My life had been so washed out before she came into it, and now it was like living in a cathedral, the stained glass backlit by the sun.

The boys were happily settled back in their paddock when Aaron came down to say goodbye, stealing my last few minutes with her, an envelope in his hands that made me smile. Her brow furrowed when he held it out, and she opened it cautiously, eyes widening at the check inside. "What is this for?"

"It's compensation for your work this last weekend, with a small bonus for all the work you did when you didn't have to."

He offered, grinning like a clown as she pulled it out to study it, as if suspecting a joke.

"Okay, I appreciate that, but I certainly wasn't expecting anything." She groused, still reading the lines that describe the taxes pulled from the total. "What is this tax for?" Her fingernail underscored the twelve bucks and fifty cents that held no signifier other than P.I.T.A. and I turned sideways to punch Aaron in the arm.

"Oh, that was Bart's idea." He snickered like the idiot he was, pointing at me with one finger even as he rubbed his arm.

"I was joking, you moron." I grumbled, folding my arms across my chest to keep from throttling him again. "I didn't mean for you to actually do it."

"He thought maybe we should impose a tax for every time you sassed us."

Clever as a fox, she flipped the joke on its ear with casual smile, taking us both in with a calculating eye. "Indeed, I'd like to see the breakdown on that. The figures must be fascinating. How much does my insolence cost me?"

"Fifty cents an infraction." Aaron responded quickly, not realizing she's baiting him. I bit my lip to keep from smiling, watching the incoming shot with awe.

"Really?" She took her time folding the check and tucking it in a back pocket, her lips pursing thoughtfully. "Well, if that's all it costs me to run verbal circles around you, I'd call it a bargain. Expect the amount to increase for subsequent checks."

Aaron sputtered as she headed toward the front of the barn, and my chest tightened a little when she looked back at Ro one last time, a flash of vulnerability amidst her strength. I'd make sure to send her updates on him so she didn't worry too much. We walked her to her car, bags already stowed in the back seat, and Aaron actually hugged her, claws of jealousy lancing my chest. Before she could climb in I gathered my courage and tempted fate, like a little kid taunting a dog behind a rickety fence. "Hey, where's mine?"

She startled, like the doe we'd surprised in the woods that morning, eyes soft as she swiveled my direction. I held my arms out playfully, like my whole world wasn't hanging in the balance as she stepped closer. With her height, I didn't so much fold myself around her. It felt more like fitting two matching puzzle pieces together, all her lines a perfect complement for mine as she slid her arms around my back, her chin raising slightly to rest on my shoulder.

Pressing my cheek against her temple, I squeezed her gently, like the friend I was supposed to be, drawing in the scent of her vanilla shampoo and a hint of the horses we both loved.

"Come back soon, Josephine." I risked murmuring before letting her go, immediately missing her warmth. Hell, I could still point to the exact spot she had kissed on Saturday night, sweetness in the midst of her own pain.

She smiled a little too brightly, like a wrong word might make her bolt, but there was a softening in her shoulders when she answered me. "Wild horses couldn't keep me away."

Minutes later, as I watched her car head out the gate, Aaron clapped me on the back. "Don't worry, dude, she'll be back. We have her horse."

His jovial tone scraped my freshly exposed heart, and I walked back to the paddock to be close to the one thing that still linked us together. Ro and Eros both closed in on me, offering support and I shut my eyes to get my emotions in check. They knew what Aaron didn't—while Jo had been earning her way into Rowan's heart, she had also been chipping away at the armor on mine.

-Fini-

Hard Charging Hearts

Now Available

Josephine Bowen is a strong willed woman with a sword sharp wit, stainless loyalty, and a priceless heart. After enduring a host of physical and emotional challenges in order to become a modern day jouster, she's finally earned her knighthood. Now, it's time to go on the road with the Gallant Company to earn her keep. She faces both bodily injury and the doubts of outsiders as her jousting skills are tested and honed. Strengthening her relationship with both her horse and her best friend (who is perhaps something more) proves riddled with challenges and tears. Yet, no matter the trials before her, she continues to surprise, because if jousting has taught her anything it's that some things are worth the risk.

For more information about

The Gallant Company of Knights

Follow us on Facebook
to get series updates and teasers on all the upcoming books!
Just search for the **Gallant Hearts Groupies** and join in the fun.
I'll see you there!

Or find us on the Web
www.gallanthearts.com

Appendix-

Welsh-

Cawl cymraeg- Welsh broth
Fy annwyl- my darling
Adfyd a ddwg wybodaeth, a gwybodaeth ddoethineb-
Adversity brings knowledge, and knowledge, wisdom.
Dywed yn dda am dy gyfaill, am dy elyn dywed ddim- Speak
well of your friend, say nothing of your enemy
Tylwyth Teg- fair family, term for the fairy folk of Wales
Cynefin- A place where a person or even an animal feels it
ought to live. Where the nature around you feels right and
welcoming.

Armor-

Buffe- bolts on beneath the grand guard, deflecting blows that
skip up toward the neck and head
Cuirass- refers to both the breastplate and back plate that
protects the jousters torso
Cuisse- section that covers the thigh
Gorget- protects the throat
Grand Guard- A target bolted to the jousters left shoulder to
receive blows, often gridded to catch and break the lance more
effectively
Grapper- metal back plate on the lance that supports it against
the torso
Helm- essential protection for the head, with several hinged
sections to allow it to fit closely to the skull and jaw.
Manfair- a gauntlet that covers the jousters left hand, just in
case a blow goes awry
Pauldron- covers the shoulder
Vamplate- metal front plate on the lance that protects the hand

Want to see full contact jousting near you? Here are a few companies to check out!

Knights of Valour
http://www.knightsofvalour.ca/

Knights of the Rose
http://theknightsoftherose.com/

New Riders of the Golden Age
http://www.warhorse.com/

Knights of Mayhem
http://www.knightsofmayhem.com

Acknowledgements:

This book would never have made it through its first draft if not for the cheerleading and encouragement of the first Gallant Hearts Groupie, Jessica Post. Not only is she an actual full contact jouster, she's an exceptionally loyal friend and gracious source of fodder.

Also, to J.A. Campbell, an author who encouraged me as I stumbled through this journey.

Vivian Caethe, editor extraordinaire, for seeing something in this story that elevated it to the next level.

Auburn McCanta, Fellow author and proofreader of exceptional quality, thanks for y.

Kimberley Carman, for your excellent embroidery work and long suffering endurance.

Kat Moran, where would I be without your gift for graphics? Still trying to muddle through, that's what.

To my proofers, Gesa, Elizabeth and Katherine, I owe you chocolate. So much chocolate.

Lastly, and always, I have to thank my husband, henceforth referred to as Nog. For believing in me so much that you endure your status as a writer's widower with grace and compassion (as if the horses didn't already claim enough of my time?). For listening as I discussed imaginary people as if I'd just spoken to them on the phone. You, my darling, are my knight in dented, beat up, scarred and battle worn armor. Thanks for everything.

About the Author

J.D. Harrison is a lifelong horsewoman, often found in the uncommonly intelligent company of her horse, Smoke.

She believes in soul satisfying relationships with animals, conversation with genuine people, supporting her friends and reading voraciously.

With over a decade of experience squiring at a championship tourney, and a long term love affair with all things medieval and renaissance, she brings to life the culture of jousters and their unorthodox lifestyle.

Chivalry isn't dead, it's just hiding at your local renaissance festival or medieval recreation event.

80050514R00205

Made in the USA
San Bernardino, CA
22 June 2018